THE UNDEAD DAY TWENTY

RRHAYWOOD.COM

RR HAYWOOD

ALSO BY RR HAYWOOD

Have you read?

Blood on the Floor

An Undead Adventure.

Best read between Day Nineteen and Day Twenty

‿

Bring death and bring it fast because he does not fear it now. To go back is a blessing not a curse. To go there is a victory not a loss.
Bring all of them
Bring them here

I'm not putting my cock on Dave's cup.

THE WATCHES

Gnarled hands knead the flour to make bread to feed the many that will wake in the morning. His craggy face remains impassive as he listens to the sounds of the night around him, absorbing the ambience. He pauses when a child whimpers but carries on when he hears the soft motherly tones giving comfort.

The fires in the middle of the fort burn bright, ready to bake and cook. It's hot but he works on with a steady energy while others sit on the shore at the back, their feet dangling in the cool waters as they cast rods into the black sea to catch fish to feed the many that will wake in the morning.

The patients in the medical bay sleep drug induced and quiet. Others in the fort wake gasping in the grip of nightmares. Some can't sleep at all for fear of the nightmares coming back so they walk the walls with drawn expressions.

Sentries at the gates talk quietly, sip coffee and turn at the screams of the children that sound out from those nightmares.

The sea surrounding the fort is a mirrored surface with barely a ripple of motion. The very air seems to hang low from the heat. A flash of silver scales breaks the surface then it's gone to dive down and feast on the corpses that are quickly being stripped of their flesh.

Those same waters lap softly at the sand on the horseshoe bay where mounds of goods left stacked on the beach wait to be taken over.

Nothing stirs. Nothing moves. The air is heavy and humid. The windows of the last house on the bay are all open. The doors too. They sleep without covers. Waking frequently from the uncomfortable warmth.

Howie and Marcy finish their watch. Marcy goes inside to make tea for Clarence. Reginald sits in the kitchen. Impervious to the heat despite the sweat forming on his head. By candlelight he reads. By candlelight he reads again and again to be sure, to understand, to seek knowledge to be one-step ahead of the other player to win the game.

Marcy offers tea. Reginald lifts his head, startled at being distracted. Marcy smiles warmly, resting a hand on his shoulder as he goes back to reading.

'What's that word?' She asks, resting a finger on the notepad.

'Catholicon.'

'What's it mean?'

'Er...it's er...'

'Never mind, do you want tea?'

'Tea? Yes. Yes. Peppermint tea.'

Tea is made. Peppermint for Reginald. Builders tea for Clarence in the biggest mug she can find. A plate is loaded with biscuits from the packets she carefully secured the previous day. Custard creams, digestives, pink wafers, shortbread fingers, bourbons and nice. She smiles as she works. It's the small things that make the difference in this world now.

'Tea,' she places Reginald's cup down. He doesn't reply. He is too absorbed. She treads softly upstairs and wakes Clarence before taking his tea and biscuits outside.

The big man creaks through the house in the manner of a bear creaking through a house. The floor in his room creaks, the door creaks, the floorboards on the landing creak, the stairs creak, the landing at the bottom creaks. He's a big man, what can he do?

'You eating my biscuits?' He rumbles, smiling at Howie eating a custard cream.

'Yep, this one is mine...and this one...'

'Anything?'

'Nope. All quiet. I'm going in. You okay?'

'Fine. Night.'

'Night, mate.'

The Second Watch commences. Meredith is there. It is ordained that she will take Second Watch with the big man and eat biscuits. She whines softly as he eases his bulk down on the back step of the Saxon after several minutes of standing silently to absorb the sound of the night.

'Where is she?' Clarence asks, smiling at the dog. 'We're not all here...'

Jess snorts in the garden. It is ordained that she will take Second Watch with the big man and the dog and eat biscuits. She pushes the fence, testing the resistance. She turns and looks round, eyeing the back door and the glow of the candles within.

'I've got tea,' an absorbed Reginald tells the horse as she walks through the kitchen, clip clopping on the wooden floor dragging a stool with her.

Jess walks down the hallway. Her sides touching both walls, her ears brushing the lampshade hanging from the light fitting on the ceiling. She stops to look in the designated barrack room of the lounge and snorts air through her nose at the smells. She backs out and stops to stare at the small man on the stairs before deciding he doesn't have the sugar she can smell. Dave sheaths his knife and goes back up the stairs. His face as devoid of expression as ever.

Clarence grins. Meredith turns and whines with an urgent look at the plate of biscuits. All members are now present.

The Second Watch Biscuit Club commences. Three huge beasts munching at the back of an army truck.

Inside the house Howie and Marcy clamber into the double bed of the room set aside for them. They cuddle at first but it's too hot so they separate and lie apart to sink down into deep sleeps.

Paula and Roy mimic the actions. Lying apart without covers. Nick and Lilly, younger, hardier and more enraptured with true love withstand the heat to lie entwined and spooned. They wake frequently to feel the other's presence and drift back off to sleep with smiles touching the corners of mouths.

The night passes. The Second Watch Biscuit Club comes to an end. Jess remains out the front, cleansing her palate with the lush grass on the verges. Meredith dozes, her ears pricked and listening.

Mo stirs. He has been waiting for this all day and all night. It couldn't come soon enough. When he went to sleep, he positioned his bedroll carefully, leaving Dave only one route to him and that being from the lounge door. As he detects movement so he grins and points to where he knows the lounge door is.

'Wrong,' Dave says from behind him. Mo opens his eyes to look round. 'Good attempt,' Dave adds, his voice as flat as ever.

'How long you been there?' Mo asks, not bothered in the slightest at the thought of Dave creeping about in the night. This is the game.

'Three minutes. Training. Outside.'

Mo moves fast. His kit already laid out ready for dressing. Socks on. Trousers on. Boots on. Top on. Pistol checked. Rifle checked. Bag grabbed.

'Adequate,' Dave says in acknowledgement of the time keeping. 'Fruit. Water. Eat. Hydrate.

They eat and hydrate as Clarence creaks his way back through the house. Blowers stirs and rolls, tutting at the heat. Charlie wakes and blows air through her cheeks. Blinky farts. Cookey murmurs. Charlie looks over at the sound of his voice, staring intently in case of a nightmare and ready to give comfort. Cookey chuckles and mumbles *it's my chocolate cake.*

The first blow comes as Mo stands from putting his bowl on the floor. This is the game. The rules have been set. Mo reacts, dancing back to block with a grin on his face.

'We ain't warmed up yet.'

'Yes. I am sorry,' Dave says, stopping the attack. 'Wrists.'

Mo narrows his eyes as Dave starts circling his wrists. Dave watches Mo narrowing his eyes but portrays no reaction. Mo stiffens ever so slightly and starts circling his wrists while watching Dave like a hawk. Dave whips a hand out with a blur of speed as Mo leans back and away from the strike.

Mo smiles again. An energy between them. A bond of understanding. Mo thought about this all day yesterday. The motions, the feints, the dodges, the grips, locks, moves and counter moves. The toe taps, leg hooks, the pressure of the body and the suppleness of motion. He thought about every single movement and the speed it will take to land one on Dave. He dissected it. He absorbed it. He pondered, imagined, ran scenarios through his mind and cursed himself for every mistake he made.

Dave senses the energy between them. Dave has trained many people before, for single objective missions and for greater overall combat training. He trained Jamie and Jamie was good. Jamie was fast. Jamie was not boastful and looked at the training for what it should be, which is an enhanced set of skills that are continually improved upon.

Mohammed is not Jamie. Mohammed is entirely and uniquely different to anyone Dave has ever trained before. Mohammed is faster than all of them, quicker witted and with a cunning ruthlessness. He has fear but that fear is for the perception of failure and not the fear of injury or harm.

'Knees,' Dave says, standing on one leg to swinging his lower leg forward and back from the knee joint. 'Jess is over there.'

'Yep....ow!'

'Yes not yep.'

'Hips,' Dave says, placing his hands on his own hips as he starts circling.

Mo smiles, holding eye contact for the briefest of seconds before nonchalantly looking away. 'Yeah...' the word hangs in the air. Dave doesn't show outward reaction but Mo has to suppress the urge to giggle. The tension builds. Mo knows it is coming. He pauses his hip swing, lowering his head a fraction of an inch to widen his peripheral vision. Dave watches him, knowing the expectation is there, knowing the bait has been laid. He knows he should not strike Mohammed as that is what Mohammed wants and they should never do what is expected. However, the lure is too great, the sense of play is too strong and the glint in Mohammed's eye is too much to deny.

A smile is a rare thing for Dave. He doesn't smile now but the corners of his lips do give a certain twitch as he lashes out with a half speed barrage of straight punches that Mo reacts to with excellent precision.

There it begins but Dave doesn't do anything without reason and the warm up is completed within the combat training. Not that Dave expects Mo to notice or know the warm up is still being given.

Mo does notice though. He notices that Dave's punches are designed to make him swing left to right to finish the movement of his hips. He knows the greater distance Dave then leaves is to invite Mo to give low sweeping kicks to warm up his legs. He notices that Dave builds the pace gradually until their bodies are starting to thrum and their muscles are buzzing with energy.

Meredith watches them, her tail swishing as she senses the play being given. This is the way of training as training should be. Pups learn through play. They learn the pressure of the bite. They learn motion, speed and power. She knows what they are doing and dozes contentedly with soft brown eyes flicking open every few minutes.

'You are warmed up now,' a statement not a question but the invite is there and Dave lays his own bait, watching Mo with expressionless interest to see what the response will be.

Mo nods, serious and solemn. 'Yeah.'

They go again. Dave attacking and Mo defending. Simple punches and kicks that Dave knows are no threat to Mo.

'Yes not yeah,' Dave says, giving a flurry of blows into Mo's lower back as the lad spins round to fend off.

'Yeah,' Mo says, unable to suppress the giggle this time.

Dave gives a flash of true speed and power. A wrist grab, pulling Mo in. A leg hook unbalancing the lad. A gentle shoulder barge to take Mo down. A second wrist grab to grab the arm that he knew Mo would send at his head. He moves deftly, drawing Mo's arms across his body while holding him just below the point of balance.

'Yes not yeah,' Dave says, staring down at Mo who is frantically thinking how to counter move. He tries to kick but finds Dave foot blocking him. He tries to roll but the position prevents it.

'How do I get out?' Mo asks, examining the holds and position.

'Yes not yeah.'

'Break the lock?' Mo asks, grunting to try and counter turn Dave's grip on his wrists.

'Yes not yeah.'

'Okay okay,' Mo says, nodding quickly as though in preparation of submission but Dave has seen the glint and knows Mo will try to lift both his legs to make Dave either hold his weight or drop him, either way it will break the lock. Mo does try that move. He flexes from the core to flick his legs up towards Dave's neck for a scissor grip but Dave simply lets go and steps back as Mo flops down with a dull thud.

'Good,' Dave says, nodding once.

'I ain't disrespecting you when I say yeah.'

'I know,' Dave says simply. 'Get up,' he reaches out to offer a hand to Mo who takes it while knowing the rules of the game and surges up using Dave as leverage. Dave knew it would happen and allows the attack to come. He gauges Mohammed's speed, dexterity and fluidity of motion to match his own body just above the level Mo is capable of achieving.

The close quarters fight is a blur of arms and legs moving at stunning speeds but each movement is only that which it should be. Dave leads Mo down the street simply blocking each move and feeling Mo's speed increasing. Mo goes for a wrist grab that is turned away, he tries again and is countered but keeps trying with a flurry of hands trying to grip and hold. Dave goes for his own lock but slowly enough to let Mo deflect and counter. Back and forth and for those few minutes it is just wrist and arm locks being attempted until Mo is sent spinning away and now takes his turn to parry the incoming attack. A withering speed from Dave. Hard hits given that land on Mo's cheeks with ringing slaps. He cuffs the back of Mo's head to fuel the anger he knows is bubbling under the surface. This is play but Mo has to be able to fight through his emotions. Mo senses the taunt and it stings. It stings his pride that he is being toyed with so easily.

'You are angry,' Dave says in that awful cold monotonous voice. He slaps Mo again. Mo snarls and turns back, faster and harder now. He storms in with lightning speed to feint left then right while ducking to grab Dave's ankle that is slipped an inch out of reach. As he lifts he tries to punch into the side of Dave's kneecap but strikes the hard top of the patella instead. A grunt from the pain in his knuckles.

'You are weak.'

Mo feels the rage spilling up. The cold hard lust for battle. He spins and launches into attacks.

'You are a child.'

The rage turns incandescent. The dent of his pride. The frustration at being denied the chance to score a point. Still he goes faster. Drawing energy and power from his core to deliver devastating blows that hit empty air and the place Dave was at a split second before.

Dave goads him. Dave taunts him. He mocks and cajoles in that terrible cold dispassionate voice. He slaps again and again. He flicks Mo's ears and tweaks the end of his nose. He kicks him in the backside and boxes his ears but lets Mo keep coming until suddenly he grips and locks Mo up in a blur of motion until the lad is pinned down with Dave leaning his weight into the back of Mo's elbow, easing towards the break point.

'Did that anger aid you?'

'Fuck you...'

'Did that anger aid you?'

'I'll fuck you up...'

Dave lets go. 'Try then.'

'Cunt,' Mo's up and in. Lashing forward. Dave hits harder now. Slapping with greater force that knocks Mo's head to the side. Mo becomes unrestrained, wild with rage that sends him into a fury of uncontrolled movements. Dave grabs an arm that is pushed up behind Mo's back, gripping him hard while turning him in a tight circle.

'Did that anger aid you?'

Mo can't speak. He cannot form words. He tries to move out of the lock but his mind is too fogged. A foot strikes the back of legs. He sinks down. His hair is gripped. His head pulled back.

'Did that anger aid you?'

'Fucking...'

Face down now on the ground in the dirt at the side of the road. Dave on top grinding his head into the mud.

'Do not ever allow your emotions to overcome your capabilities. Break. Hydrate.'

Dave walks away barely breathing harder than normal as Meredith watches lazily from the back of the Saxon. Her ears pricked as her eyes blink heavily on the cusp of sleep. The pup is annoyed. The pup wants to run and jump before he can walk. No matter. She dozes back off to sleep as Mo walks slowly towards Dave.

'Sorry,' Mo says after a few minutes of silence with shame creeping into his cheeks.

Dave shrugs.

'I's don't like people takin' the piss like that...'

Dave looks at him, staring without expression. 'You are not what you were.'

'What?'

Dave doesn't reply but simply looks at him. 'This is training.'

Mo nods and swallows the rush of emotions. The shame at being taken to anger so easily and the sting of being toyed with and beaten so easily. He'll never match Dave. Nobody can ever match Dave. Mo feels too heavy, too slow and cumbersome. Like an elephant chasing a fly.

Dave looks up at the sky then out to the horizon of the sea and the fort in the distance. 'You are less than half my speed.'

Mo nods again. Chastised and repentant of his failures.

'You are twice faster than yesterday.'

Meredith senses the change in dynamics. The way the pup suddenly looks up with wide eyes.

'Ready?'

'Yeah.'

Meredith's tail swishes as the pup smiles youthful and full of play once again. She watches them fight and run back and forth as the wooden spatula is drawn and used. She dozes then comes awake when Mo starts dry firing his pistol at given opportunities and she flicks her ears at the sound of skin on skin when Dave delivers a strike. If the other pack members saw the pup being hit they would become angry. They don't like their own pack being hurt but the teacher is doing the right thing. The pup has to learn the pressure of the bite and besides, she's watching and as fearsome as the small man with the strange energy is, she'd still rag him down the street.

Mo is taught left hand firing. To draw and dry fire with his weaker left instead of his dominant right hand. He takes to it quickly, learning the adjustments needed. He is passed Dave's empty pistol and taught to hold both but never to fire at the same time. Always one after the other. Aim, fire, aim, fire. Every bullet should hit a target. Every aim is calculated. They are always several moves ahead of the enemy. They are different. They think faster. They move faster. Draw both. Aim, fire, aim, fire.

'What about loading? I got's both hands full?'

'Put one away.'

'Can't you re-load both at the same time?'

'It is possible but you will not learn this now.'

'Show me.'

'You will not learn this now.'

'Can you do it?'

'Yes.'

'Can I see?'

'You will not learn this now.'

'Just once? Show me just once...'

'I will show once...give me your pistols. My magazines are here on my belt. I know where they are. I lift the pistols to give height and space. I eject the magazines. They fall away. I release the pistols, grab the magazines, lift them up as I let go and catch the pistols to push them down into the magazines...'

'That ain't possible.'

'It is possible.'

'Ain't.'

'It is.'

'Show me then.'

'Watch.'

Dave does it. A speed of motion that Mo tracks. His hands lift the pistols to head height then let go. The magazines are launched into the air with a movement that keeps them straight. His hands grab the pistols and slams the butts down onto the magazines. The downward motions continues as he rams the butts into his thighs. A flick, the pistols twirl so he can grab the top. Another flick forces the slides back, chambering the first rounds, another flick and the pistols are held ready.

'It is possible.'

'Fuck.'

CHAPTER ONE

In the communal barracks of the lounge, Blowers comes awake at hearing Mo Mo rustling about. He sits up, yawning sleepily to see the lad drying himself with a towel.

'You alright?' he whispers, looking over at Mo.

The lad gives a wide grin, 'yeah...you?'

'Fucking hot. Training okay?'

'S'good,' Mo whispers as Blowers leans closer.

'Dave got you a few times then.'

'What?'

'Your cheeks.'

'S'hot.'

'That ain't heat...come here a bit,' Blowers says, sitting up to stare harder with an expert eye. 'Dave's bruised your cheeks.'

'Has he?' Mo asks, feeling his face again. 'They's feel alright.'

'You'll be fine but keep your head down round Paula. She'll go nuts if she sees your face.'

'Okay, cheers, Blowers.'

'Get something cold on them, wet flannel or something. Bring the swelling down.'

'I will, thanks.'

Blowers looks round at Blinky still fast asleep, Charlie murmuring softly and Cookey face down with his sheet bunched up over his legs. Biting his bottom lip, Blowers eases from his bed and motions for Mo to stay quiet with a finger pressed to his mouth. Mo frowns, smiling and watching Blowers grab a bottle of water from the floor then point at Cookey with a big grin. Mo nods. Instantly onside. Blowers points to Blinky, nodding for Mo to wake her up. Mo drops to her side and rests a hand on her shoulder while pressing a finger to his own lips. Blinky snaps wide awake in an instant. She frowns and follows Blowers pointing at Cookey while waving a bottle of water in the air. She nods. Instantly onside.

Mo points to Charlie, a questioning look on his face. Blowers nods. Giving the order. Mo gets to Charlie, drops and rests a hand on her shoulder while his finger remains at his mouth. Charlie wakes and smiles at Mo trying not to giggle. The lad points at Cookey, Charlie looks up, seeing Blinky crawling towards Blowers who is waving a bottle of water while pointing at Cookey. She grins and nods, instantly onside.

The plan forms. The attack commences. Blowers leads his team and indicates for Charlie to get the sheet free from Cookey's legs. She goes gently, easing the bunched material out that gets lifted and held by Mo and Blinky. Blowers stretches his hands out, motioning for them to bring it down over Cookey. Giggles are suppressed, bottom lips are bit, heads turn away to stop the risk of laughing coming out. The sheet is laid over Cookey. Blowers motions with his hand to lift it higher. Charlie nods, suddenly understanding and eases the sheet up to cover Cookey's arms. Blowers gives a thumbs up and guides Blinky to stand on one end of the sheet then Charlie and Mo the other side. They go stealthy and silent. Creeping over the sheet to gently draw the tension over Cookey who sighs in his sleep. Blowers makes a fist. They hold still.

Sensation of movement. They look round to see Dave standing

in the doorway watching them. Guilty looks creep across faces. Dave stares, taking it in. He looks down at Cookey slowly being pinned under the sheet and the bottle of water in Blowers hand. He comes forward, silent in his steps before stopping and pointing at Cookey's legs poking out the bottom of the sheet. He makes flat hands and presses down, indicating the legs should be held. Blowers' mouth drops open. Mo manoeuvres to Cookey's legs, lowering to hold his hands an inch from Cookey's ankles then looks up to Dave who nods once and walks off as silently as he entered.

The sheet is ready. Charlie on the left side. Blinky on the right. Mo on the legs. Meredith sits on Blowers bedding watching intently. Blowers wishes Nick was here to add his weight but they must prevail and work with what forces they have. He goes forward, ready to execute the plan then stops to hold his breath to stop the giggle coming out. His face sets Charlie off who has to turn away. Mo's face scrunches up as he looks down, his hands trembling from the laughter locked inside. Blowers steels himself and draws resolve to keep going. He mouths *on three*. Charlie snorts softly then winces an instant apology as Cookey stirs. Blowers pauses, waiting for Cookey to go silent. He lifts a finger, *one*. He lifts a second finger and makes ready, *two*. He creeps to get his feet either side of Cookey and lowers to a squat as his third finger comes up. *Three*.

Perfection of execution. Charlie comes in closer, applying pressure on her side of the sheet. Blinky the same. Mo's hands drop to grip ankles. Blowers lowers and aims the bottle as he drops his weight to open fire. Cookey gains the sensation of pressure first as the sheet is pressed over him. He feels the hands on his ankles and starts the journey up through the layers of sleep. Something comes down hard as water is sprayed in his face. He gasps and turns his head as water spurts up his nose, in his mouth and in his eyes. He tries to fight free but the room comes alive with the sound of giggling. In that split second he knows this is play and reacts accordingly. His ankles are held. His body covered. His face drenched. He sputters and yacks as the others burst out laughing. Cookey is strong though, he bucks to shift Blowers with a hand snatching out to grab the bottle of water. Charlie dives in, pinning the arm into Cookey's chest while giggling like mad. Cookey snorts and turns his head while bucking to get his legs free as Mo lunges in to apply his body weight. Cookey's other hand gets free and makes a desperate grab for the bottle as Blowers tries to hold his balance. Cookey gains the bottle and squeezes the plastic sides, sending a jet of water out into Blinky's face. Charlie spots another lying in arms reach and wriggles to get more ammunition. Blowers and Cookey battle over the bottle, laughing and giggling like schoolchildren. Cookey gets the aim and squeezes but Blowers is fast and dodges the incoming strike that swooshes past into Mo who tries to duck and cover. Charlie gets the other bottle and turns to spray into the side of Cookey's head. He sputters and turns to see Charlie laughing so hard the bottle wavers in aim.

Dave stands in the doorway watching. His face impassive. His whole bearing revealing nothing as he watches Cookey fighting valiantly but unable to defend all sides without taking hits. Dave watches Blinky grab Cookey's free arm and Mo shifting up to add weight with Blowers on Cookey's mid-section. He watches Charlie take aim and fire and Cookey sputtering to spray water from his mouth while laughing hard.

Dave doesn't understand finer social skills but this is not fine social skills. This is overtly play. He understands and his deft touch, he bends down to grab a bottle, aims and fires into the battle.

Dave firing anything is perfection of movement with head strikes gained. Water hits Blowers first who gasps and turns in shock to get another spurt. Blinky is next, a twitch of aim and Mo is given a blast, another twitch and Charlie is soaked. They all sputter in shock, buying a second for Cookey to get a hand free and fight back.

'Thanks, Dave,' Cookey gasps between laughing.

SHE COMES awake to the sound of laughter and like a mother the reaction within her is two-fold. The sound is lovely and represents play in a world where everything else has gone to shit. The other side of her wonders what they are up. There is a lure too. A weird feeling that makes her want to go down and join in with whatever they are doing, or just to watch with a coffee.

Instead, she stares at the ceiling then over to the window. The dawn is just pushing the night away. A battle of perpetual motion that will always play out. The night chases the day that chases the night. A world that turns. A planet that spins in orbit within a scale of such size it renders anything done on the surface as utterly meaningless.

Ah but it is a new day in the new world and as nihilistic as it all may seem she still blows air out through her cheeks and wishes it wasn't so bloody hot. A sheen of sweat covers her skin. Strands of hair lie plastered to her scalp and forehead. She glances at Roy lying on his side and pulls a thoughtful face that holds for a few long seconds before she decides the pressing on her bladder is taking priority over anything else.

She rises in bra and knickers to tread softly to the door and feels the trickle of sweat rolling down her cheeks and chest. She stops in the darker hallway, listening to the low giggles from downstairs. A smile forms from a sudden thump, a gargled yelp, the sound of water being sprayed then a fresh fit of giggles instantly followed by a chorus of voices all shushing each other.

Waking up happy in this new life is messed up. Everything is messed up but truth be told she wouldn't change it for anything. She holds still with her hand on the bathroom door handle, listening with that smile etched on her face. Clarence opens the door. His natural strength swinging so hard it drags Paula inwards who falls in with a yelp. Clarence reacts with lightning speed to bring her back up to her feet in one smooth motion of immense strength. She comes back to her feet, stunned for a second at the world shifting around her so fast.

'You okay?' Clarence rumbles, standing over a head taller and many inches wider. His enormous hands holding her elbows gently as he peers down with concern.

She blinks and looks up. Her eyes travelling over his bare chest to his thick neck and up to his soft eyes. The time to reply and say she's fine comes and goes. The silence extends. The way he stands so high over her. The strength in his hands holding her so gently.

'Paula?'

'Huh? Fine,' she grins wide and stupid, hoping to hell the shadows are hiding her blushing cheeks. 'Do you need more socks?'

'Socks?'

'Yeah er...' she blinks again and slowly thinks to stand properly to support her own weight. Clarence smiles softly, his hands slowly leaving her arms but tentative as though ready to catch her again.

'Sure you're okay?'

'Fine,' she nods quickly, too quickly and swallows as he goes to move past. She steps back into the doorframe. The pair of them acutely aware of being in underwear. 'Sorry,' she whispers.

'My fault,' he says politely, pointedly looking away.

'Er...after you,' she slides into the room to give him space to get through.

'Thanks,' he rumbles deep and shy, lifting a huge hand. As he passes through the hallway so the weak light of the new dawn bathes his face showing her the blush in his cheeks. She closes the door quickly, staring wide-eyed and frozen still.

No. Shaking her head she yanks her knickers down and sits on the loo to tinkle in the bowl. What the hell was that?

Paula razed a town to the ground on her own. She slaughtered hundreds of infected by careful planning and has earned her place to lead. She sees them all as family. Closer than family. They've killed together, wept and laughed, they've held each other at the worst of times and slept in the same room for fear of separation.

They cling to each other while all the time doing something of such magnitude it has made them living legends within a bare couple of weeks. They ground each other against the horror and terror and the rumours that follow them.

She adores Howie with something akin to worship and would follow him into the fires of hell. They all would, but she also knows they would all go in dirty pants, worn socks, dirty hair and stubbly chins. Howie is relentless in his nature. He is unforgiving and sometimes forgets others don't have his abilities. She offsets Howie's brutality and in so doing, she is perhaps closest to him than all of them. Howie listens to her, he respects her immensely and she knows the deep respect is returned, but she has never looked at Howie in that light. Not in the way a woman looks at a man. She sees the appeal of him. She sees the dark brooding nature and the sheer ferocity within him, but not like that. Howie is like a brother, closer than a brother. It is the essence that Meredith gave them during the big battle. They are pack and that feeling goes way beyond the human concept of family. What they saw through Meredith, what they felt and what came into them was a plane of existence completely different to anything they could ever comprehend and so the titles formerly attached become meaningless.

The lads are like children but not like children. They are exceptional killers bound with an unbreakable bond and a loyalty that comes from the heart but the organic view of them touches on the concept of *being* child-like because they are younger in years.

Paula isn't old enough to actually be their mother but that is the closest way she can describe it. She feels a special warmth for all of them. Especially Mo. That lad needs mothering too. She doesn't know anything about Mo's life before this, only that it was harsh and violent. There is a unique perception of each of them. There is a unique bond from her to them, from them to her and between each and all. That is pack. That is what Meredith showed them. Achieve that and live a different life. Think a different way. *From the heart.* She nods as she remembers.

Clarence though? She stares into space at the special warmth she feels for him and in the quietness of the dark bathroom, she lets the thought run longer than it should before chastising herself harshly and standing to rinse her hands.

CLARENCE EASES INTO HIS ROOM. As much as a giant can ease into a room that is. His mere presence seems to make the door squeak in fear as his fist grips the door handle for a second too long and holds a tad too tight as the poor thing starts to buckle. He shakes his head, dismissing the notion instantly. He has honour. Deep honour and will never allow such a thing to remain in his mind.

Instead, he looks at the window and the new dawn bringing a new day. He cocks his head at the sounds of the lads downstairs and smiles at the play obviously underway. Might as well stay up now. Get a brew on and sort some kit out. The GPMG needs a clean. His rifle could probably do with a clean too, and his pistol. Yep, plenty to do. Get a brew, get some work done.

'Clarence, are you okay?' Reginald asks, staring over from his bedroll.

'Hmm?' Clarence says, struggling to get his foot into his trouser leg. 'Yeah, why?'

'Those are my trousers.'

HOWIE HEARD something once that people in modern life were more stressed than people were during the blitz in London during the war. That stuck in his mind. There was a real daily risk that a German plane was going to drop a bomb on your head. Every day they had to dig through piles of rubble trying to rescue those alive or gather enough body parts together for the funeral.

He dismissed it at the time as bollocks. It was just tripe. Some dick had plucked something from the air that *sounded* good and it was repeated enough times by mainstream media to be believed.

For a start, how did they know what the stress levels were like during the blitz in London? Did someone invent a time machine and go back with a load of those high-vis tabard laminated badge-wearing teenagers to stand in High streets and ask questions?

Hi, we're doing a survey on stress. Do you have a few minutes?

Not right now. My house just got bombed by the Luftwaffe.

But you can win a prize!

So how did they know? Did they go and ask a bunch of old people in care homes? *Hi, are you more stressed now than you were during the war?*

Thing is, if someone caught him at the wrong time in a normal working day and asked him that question he would have said yes, right now he is more stressed than at any other point ever but only because the emotion of the situation was at the forefront of his mind.

So some boffin said, apparently, that people were more stressed in modern life than during the blitz and you know what? Right now, on the morning of the twentieth day since everyone started eating each other, he does actually agree with them.

His washing machine broke a few months ago. He needed a new one. He went online and bought a new one. It was super easy and a marvel of the modern world. The day of delivery, he popped out to get something and missed the delivery attempt. Thereafter, it became a living hell of trying to communicate with a faceless corporation whose front line existed in the way of poorly trained low-paid advisors. He was put on hold and transferred so many times he lost track. He had to explain the issue over and again. He had to *pass security* again and again. It took a whole day to resolve and by the end of it, he felt exhausted, distracted, drained and bordering on a psychotic episode that manifested in a fantasy of finding the owner of the company and punching them in the nose.

He does not have that now. Those days are gone. Everything became too big. They became machines and lost the humanity of existence. They *centralised* to make things cheaper and in so doing, they fucked themselves over and lost the spark of life.

So yeah, right now, he gets it. They are at constant risk of death. They are under threat. They have seen their mates killed. They have killed their mates. They have seen and given more death than anyone has a right to see or give. They have cried, wept and felt so forlorn, so wretched that they wanted nothing more than to curl up and sleep the eternal sleep of the deceased. They demanded justice from God for the awfulness of what was happening. Then they realised God is a dick so they went out and spanked the baddies themselves.

They laughed too. Howie has laughed more now in the last twenty days than he did in the last ten years of his life before this happened.

He is in a house that is not his. He does not know who built this house, who owned it, who lived here or anything other than it is the last house on the bay opposite a fort that now stands on an island. He is staring out the window to that fort right now. He can see it. He can feel the heat of the day on his skin. He can smell the salt of the sea. There is a double bed behind him with a woman snoring gently upon the sheets. Downstairs he can hear laughter and play being given.

They have a horse. They have a dog. They have a Dave and a Clarence. They have a Nick who can fix shit. They have a Mo who can break into shit. They have a Roy who can fix people, sort of, kind of. They have a Paula and a Marcy, a Charlie, a Blinky and a Saxon that is big and mighty and wants nothing more than to go with them and spank the baddies. They now have a Reginald who is smarter than they are and will fuck 'em over for the sheer pleasure of winning and proving his intellect is better than theirs. They have ego and pride. They are humans flawed beyond comprehension. An Autistic ex-Special Forces soldier that was not actually

Special Forces but something much more sinister and deadly. He doesn't think the SAS blow cows up for a start and make things go bang so much they can be seen from space. Marcy is vain as fuck. Paula is a control freak. Roy is just messed up. Mo should really be in prison. Blowers and Cookey take the piss out of everything. Seriously, if God actually walked into this house right now and said *hey mortals, I am God, I am powerful, and you are puny.* Those two would call him a dick and make totally inappropriate gay jokes. God could smite them both to death and they'd go all smited and in pain but still taking the piss.

What the fuck? Howie shakes his head at the tangents of thought popping up. Is there a word for that? He bets Reginald knows. He'll ask him later. For now though he shall saunter across this room, ease himself down on this bed and bite into the bare arse he can see before him. Actually, that might be in bad taste. Darren bit her arse so maybe Howie biting her arse isn't such a good idea. Okay, no bum biting. He really wants to bite though. Not hard like to actually hurt or anything, but you know that urge you get? Just to nibble a bit and make gnawing noises? He has that now.

Hmmm. Not the arse then. He could go lower for some thigh. Or higher for some back or shoulder. Maybe some neck? An arm?

'Go back to sleep,' she murmurs all murmuring and sleepy like.

'I'm a zombie,' he tells her. Which also is perhaps a stupid thing to say, seeing as she was also a zombie, which came about from being bitten on the arse by Darren.

'Twat.'

She appears not to have taken offence and instead has called him a twat in that sleepy murmuring way. He bites down into her neck which makes her squeal, scrunch up, roll over, laugh and beat him off all at the same time.

'I'm a zombie...'

'Get off!' she squeals again and giggles at his mouth descending once more to her neck.

'Is this in bad taste?' he asks her, pulling back a few inches.

'What?' she asks, still giggling and blinking her eyes open.

'Being a zombie.'

'Um...nah,' she says, smiling a flash of white teeth.

'Cool...you okay?'

'Mmmm,' she says, stretching all languid and just so fucking sexy it makes him stare down and want this second to become infinite. 'Is it early? I bet it's early. Go back to sleep...'

'But...'

'If it's twat o'clock I...' she trails off, stretching to look at the window and the sky that snitches on Howie by being all dawn-like with purples and blues and pinks. 'Fuck's sake,' she groans then reaches out to pull him down to squash his face into her boobs then commences a rather hard patting stroking like motion on his face. 'Go back to sleep,' she pats / strokes while he suffers death by boobs. 'Actually sod off, it's too hot,' she rolls away to lie face down and grooves into the bed with a long sigh of more sleepy murmuring.

'Fancy a coffee?'

'In bed?' she asks, her voice muffled from the pillow.

'I'll bring it up.'

'Awesome,' she flaps a hand in his direction.

He slides off the bed and pulls his trousers on, grabs his clothes, kit, bag, weapons and with his arms full of gear he heads down to the bathroom.

His *ablutions*, as Dave calls them pass without incident. Other than some weirdo staring at him from the mirror. Howie doesn't like the look of him so he avoids eye-contact in case he mistakes it as an invite to commence conversation. Instead, he urinates, brushes his teeth and showers under freezing cold water that feels divine after such a hot steamy night. Not steamy as in sex-steamy. Steamy as in just bloody hot and sweaty.

'Fuck,' he mutters under his breath standing nudey in the bathroom and realising he has no clean pants or socks. He puts yesterdays on with a grimace then curses again when he realises he's down to his last clean top too.

He comes out to nod at Paula emerging from her room.

'Morning, Mr Howie.'

'Morning, Miss Paula.'

The leaders of the living army. The fearless warriors of heart and sinew that hold their band of fighters together with grit in their eye and a snarl on their lips.

'Run out of pants and socks,' Howie says.

'Okay,' Paula says.

The leaders nod at each other as the door opposite opens to reveal a man mountain silhouetted by the light of the window behind him. A Viking from days of old. A Berserker of Biblical strength.

'I'm out of boxers,' Clarence says.

'Okay,' Paula says, trying not to think of seeing Clarence in his boxers a few minutes ago.

'And socks,' Clarence adds, remembering her asking him if he needed socks a few minutes ago and trying not to think of her in underwear.

'Okay,' Paula says.

'HAIRBANDS,' Marcy bellows, sleepy, languid and now not murmuring but shouting from the bedroom.

'OKAY,' Paula calls up.

'Arrows,' Roy calls out, sleepy, languid and stretching in bed.

'Okay,' Paula says.

'Knives,' Dave calls out from outside the front door, on watch but listening as ever to the motion of every living thing near him.

'Okay,' Paula calls down.

'My last clean top,' Howie says, plucking his tight black wicking top away from his chest as though Paula wouldn't know this was the top he was referring to.

'Okay,' Paula says.

'Mine too,' Clarence says, also plucking his top out from his body.

'Think I'm on my last one,' Roy calls out.

'How strange,' Howie says.

'Not really,' Paula says. 'We all got the same amount three days ago…which was three…three days ago…'

'HAIRBANDS…'

'Heard you,' Paula calls back.

'WHERE'S MY COFFEE?'

'YOU ASKING ME?' Paula shouts.

'NO. HOWIE. HE SAID HE WOULD BRING ME COFFEE.'

'Okay,' Paula says. 'Shopping day then.'

'Oh fuck,' Howie says.

'Bugger,' Clarence says.

'Arse,' Roy mutters, rolling over.

'YAY,' Marcy shouts.

'How the fuck?' Howie asks, shaking his head in the direction of his room. 'She's got the hearing of a bat…' he mutters under his breath.

'BATWOMAN.'

'Coffee,' Howie says.

'Coffee,' Clarence says.

'Okay,' Paula says.

'Arse,' Roy mutters.

'I'M A BATWOMAN…'

The three fearless leaders traipse down the stairs as Batwoman groans in irritation at needing a wee. They stop at the door to the barracks, also known as the lounge, and stare in to see three young men and two young women sat on their arses in underwear, soaking wet and giggling with red cheeks.

'Sir, morning Mr Howie, Sir. Miss Paula, Sir…and er… Clarence, Sir,' Blinky blurts, launching to her feet to snap a salute.

'Right,' Howie says slowly, grinning at the sight.

'Dave,' Cookey starts to say then stops due to the giggles cutting him off. He composes himself, draws breath and tries again. 'Dave saved me...'

The three fearless leaders do an eyes right order to the front door and the small man outside staring in as devoid of expression as ever but with just the merest hint of reproach in his eyes, *as if I would*.

'He did!' Cookey exclaims.

'Coffee, Mr Howie?' Paula asks.

'Aye, coffee, Miss Paula, Sir,' Howie says, adding an *as you were* nod at the barracks.

The three launch the attack into the kitchen. Clarence goes for the big pan, pouring water ready for heating. Howie makes fire, manly and heroically striking the match that flames to ignite the gas pumped from the jets. Paula manhandles the mugs, forcing order from chaos.

Water pouring. Fire igniting. Cups clattering. Feet thunder on the ceiling above their heads as Batwoman decides that having a wee and getting ready for the shopping day are actually far more enticing than being served coffee in bed. More floorboards creak. A door opens.

'Fuck it,' Nick's voice floating down as he comes out of his room to spot Marcy securing the bathroom ahead of him. Feet on the stairs, thudding fast and fluid as Nick runs down to stop with a bemused look into the lounge.

'Morning fucktards...what the...actually I need a piss,' he runs off for the downstairs toilet.

'How many of us?' Paula asks, pausing to squint while sorting the mugs. Howie and Clarence exchange glances. Shaking heads and shrugging.

'Twelve?' Howie suggest.

'Thirteen?' Clarence offers.

'Fourteen,' Paula says, resuming the placing of the mugs. 'Lilly is upstairs...she doesn't have sugar does she?'

'Er,' Howie says.

'Um,' Clarence says.

'We'll just put a sugar pot out,' Howie says.

'No she doesn't have sugar,' Paula says, nodding to herself. The two men watch as she deftly adds spoonful's of sugar to mugs, one in this one, two in this one, one in this one, miss one, one in this one.

'Do you actually know who has what?' Howie asks.

'Yep,' Paula says, hesitating with a glance back at the row of mugs then resuming confidently.

'No way,' Howie says, he steps over and points at a mug, 'who's that for?'

'Nick, white, two sugars in the morning, one sugar the rest of the day but he will drink it black and without if need be.

'Fuck,' Howie says in genuine admiration. 'What about this one?'

'Marcy. No sugar, only a dash of milk or half a portion of those little pots...'

'This one...'

'Roy, no sugar, normal milk or one portion.'

'She's a witch,' Howie whispers to Clarence. 'We should burn her.'

'We should,' Clarence whispers back.

'Idiots.'

'How do you do that?' Howie asks.

'It's in order of us...' Paula says. 'I mean in order of us in my head...don't you do that?'

'Er, do what?' Howie asks.

'So it starts with you,' Paula says, tapping the first mug. 'So... Howie, white or black, one sugar prefers milk and actually doesn't like instant coffee but will drink warm piss if it has caffeine in it. Then me, white no sugar. Clarence, he prefers tea but goes with coffee and likes it white with one sugar, Dave black no sugar,

Blowers white one sugar but will do black no sugar and he does like tea but only if we have milk and he likes his tea strong. Nick white two sugars, same with tea but he can drink both without, Cookey white two sugars but will take black without and he prefers it milky so I always put two or three portions in his. Er...Charlie, white no sugar and loves herbal tea but will do black. Blinky, black for tea and coffee, no sugar. Mo Mo is the same as Cookey and has two sugars and likes it milky. Roy no sugar with only a dash of milk. Marcy, no sugar and only dash of milk or half a portion pot and Reginald has herbal tea...so er...oh and Lilly of course, who doesn't have sugar.'

'Oh,' Howie says simply.

'Needs burning,' Clarence whispers again. 'I don't know how you do that, Paula.'

'Magic,' Paula says.

Upstairs, Lilly moves down the hallway but stops at the bathroom door on hearing movement inside. She goes to retreat in the way of good manners and the etiquette of not being caught waiting for the toilet.

'Hey you,' Marcy says, having detected movement outside with her hearing of a bat and opening the door to peer out with her toothbrush in her mouth.

'Morning, Marcy,' Lilly says politely. There are degrees of connections and even though Marcy is one of the group, Lilly hardly knows her so she retains the polite formality.

'Need a wee?' Marcy asks, not detecting or simply just ignoring any sense of formality.

'I can wait,' Lilly counters, still polite.

'Pah,' Marcy says and waves the bathroom. 'Go on, I'll wait out here.'

'Er,' Lilly hesitates. Marcy is in her bra and knickers and completely unbothered at standing in the hallway in such a state of undress. 'Honestly I can...'

'Go on,' Marcy says, pulling the toothbrush out to smile with a level of natural warmth that makes Lilly feel more comfortable. She goes inside while Marcy hums and brushes her teeth.

'Thank you,' Lilly says, opening the door.

'Anytime,' Marcy goes in to rinse and spit, using a bottle of water instead of the tap. She was infected so whatever might be in the water cannot harm her but the thought of rinsing or drinking with tainted water revolts her. She glances at the door to see Lilly hesitating as though suddenly unsure of something. 'You okay?' Marcy asks, moving towards the girl. 'How was last night?'

'Oh fine. Yes fine. Thank you,' Lilly says, still prim and proper.

'No no no,' Marcy draws her back into the room and closes the door, sealing them in the bathroom. 'What's up? You okay?'

'Um,' Lilly pauses, the mask of cold ruthlessness slips as she suddenly looks the sixteen year old girl she is.

'Hey,' Marcy pulls her in, rubbing her back. 'It's okay...you're okay. Was it your first time?'

Lilly nods. Her eyes filling with tears. She doesn't reply but she doesn't need to reply.

'It's okay,' Marcy says softly, rubbing Lilly's back. She remembers her first time with a man. It was awful and horrible and seedy and drunk. All she wanted was her mum but Lilly doesn't have that. Lilly doesn't have anyone now. 'It's okay,' she says instead, rubbing and soothing. She pulls back to kiss Lilly's head with an act that brings the tears flooding from Lilly's eyes to roll down her cheeks. 'What's wrong? Did something happen? You can say, Lilly...'

'No no, it's nothing...' Lilly sobs the words out, half crying half smiling. 'It was so nice.'

'Oh bless,' Marcy's own eyes fill as she pulls her back in for another hug. 'Had me worried then...christ, there's not many girls that can say that...It's just emotions coming out...did it hurt a bit?'

Lilly nods, 'Nick thought he hurt me...'

'No. No he didn't. It happens to everyone. Bit of blood too?'

'Only a bit...he was so gentle...'

'It's Nick,' Marcy says as though that explains everything. 'He's a keeper alright. So nothing hurts now does it?'

'No no, I am fine. Honestly. I do apologise.'

'Oh don't be silly,' Marcy says kindly, 'you're lucky. I remember my first time. God it was awful. I was so drunk and he was a disgusting pig.'

Lilly snorts a laugh and gently pulls back.

'It's easy to forget how young you are,' Marcy says, examining the girl closely as she smooths Lilly's hair back. 'It's normal. What you're feeling now I mean. Your hormones will be all over the place for a few days but it'll settle. Nick adores you, you know that. Don't doubt that for a second. We all adore you.'

Lilly nods again, the composure coming back steely and cold.

'Good girl,' Marcy says, seeing the look coming into Lilly's eyes. 'New world now. New rules. With us it's safe but fuck everyone else...you are so beautiful, Lilly,' she smiles warm and sad, worried and full of hope all at the same time. 'We'll go soon. Howie won't stay here, you know that right? Nick will want to stay here with you but he won't. He'll go with Howie the same as the rest of us but that doesn't mean Nick doesn't want to stay with you...'

'I know,' Lilly says quietly. 'Nick said how many you face sometimes...'

'It's insane,' Marcy says, meaning every word. 'Howie needs Nick...but...what you did before, you do that again if you need to. If you have to kill then do it. Don't hesitate. Don't let it get bad enough that you can't react.'

'Okay.'

'Good,' Marcy says, holding a serious expression that melts as she smiles and winks. 'Now, did you use a condom or are we all having babies in nine months?'

CHAPTER TWO

The boat glides gently onto the beach, the hull scraping on the soft sand. Dawn and the night is still lifting but the promise of another scorching hot day is there to be seen.

Maddox goes first, leaping over the front onto the sand and turning quickly to grab the front of the boat to hold it steady. He offers a hand.

'Thank you,' Pea says, taking his firm grip to drop from the boat.

'Sam?'

'I'm fine,' Sam says coldly, avoiding eye contact to clamber from the boat herself.

Maddox shows no reaction but offers his hand to the next person instead, 'Joan?'

'No thank you,' she says brusquely.

'Kyle?' Maddox says, looking at the craggy face. 'Want me to take that?'

'Ah now, that'll be a kind thing of you,' Kyle says, passing the basket over before jumping deftly down onto the sand.

'You move well for an old man,' Joan says with an arched eyebrow.

'You move well yourself,' he says, smiling kindly as he takes the basket from Maddox.

'I don't overeat,' she says stiffly. 'Shall we? No point in dilly-dallying here all morning. I cannot abide dilly-dallying.'

'Oh I like a dilly dally now and then,' Kyle says easily.

'Are you being rude? I cannot abide rudeness.'

'Ah you're a feisty woman so you are there, Joan.'

'Do not use that Irish brogue on me young man.'

'Irish you say? My accent is not Irish.'

'Your voice is Irish. You are Irish. I tell it like it is.'

Pea pulls a face at Sam who shrugs and scowls at Maddox trying to smile at her. She's got a rifle on her chest and a pistol on her hip. Joan and Sam the same. Maddox might be armed but he's outnumbered and so the confidence is there to show overtly what she thinks of him.

They thread round the piles of goods on the beach to gain the road. Walking down towards the lone figure of Dave standing like a sentinel with his legs planted and his rifle held ready but lowered.

'Morning, Dave,' Joan says, her tone as blunt as ever.

'Morning,' Dave says, his tone as blunt as ever.

'Are they up yet?'

'Yes.'

'Good. We'll take over watching. You can go and eat. Tell Lilly everything is fine in the fort. Billy slept soundly. The children are all fine and the rest will be over once they've finished eating.'

'Dave,' Maddox nods respectfully once Joan finishes issuing her instructions.

'Maddox. You will not come into the house.'

Maddox holds still, his face impassive while he thinks quickly. 'I'll wait,' he says.

'You will wait outside. You will not provoke my team. You will not speak to Mohammed. Do you understand?'

'I understand, Dave.'

'You will address Mr Howie as Mr Howie. If you pose any threat or risk to my team I will kill you. Do you understand?'

'I understand.'

'If you point your weapon towards any members of my team I will kill you. If you show anger towards any member of my team I will kill you. I am only not killing you now because Mr Howie has not told me to kill you. If Mr Howie tells me to kill you I will kill you.'

'Fuck me,' Sam mouths, wincing at the dull tones that sounds so much worse for the absolute certainty projected within the words.

'Good stuff,' Joan says, nodding at Dave. 'I like a man who speaks straight. Needed to be said. Chest straps,' she says, holding a bag out for Dave.

Dave nods, takes the bag and starts walking towards the house.

'Kyle has bread,' Joan says after him.

'Kyle is trusted. He can come into the house.'

Joan looks at Kyle sharply, raising yet another eyebrow as he smiles back, toothy and full of mischief.

'Will you look at that now,' he chuckles, following Dave.

'Irish,' Joan says.

'Maybe I am...or maybe not...'

'Irish,' Joan says, watching the old man enter the house and go straight into the lounge then switching her gaze to look at Sam and Pea. 'Stop that grinning right now.'

'Such a flirt,' Sam says.

'Flirting? Women my age do not flirt. We converse.'

'That was flirting,' Sam says, pointing at the front door.

Joan tuts, huffs and stands stiff. 'It was no such thing.'

'Someone coming already,' Maddox says, staring up the road as three women move out to see a white van coming towards them. 'I'll take this one. You get coffee and...'

'You are not in charge here, Maddox,' Joan cuts across him, her tone biting in delivery as she strides out to motion at the driver, telling him where to stop. Maddox hides the flinch at the sharpness of her tongue and walks across the road. It will take time to win them over again. He knows that.

The white Ford Transit stops next to Joan who takes in the adult male driving and the adult female in the front passenger seat. A sliding door on the side. Pea and Sam hold their rifles as taught by Joan, ready but lowered. Maddox stands back, his rifle also held ready and lowered as he fixes his eyes on the sliding door.

'Welcome,' Joan says in that curt tone. 'How many of you?'

'Er...' the woman hesitates, looking at the man. 'Was it six we picked up?'

'Six,' the man says with a nod.

'So six...seven eight...nine...ten...ten of us,' the woman says, nodding at Joan. 'The rest are in the back...'

'Obviously,' Joan says, pulling the sliding door back to look inside. She counts the people, reaching ten and nodding once. 'We'll need to check you all. Out you get...'

'Is that the fort?' The woman asks.

'It is,' Joan says, leaning into the van to take in the six exhausted filthy looking children. Three white kids, three Indian kids. 'Your children?' Joan asks.

'God no, we found them,' a woman in the back of the van says. 'About twenty miles back...the two older ones were pushing the rest in a wheelbarrow. Said they'd been attacked all night and had to run for it...bless 'em, half delirious. Keep talking about that actor, Paco Maguire?'

'Paco,' a small voice murmurs.

'What was that?' Maddox asks, striding towards the van.

'Tired children,' Joan says. 'We'll have to...'

'Did you say Paco?' Maddox asks, cutting across Joan to lean into the van.

'Yeah,' the woman says, shrugging and lifting her hands. 'They're exhausted...'

'About Paco,' Maddox presses.

'That one,' the woman says, showing confusion on her face and pointing at a little Indian boy.

'Hey,' Maddox says softly, touching the boy's shoulder. The boy mumbles, opening his eyes that close again as he drifts back off to sleep. 'Wake up,' Maddox nudges him gently, holding a soft tone.

'I think they need rest,' the woman in the front of the van says.

'Hey, wake up,' Maddox nudges a bit harder, the boy blinks and looks with wide eyes at Maddox. 'Hi, what's your name?'

'Rajesh,' the boy says, clearly frightened. He looks round for his big sister, reaching out to grab her arm. 'Subi...Subi wake up...'

'What?' Subi says, blinking awake to look in shock at Maddox.

'You said Paco?' Maddox asks, 'Paco Maguire? The actor right?'

Subi nods, her face showing fear. 'He got us here...and Heather...'

'Get Howie,' Maddox says, calling out to Sam and Pea.

'Whatever is...' Joan starts to say.

'Now. Get Howie now,' Maddox says. 'Heather?' He asks, looking back at the Indian girl.

She nods, wide eyed and moving to shield her little brother.

'You're safe now,' Maddox says. 'You're at the fort...who is Heather?'

'She found us,' Subi says. 'With Paco...'

'Are you sure it was Paco Maguire?'

'I am sure,' Subi says.

'What on earth?' Joan snaps, furious with Maddox for interrupting and talking gibberish about an actor.

'They got the dog from Paco,' Maddox says, running towards the house. 'She killed him...' he goes through the door as Blowers steams from the lounge door slamming him back outside.

'Fucking prick,' Blowers growls, pushing Maddox away, his face twisted with hatred.

'I need Ho...I need *Mr* Howie,' Maddox says, still holding his hands away from his body.

'You need a fucking spanking,' Blowers seethes. 'You fucked with Lani...you locked her in the hospital...the boss said on you, Maddox. Remember that? He said that. He said on you...'

'Blowers, I need to...' Maddox words cut off as the punch hits him full in the mouth.

'He fucking said on you...' Blowers says, pacing after Maddox scrabbling back. 'Come near us and I'll kill you...'

'Easy now, son,' Kyle's hand comes to rest gently but firmly on Blowers shoulder.

Maddox stares up at Blowers then past him to Cookey and Nick both hard faced. Two girls he doesn't know, one blinking furiously and the other with a huge cut down one side of her face. Lilly strides out. Her face a mask of composure.

'That's enough,' she says, her voice cold as ice.

'Yes, Ma'am,' Blowers stands down instantly, showing Maddox that Lilly has authority. He even turns to nod at her, giving respect with that discipline.

'What the fuck?' Howie asks after rushing down the stairs and now staring between Blowers standing over Maddox and Maddox lying on his back. 'Maddox? What...fuck me...is that bread I can smell?'

'Kyle made it,' Cookey says.

'Smells so nice,' Howie says, 'morning, Kyle.'

'Morning, Mr Howie.'

'Maddox, what you doing down there?' Howie asks.

'I tripped...'

'I hit him,' Blowers says without apology.

'Fair one,' Howie says, 'you pulled the punch then?'

'Just a bit,' Blowers mutters.

'Paco...the kids in that van said Paco got them here,' Maddox says, rushing the words out.

'Do what?' Howie says.

'Paco Maguire,' Maddox says, still on the ground and wanting to get up but sensing that getting to his feet right now might not be the best tactical move. 'They said Paco Maguire got them here... with a woman called Heather...said they were attacked all night... twenty miles from here...'

'Paco's dead,' Howie says, 'get up...Blowers, don't punch Maddox again.'

'Roger that.'

'Can I?'

'No, Blinky.'

'Sir.'

'Where are these kids? In that van?'

'Yeah,' Maddox says, moving slowly back to his feet while holding his hands away from the pistol on his belt. 'Can I pick my rifle up?'

'Eh?' Howie asks, 'er yeah sure...don't point it at anyone'

'What's going on?' Paula asks, coming out and sniffing the air. 'Is that bread?'

'Kyle made it,' Cookey says again.

'Smells so nice. What's going on? Maddox? Who hit you?'

'I did.'

'Christ, pulled the punch then,' Paula says, blinking quickly. 'He's still alive. Bloody hell that bread smells nice. What is it...if anyone says bread I will be cross.'

'Bread rolls,' Cookey says.

'Ooh get me one, Cookey. Howie? Want a bread roll?' Paula says.

'Yeah, yeah I'd love one cheers.'

'Want jam?' Cookey asks.

'He's brought jam?' Paula asks. 'What flavour?'

'Dunno...Kyle?' Cookey asks, turning round to see Kyle has gone back inside. What flavour jam is it?' he calls out.

'Blackcurrant.'

'Blackcurrant,' Cookey says.

'Ooh yeah, yeah bread and jam,' Paula says, pulling her hair back then tutting on realising she doesn't have a hairband.

'Here, Paula...' Charlie says, sliding one from her wrist.

'Thanks, Charlie...er...I can't let it go now...'

'I'll do it, ponytail?'

'Yeah please, nice and tight...thanks.'

'Boss? You want jam on your roll?' Cookey asks.

'Yeah please, mate. Everyone else having jam?'

'I'm having jam,' Clarence says, walking out. 'Blowers?'

'Yeah, cheers, Cookey.'

'What the fuck? I'm not making everyone's.'

'I'll help you,' Charlie says.

'Fuck yes! Best day ever. Maddox got twatted and me and Charlie are gonna fall in love making jam rolls.'

'Right so...oh yeah, Paco?' Howie asks, finally turning back to Maddox. 'Paula, some kids in that van said Paco got them here.'

'Paco Maguire? I thought the dog killed him.'

'She did,' Clarence says.

'Can't be then,' she says obviously.

'Go and ask,' Howie says.

'Me?'

'Yeah, you're good with kids...'

'You want me to ask if a dead Hollywood actor brought them here?'

'Yes.'

'The same bloke you all saw being killed by Meredith.'

'Um...yes.'

'Okay...fine. I'll go and ask that then.'

'And they said they were attacked twenty miles away.'

'By the dead actor or someone else?'

'Dunno I wasn't there...'

'Wasn't where?' Marcy asks, walking out to look at Maddox's bleeding lip questioningly.

'I did,' Blowers says.

'You did?'

'Yeah.'

'He's still alive.'

'Didn't hit hard.'

'Lucky you,' Marcy tells Maddox.

'Want a bread roll with jam, Marcy?' Cookey asks.

'Bloody do I? Yes! Yes please, Cookey.'

'Marcy, give me a hand,' Paula says, nodding at the van.

'With what?'

'We've got to ask some kids if a dead actor got them here.'

'That makes total sense,' Marcy says.

'Kids said Paco Maguire got them here,' Howie says.

'Paco? He's dead…didn't Meredith kill him?' Marcy asks.

'She did,' Clarence says.

'And they said they were attacked twenty miles away,' Howie says.

Marcy nods, nothing in this world is surprising anymore, apart from the smell of fresh bread that is. That's surprising. And jam too. 'Okay,' she says simply, following Paula to the van.

'Do Pea and Sam and Dave's mum want a bread roll with jam?' Cookey shouts from the house.

'Sam? Pea? You want a bread roll with jam?' Howie calls out. 'Is Dave's mum with you?'

'At the van with Paula and Marcy,' Pea says, 'and er…only if there's enough for you first.'

'She is not my mother.'

'Got loads,' Cookey shouts from the house.

'Howie…Nick…come here,' Paula calls out.

'Me?' Nick asks, 'why me?'

'Something needs burning down,' Blowers mutters.

'Funny,' Nick says, walking past Maddox, 'prick…'

'Nick,' Maddox nods politely.

'What?' Howie asks, reaching the van with Nick and seeing Meredith's arse and tail poking out the side opening.

'Meredith,' Marcy says, motioning towards the dog.

Howie and Nick go forward, exchanging *what the fuck* glances before seeing Meredith sniffing every child within the van. Not just sniffing but examining, assessing, inhaling deeply and whining while doing it with a keening noise that comes from her throat.

'She won't hurt you,' Paula says again to the children inside. 'She loves children...'

'And penises,' Nick whispers as Howie snorts a laugh.

'Nick,' Marcy laughs, hitting him on the arm.

'She's going nuts,' Paula says, 'look at her...think she can smell him?'

'Dunno, have you asked her?' Howie asks, getting a look in return.

'Why am I here again?' Nick asks, worried that his bread roll with jam will get eaten.

'She's your dog,' Paula says.

'She's not my dog,' Nick replies then looks at Marcy, 'she's not my dog.'

'Nick, think she can smell something?' Howie asks, watching Meredith closely.

'I don't know, Boss. She's not my dog...er...yes, yes she can... may I?' He goes closer, watching Meredith and the way she moves from hand to hand. Pushing her nose to open fingers to smell palms. She stops at the smallest child, a little Indian girl who grins widely at the dog and starts rubbing her head. Meredith keens more, her nose moving over every inch of the girl.

'Are you sure it was Paco Maguire?' Paula asks the same question again, getting nods coming back.

'Bread rolls,' Clarence says, walking into the group with his hands holding several jam filled weirdly shaped lumps of bread.

'Cheers,' Howie says, taking one.

'Want one,' the little Indian girl says on sight of the rolls.

'Amna,' Subi says, 'that is rude.'

'She can have mine,' Howie says, offering the roll to the little girl who beams with delight.

'Here, honey,' Paula says, offering her roll to Subi. 'Go on, we've got plenty.'

'Why is she sniffing that girl the most?' Marcy asks, offering her roll to the children.

'Dunno,' Nick says, thinking hard. 'Did Paco carry you? Did he carry this girl?' He asks the older children who nod.

'No way,' Howie says. 'Paco?'

'Hey,' Paula says, crouching at the side of the van. 'Did Paco have any injuries anywhere?'

Subi nods, her hand lifting to touch the base of her neck. 'Here.'

'He couldn't speak,' Rajesh says.

'He did speak, Raj,' Subi says. 'He said dog and girl and Heather...'

'Howie, want to get everyone ready?' Paula says softly. 'I'll find out the rest.'

'Yep.'

'Save me a roll,' she adds.

'And me,' Marcy says.

'Yep,' Howie calls out, rushing back with Nick and Clarence.

'She killed him,' Clarence says. 'We were there. We saw it.'

'Maybe she didn't,' Nick says.

'What's going on?' Blowers asks, eating a bread roll with jam.

'Get ready to go...Paula's finding out the rest but it's looking likely.'

'No way,' Blowers says, shaking his head.

'Is Maddox having a bread roll with jam?' Cookey shouts, 'cos I'll shit in it if he is...'

'I'm fine, thank you,' Maddox says, holding his impassive expression.

Chaos erupts. An explosion of activity of many people moving through a house while finding socks, boots, clean tops and eating jam filled bread rolls. Rifles are checked, fresh magazines loaded. Pistols the same. Dull metallic clicks sound from every room. Voices arguing over space and kit. The bathroom is used. A constant flushing of the toilet. Kyle moves amongst them, passing rolls into hands to make sure they all get something.

Charlie goes into the back garden to get Jess ready before going back into the house with a thoughtful look on her face. The cut on her cheek is itching already. She scratches it gently then the top of her ear too, feeling the new shape under her fingertips. She stops outside to look down at Jess munching happily on the grass verge.

'Why is Jess out the front?' She asks, going back into the house.

'My fault,' Clarence calls down from upstairs. 'She came out last night...'

'How did she...'

'Through the house. I had biscuits.'

'Oh. Oh I see. Right...'

'Is that okay? Can she have biscuits?'

'One or two now and then won't harm her.'

'Er...roger that, one or two....now and then...roger.'

She goes back outside to get Jess ready, checking the big animal over before leading her to the horse box at the back of Roy's van.

Maddox waits on the path outside the house. Watching and listening and feeling very alone. Pea and Sam eat bread rolls and move amongst the team with ease, sharing jokes and comments. Joan stays at the van with Paula and Marcy. Everyone ignores him. His lip stings a little but it's not the first time he's been hit and he knows Blowers pulled that punch a lot. That thought alone tells him there might be a chance to earn back the respect he had before. Still, it was a bloody hard punch though. He hasn't been put on his arse for a long time. Not since he was a kid.

'Twat,' Cookey mutters, rushing past to get the Saxon ready.

'Cookey,' Maddox says, still holding that polite tone.

'Cunt...'

'Who are you?' Maddox asks.

'Blinky,' Blinky says, stopping as she rushes behind Cookey. 'I blink a lot...'

'Oh...I'm Maddox.'

'I know.'

'Okay.'

'Bye.'

'Er...bye,' Maddox says as she runs towards the Saxon. 'Hey,' he looks down at feeling Meredith's nose sniffing his leg. He drops to a squat, rubbing her head and ears. 'Do you hate me?' She runs off back to the van and smells inside. 'Figures,' Maddox mutters, standing back up.

'We ready?' Howie asks, coming down the stairs with his hands full of kit. 'Marcy, your stuff is here by the door.'

'Ta,' she shouts from the van.

'Maddox.'

'Hi,' Maddox says, nodding at Roy coming out the house. 'How are you?'

'Fine...got a weird pain in my mouth though. In the right cheek...might be a growth.'

'A growth?'

'And I'm sure my neck doesn't feel right...' Roy says, turning his head side to side. 'Feels knotted...must be something bad.'

'New pillows?' Maddox asks.

'Ah could be...' Roy says, looking at the younger man thoughtfully. 'Blowers hit you?'

'S'nothing.'

'Bit swollen. I've got a medic's bag from the hospital section yesterday.'

'That's er...that's good.'

'Red.'

'What?'

'The bag. It's red. Got loads of stuff in it. I really want a defib though. We should have a defib.'

'Cock,' Cookey mutters rushing back into the house.

'Other than that I think I got some good stuff though. Have they got any over there?'

'Any what?'

'Defibs?'

'Er...I don't...yes, yes they have.'

'The mobile ones in the yellow case? It's all self-contained...has a voice that tells you what to do...'

'I'm not sure.'

'Cock.'

'Cookey,' Maddox says, nodding politely again.

'Course I said I'm not a medic but Howie seems to think I am.'

'Hey, Maddox.'

'Blinky.'

'Cunt...why are we calling him names again?'

'He locked Lani in the...'

'I could probably set a broken arm. Maybe a broken leg...you know, splint it up. Cuts and bruises are easy enough too. Did you see Charlie's face?'

'Er...the girl with the cut,' Maddox says, touching his own cheek.

'Yes, the same. I steristripped that wound. Doctors said I did a good job too.'

'That's good.'

'Roy.'

'Blowers,' Roy says, turning to the door as Blowers comes out. 'Pulled the punch then.'

'Bit. You ready?'

'Yep, all ready,' Roy says, nodding at his bow and kit bag at his feet. 'Am I taking my van?'

'Probably,' Blowers says, avoiding looking at Maddox. 'Can't be Paco...the dog had his throat out.'

'Maybe she didn't kill him,' Roy says. 'Did any of you check?'

'Check what?'

'His heart or pulse.'

'His throat was ripped open.'

'Still...look at Cookey's back and Charlie's wounds. There's a chance she left him alive...well, she must have done if he *is* alive.'

'Cookey's back?' Maddox enquires.

'Go fuck yourself,' Blowers mutters.

'Infected ripped his back open,' Roy explains. 'Healing well mind.'

'Ready,' Howie says, dumping kit bags on the floor as the others pile out.

'Will you be coming back here today?' Kyle asks, coming to the door.

'Hope so,' Howie says. 'Where's Reggie?'

'Behind you.'

'Oh, you read all that stuff yet?'

'I have and I need to read it again.'

'Righto, we'll be doing this for a bit. Paula? Marcy?'

'Two minutes,' Marcy says, leaning round the back of the van, 'did you save us some rolls?'

'I have them here,' Kyke says, holding two rolls wrapped in silver foil in the air.

'Don't let Nick eat them.'

'He's had four already so he has.'

'Four?' Blowers asks, leaning round Howie to look at Nick. 'You fat fucker.'

'Get bent.'

'Blowers is,' Cookey says, rushing past to the Saxon. 'Twat...'

'Cookey,' Maddox says, noticing as the last two come out the house. 'Mo Mo,' he says, nodding at the young lad.

'What did I tell you?' The space falls silent at Dave's dull hard voice.

'Awkward!' Cookey shouts from the Saxon.

Mo looks different. Older, harder, his eyes are like the rest of them now. Never still but always watching, always scanning. He doesn't slouch but stands straight and he's had a shave too. All the wispy hairs from his jaw and chin are gone. Like Dave he wears a pistol on each hip with the butts facing in to be cross drawn. Knife hilts on his belt. His bag secured with the chest and waist strap fastened. Like Dave. Mo looks like Dave. Dressed the same. Standing the same.

'Right,' Paula says, coming down to the group with Marcy. 'Everyone here?'

'Cookey and Charlie,' Howie says.

'Cookey? Charlie?' Paula calls out.

'Yep, coming,' Cookey says, dropping from the Saxon.

'Here,' Charlie says, rushing from the back of the horse trailer.

'What we got?' Howie asks.

'Everyone listening?' Paula asks, 'no funny comments from anyone...Cookey...'

'Roger that.'

'Lady called Heather and Paco Maguire find three Indian kids hiding in Tesco in a town called Boroughfare...'

'Do what? That's my town,' Howie says, looking at Dave. 'Where me and Dave worked...in that Tesco...'

'She said it was piled up with bodies.'

'Yeah, Dave did that...in the middle aisle.'

'I didn't ask what aisle funnily enough. Anyway, she said the smell kept the infected away.'

'Boroughfare? Seriously?'

'Yes. Boroughfare. Anyway, so this Heather and Paco found them a few days ago. The kids are filthy, living in this Tesco, so Heather takes them with her and Paco. Now they...what?'

'That's our Tesco.'

'Yes, Howie. I know. Heather gets them cleaned up and ends up handing them over to another group of survivors...they said Paco was all injured on his throat and his eyes were red. They said Heather bandaged him up and...'

'She a doctor then?'

'I don't know, Roy.'

'Oh, okay.'

'Tesco? Seriously?'

'Yes, in Boroughfare. So they are one hundred percent sure it was Paco Maguire. Said he was strong...like able to throw people and carried the kids all day and never got tired...'

'Why you all looking at me?' Clarence asks.

'...and also that he couldn't speak.'

'They said he did speak,' Marcy says.

'I haven't got to that bit.'

'She might be a doctor.'

'Me and Dave worked in that Tesco.'

'Fuck's sake...listen! Right, so Heather and Paco give the three kids to another woman. They end up getting attacked at which point Heather and Paco come back...now from what I can gather... they were near the towns we were fighting in two days ago when we took on the ten thousand...'

'Ten thousand?' Maddox asks, stepping forward.

'Yep, now...they get into a town...they said it had a square and that square was full of infected. They said they hid in the top floor of a flat and saw blue and red flashing lights outside during the night....lots of gunshots and explosions...'

'No way,' Nick says, 'they were there?'

'Sounds like it,' Paula says. 'So Heather and Paco get seven kids moving out that town to get them here...yesterday evening they find a house and try and get inside. One of the kids got killed, shot by a shotgun...'

'That's awful,' Clarence says, shaking his head.

'Heather tried saving her but that's when they got attacked. They said the infected kept coming all night. Lots of them. Said Paco and Heather kept them running and were fighting the infected. In the end they get trapped...Heather kissed Paco...big fight, lots of infected. This is where it gets interesting...'

'Yeah cos all of that was so boring.'

'Cookey, I said no comments.'

'Sorry.'

'Heather was bitten but carried on fighting. By this time Paco is speaking but his voice is all wrong...'

'Fuck me,' Nick mutters.

'They get the kids through a hedge and tell them to run...the kids run...find a stable and use a hose to get water then a wheel-barrow to push the youngest kids. Little bit later they get found by that van and brought here. Twenty miles away.'

'Shit, all that was going on twenty miles away?' Howie asks.

'Looks that way.'

'Got a map,' Marcy says, holding out a piece of paper. 'The oldest girl, Subi?'

'Yeah Subi,' Paula says.

'Genius little girl...she drew a map from where the van picked them up back to the stable.'

'Fuck...can the van show us where they found them?' I ask.

'They're ready to go,' Paula says.

'Let's go. Load up...Maddox, what you doing?'

'I would like to come with you.'

'Fuck off.'

'Get fucked...'

'Not a fucking chance...'

Howie pauses to look at him. 'Can you take instruction?'

'I can. I'd like to...I want to...' he stops to drop his gaze.

'Cheeky fucking twat,' Cookey says, shaking his head.

'He's not immune,' Nick says.

'How do you know?' Maddox asks, keeping his tone respectful.

'You got tazered eight times and took two day to recover,' Blowers says. 'Charlie got her ear bitten off yesterday and fucking laughed about it...'

'It was just the top of my ear actually.'

'I can fight,' Maddox says, looking at Howie. 'I don't blame Lilly for what she did...'

'You fucking...'

'Easy,' Howie says to Blowers without looking at him. 'You'll work under Blowers on his team. You'll follow his instructions. Clear?' Howie says after getting a nod from Clarence.

'Boss?'

'Mr Howie is giving an order, Simon.'

'Yes, Dave.'

'Likewise Maddox will follow your instructions.'

'Yes.'

'To the letter,' Dave adds, looking at Maddox.

'Yes.'

'Yes, Dave,' Dave says, still managing to make *Dave* sound like *sarge*.

'Yes, Dave,' Maddox says.

'Load up. We're going. Charlie? Jess ready?'

'Ready, Mr Howie.'

'Reggie? You staying or coming with us?'

'Do I have a choice?'

'Stay here if you want, mate. Read the books in peace...'

'Oh gosh that is a nice idea. Yes a wonderful idea but I fear you will charge a horde and spend all day fighting with spoons if I am not there. Am I given to understand we are simply looking to secure this man and woman and then returning here?'

'Yep.'

'That won't happen,' Reginald says to himself as he runs behind the rest.

CHAPTER THREE

S ilence. Cramped hot and quiet. They sit shoulder to shoulder. Paula and Marcy near the front leaning over the hand drawn map. Dave and Mo by the back doors. Meredith in the middle panting at the heat and excitement of being off with the pack. Clarence in the passenger seat. Howie driving. Everyone else silent. Charlie looks down at her rifle between her legs and fingers the wound on her face.

'Itchy?' Nick asks.

'Very itchy,' she replies, flicking her gaze to Cookey and waiting for the offer but Cookey is busy staring ahead to the quiet man seated opposite. She taps his leg with her foot, smiling when she sees that hard look in his eyes soften as he looks at her.

'We're going in hot,' Clarence says, leaning round in his seat. 'Clear the air...now.'

'You're a fucking cunt,' Blowers growls across the gap, making Charlie blink and everyone else look at him sharply. 'But you'll stay with me at all times. Where's your bag?'

'Bag?' Maddox asks.

'Where are your spare magazines? Where is your water?'

'I didn't bring any,' Maddox says, cursing himself inwardly.

'Paula, we got a spare bag?' Blowers says.

'In the locker under Charlie.'

Charlie looks to Cookey again, waiting for the *I'll get it* comment but Cookey eyes stay fixed on Maddox. She never met Lani but now realises the depth of feeling running through the others at having Maddox with them. She reaches down, mooching through the small space to pull a bag free.

'Thanks,' Maddox says, taking the bag.

'You're welcome,' Charlie says politely.

'Everyone dig a spare magazine out and give it to Maddox. We haven't got time to load fresh ones now. How many magazines you got for your sidearm?'

'One.'

'Be specific. One in the weapon and one extra or just one?'

'One in the weapon.'

'Dave, you got any spares? Charlie, pass it down, please.'

'Thanks,' Maddox says, opening the bag.

'Water bottle,' Nick says, throwing it at Maddox's feet.

'Thanks.'

'Drink now...hydrate while you can,' Blowers says.

'I'm fine.'

'It's hot. You'll sweat and we might be engaged for a length of time. Drink now. Same for everyone else. Hydrate.'

They do it too. All of them lifting water bottles to drink deep while Maddox takes in the confusing and messed up dynamics.

'Mr Howie gives the orders,' Blowers says. 'He leads from the front. That means he will generally be ahead of us...'

'I know what leading from the front means.'

'I don't give a fuck what you know. I care about my team and your ability to function in it. Mr Howie leads from the front. Dave stays close to him. Clarence works independently as he sees fit. Paula and Marcy will either be close to the boss or with me in my team. If we have higher ground Roy will work overwatch. That means he stands apart from us to gain a view of the fight to use his bow, if not then he works in my team, which works as a unit. We do not work independently. We cover the flanks and the rear unless otherwise instructed. We shout magazine when our magazines run out. We count the rounds we fire so we know when that will be. We fire single shot unless we are overwhelmed at which point everyone around you will be firing bursts and you will know when that is. If we become compressed, we revert to hand weapons. Do you have a hand weapon?'

'No.'

'Dave, do you have a spare knife? Charlie, pass it down, please.'

'Thanks,' Maddox says, taking the sheathed knife.

'If we revert to hand weapons you will fight what is in front of you. Everyone else knows what they are doing and will work to cover your sides. If you are bit or cut by an infected you will make that known straight away. We fuck about when we are not fighting but we are serious in the application of our work. Do you understand all of that?'

'Yes.'

'If Roy is firing his bow do not try and compensate for where you think he may fire. Roy will work around you. Nick, you got a spare radio?'

'Yep.'

'Radio goes on your belt, thread the microphone up inside your shirt and clip it on. Press the button to transmit. Keep the earpiece in at all times. Hand me your sidearm.'

Maddox draws his pistol, flicking it round to present the butt to Blowers. The weapon is stripped quickly, the moving parts checked before being re-assembled and handed back. 'Rifle...'

He does the same again. His hands working fast, checking the working parts and listening to the firing mechanism.

'Loaded, made ready, safety on,' Blowers says, passing it back. Paula and Marcy watch him closely, both of them fascinated by everything he just said and the way he said it. They share a glance, mouths turned down and eyes wide.

'Any questions?'

'No.'

'Good,' Blowers looks away to the front, his hands resting on the assault rifle between his legs.

The silence extends again. Awkward and uncomfortable.

'Put another two water bottles in your bag,' Blowers says after a few minutes.

'Van's pulling over,' Howie calls back. 'They're waving...there's the wheelbarrow. Paula? See it?'

'Er...yep got it.'

'I'll tell the van they can go back,' Clarence says, dropping out to run ahead.

'Right,' Paula says, spreading the piece of paper out. 'So this line is the road we're on...she said we go back up the road to a junction...so that will be on the left?'

'Right,' Marcy says, 'right side.'

'Is it? Oh yes, yes you're right.'

No Cookey jokes about being lost already. No comments from Nick that even he could read it better. Nothing from Howie. Nothing from anyone. Just a heavy silence that Maddox knows his presence is causing.

'Right,' Clarence says, clambering back in. 'Which way?'

'It's one road,' Howie says. 'We can only go one way.'

'Good point,' Clarence says easily.

'Keep going until we reach a junction on the right,' Paula says.

The Saxon pulls away. The big engine rumbling deep and strong to roll the vehicle on the road. Nick stretches his neck, rolling his shoulders. Cookey entwines his fingers and stretches his arms forward. Blowers inhales deep and long. Blinky pulls her head back trying to stop the urge to puke. Mo stares at the back doors, his hatred for Maddox palpable and obvious.

'Junction,' Marcy says, calling out and pointing.

'Is it?' Howie asks. 'I would have gone straight past it too.'

'Funny.'

'I try.'

'You're very trying...'

'Down this road and she said we go straight over at the next junction...she said they stayed on the wider road.'

'Roger,' Howie says, building the speed up.

'Open the back doors, Mo. Hot as fuck in here,' Nick says.

Dave nods, Mo releases the lock to push the doors open filling the interior with the noise of the tyres on the road. Roy's van behind them.

'Straight over?' Howie asks.

'Yep, stay on the wider road,' Paula says. 'Should be a gate down here somewhere, she said it leads to the stables...the big fight was across the field from that stable.'

'There,' Clarence says, pointing ahead.

'Got it,' Howie says, easing the speed down. 'We'll go on foot from here. Everyone switch on...out we get.'

'With me,' Blowers says, staring at Maddox. Mo and Dave drop out. Charlie and Blinky next.

'On Jess?' Charlie asks.

'Go for it,' Blowers says.

'Work with Simon's team for now,' Dave says to Mo, walking off to the front. Mo nods, scowling at the ground to avoid eye contact with Maddox.

'Fan out and cover the back until Charlie's up,' Blowers says, leading Maddox down past Roy's van and the horse trailer to stand facing down the road. Maddox stays at his side, copying Blowers and everyone else when they pull bolts back and flick safety switches off. 'Cookey, you got a view of that side?'

'Yep.'

'Blinky, Mo...other side.'

'On it,' Blinky says.

'Fasten the top of your holster,' Blowers says, without looking at Maddox. 'Thirty rounds in the magazine. Count them if you fire. We've got both sides of Roy's van covered so that means we can see down the line towards the front and the rear. Once Charlie is mounted we'll have a view over the hedgerow.'

Maddox watches them work. Charlie getting Jess out. The huge horse surging out the back of the trailer to spin round in the road, snorting and rolling angry eyes while taking oversized steps. Maddox backs away to give space. Everyone else stays put. Charlie gets on smoothly, settling the horse with soft words and a hand stroking her neck.

'She can smell them,' she says quietly.

'Boss,' Blowers says, dipping his head to speak into the radio under his shirt.

'Go ahead, mate.'

'Charlie said Jess can smell them.'

'Yep, got it...everyone stay alert. Charlie up front once you're ready.'

'What the fuck is that?' Cookey asks with a laugh. Maddox moves back to see Roy pulling a bright red rucksack on his back, the top filled with arrow shafts poking out.

'Medic bag,' Roy says.

'It's bright red,' Cookey points out helpfully.

'It's a medic bag. It's meant to be red.'

'It's got a fucking great big white cross on it,' Cookey says.

'It is a medic's bag,' Roy says again, his tone dropping a notch. Maddox watches the man sling his rifle and pull a big bow from the van, testing the ends and the tension on the string. 'Where am I?'

'With me for a bit if that's okay,' Blowers replies.

'Everyone, It's Roy. Just to let you know I have the medic's bag now...in case of injury or anything...'

'Er yeah, cheers for that, Roy,' Howie's voice sounds in their ears.

'And it's bright fucking red...'

'It is a medic's bag, Cookey. It is meant to be red.'

'Focus,' Blowers says, bringing them to quiet. Charlie trots on, taking the horse down the side of the vehicles to the front. Maddox watches her go, wanting to move to the front. He doesn't do the back. He's a leader, not a follower.

Blowers glances at him. At the strong proud face staring after Charlie and Jess to the front.

'Simon?'

'Here, Reggie.'

'What am I to do? Is anyone staying with the vehicles?'

'We're on foot from here, Reggie.'

'Foot? On foot? We have perfectly good vehicles to use. Why are we on foot?'

'Because we are,' Blowers says, his tone respectful yet firm.

'Gosh. Gosh and damnation. I shall get my books. Please wait for me. I shall be only a minute...on foot. On foot he says. *Mr Howie, I am gathering my books. I understand we are on foot? Is that correct?*'

'Yep. We are.'

'Oh dear. I shall get hot and sweaty. I really do not like sweating. I must find a sunhat. On foot? We have perfectly good vehicles and he wants to walk. Okay yes, yes I am ready. I am not carrying a weapon though. Dave said I am not to have one. He said that. I almost shot everyone and they are really very heavy and I have my bag of books...'

'It's fine. Mo, keep an eye on Reggie.'

'Will do.'

'Got a bodyguard, Reggie,' Blowers says.

'That is good. Yes, yes that is most good. Thank you, Mohammed. These books cannot fall into the other player's hands. We really must protect them, and when I say we I mean you of course.'

'We ready at the back, Blowers?'

'Ready and waiting, Boss. Reggie is with us. Mo's on him.'

'Moving out...Charlie, you go forward.'

'Good lord it is hot already,' Reginald says, muttering as he peers round at the high hedges.

The rest stay quiet. Walking slowly past the vehicles until they reach the empty lane in front and the five bar gate standing open ahead. Maddox spots the lane veering sharply to the left and the way Charlie trots ahead to gain the view before lifting a hand with a thumbs up to the rest.

Howie leads from the front, literally moving ahead of everyone else with Dave at his side and Clarence only a few feet behind. Paula and Marcy walk in the middle, still holding the map and talking quietly.

Blowers checks the spacing between them all then looks ahead to the corner, then over to the gate and round to check behind. The hedges are thick and high, giving a sensation of being contained. He listens intently, absorbing the noises around him. As Howie goes through the gate Blowers turns to his team behind him and points at his own eyes with two fingers. He points to the gate and swings his right hand back and forth before placing both hands together as though in prayer. He pushes his hands apart, flowing out to the sides. The others nod. He points at Cookey and Nick with his right hand then at Blinky and Mo with his left. He motions to Roy, points at his own eyes then up to the corner of the lane. *We go through the gate. Cookey and Nick cover right. Blinky and Mo cover left. Roy at the back to watch that corner.* The whole thing is done in seconds. Understanding all round. No need for speech. Blowers faces forward, feeling Maddox watching him.

He checks the spacing again. Watching as Howie leads through the gate into the field. Clarence and Dave with him. He spots Meredith running ahead with her nose to the ground. Paula and Marcy go through. He flicks his right hand out. Cookey and Nick move to the right inside the gate. Blinky and Mo go left. Roy turns to face down the lane, an arrow already nocked in the bow. Blowers stays in the middle of the gate, staring round at the landscape.

'Buildings,' he whispers to Maddox. 'Stable block there...barn there....looks like a path goes down that side to a lower field. See that gap in the hedge? Point of danger. The stable and barn are points of danger. Charlie is moving round the field to gain a view. We watch those buildings and that access gap down the bottom.'

'What she doing?' Maddox asks, watching the dog run with her nose seemingly glued to the ground.

'Doesn't matter what she's doing,' Blowers replies curtly. 'We watch the points of danger...keep your eyes on that gap down there.'

'Blood on the floor,' Dave says, pointing at the concrete hard-standing next to a hose stretching back to the stable building.

Blowers glances over. Seeing the others cluster round the stains on the ground. In his mind they are the elders. That's the title he attaches to them. Howie, Paula, Clarence, Dave, Marcy and Reggie. The elders. He looks back to Roy, watching as the bowman probes the inside of his mouth with his tongue, pushing his cheek out. He sees the familiar frown of worry on Roy's face and knows that's the thing that keeps Roy from being an elder. The man is focussed solely on his own issues. He looks at Reginald and smiles wryly to himself, seeing the struggle taking place. Reggie wants to stay close to Mo. Mo protected him yesterday, using the skills taught to him by Dave, but he can also see Reggie craning his neck to see what the others are looking at. His intellectual curiosity is too great to deny. Blowers counts in his head, getting to five before Reggie mutters something to Mo and heads off across the field towards the others.

'I'll er...just seeing what they have,' Reginald says politely as he passes Blowers.

'No worries,' Blowers says, turning to give a quick heads up at Mo.

It's a feeling. A sense of order and discipline. That's what Blowers strives for. Right now, there is order and discipline. The sides are protected. The rear is safe. Charlie is ranging out. Dave is with the elders. Right now they are safe. They have order. It doesn't matter to him what they are doing or where they are going.

Whatever the elders decide is right. He knows Reginald will now join in and together they'll form the next phase of the plan and he'll be ready whatever that is.

'Right here by the looks of it,' Howie's voice comes over.

'Subi said they stopped here,' Paula says. 'Said they used that hose...' she points down the field towards the access point to the lower section. 'Must have come through there.'

'She's off,' Clarence says, watching Meredith start following a trail across the paddock.

'That way,' Howie calls out, motioning towards that access point. Blowers nods, his mind already assessing the next phase.

'Line across the rear, watch that gate,' he calls back and waits with Maddox for the others to fall in at either side. 'Even spacing,' he says quietly, watching with an expert eye as they move further away from each other while walking ahead behind the elders.

The feeling comes back. Order and discipline gained. He looks ahead, seeing the gap and knowing Charlie will get there first.

'This what you do?'

'Shut up,' Blowers snaps the words out, silencing Maddox. He needs to listen and be ready. He watches the hedge, spotting the gaps between the tightly woven branches. Meredith pushes on, following a straight path down.

Maddox suppresses the urge to exhale noisily knowing it will be a show of his frustration. Earning his place in his mind meant being at the front with Howie. Not at the back with the followers. He bides his time, waiting for a chance to go forward and show he can lead and make decisions. He knows the damage done by his actions with Lani and although he stands by his belief, and was later proved right by the fact she turned, he also knows he made mistakes in *how* he did it. He knows he relied on the numbers in his crews and the use of force whereas it was a time for diplomacy instead of violence.

He finally came out of the medical section last night and saw first hand what Lilly had accomplished, which brought an immediate conflict within him. He was deeply impressed but he also realised it was done without him. He wasn't needed. There were no armed guards inside the fort. No men with guns. Instead there was a weird feeling of peace. Lenski sensed the change too and it was her that told him to go to Howie and earn his respect back, either that or they leave. He didn't do anything at first but then started to see the remaining youths from his crews here and there. They looked different too. None of them were in black for a start and all of them kept their distance from him.

'Mr Howie, it's Charlie...there is a big gap in the hedge at the bottom of the field. Lots of bodies here...'

'Roger, stay back. We'll come to you.'

Blowers picks the pace up, closing the gap between his team and the elders with an instinct that tells him Howie will push on faster. He does too. Howie starts jogging but the pace is already there and holding that distance steady. They go through the access gap to a furrowed field enclosed on all sides by thick hedge. Charlie at the far side on Jess aiming her rifle into a visible gap in the gnarled branches.

'Slow down,' Blowers says, sensing the urge in Maddox to rush forward. Maddox is not a leader here.

He scans the field, looking for points of danger. All of them do. All of them with eyes up, watching and scanning. The two gaps are the only obvious points of danger. As they reach the bottom so Blowers allows his line to collapse in to join everyone else.

'Smell that?' Blowers asks, glancing at Maddox who inhales the air before screwing his face up in disgust. 'Infected. The smell gets worse every day. Shit, blood, piss...you smell that and you know they're close.'

Maddox looks at the gap in the hedge, seeing the freshly snapped branches showing stark and obvious. Bodies everywhere lying torn and twisted. Mouths hanging open. Red eyes staring lifelessly. Flies buzzing to land and feast on the wounds. The stench is almost overwhelming.

'Mohammed, to me.'

'Yes, Dave,' Mo runs forward, ignoring Maddox as he passes.

'See the branches. The angle they are damaged point inwards from the road. The damage was done from the road. The access point is from the road into this field.'

'Got it.'

'What else do you see?'

'Er...' Mo casts about, watched intently by Maddox and everyone else. 'Er...it's wide so a few came through...the bodies here are all heading into the field so...so they's came in from the road to be killed here, you get me?' he goes forward to look through the gap to the road on the other side. 'They's got pushed back out... they's all piled up, like a defensive point was made.'

'Good. The bodies.'

'Er...' Mo looks round, nervously glancing up at everyone watching him. 'Necks. Broken necks... and that one's been bitten... human mouth?'

'It is.'

'Another one there, Dave,' Mo says, shoeing a body over onto it's back. 'Right in the throat...'

'What else?'

'Else? Fuck me...er...'

'Big man,' Clarence coughs into his hand.

'Big man? What big man? Oh...oh...' Mo grins sudden and delighted. 'Yeah that one...he got thrown from the road...you can see how he landed...strong fucker threw him...like Clarence does.'

'Good. Go through and report.'

'You sending Mo through first?' Paula asks.

'Yes, Miss Paula. Mohammed, go through and report.'

'Yes, Dave.'

Mo goes through, ducking to gain the other side. He drops down onto soft bodies and out to gain the road. His eyebrows lift. His face showing surprise at the sheer numbers of infected lying dead.

'Report,' Dave says.

'Give him a chance,' Paula says.

Mo holds his rifle across his chest, his eyes scanning the ground and up to both directions of the narrow lane. 'Came from both sides...' he calls back. He spots something poking out under a body. The butt of a gun. He kicks the body over to look down. 'Shotgun here, broken...used like a club...no gunshot wounds. Broken necks, bite marks...bladed weapon used but it was blunt.' Mo stares round, seeing more as he looks. His eyes alive and twinkling. 'Two sides, Dave. They fought on two sides and fell back to that gap in the hedge...bladed weapon used on this side.' He back steps away to the epi-centre of the battle. 'The strong fucker was on this side... broken necks everywhere and that big bloke was thrown from here...'

'Good,' Dave says, coming through the gap to drop lightly into the road. 'Anything else?'

'Er...' Mo frowns, pursing his lips while examining the sides, both directions, the bodies, the gap in the hedge. 'Nah, got fuck all, Dave.'

'No, Dave.'

'S'what I said.'

Everyone bar Maddox on the other side of the hedge pulls a face at the backchat from Mo to Dave, expecting a harsh response.

'Which direction did they come from?' Dave asks instead.

What the fuck? Howie mouths. Clarence shrugs. Blowers shakes his head.

'I don't know,' Mo says from the other side.

'Look.'

'At what?'

'Both ends.'

'Both ends? What's that mean?'

Howie's eyes widen. Clarence winces. Blowers looks down at the ground waiting for Dave to bellow.

'Be clear, Dave.'

'Holy fuck,' Cookey mutters, taking a step back from the hedge.

'My apologies, Mohammed. Look at both ends. One direction will have less bodies.'

A stunned silence.

'Ah got it, yeah...yeah none this way...so's they came the other way right?'

'Yes.'

'HA! Got it. Fuck yeah...'

'Yes not yeah.'

'Fuck yes. Can I say fuck yes?'

'Yes.'

'Ha! Fuck yes. Did I miss anything?'

'Not of importance.'

'Eh? What'd I miss?'

'Footprints in the blood. The defenders were male and female. Both adults. The male was large build, the female was smaller build.'

'How the fuck?'

'This footprint is the same size as Marcy. More here on this side working back towards the access point to the hedge. The male's feet are almost as large as Clarence's feet.'

'Yeah...I mean yes, yes I see that, Dave.'

'Report back to Mr Howie.'

'Got it.'

'I heard it all, Dave.'

'Mohammed needs to learn reporting back, Mr Howie.'

'Righto.'

'Mr Howie,' Mo says, grinning widely as he climbs back through the hedge.

'Mo,' Howie smiles.

'I er...I's ready to report, Mr Howie.'

'Okay, mate. Report.'

'Dave?' Mo asks, looking back at the hedge.

'Yes. Mohammed?'

'Can I do it in my words?'

'The report must be understood, Mohammed.'

'Do it in your words,' Howie says.

'Sir...' Mo says, forcibly trying not to stop smiling. 'So...big fucker and a woman same size as Marcy came from that way...'

'Children's feet here too, Mohammed. Six.'

'With six kids,' Mo says. 'And they had a big fight...the woman had a blade but it was blunt as fuck, like a big blade...not an axe or a knife though...'

'Machete.'

'We think it was a machete innit...so they got trapped here. The big fucker threw another big fucker through that hedge and they got the kids through and held the infected back until the kids got away across that field. Someone was biting them too...hang on...' He says suddenly, moving forward to peer at Marcy's mouth then dropping to look at the body with the throat bitten out. 'The woman did the biting, Mr Howie...same size mouth as Marcy...cos like Clarence's mouth is massive you get me? Dave, I think it was the woman that did the biting...'

'It was, Mohammed.'

'It was,' Mo says, nodding at Howie. 'Er...that's my report.'

'Fucking brilliant,' Howie says as Mo is sent sailing five feet to the side from a pat on the arm from Clarence.

'I bloody adore you,' Paula says, grabbing Mo's face to kiss his forehead.

'Mo Mo Dave Two,' Cookey says.

'Fact,' Nick adds.

'Fall back in with your team, Mohammed.'

'Yes, Dave,' Mo says, still grinning as he heads back.

'Well done, mate,' Blowers says, patting him on the shoulder.

'Cheers, Blowers,' Mo says, the grin on his face dropping the second he looks at Maddox. Coldness in his eyes. The eyes of a killer. In that second Maddox sees the total change in Mo. The old

Mo would never have sought validation from others like that. The old Mo would have sucked his teeth and skulked with his head down. Mo falls back in, laughing again as Blinky punches him on the arm.

'So what now?' Howie asks. 'They came from that way,' he says, pointing in the direction Mo indicated. 'But came through here...they must have gone up to that stable...'

'Really?' Marcy asks, staring at Howie. 'We said that. We said Subi said that. We said they came through the hedge across the field to the stable and out through the gate. We've got a bloody map that says that.'

'Then why are we down here?' Howie asks. 'We should be up there...everyone back to the stables.'

They head back across the furrowed field, tripping and cursing over the valleys and troughs made by a tractor that will forever now lie silent until it rusts away to become nothing more than a heap of slag.

'This is another morning without coffee isn't it,' Howie asks, making a statement more than asking a question.

'Flasks,' Paula says, clicking her fingers. 'We'll get flasks.'

'Flasks?' Howie asks, looking down the line to Paula.

'Flasks. For the storage of hot beverages.'

'That's a good idea,' Clarence says.

'I had a good flask,' Roy says. 'Stayed hot for hours.'

'Yeah?' Howie asks.

'Come a long way flasks have,' Roy replies knowingly.

'We should get flasks,' Howie says. 'Nick? Can we rig a hot water thing in the Saxon?'

'Er...Roy's van will be easier.'

'Hey now,' Paula says, nodding in admiration. 'Good idea that, Mr Howie.'

'Thanks, Miss Paula.'

'Nick, Roy...you are tasked to get hot water in Roy's van,' she says, turning to look at them both.

'Maybe I don't want hot water in my van.'

'We'll add it to Reggie's duties...other than being the brains of the team he can brew up.'

'Good Lord I will do no such thing...'

Mindless. It's mindless words spewing from mouths talking shit. Maddox listens, turning to each as they add increasingly stupid comments while walking across a bloody field after staring at dead bodies for ten minutes. Is this it? Is this what they do? He watched them when they found the bodies and the lack of any shred of reaction to the torn up human forms laying at their feet. Maddox has seen and given death but even so, even he felt repulsed by the sight. They didn't. They didn't show anything. Now they're talking about flasks and a hot water urn in that cash in transit van.

Blowers smiles at the thought. A hot water urn in Roy's van is the best idea they've had for days. They can brew up wherever they go. You can't put a price on the morale boost brewing up gives. The making of it, the communal drinking and the idle chat. Nothing beats a brew up.

'Is it hard to rig up?' he asks.

'Easy enough,' Roy replies. 'It drains power though.'

'Not from the main battery,' Nick says. 'The split charges the back up and that lasts for fucking ages.'

'What about that Tassimo Lilly had?' Howie asks. 'Would that work?'

'He's on fire this morning,' Marcy says.

'Someone will be if I go all day without coffee again.'

Maddox hides his scowl. Blowers chuckles. They walk across the field.

CHAPTER FOUR

'Shit...Charlie...stay with her... everyone else back to the vehicles.'

Charlie canters on down the road, following Meredith as she runs from the gate into the country lane following the scent trail hovering in the middle of the road. She knows it's him. He smells different now. Like Marcy and Reginald. Different like that but it's him. She has to find him. She runs on sucking air up her nose into the filters in her brain that breaks those smells down to a molecular level.

Blowers breathes out, feeling the small pulse of adrenalin at having to something to go after. He goes to make a comment but stops at the sight of Maddox opposite him in the back of the Saxon. The smile fades. The humour drains from his eyes. Lani didn't deserve that. Not like that. Lani might have turned back regardless of what happened but she should have been with her team. Not isolated and left on her own. Soldiers don't ditch their mates. Maddox is a street brawler and a hard man but he isn't a soldier. Soldiering isn't just about fighting. Soldiering is professional. It's structure and knowing your place in the machine. Why the fuck did the boss bring him? He knows why. He knows exactly what the boss was thinking. Paula too otherwise she'd have said something. They all know it. They were thinking that this will be good for Maddox and show him how it's meant to be done. Teach him some respect or something. He needs it but he still shouldn't be here. Not with them. Not after what he did.

'What will you do when you find him?' Maddox asks once everyone settles.

Silence comes back. An unwillingness to reply. Paula tuts, casting a look at the lads. 'We'll figure it out when it happens.'

Maddox nods, his face remaining impassive which conveys an air of disapproval at the lack of a plan.

'Marcy and Reggie were turned,' Paula explains. 'If Paco was turned but now turning back then he could be like them...same with that woman Heather. That girl said Heather was bit but carried on fighting...'

'Ssshhh,' Blowers says, 'Maddox might lock him in the hospital.'

'Away from his mates,' Nick adds, looking down to the back doors.

'And tazer him like a fucking coward.'

'Cookey, that's enough.'

'Roger,' Cookey mutters.

Silence.

'So,' Maddox says, shuffling further back into his seat while looking at Marcy. 'You and Reginald were both infected...but you're not now?'

'Don't even look at Marcy...'

'Cookey, enough. It was a question,' Paula snaps.

'We don't know,' Marcy says flatly, looking away.

'But your eyes aren't red...have you got any symptoms?'

'What the fuck has it got to do with you?'

'Nick! All of you pack it in. Maddox, we don't know any answers. Reginald is trying to work it out.'

'We shouldn't tell him anything,' Blowers says.

'Lani turned. I was right...' Maddox states, fixing his gaze on Blowers.

'You fucking...'

'She should have been with us,' Cookey shouts.

'Jesus Christ, enough!' Paula snaps again.

'If she'd been with us that fucking mess wouldn't have happened...'

'Cookey...'

'You locked us in a room with dog shit...you took our fucking weapons away and made us crawl through a fucking tunnel...'

'You chose that...I kept Lani isolated in case she turned which she did.'

'If she'd been with us we would have contained it you stupid fucking prick...'

'I did what I thought was right at the time...'

'What happened after that?' Nick asks quietly, driving the atmosphere down through the floor. 'Go on? What happened after? What happened to Lilly?'

'That wasn't...'

'Your crews, Maddox,' Blowers says.

'Darius was...'

'Yeah cos Lani killed him like she killed Jagger...' Nick says.

'She turned...'

'You best be shutting your fucking mouth...' Nick says, his face hardening.

'Nick, stop it...'

'Lani turned. She was infected...'

'You fucking...' Blowers spits the words out.

'She turned. She was infected. How would I know what she'd do?'

Voices shouting. The lads edging closer on their seats. Blinky grabs Nick and Cookey to push them back as Paula leans towards Blowers. Mo's eyes flash at the mention of Jagger with the cold look of Dave on his face. Spittle flies from mouths. Accusations back and forth. Maddox fires back at them, leaning forward as Marcy pushes in front of him.

'STAND DOWN.'

Dave's voice. The three lads fall silent, breathing hard with pure hatred showing on their faces. Paula glares round with a rare look of disgust shown to the three young men she admires so much.

'Not another word,' she whispers, pointing at each in turn. 'There will be a time for this but not now and not here. We're working. We are at work. Do you understand?'

'Ma'am,' Blowers says, sinking back in his seat.

'Cookey?'

'Yes, Ma'am,' he says, copying Blowers without realising he is doing so.

'Nick?'

'Sorry, Ma'am.'

'Stop with the ma'am...Maddox? Not another word about Lani.'

'Yeah...'

'Yes, Ma'am,' Dave says.

'I said yeah...I ain't one of you...' Maddox sneers.

'You fucking arrogant piece of...'

'Oh for the love of God...Howie!'

'Ah pack it in,' Howie says calmly without turning from watching Charlie and Meredith ahead. 'Haven't had enough coffee yet...seriously, any more shouting and I'll get cross.'

A switch flicked. An instant change in atmosphere. The tension eases, dropping away from a few quietly spoken words. Maddox stares at the back of Howie's head, sensing someone watching him. He looks over to see Marcy staring at him. The woman is breath-taking in her beauty but that same coldness Mo had is right there staring through him. She finally blinks, breaking the eye contact to look over at Paula.

'Entrance ahead...Meredith is veering towards it...hang on...yes, yes she's going in...'

'Yep, got it. Hold at that entrance. We'll go in together... Everyone hear that? Driveway ahead. We'll pull up just back from it. *Roy? We'll stop before the driveway and go on foot.'*

'Understood.'

'Contact contact...one ahead...Meredith's on him...she's running on...HORDE...CONTACT CONTACT...'

'OUT GO...' Howie brings the Saxon to a slewing halt bursting from the driver's door to drag swing his axe up and down behind his bag. His rifle already gripped as he runs to join Clarence.

'With Blowers,' Dave drops from the back doors to sprint on down the side. Mo backs up to give space for the rest piling out.

'LOTS MR HOWIE...' Charlie's voice in their ears. Hearts thunder with beats per minute. Adrenalin courses making vision sharper and voices louder.

'Rear guard, secure the lane...' Blowers orders his team. 'Roy, straight in. Marcy, Paula with me...REGGIE?'

'Gosh I am coming...I am running I am...'

'Stay with Mo at all times...'

'I most certainly....'

'SURVIVORS IN THE HOUSE...'

'GO GO GO,' Blowers shouts. As one they run. As one they sprint hard down the side of the Saxon veering sharply into the driveway. Weapons held ready. Blowers drives power into his legs to gain the front of his team. Maddox at his side. A gravel driveway underfoot. The sound of stones crunching under boots. He spots Howie, Clarence and Dave ahead slinging rifles to draw hand weapons.

'HAND WEAPONS,' Blowers slings his rifle and reaches back to pull his axe. The action is copied down the line. Rifles pushed back. Axes pulled free from bags. Mo draws his knife, flicking the hilt to rest the reverse side of the blade against the inside of his right forearm. His left hand on Reginald's shoulder keeping the terrified man close.

Blowers reaches the corner of the driveway to gain the view of the big house. A split second for his expert eyes take in what the elders saw first. A thick horde between them and the big country house. The ground floor windows all boarded with thick planks. People at the upstairs windows staring down in terror. To fire into that horde risks the bullets going through into the building. A stray shot from an assault rifle will go through a wooden door and boarded window with ease. They cannot fire unless they can move to the side but both sides are blocked by the infected laying siege.

'CHARLIE...CLEAR THE FRONT DOOR...' Howie shouts, glancing back to make sure Blowers is close.

'COME ON...INTO THEM,' Charlie roars with a pulse of energy sent into the horse that rears high, kicking her front legs out before landing with a snort, bunching up and charging on with pure aggression in her eyes. The impact is beautiful. A path carved through the undead battered aside as the scarred face of Charlie screams to swing the axe side to side, chopping down to an explosion of blood and brains.

'HAVE IT...' Howie runs in behind them. Charging across the once perfectly manicured lawn with Dave and Clarence veering to his left and right to slam into the ranks in a desperate push for the door.

'Marcy, Paula on Reggie...Mo with us...Roy, that shed any good?' Blowers words fired fast and hard. Paula and Marcy drop back to cover Reginald as Mo comes forward to join the line. Roy spots the shed and the bench next to it and runs hard to vault once and vault twice to plant his legs either side of the apex on the pitch sloping roof. Arrow nocked, pulled, lifted and aimed. He fires the first shot that takes one lunging for the back of Howie through the neck.

'OUR TARGET IS TO CLEAR THAT SIDE...' Blowers shoots an arm out with a flat hand to the right side of the horde. 'GO GO...'

Soldiering is the professional execution of warfare, and right now it means to charge in against a much larger opposing force and match their aggression with teeth showing and lips pulling back. It means to take that gut wrenching fear screaming in your head to run away and use it as fuel to remember your training and discipline. It means there is a time to stand back and fire from safety and there is a time to fight hand to hand and feel the hot blood of the enemy on your skin.

He goes in fast with Cookey forever at his side. The two of them cleaving with axes that fell many in that first strike. They go deeper. Side to side. Always knowing where the other is. They go hard, screaming for the pure glory of the fight. Nick comes after them, sensing the closeness of Meredith ragging bodies to his side.

'CUNT CUNT CUNT...' Blinky was born for this. Born to fight. Born to be a warrior. She goes in with years of hard tackling and learning fast feints to wield an axe. She takes the head of a woman from her neck and boots the body back into two more and attacks them with the same with controlled frenzy.

Mo comes in last, veering off at the last second to whip through the lines to start his attack from within. This is it. Maddox is gone from his mind. Jagger is gone from his mind. Everything apart from Dave is gone from his mind. He slashes a throat, spinning on the spot to take two more down and spots the next four targets. Mo goes to work. He spins again, going through a gap left by two lunging at him. Two flicks and they drop with throats cut. A backstab into the throat of the one behind. He lets the knife go and grabs the hand coming to rake his face. The first twist breaks the wrist. He pivots to use the held body as a shield and breaks the elbow. He pivots again, blocking the next attack while dislocating the shoulder with a motion that brings the head into his arms that is snapped quickly to the side. As that one falls he turns and plucks the knife from the throat of the one he stabbed that falls to join the others.

On the driveway two women stand with rifles braced in shoulders. Single shot selected. Behind them hides Reginald. His face a picture of fear and intense worry, his arms holding the bag of books close to his chest. One streaks out, spotting the three isolated. An arrow takes it down. Neither woman flinches but tracks and watches the battle underway. They can both fight and have proven it but they cannot match what the others can do. It isn't sexism. It isn't anything other than the use of skills for the job at hand and if cornered they will draw knives and show teeth but for now they will stand guard over Reginald.

Maddox stays close behind Blowers and Cookey. This is chaos. This is a high speed burst of pure instinct. He can fight. He can kill. He can think fast and make decisions under pressure, be they right or wrong, but this? This is something else. It all happened within a few seconds too. In the Saxon. Running then charging and now he's in it. Blood everywhere. The heat is immense. The stench is indescribable. The compression is stifling. The aggression they show is staggering. He learns fast though. He learns within the first few seconds this isn't a street fight but a fight to kill. He stabs a chest, instantly seeing the lack of reaction in the man still pushing at him with bared teeth. He twists to the side, pulling the knife free to stab into the throat. Something touches his back. He lashes round, slicing the blade across a face but again not a killing blow. He brings a knee up making the beast bend double from the impact before stabbing down into the back of the neck.

'MADDOX...SLICE...DON'T   STAB...STRIKE   AND MOVE...'

Blowers' voice. He prickles from being told what to do and slashes into a neck, cutting deep into flesh that peels apart down to the artery that spurts hot blood into the air.

'STRIKE AND MOVE...DON'T FUCKING STAND THERE...'

Nick now, shouldering one away to bring his axe down into the head. Maddox goes the other way, his eyes flicking to the potential targets in front of him. He goes for one as Meredith launches up to rip the thing from its feet. He locks on for the next that is taken down by Blinky cutting it in half. He snarls in frustration at not being given the chance to impress and show he can lead. He goes in with a knife that stabs and slashes wild and hard. He kicks, feints, dodges and shows the years of nasty fights born on the streets of social housing estates where you either lie in the gutter or stand up to be counted. He fights because he can. He learns and fights faster. Slashing throats and driving the point of his knife into eyes. He kicks legs out, making them tumble with dirty tricks learned hard and fast. He stabs back into groins and slices stomachs open for innards to fall out. He drives his thumb into another eye while stabbing repeatedly into the neck until he sees the spurt from the de-pressurised artery. He twists, moves, ducks and kills.

'LINE...FORM ON ME...'

He glances up to see Blowers and Cookey side by side with their backs to the garden wall and rushes to join them. Nick after him. Blinky and Mo coming from the ranks of the horde to make the line.

'FIRING LINE READY...'

'**HOLD...**' Dave's voice.

They fight on. Holding the line as the infected charge at them. Blowers senses the subtle change in them again. The greater control they have. The speed and reflexes showing in their movements. Something like intelligence in their dead eyes, dull and weak but there nonetheless.

'WE HAVE THE DOOR...'

Dave's voice again. Blowers flicks his eyes to see Charlie still within the ranks, spinning the great horse round as she lashes down with the axe now secure on her wrist. Ripples of motion as the horse's rump slams the horde that stagger but rally and charge back.

'CHARLIE OUT...'

'COME ON,' she screams again, geeing the horse to propel forward towards Roy as an arrow flies an inch past her head taking one of its feet behind her.

'MAKE SPACE...' A lunge from the line that goes forward on

Blowers command. Maddox wasn't ready. He didn't know the command. He falters and follows a second behind them as they attack to drive the infected back. 'BACK NOW....BAGS DOWN RIFLES UP...'

Back they go. At speed too. Rushing back to the wall to drop hand weapons and bags at feet to pull rifles round. Again Maddox is a second behind them. Running to gain the wall to drop his knife and scrabble for this assault rifle while trying to wrench his bag from his back.

'BLOWERS CLEAR...'

'FIRE...' Blowers gives his command. Five rifles fire a single round each in perfect unison while Maddox snarls and brings his rifle up with his bag still hanging off one arm. The rifles fire quickly. Single shots to burst firing. Paula and Marcy cover Reginald to bring him down, joining the firing line. Reginald stays low, running ducked to get behind Mo who shuffles forward a step to give the small man enough space.

The effect is outstanding. Bullets beats axes. Bullets beats knives. Bullets beats brains from heads that burst from skulls exploding with pink mists. Bodies are blown back. The horde is withered.

'MAGAZINE,' Blowers first, dropping to a crouch to grab one from his bag as the used one is ejected. As he rises so Cookey shouts the same and drops.

'I'M OUT,' Maddox shouts, dropping to tug his bag free from being tangled on his arm and rifle sling. He pulls at the flap, his hands working to grab a magazine that gets pushed in, bolt back, up he stands to aim and fire.

'CEASEFIRE...'

Instant silence. Ears ringing from the retorts of the weapons. Rifles remain in shoulders, aiming into the downed horde.

'Crawler,' Blinky says, firing once to strike a head.

'Shot mate,' Nick mutters.

'Fuck yourself,' Blinky mutters as Nick chuckles.

Meredith runs through them, snapping jaws left and right to finish them off before seemingly remembering why they are here and running flat out for the door.

'CLEAR OUTSIDE,' Blowers shouts.

'CLEAR INSIDE...COME IN,' Clarence shouts back.

'Fuck,' Blinky coughs, bending double to spew vomit on the ground.

'She alright?' Maddox asks.

'Fine,' Blinky shouts, waving a hand in the air.

'Injuries?' Blowers asks, changing magazine. 'We'll go in... Blinky and Mo cover the rear when we enter. Reggie...'

'Stay with Mohammed...yes yes, I most certainly will. May I say, Simon, that was very well done.'

'Thanks, mate,' Blowers says easily.

'From the side was a very good tactic. Indeed yes, yes it worked most assuredly.'

'He likes it from the side,' Cookey says.

'What?' Nick asks.

'Dunno, made it up,' Cookey says, grinning as he swaps magazines.

'Mo, good skills there, mate.'

'Cheers, Blowers.'

'Everyone ready? We'll go in...COMING TO YOU...'

'YEP,' Clarence shouts back.

'Magazine not *I'm out*, Maddox. Keep your bag straps and rifle sling clear of each other. Put the magazines at the top of bag so you can get them.'

Maddox doesn't reply but walks with the line across the battleground towards the front door of the big old country house. Bodies everywhere. Blood everywhere.

'Roy, Charlie...you cover outside.'

'Will do,' Charlie calls back.

'Love you, Charlie.'

'Love you too, Cookey.'

'She loves me. She said it. We're getting married and having babies.'

'Are we?'

'How the fuck did you hear that?'

'Focus,' Blowers says, smiling at the post-fight energy flowing between them all. 'Hey, you got him?' he asks, reaching the door to see Clarence holding sentry.

'Nope, out the back apparently. Come through,' Clarence says. 'Nice work, Blowers.'

'Thanks, Boss,' Blowers gives his easy response, his rifle held ready but lowered a few inches. A large gloomy hallway with light pouring through the cracks of the boards on the windows outside. A wide wooden staircase on the right. Doors ahead and on the left.

'They only came a few minutes ago. Straight after the big man and the woman...'

An old woman stood with her hand pressed to her chest looking very shaken speaks in a trembling voice to Howie and Dave. Blowers moves to the stairs, mounting the first few to gain a view of the top. Movement. People standing back. Whispered voices. He goes up quickly, holding the rifle with his right hand while his left waves for someone to follow him.

'Behind you,' Cookey whispers.

'How many upstairs?' Blowers calls out, ascending to see a small group of men and women cowering in a large doorway to one of the rooms.

'Five,' a man blurts the words out. 'Who are you?'

'From the fort,' Blowers replies, sweeping his gaze over each in turn. 'With Mr Howie...'

Blank expressions, the name doesn't mean anything to them.

'How long have you been here?' Cookey asks, turning to see Maddox coming up behind him.

'Since it started,' the same man says, his eyes catching sight of Maddox coming into view. 'Are you soldiers?'

'We're...' Maddox starts to say.

'We are,' Blowers says, cutting in quickly. 'The fort is twenty miles away. Why are you still here?'

'Fort Spitbank?' The man asks, showing confusion.

'It's down the road,' Blowers says.

'I know where it is,' the man replies stiffly, 'is it in use? Have the government taken it over? I said we should bloody check it,' he mutters to the other people around him.

'It's a safe place. We advise you go straight there...if you are quick we can escort you.'

'Have the government got it?' The man asks again.

'Has the army mobilised then?' Another asks.

'Is it ending?' A woman asks, moving out a step from the group.

'Blowers?' Howie calls out.

'Yep, up here,' Blowers shouts down. 'Got five survivors.'

'Paco went straight through to the summer house out the back...'

'Coming,' Blowers shouts back. 'Listen, get ready to go. You can't stay here now...'

'Why ever not? We've got food and...'

'They know you're here now. They'll come back. Get ready to go...' Blowers says.

'Are you ordering us to leave?'

'Nope, your choice. Do what you want,' Blowers says, heading down the stairs after Cookey and Maddox.

'Fifty two,' Reginald says, walking into the hallway with a pensive look on his face.

'Fifty two what?' Howie asks.

'Bodies,' Reginald says, his face reflecting his deep thoughts.

'Right, a big man went straight through carrying a woman in his arms...' Howie tells everyone, glancing at the old woman.

'The summer house,' the old woman says. 'He carried the woman to the summer house. Didn't say a word. Covered in blood they are...we offered help of course but...well, he looked dangerous,' she adds in a lower voice. 'Big chap too, nearly as big as you,' she adds, looking at Clarence.

Meredith scratches at a closed door, whining for someone to open it. She backs up, giving high pitched barks, expressing urgency.

'Sounds like him...' Howie says, looking round. 'Blowers, Cookey, Nick, Clarence, Dave, Paula and Marcy with me. We'll go down....everyone else stay here and get these people ready to go.'

'Go?' The old woman asks. 'Go where?'

'Reginald, you explain,' Howie says, 'we're going before the dog busts through that door.'

CHAPTER FIVE

H e stays at her side. His red eyes watching her breathe. He washed the blood from her face when she woke but more blood has come. He struggles to understand what to do but knows he will always stay with her.

For nine days she has been at his side. She cleaned him. Bandaged his wounds. Fed him. Gave him water and comfort and in turn he killed the infected to keep her safe. Now she is hurt and he doesn't know what to do.

Paco Maguire was bitten by an infected eleven days after the outbreak started. Paco found courage after days spent hiding in fear and fought to protect her when the infected came to kill her. The dog was at his side when he went down. He died and came back in the true state of being. He came back changed. His cells forever different. His blood tainted. She bit him. The dog he protected knew he was no longer what he was, so she bit deep into his throat, with what at any other time, would be an attack to kill.

He was dead again. So they thought, but the infection that killed him the first time kept a flicker of life inside his body. That flicker generated a heartbeat that sustained and gave another. Throughout the night he remained with the fallen until he finally woke with his throat torn apart and his body rendered weak but in the true state of being. He was turned. He was one of them.

Then Heather found him, or rather, he found her. Something in him prevented him from taking her. She ran. He followed. She hid. He found her again. At first she used him as a shield but as the days went on she learnt to trust him and finally to give something more. The infection healed his body. The memory of a dog stopped him turning and the love of a woman made the confusion and rage go away.

Now, on the twentieth day since the outbreak started, he still does not have full cognitive function. Heather told him it would come. She helped him say words and held his hand and kissed his head. He liked that. He liked her touch and her soft voice. He grew strong again. Stronger than he was before, faster and harder than he was before but it was Heather that guided him and kept him clean. His mind wasn't open enough for anything other than following Heather and killing the things that came close to her. It was Heather that kept the children safe and gave them to another family. When that family were attacked she went back and found the children again. She gave everything to keep them alive and get them to the fort. Heather hates people. She was terrified of being near anyone but Paco was different. Paco wasn't a person. Not in that sense. He did not speak or judge her. He did not ask questions about her life that made her want to run away and cry.

Then, as they neared the coast where she believed the fort to be, the infected came. They came all night. Running to attack to take the children and kill Paco who was one of them before but now something else. They fought together. They kept the children alive until they were trapped by the hedge. Heather was bitten and beaten close to death but she didn't die and she didn't turn either.

The children escaped and when the last infected died so Paco carried her slumped form to the stable to rinse the blood from her body as she did for him. She came awake, just for a few seconds. He carried her again. He could hear them coming. More of them.

More than he could fight. He found the house and went through the door, his mere presence, size and the fact he was torn to bits and covered in blood kept the people back.

He didn't know what to do but did not want the people touching her. No one could touch her. No one *will* touch her. No one will come close. As long as he has life in his body he will not allow it. He saw the summerhouse with a flash of a memory of a barn and a time with Heather eating tinned food. He went for it. Gained it and lowered to hold her close. They will come. The infected will come. He cannot run now so he will fight instead.

Shouts in the air. Gunshots. The sound of fighting then silence. He doesn't know what that means but it matters not. No one will touch her.

She can smell him. It's him. The man-child that she kept safe until he found his courage. The smells hover over the ground like colours holding form and shape. Denser shades that tell her his feet landed here and here. She follows that trail to another set of doors and gives furious voice that she cannot get through. She launches up. Scrabbling at the place she knows will open it. The pack leader comes. The pack leader makes the door not be there. She runs out. The colours holding the scents of his life on the ground are strong and clear. She races flat and fast. He's close. Him. It's him but different. She can smell the things in his blood. She barks. She gives voice. She tells him she is coming.

He hears a bark. He turns, his face showing pure violence to defend Heather. He rises smoothly. The muscles in his arms bulging. His chest inflating as he draws air to fight and kill.

She barks again. Running over the grass that holds his scent so strong. She can see the building. He is in there. She knows it.

He goes to the door and pauses to look back with softened eyes at the woman he adores more than anything in the world. Sadness inside. His mind unable to form sentence to give coherence to his emotions. The bark again. He goes through the door, ducking his head to get through and watch the dog sprinting flat out towards him.

A pulse. A sensation. A feeling. A memory. A dog. A girl.

'Dog...' his broken voice says the word he now knows. 'Gerl...' the dog is a girl. He tried telling Heather that. 'Dog...'

That pulse again. That sensation grows stronger. The memories surge in his mind and heart. She barks. She gives voice.

He goes forward with only instinct in his reactions. His heart hammering. A dog. The dog was a girl. He remembers a dog. That's the only thing he could remember.

She charges in. He runs out. She barks. He runs faster. She barks again. He sprints as she leaps at him, taking him down from the massive weight slamming into his chest. A dog. He had a dog. The dog kept him alive when he was afraid. The dog saved him. This dog. This girl.

She whines with happiness bursting in her heart. It's him. He was dead but now he is not. Now he is here. Him. She cannot lick him fast enough. She cannot show him her emotions. She cannot be close enough.

His arms come up. His face streaked with tears. A rough tongue on his face. He remembers her licking him before. He remembers those noises she makes. He remembers the feel of her, the size of her, the soft fur and the even softer brown eyes.

The long nose nuzzles his face, his jaw, his chin and hair. She flattens on him, pressing into his body, absorbing his smell. He is the link to her little one. He *was* a little one until he stopped being a pup and became strong. Now she cries and whimpers to lick and push.

He cries too. He cries with his heart surging and his arms wrapped round her. He weeps tears that she licks away.

It matters not to either why or how they are here. Only that they are. It matters not what caused this. Only that it is happening.

'Paco?'

On his feet. His face morphing into violence to snarl and stand ready. People come. People with guns. People that run towards him. Towards Heather. His arms tense. His head lifts. He readies to fight. Meredith snakes round his legs, whining and jumping up. *Pack. Friends. Not enemy.*

'Slow down,' Howie says, holding a hand out.

Blowers breathes hard. The sprint across the grass was longer than they all thought. Marcy bends forward, resting her hands on her knees while wishing she had put the bloody sports bra on. Meredith went off like a rocket and they all saw him come running from the summer house. For one awful second it looked like Meredith took him down. Then they saw his arms come up and her tail wagging faster than ever before while she licked his face and dropped to lie on him.

They come to a stop. All of them seeing Paco Maguire. The same man they fought next to for the safety of a dog that later proved she was tougher than nearly all of them. They saw him fall. They heard him shout the name Meredith which came to be hers. They saw him come back too and saw Meredith go for his throat. Those injuries are clear now. His throat is damaged but healed only in the way the infected do. The way Charlie is healing. The way Cookey's back is healing. The way the hundreds of cuts, marks, bites and bruises on all of them heal. They also see the lack of recognition in his expression that now looks so different.

Blowers holds back a few steps from Howie. Lowering his rifle and checking Nick and Cookey do the same. Dave slings his to the back but rests a hand on the butt of his pistol. The boss is safe. Dave can draw and fire faster than Paco can move.

'Paco...it's us...' Howie says softly. 'Howie...do you remember?'

They can see his eyes. They can see the aggression pouring from him. The way he looks to each in turn as though assessing the threat and the way he rests those red bloodshot eyes on Clarence as though calculating the bigger man's size and weight. He stands his ground though, and without a shred of fear either.

'Clarence...' Howie says, pointing at Clarence. 'Dave...Blowers...'

'Paco,' Blowers says, inclining his head.

'Cookey...Nick...'

'Hey.'

'Paco.'

'That's Paula...that's Marcy...'

'Hey,' Paula says, smiling softly. 'You're hurt,' she adds, nodding at him. *'Roy, come down...bring your med bag.'*

'On way.'

'We were with you,' Howie says. 'With Meredith...'

Paco looks at Howie. Recognising the names they say. They are familiar...something about them. Heather would know if they can be trusted but Heather is hurt so he stands ready to fight.

'You saved Subi...'

His eyes flick to the woman.

'And Rajesh? Amna? You saved them with Heather...'

His head inclines a touch. His body stiffening in response to hearing her name.

He goes to speak, his mouth forming sounds, 'Ether...' he growls, broken and hoarse.

'Heather,' Paula says, smiling gently. 'Where is Heather?'

He stiffens again. His body tensing. Suspicion in his eyes.

'Is she hurt? Paco? Is Heather hurt? Subi told us to find you....Subi is safe...'

'Zuuubi...'

'Yes, yes Subi is safe. She is safe, Paco. Rajesh and the children are safe. Where is Heather?'

'Ether...'

'Where is she, Paco?'

He stays where he is. Meredith whines round his legs. He looks down at her, his expression softening for a fraction of a second. 'Dog...gerl...'

'Meredith,' Paula says. 'The dog...she was with you...'

'Gerl...'

'She is a girl. Meredith is a girl...Nick, call Meredith, show him she accepts us.'

'She isn't my dog...Meredith! Here girl...come here...hey who's a good girl....yes you are...' He drops to rub her head and ears. Smiling as she snakes round his body pushing against him.

Paco watches intently. Seeing the man smile and fuss the dog. The woman moves. He flicks his eyes to stare at her.

'Heather? Where is Heather? Is she hurt? Is she in there?' Paula points to the summer house. 'I need to see, Paco...'

'Paula...' Howie says quietly when she moves a step towards him.

'Show me,' Paula says, 'Paco, show me Heather...show me...' She goes forward again. Paco stiffens, his head lifting. 'I will help. Heather is hurt. Show me,' Paula says. 'Meredith...here girl, good girl...see? Meredith is one of us. Where is Heather?'

'Ether...' Paco says, twitching his head towards the summer house.

'Show me,' Paula takes another step then another until she is walking steadily towards Paco who looks over at Dave moving out to keep a clear line of sight. 'Show me Heather,' Paula says. She goes close to him, standing only a foot in front. 'Show me... Heather...Show me...'

It's Meredith that makes it okay. She runs to the summer house. Smelling the blood inside. Smelling the hurt woman. Paco turns sharply, glaring as the dog disappears inside to whine and make noises.

Paula goes after her with a purposeful tread while giving thanks Dave is at her back. Paco rushes to get there first. Running into the summer house to see the dog licking Heather's face. He drops at her side. His eyes transformed to show hurt and worry. He looks down hopeless and lost. Not knowing what to do. She woke up but now she won't wake up.

'In here?' Paula says, knowing the answer but giving some

voice to show she is coming in. He looks round, showing her that hurt and pain on his face.

'*Roy, need you now...*'

'*Coming...*'

'Paco, move back...move back,' she says, shunting him over with her body. Bites and cuts all over the woman's body. Her arms, legs, her stomach...just everywhere. Blood all over her face. Blood on her hands and arms. Blood on the floor. She leans over the woman, gently easing an eyelid back and breathing a sigh of relief at the lack of any red.

'She's still breathing,' Paula murmurs, pressing a finger into the woman's neck.

'Can I come in?' Roy asks, breathing heavy from the sprint across the rear grounds.

'Yep,' Paula says, sitting up to rest a hand on Paco's arm when he twitches to stare at Roy. 'Friend,' she says simply. 'Roy...friend...'

'Heather?' Roy asks, easing his red medic bag from his back.

'She's in a bad way.'

'Might look worse than it is. Is she breathing?'

'Yeah but I can't find a pulse.'

'Don't worry. May I?'

'Yeah go,' she pulls back to let him in. Roy examines visually first. Seeing her breathing unaided. Noting how far her chest rises as she breathes. There's too much blood to see the wounds. She's breathing so he chooses to focus on identifying the injuries first. 'get some water...go round the other side. We need to look for injuries...'

'Marcy...hand please...'

'Coming.'

Paco moves back. Watching closely as three strangers pour water over Heather's body gently washing the blood and filth away.

'Wound here,' Marcy says, holding Heather's arm.

'Bite,' Paula says, staring at the woman's shoulder.

'Look for anything still bleeding...' Roy says.

They work fast but gentle. Washing blood away. Cutting the legs of her trousers off to inspect her skin. The same with her top until she's in underwear on the floor of a summer house being watched by the red eyes of a man who hates her being touched but with an instinct telling him this is okay.

'Christ,' Paula mutters at the number of bites on Heather's body. Teeth marks everywhere.

Roy feels her skull for breaks or fractures. He fell over once and banged his head. He called the ambulance himself and put himself in the recovery position until it arrived. Then he made the paramedics examine him fully before they declared he was fine and told him to stop phoning ambulances unless he was actively dying. The paramedics examined his head and spine and told him they were looking for anything that *didn't feel right*. Roy even went to the hospital later, in his own car, and demanded a doctor check him properly. The doctor did the same thing, with lots of tuts, huffs and deep sighs. Now he does it. He feels the skull and down the vertebrae in her neck for anything *that doesn't feel right*. With Paula and Marcy's help he lifts her enough to feel down her spine then down her legs, visually checking for any deep lacerations.

Her legs move like they should. Her arms too. He goes back to the head now looking for contusion marks that could explain concussion. He opens her eyes, shining his torch at the pupils in turn and noting they retract and both look the same. There's no blood coming from her ears. She's breathing unaided. He finds a pulse and waits with a pensive look on his face. Deep and strong.

'She okay?' Paula finally asks.

'I'm not a doctor, how would I know?'

'Fuck's sake, Roy.'

'Seems fine. Nothing obvious that I can see...she's got colour in her cheeks which seems to suggest she hasn't lost too much blood. Maybe she's just tired.'

'Tired?' Paula asks. 'You saying she's asleep?'

'Passed out...exhaustion or shock.'

'Shock's dangerous isn't it?' Marcy asks.

'Oh very,' Roy says.

'What do we do?'

'I don't know. I'm not a doctor.'

'We just cut her clothes off,' Paula whispers. 'She's asleep and we cut her clothes off...'

'She's not asleep.'

'You just said she was tired.'

'I said she might be tired...as in collapsed...exhausted...fatigued...a general state of being bloody knackered...'

'I know what you meant, Roy. If she was just tired she'd wake up wouldn't she?'

'Not if she's unconscious.'

'Unconscious now is it? You just said she was tired.'

'I'm not a doctor.'

'Well what do we do now?'

'I don't know. We need a doctor.'

'Fuck me...' Paula says, leaning closer to him, 'now we look really stupid.'

'What about internal bleeding?' Marcy asks.

'What about it?' Roy asks.

'Her boyfriend is right there...' Paula whispers. 'And he's bloody huge...'

'She might have internal bleeding,' Marcy says.

'She doesn't. It discolours the skin.'

'Oh...'

'Right, just blag it.'

'Blag what?' Roy asks.

'Blag it,' Paula says again. 'Pretend to do something.'

'What?'

'He's right there. He just watched us cut her bloody clothes off...'

'We're only twenty miles from the fort aren't we?' Marcy asks.

'Brilliant,' Paula whispers then leans back. 'Yeah so...you think she needs to go in then?'

'In what?' Roy asks.

'Into the fort for examination,' Paula says, glaring at him.

'Yeah I suppose so, or...'

'Or what?' Paula says, shaking her head in frustration when he doesn't finish his sentence.

'Or you know, just let her rest.'

'With no clothes on?'

'It's a hot day.'

Strange voices in her head. Strange hands on her body. Heather surges to consciousness to snap her eyes open and stare at three strange faces hovering over her.

'PACO,' she screams out in fear. She's naked. She's vulnerable.

She rises quickly, scrabbling away as Paco moves in, sweeping them aside to scoop her up into his arms. She clings to his form, hyperventilating from shock as he strides outside. Men with guns. A dog barking. Soldiers. The army. They'll hurt Paco. They'll see his red eyes. They'll shoot him.

'RUN...'

He runs. He runs because Heather tells him to run. He can sense her fear. She is awake now. She is back. She doesn't trust these people.

'Wait,' a man with dark curly hair shouts after them, running behind them. The others run too. A huge man with a bald head. She saw him. She saw the man with curly hair too. She heard about them. She's confused. The fight. The children. Running all day and night. She can't breathe properly. She was bitten. She is turned. She's one of them. She's infected. Paco runs hard, powering on with her held in his arms. She clings to his neck. Looking but not seeing. Hearing but not understanding.

'Heather...' The man with curly hair shouts her name. He has a big gun. They all do. The dog is chasing them.

'HE'S NOT INFECTED...' she screams the words out, jolting in his arms as he runs. 'LEAVE HIM ALONE...'

'It's fine...it's fine...It's Paco...we know him...Heather, it's fine...' the man with the curly hair shouts again. His voice isn't angry. The guns aren't pointing at them. The dog is running but not chasing. She looks but doesn't see. She hears but still cannot understand.

'Subi!' A woman shouts, running with the others. 'Subi told us to find you...'

The first prickle of comprehension. The first nudge of awareness in her mind that woke too quickly. Subi. Raj. Amna...the children...the fort...Howie...Mr Howie...

'Mr Howie...' she blurts the name.

'Me! I'm Howie...that's me...Subi told us to find you...'

She swallows and looks round at them again, 'stop,' she whispers. The big man slows but holds her close, pulling her into his body, ready to run again. She clings to him, feeling his body pressing into hers, feeling the heat from him. Paco is safe. Being with Paco is safety. She protected him. She fed him. She cleaned him. He killed for her and she killed for him.

'Thank fuck,' a beautiful woman gasps for air, rubbing her boobs, 'didn't put a sports bra on.'

'That was silly,' the other woman says quietly.

'I'm Howie,' the man with curly hair says, standing back. 'That's Dave...' the man gasps, 'and...other people...shit a brick he runs fast...'

'He's not infected,' Heather says.

'We know,' Howie says, lifting a hand.

'Well actually...'

'Not now, Roy,' Howie says. 'You're Heather?'

She nods, still unsure. Every instinct tells her to go. People are bad. People with guns are dangerous but she knows who these people are. She saw them. She watched them fight in the square when they had thousands against them. She was hiding in the top flat of a building on the other side.

'I saw you.'

'Subi told us,' the woman says. 'I'm Paula...'

'You have that army truck.'

'The Saxon,' Howie says. 'We know Paco...before he...before he died. We were with him when it happened.'

'He's getting better,' Heather says, her voice low and showing the distrust.

'He will,' the beautiful woman says. 'I was infected...another one of ours was too...'

'You were bitten,' Paula says. Heather twitches her gaze. 'I was too,' Paula adds.

'And me,' Howie says. 'Those men are Blowers, Nick and Cookey...they were bitten too...we didn't turn...'

'There is immunity,' Paula says.

'Well actually...'

'Not now, Roy,' Blowers mutters.

'We don't know what we are,' Howie says, 'but one of our team is trying to work it out...'

'The children? Where are they?'

'Safe,' Paula says. 'They're at the fort.'

'How many?'

'Six...Subi said one was shot?'

Heather nods. 'Man in a house...I tried to...I couldn't save...'

'You saved the others,' Howie says quickly, seeing the pain in her face. 'They're safe now. We came to find you...we'll take you back and...'

'No.'

'Er...' Howie falters, watching her intently.

'We'll go,' Heather says.

'Go where?' Paula asks.

'Doesn't matter. We'll go.'

'Why? We're no risk to you,' Paula says. 'We just gave you medical aid...'

'Is that what it was?' Marcy mumbles.

'I said I'm not a doctor.'

'Few minutes,' Paula says, shooting dark looks at Roy and Marcy. 'Just a few minutes, and besides...your er...your clothes are all torn up and...probably from all that fighting you did so you need new clothes. We'll get you new clothes...and weapons too, you'll need a weapon if you're going...'

Paula is a bloody genius. Blowers listens to her, the way she uses her tone of voice to inflect meaning and sincerity. Her facial expressions, the way she stands. He watches the woman being held by Paco and the way he doesn't tremble from the weight in his arms. He watches Paco turning slightly to see them all and the passive look now on his face as he simply holds Heather and waits. An idea comes to mind. He glances at the boss then at Paula before slowly drawing his pistol that he flicks round to present the butt towards Paco and Heather.

'Take this,' he says. 'You're armed then...'

Blowers is a bloody genius. Paula watches him, seeing his earnest expression and the respectful tone of voice. She could kiss him right now for this simple act.

Heather stares at Blowers then down to the gun in his hands. She doesn't know how to use it but having it would make them safer than not having it. She eases from Paco's arms, dropping lightly to the floor. Paco moves with her, steadying her drop until he's sure she is stable on her feet. She keeps one hand on his arm as though just feeling him close gives safety.

As one the men turn their heads, looking away while one of them holds the pistol out towards her. She frowns, unsure of what just happened.

'Clothes, honey,' Paula says gently, smiling with pride at her boys all looking to the right. That does it. That show of dignity and respect is seen and understood. Paula takes the pistol and walks towards Heather.

'Loaded, made ready, safety on,' Blowers says.

'Here,' Paula says, holding the gun out. 'Know how to use it?'

'No...'

Paco does. He takes the pistol. His brain is wired differently now. He cannot form thoughts as he should, he cannot extrapolate and reach the logical conclusions that coherent thought processes give, but he does know how to use a gun. He was a soldier, an assassin, a cop, a detective, a superhero, a rogue agent. He was in the FBI and the CIA. He protected the President. He saved the girl and he used weapons in every single one of those action films. He was taught to fight, to shoot, to re-load, to strip weapons and reassemble them. He was taught safe practises by experts and was drilled to perfection to give the sense of realism that his films presented. He knew he couldn't act that well so he made up for it with everything else. He takes the pistol, ejects the magazine, slides the top back and catches the round that comes out. He turns away, dry firing to feel the weight and balance. He thumbs the top of the magazine checking for pressure and slots the spare round back in. He slams the magazine home, slides the top to chamber the first and turns back with the weapon now held in front of his stomach pointing down to the ground.

'Oh my god,' Heather says, smiling at him with that look that makes his heart feel funny. 'That was so bloody cool, Paco...'

Paula smiles at the complete change in manner as Heather speaks to Paco. The overt show of emotion and the use of facial expressions, the warmth in her voice and the way Paco smiles back at her with such a look pure love in his eyes that it makes her feel weird for a second. Like she is seeing something that should be for them alone, that she should turn away and give them privacy. Without conscious thought she glances to Clarence, catching him watching her before he blinks and looks away.

'We're not going to the fort,' a hard tone and blunt words. Paula looks up to see that emotion and meaning are now gone from Heather as she addresses the group with Paco standing very tall behind her.

'It's only twenty miles from here...'

Heather shakes her head. Making her intentions clear. 'No.'

'May I ask why?' Paula asks.

'They'll hurt Paco. I won't risk that. If they see him they won't understand...'

'I'm so sorry,' Howie says, cutting across her. 'I don't think you understand. See that man? That's Nick. His girlfriend runs the fort. We run the fort. It's our fort...'

CHAPTER SIX

'Just a few minutes,' she tells him. He looks down at her hand on his arm, his eyes expressive. 'I mean they seem nice enough,' she adds, speaking low and quiet. 'What do you think?'

Paco does not reply. The equilibrium in his head is back to where it should be. Heather is awake, talking, smiling and touching his arm. The infection inside was like a pendulum swinging back and forth. It suppressed his memories of the dog and his life before while something inside of him suppressed the need to bite and pass the infection.

He is not what he was before he was bitten. He is not what he was when he woke in the true state of being. He does not know what he is. He does not think to know what he is. He has Heather. Heather is safe. That's all that matters.

She fingers the shreds of her top and looks down at the remaining strips of her trousers. They cut her clothes off. She's been washed too. So many bites on her skin. She remembers it happening. The teeth sinking into her shoulder and knowing she had about two minutes before she went down. Except she didn't go down. She stayed fighting and took more punishment than anyone had a right to take. She thinks back to the days since meeting Paco and the times she watched him taking down dozens of the infected at a time just with his bare hands. Ripping them apart, stomping on heads and breaking necks with that trademark film thing he does. Paco was bitten and raked open in nearly every fight. He was cut, bruised, hit, struck, kicked but never once reacted to any sense of pain.

'I don't h‿rt,' she tells him, speaking her mind in the way she has come to do with him. 'Tender but...' she frowns and pokes a bite mark on her stomach. She should be in agony but instead it's just a bit sore. She pokes another one, then spots a cut made by a dirty jagged fingernail and pokes that too. She pokes more, pressing and digging the tips of her fingers in until his hand reaches across to stop her. She blinks up at him, surprised at his action. The world is nuts. Everything is crazy. She saved six children and ran all day yesterday and has fought a running battle all night. She was exhausted to the point of passing out a little while ago. Now she feels okay, a bit tired but nothing like she should. She shrugs and pulls a face at him. 'Did you give me zombie?' She looks ahead to the group of people in front of her. 'Did Paco give me his zombie thing?' She asks, her tone instantly changing from the softness she uses for him to the general blunt expression of her hatred for humanity used when addressing any other human being.

'Er...' Paula hesitates, looking back while walking on.

'We don't know how it works,' Howie says without turning. 'Hopefully Reggie might figure it out.'

'Reggie?'

'One of our team,' Howie says.

Team? Heather doesn't like the sound of that word. It implies people working together. It implies teamwork and sharing things with other people. She doesn't like other people. People are bad. They ask stupid questions that make her feel uncomfortable. She survived for days hiding in a church when it first happened. Not from any religious beliefs but because it was isolated and had thick walls and miles of open flat land round it. She simply got bored in the end and went looking for supplies which is when she met Paco, or rather, when Paco chased her and tried to eat her. He didn't eat her.

She looks up at him, remembering when he didn't eat her. Team sounds bad. Get some clothes and they can go somewhere else. Walk and find a nice barn to stay in. Just her and Paco.

She heard about Mr Howie and Dave a few days ago. She heard they had a fort and were fighting back. She even saw them at different times. The world had suddenly grown very small and it appeared all lives were crossing paths or some other weird shit was going on. She saw Clarence going nuts when the Saxon broke down about two weeks after the outbreak started. She and Paco were hiding in a building nearby. She saw the Saxon and a blue armoured van driving through another town after the bad storm that made everywhere flooded. She felt something then. A sensation at seeing them and hearing their names. She felt a pull to them. An instinct that her own kind were fighting back and she should be doing something to help. That was offset by her own deep wariness of other people. She even watched the battle against the ten thousand while keeping the children hidden. She saw so few go against so many and felt the rage inside when they charged out in response to the little girl screaming in torture. Paco felt it too. They both did.

Now they are walking behind them and her instinct to be away and on her own is proving the stronger of the two. Get clothes and get away. That's the new plan.

Blowers walks on. He wants to turn and check but the woman is pretty much down to her underwear so he can't. He doesn't like someone having a loaded gun walking behind them. One pull of the trigger could kill the boss. He looks across to Dave, seeing the small man's hand is resting on the top of his pistol while his head is cocked as though listening intently. Clarence is walking behind Howie too. Using his bulk to break the line of fire.

They walk in silence. He looks at the back doors ahead, then along the building line noting the ground floor windows are all boarded up. He checks the sides and any possible points of danger. Hopefully they can go back to the fort and ditch Maddox. Get some coffee, get cleaned up and see what the elders want to do next. That's the hierarchy in his head and it's fine with him. Whatever they have between them works. They've fought battles they had no right to walk away from so he doesn't question it now but focusses on his role and his team to keep the cogs of the machine working.

'We'll go ahead,' he motions to Nick and Cookey. The three of them speed up as Maddox appears in the doorway.

'What are you doing? I said to stay out the front...'

'You told Mo and Blinky to remain at the front. I was checking the back.'

'Prick,' Cookey mutters under his breath, walking past Maddox into the room.

'You found him then.'

'Get fucked,' Nick says, passing on his other side.

'Is that Heather?' Maddox asks, ignoring Nick.

'Back out the front.'

'Why?'

'Because I said so and that's the point of danger...'

'They've got radios if anything happens.'

'Listen you fucking...'

'Clear?' Howie asks, walking into the room with a look at the pair of them.

'Clear,' Maddox replies quickly. 'But they don't want to leave here.'

'Can't make them,' Howie says, moving aside to let the others in.

'We can't just leave them here,' Paula says, hearing the conversation.

'I tried talking to them,' Maddox says.

'You and Marcy have a go,' Howie tells Paula, glancing at Paco in the doorway with Heather standing behind him. 'You two want to get cleaned up here?'

Paco looks at Howie then at Clarence, at Paula, Marcy, back to Howie then to Maddox who he stares at for several long seconds before going back to Howie.

'Er...Heather?' Howie says at the lack of verbal response. 'You want to get cleaned up here?'

'We're not going with you,' Heather says, leaning Paco round to look at Howie.

'We said down there,' Howie says, motioning with his head to the grounds behind her.

'I said I'd talk to you for a few minutes.'

'We can talk at the fort. It's like twenty miles from here.'

'We can talk here just fine.'

'Okay,' Paula says, stepping in diplomatically. 'Heather? Want to come with me? We'll have a look for clothes.'

'I'm staying with Paco,' Heather says, her tone blunt and hard. Paula goes to reply as Marcy lifts a hand and peers round Paco.

'Nothing bad will happen.'

'I said...'

'Heather, Subi told us to come and find you. We've done that. We killed them to get in here. We've got the house secure now... you need to get cleaned up.'

'It's only upstairs,' Paula says.

'I think the old woman is making coffee,' Maddox adds, detecting the fear in the woman and trying to help.

'Just a few minutes,' Marcy says, watching Heather's reaction and the look of panic on the woman's face. 'Hey, it's okay...what's wrong?'

'Nothing. We're going. We have to go...'

'Go where?'

'We just have to go.'

'Okay, that's cool,' Marcy says easily, 'it's fine, you can go when you want.'

'We will,' Heather says, feeling the pressure of too many people being near her. Too many eyes facing her direction. Too many questioning looks. They'll ask things. They'll want to know who she is. She can't handle that. She can't be in crowds or with people. Paco stiffens in response to her tone behind him. His head lifting an inch. His eyes growing hard.

'Easy,' Clarence rumbles, looking at Paco. 'No threat here...'

'Paco, it's fine,' Heather says, rubbing his blood stained arm. He's covered in blood from the fighting last night and probably her blood too. She can't remember when they last had food or water either. She was looking for these people but now she's found them she can't deal with it. She has to deal with it. Too many questions form in her mind. Her fear of crowds and people making the thoughts confused and jumbled. This is what happens when people ask questions. She gets panicked and feels like she's backed into a corner.

'You fought last night?' Howie asks, his tone low and easy.

Heather nods, then realises he can't see her nod. 'Yes.'

'How many did you kill?'

She shrugs then winces at herself, hating her own stupidity. 'Few.'

'We found the hedge you went through...by the stables. It was more than a few.'

'Then why ask?' she says bluntly while looking at Paco's back and wishing the beautiful woman would stop staring at her. Her hand on his arm, feeling the hairs and picking at a dried patch of blood without realising it. 'They came all night,' she finally says.

'You did well,' Howie says, staring down at the ground. 'Just you two against so many.'

She frowns. That wasn't a question but a statement and he left it hanging like she should respond. 'We...I had a shotgun but...'

'It broke. We found it,' Howie says. 'So you saw us...that day in the square, that right?'

'Yes.'

'You heard the girl screaming?'

'Yeah,' she says, her voice low and hoarse.

'Mr Howie?'

'In here, Reggie,' Howie calls out.

Heather peers round to see a small man wearing glasses holding a bag clutched to his chest rushing into the room.

'Did you find them? Ah yes, yes indeed' Reginald says, spotting Paco in the doorway. 'The woman? Is she not with him?'

'Behind him,' Howie says.

'She's half naked,' Marcy adds.

'Half naked? Whatever for? I say, hello? Can you hear me? Ah yes, yes there you are. I'm Reginald...'

'Heather,' Heather says.

'Good gracious you are half naked, oh my...well indeed, yes you should get changed. Indeed you should...Hello? You must be Paco...'

'He doesn't speak,' Howie says.

'Right, gosh...no speaking.' Reginald says, his curiosity once again overcoming his fears as he walks to stand close and peer up at the famous man. 'Hmmm, very interesting. Yes indeed. Red eyes. I say, they are still very red...have they reduced in the redness at all?'

'A bit,' Heather says, watching the small man.

'Yes,' Reginald says slowly, staring hard. 'Your injuries are healing aren't they...of course it an assumption on my part that the neck is where Meredith took him. Am I correct in thinking that?'

'The dog bit his throat,' Howie says, scratching his head. 'Is that what you asked?'

'Indeed it was,' Reginald says, still staring up at Paco. 'Is he strong?'

'Very.'

'Indeed. Yes. Fast too?'

'Yes.'

'Tell me about his cognitive function...'

'He's getting better.'

'In more detail please. Can he speak at all?' Reginald asks, his eyes fixed on Paco.

'Reggie, let them get a drink and get cleaned up first,' Paula says.

'Ah yes, of course. Do forgive me...and you? Are your eyes red at all?'

'I don't know. I can't see them.'

'They're not,' Marcy says.

'Not red,' Reginald says, nodding slowly deep in thought. 'Indeed, yes...one more question. Do tell me, Heather. How many attacked you last night?'

She winces, pressing closer into Paco's back. Everyone is listening. They're asking her questions. She can't handle it but the question he asked is important. 'I don't know...they kept coming all night.'

'Hmmm, difficult to assess,' Reginald says. 'But if you had to put a number?'

She thinks back to night. A series of memories that flash through her mind.

'Over fifty...' she says, remembering the number of shotgun shells in the box she took from the house they found. Instant grief hits. One of the children died at that house. Shot by the man inside who panicked when he saw Paco. 'I had fifty shotgun things...'

'Cartridges?' Howie asks in surprise. 'You had fifty? You shot fifty of them?'

'None of those at the hedge were shot,' Dave says.

'How many were there?' Howie asks.

'Thirty nine.'

'Thirty nine! Fuck me...you killed thirty nine with just two of you? How many is that? Er...fifty and thirty nine?'

'Seriously?' Marcy asks.

'Eighty nine,' Reginald says, still thinking hard. 'Eighty nine plus fifty two here...'

'Hundred and forty one,' Maddox says.

'Clever cunt...'

'Cookey,' Paula says, her tone warning.

'One hundred and forty one,' Reginald muses. 'One hundred and forty one within twenty miles of the fort. Indeed. Yes.' He walks off towards the interior door, thinking hard at what he read last night, at seeing Paco and Heather and now hearing one hundred and forty one were killed so close to the fort.

'He does that,' Marcy tells Heather. 'He's very intelligent though...like a genius or something.'

'I *am* a genius not a something,' Reginald mutters, walking into the hallway.

'Coffee, my dear?'

'Coffee? Oh gosh no...do you have Peppermint tea?'

'Fuck's sake,' Paula says, huffing as everyone apart from her, Maddox, Paco and Heather make a beeline for the door at hearing their favourite word. 'Heather, come on...we'll get you cleaned up.'

'We can do it ourselves.'

'Okay,' Paula says, thinking she would love a coffee too. 'Er... Howie? Ask them where the bathroom is and if they've got spare clothes for...'

'They've got coffee,' Howie shouts.

'Yes I heard, ask them where the bathroom is and if they've got...'

'Coffee,' Howie shouts from the hallway.

'I know where the bathroom is,' Maddox says, seeing an opportunity. 'I'll take them...'

'Nah,' Paula says, smiling at him. 'Where is it?'

'I can take them.'

'So can I. Where is it?'

'I said I can...'

'Now, Maddox.'

'Upstairs. First on the right.'

'Thank you, earn it, Maddox. It tastes better...Paco? Heather? Come with me.'

Heather guides Paco through, her hand on the small of his back. He goes forward at her touch. Understanding in his eyes at Paula nodding for them to follow her. As they reach the door Heather glances back expecting to see Maddox staring at her but he stands alone staring down at the floor instead.

'What the...' Paula snorts laughter at the sight of Clarence holding a fine china saucer while trying to get his finger through the handle of the matching fine china cup. 'You alright there?'

'Handles a bit small,' he whispers like a bear would whisper, which isn't whispering but more like a dull roar.

'Fingers a bit fat more like,' she chuckles.

'My fingers aren't fat,' he says, ditching the idea of pushing his finger through to simply grab the cup and lift it to his mouth. She laughs again, the sight is ridiculous. The man is so big the cup looks like a toy.

'Nice coffee though,' Howie says, holding his saucer in one hand while lifting his cup with the other.

'Another one?' The old woman says, shoving a cup and saucer at Paula, 'coffee, my dear?'

Paula isn't given any choice but manages to grab the saucer before the lady turns to rush off back to the table set in the hallway now filled with more matching cups and saucers.

'Very nice coffee,' Clarence says, sipping delicately from his floral cup.

'You're a bloody bear,' Paula laughs, still watching him.

'I am not,' he says with mock stiffness.

'Coffee, my dear?' The old woman asks, shoving a cup and saucer at Paco who stares down at her then at the cup and saucer, making no attempt to take it.

'Coffee?' She asks, prodding him with it while paying no heed to the blood on his body or the red eyes watching her. 'Do you want coffee? Coffee? Coffee? Do you want coffee?' She chirrups, stuck in a loop of dazed shock that sets Cookey off, which in turn makes Charlie chuckle and everyone else look over. 'Coffee? Do you want coffee?' She prods the edge of the saucer into his hand again before a thought occurs to her. 'Do. You. Want. Coffee?' She asks, speaking in the loud clear voice used to address Johnny Foreigner. 'Coffee? Coffee? Do. You. Want. Coffee?'

Blowers snorts. Nick starts smiling. Mo fights the grin. Howie watches with his cup pressed to his lips.

'Coffee? Take it, dear...take the coffee...do you want it? Do you want coffee?'

Howie starts going. Marcy glares at him but the corners of her mouth twitch as she fights the laugh.

'I say,' the old woman huffs. 'Is he a spastic?'

Cookey sprays his coffee over Nick. Howie spurts his on his boots. Clarence chokes. Marcy coughs hers out.

'Mother!' A voice calls out in horror from a woman standing by the table loaded with cups. 'We don't say that word now...'

'No? Oh dear...' the old woman says, still pushing the cup and saucer at Paco. 'Are. You. Retarded?'

Cookey's gone. It's too much. He turns round in a circle bent forward with coffee coming out his nose. Charlie sets off at the sight of him, ducking out the house to stifle her laugh. Blinky and Mo follow suit.

'Or that!' The woman at the table shouts. 'I am sorry...I am so sorry,' she rushes over, flummoxed and red in the face. 'Mother... you are so embarrassing...'

'Well I don't know what I can say these days.'

'You can't say spastic or...'

Cookey goes down. Nick rests his head on the wall, tears rolling down his face. Howie turns into Marcy, burying his head in her hair to hide his laughing. Clarence turns away, his whole body shaking.

'Stop it,' the other woman whispers angrily, 'you're making it worse...ask his carer if he wants coffee...'

'Carer...' Cookey blurts as Blowers bends while laughing to help him up.

'I'm not his carer,' Heather says from behind Paco. Unable to stop the smile spreading across her face at the sound of everyone else laughing. She snorts a laugh and turns to see Maddox who suddenly smiles as though he gets the joke.

'Can he have coffee, dear?' The old woman asks, leaning round Paco to peer at Heather. 'Coffee? Can he have coffee? Does he want coffee?'

'Stop,' Cookey pleads. 'Oh fuck...'

'Outside,' Blowers gasps, helping him to the door. 'Nick...go outs...go outs...'

'Does he want coffee? Coffee?' She chirrups again, now ramming the spilling coffee into his side.

'Oh god,' Nick gasps.

'Coffee? Coffee?'

'Out,' Paula says, laughing as hard but trying to hide it.

'I'll take it,' Heather says, reaching out to take the now half-empty cup and coffee filled saucer. The old woman beams a smile of false teeth and glazed eyes before scurrying off to the table.

'Coffee?' Heather asks, handing the cup out to Maddox and smiling at hearing everyone set off again.

'Thanks,' Maddox says, taking the cup and offering a smile while still wondering what the hell is meant to be happening.

With everyone else now occupied, Heather guides Paco to the stairs and starts going up while glancing back to see Marcy and Paula pushing and dragging the rest to the front door. It shouldn't be funny. She shouldn't laugh but laughing is contagious. Smiling is contagious and she goes up chuckling and shaking her head.

First door on the right. The bathroom. She goes in with Paco to a white bathroom bathed in gorgeous sunlight from the unbarred windows on the first floor. It's so clean, gleaming even. The taps, the sink, the bath. Even the fluffy white towels are white and fluffy. She looks at the state of Paco then down to her own still filthy state with a deep sigh.

She strips the remains of her clothes off, tugging the t shirt over her head to cast it aside, instantly forgetting to be careful. She chuckles again at the thing that happened downstairs and the old woman.

'That was funny,' she tells Paco who smiles because she is smiling. 'Come on, strip...clothes off.'

Only a few days ago Paco wouldn't respond to anything she asked but would stand and wait for her to do it for him. Not that he was actually waiting as that implied a level of understanding, and he didn't understand anything. Now he does grasp the thing needed to be done and starts pulling his top off. From habit, and forgetting he can now do it himself, she moves to his belt and starts unbuckling it to undo his button and flies. His form is familiar to her now. She's scrubbed him clean countless times and washed the shit from his arse too. She's showered in front of him, gone to the toilet and shared pretty much the whole of their lives for nine solid days. They have kissed once. At the point of being trapped at the hedge when all hope was gone and she had to know, she needed to know before they died, what his love was. Was he a guard dog or a man?

He was a man and he kissed her like a man kisses a woman. He kissed her with passion and love that made her heart soar and wish for life more than any other time before.

'Boots,' she says, unlacing the first to tug it off. 'What am I doing?' she asks, staring up at him with a suspicious look. 'You can bloody do it now...go on...'

Paco smiles but doesn't move.

'Paco,' she says firmly, folding her arms. 'You can undress yourself.'

Paco smiles but still doesn't move.

She tuts but smiles at the expression in his eyes. 'Right fine, come on then...' she drops back down to tug his boots off and pull his filthy trousers round his ankles so he can step free. 'I'm not doing your boxers,' she tells him firmly. 'Don't look at me like that. I'm not. Paco, I said no. Really?' she asks when he lifts his arms to hold them over his head as though showing he won't do it himself. 'You're playing on this...you were talking last night. I heard you... what's my name? Go on...what's my name? Say my name and I'll pull your boxers off for you.'

'Ether...'

'You shit,' she says, laughing as she says it. 'Right fine, come here then. You've slept with like seven thousand women you dirty sod...don't think I'm falling for it. Right, have a wash then. Oh for love of...Paco, you can do it. I've seen you wash...' She berates him while twisting the shower on over the bath. Cold water jets out, thundering down into the huge cast iron tub. 'You get in first,' she says, nodding at him to get in. He goes willingly, stepping over the edge to get under the flow without a flicker of reaction at the cold water hitting his body. He turns as he goes to keep Heather in sight, his eyes always watching her, tracking her movements as he listens to her voice. She strips off, wincing at the smell of her own body and the filthy state of her bra and knickers. Everything is ruined. The last two days have been worse than hell and the emotions of what they had to do are too recent, too fresh and too strong to deal with. Instead she sighs, huffs and chats on then notices Paco standing unmoving under the flow. She stops to raise an eyebrow at him, folds her arms and adopts an unamused expression. He looks back at her and to anyone else his expression would be devoid of emotion but she can read him now and knows exactly what he is doing.

She clambers in with a tut, grabs the bottle of shower gel from the side and tells him to turn round. 'Oh you can do that alright,' she says at the very second she realises this is the first time in her life she has ever showered with another human being. She is naked in a shower with Paco, who is also naked. Is it different now they've kissed? She muses on the subject while reaching to soap his back and starts using her hands to rub the gore and dirt away. She'd had relationships before, albeit exceptionally short ones and she isn't a virgin. She'd had sex four times. All of them were awful experiences and she only did it on the belief that she should give the man sex or he'd find it somewhere else. She couldn't stand anyone touching her, let alone a man. She couldn't stand being looked at or spoken to and as she got older so those phobias got worse until she retreated from life to live like a shadow that planned everything to avoid being near someone else. Now she is naked in a shower with a famous movie actor who was a self-confessed sex addict and has probably slept with like nine hundred women. Funny how life goes.

'Turn round,' she soaps his face, smiling at him when he bends down so she can reach his head. The water runs pink and dark from the blood and dirt. Pooling round their feet to stain the once gleaming bath. She cleans his neck, moving gently to avoid damaging the injuries that have already healed so much since she met him. The skin is fusing back together so quickly. She can still see the outline of the puncture marks made by the dog but even they're closing over far faster than normal. She realises, on once again musing over his injuries, that she now has a chance to try and find out why he is the way he is, and why she was bitten and didn't turn. Those people said they were bitten too. They said they are immune, but then that man with the red medic bag and bow went to say something else but the others cut him off, and who was that small man with the glasses? Mr Howie said one of their team was trying to figure it out. That must be him. He didn't have a gun but a bag that looked like it was filled with books.

She cleans his shoulders, arms and chest and down to his legs while trying to convince herself she should stay and find out what she can while also knowing she wants only to go and be away from everyone. Before they found the children, she and Paco simply walked every day and found somewhere to stay at night. Paco could deal with any infected that came near them and in turn she kept him fed and clean. Those days were special. Beautiful. She wants only that. To walk with him and find old barns to sleep in at night.

That isn't right though. Paco is special. She's seen how many he can kill, and with ease too. One of them said she and Paco killed thirty nine at the hedge and she knows most of those would have been by Paco. He was bitten, infected but something in him seems to be fighting it off while leaving him with immense strength and an ability to heal and seemingly not feel pain. Like he is part them and part human, or something else entirely. Did he pass something to her to make her immune? Why didn't she turn then fight the infection like he did?

She freezes at his touch. So absorbed in her thoughts that she didn't see him reaching forward to lay his hands on her shoulders. She blinks up at him and smiles. Paco would never hurt her. She knows that for fact. She feels his touch on her skin as he starts rubbing as though trying to clean her. An intense look of focus in his eyes. Her mouth opens in surprise that he can form the connection of what she just did for him and do it back to her.

'Hands.'

He pulls away from her, opening his hands so she can pour shower gel into his palms. He stares for a second as though unsure what the gel is before reaching back out to start rubbing her shoulders again.

'Do my back?' She asks quietly, still stunned at him trying to clean her. She turns on the spot and steps back before glancing over her shoulder to watch him intently. He carries on rubbing but so gently, like he is afraid of hurting her. She smiles and faces forward, closing her eyes at the never before felt sensation of someone else washing her back. It feels divine. Better than divine. It's amazing. He goes lower as she eases back a touch to increase the pressure on his hands. 'You won't hurt me,' she murmurs.

He washes her back. Paco Maguire washes her back. Another

human being that is a man who is naked is washing her back and she doesn't feel the urge to stab him in the face with a pen.

He goes lower, moving down her spine and out to the sides. Rubbing gently. She feels him step closer, reaching round to open his hands in front of her. She can feel his penis touching her. She swallows and exhales while spurting the gel into his hands. He steps back and carries on. His penis just touched her. She's washed it before but that was different. This is bordering on being erotic.

His hands work steadily down to her bum cheeks. She swallows again and blinks, thinking that she will feel repulsed but it's nice. My god it's so nice. She lets the breath go and relaxes into it. Feeling his hands work down her thighs to her calves. A hand on her shoulder. She turns to face him. His hands open. She pours more gel. He reaches out and washes her face. She closes her eyes, feeling his fingers brush lightly over her skin then down to her neck. She's seen him snap bones with his bare hands. She's seen him throw big men like they were made of paper and those hands now move like silk down to her chest.

She swallows again at the first feel of his hands on her breasts. The borderline eroticism increases. He washes as gently as before. Rubbing to remove the dirt and moving down to her stomach. She licks her lips, breathing slightly harder. Her face flushes but her eyes remain closed. He washes her stomach, her hips and down over her groin to her legs once more. Again she lets the breath go, fighting the urge inside and the heat that seems to be building in her stomach. Not her stomach. Lower down. Down there. Oh my.

She opens her eyes when he stands up. He is finished. He smiles. She smiles back. A moment frozen in time until she spots his groin.

'Paco!'

He blinks in surprise at her tone.

'Put that away right now.'

He doesn't know what he should put away.

'Look at the bloody size of it...oh my god, Paco...you've got a bloody erection...'

She stares at it as it stares back at her. She goes to speak, to say something, to tell him off for being a dirty sod but she just felt the same thing so that makes it natural, normal, it makes it okay. He didn't grope her either. He didn't try and poke it in her, he isn't doing anything now either but looking at her looking at him without any shred of threat or malice in him. She even smiles, feeling a strange reaction to knowing he just got turned on by her naked form.

'Heather? Are you decent?' A knock at the door. Paula calling out.

'No!' Heather shouts, jolting guiltily. 'Er...hang on...' She pulls a face at him and looks round, spotting the fluffy white towels hanging neatly from the towel heater that will probably never get hot again. She turns the shower off and hops out, almost sliding across the wet floor to crash into the side unit, sending ceramic pots flying from the top that fall to the ground.

'Are you okay?'

'Fine!' Heather shouts back, grabbing a towel before skating back towards the bathtub. She stops in front of him, knowing she needs to wrap the towel round his waist but wondering how to do it while that thing is poking out. Does it go down or up? It doesn't look like it goes down, not when it's that big. It must go up. She loops the towel round his backside and pulls the ends round in front of him. 'Tuck it in,' she whispers at him. 'Paco...tuck it in...I'm not touching it...'

Paco doesn't tuck it in.

She tucks it in. Huffing and trying to give him a look but bursting out laughing while she does it. She holds it up against his body while wrapping the towel round to secure off. 'You can stop grinning like that too,' she tells him.

'Coming,' she skates back across the floor to the door, pulling it open to look at Paula. 'Hey...'

'Oh right,' Paula says, turning her head away.

'Oh shit,' Heather yelps, realising she is still naked. 'Hang on...'

'It's fine,' Paula says. 'Got some cream that's all.'

'Cream?' Heather asks, sliding to grab another towel that she pulls round herself.

'Doctors gave it to Roy yesterday for cuts and...well, Roy's got it in his head that we might be immune to *that* infection but there's other things that can hurt us.'

'Oh...' Heather says, now covered and glancing back at Paco still grinning from the bathtub.

'Can I come in?'

'Er...yeah, I guess...'

'Thanks,' Paula says, stepping through with only a cursory glance at the now filthy bathroom and an even more cursory glance at Paco grinning at something in the bath. 'Er, listen...'

'I don't like people,' Heather blurts. The flush from being turned on is still there, the heat in her face and the sensation at being washed and massaged all serve to imbue a sudden ability to say those few words.

'That's fine,' Paula says easily. 'Nor does Howie most of the time...and come to think about it, nor do I that much...actually...I think that might be a recurring trait. No...Marcy is good with people, Charlie too. Roy isn't. Clarence is. Reginald isn't...the lads are...depending on who it is of course, otherwise they're evil shits...'

'I...I mean I can't handle...' Heather swallows, the sensation of pressure starting to return. 'I don't like it...I mean I can't deal with people asking questions and...'

'Questions?' Paula asks. 'You're immune, Heather. Paco is too or something else probably...'

'Not that,' Heather says, frustrated at feeling herself clamming up again. 'I mean...like...'

'Like what?'

'Just...like...when people ask where you're from and...family...I can't...and when more than one person looks at me. I can't...I'm sorry...we'll go...'

'Slow down,' Paula says. 'We're not like that.'

'I can't. I just...we'll go. We'll have to go...that man with the glasses can ask about me and Paco...about what happened but then we'll go.'

'I was almost raped...' Paula says so matter of fact it catches Heather off guard.

'What?'

'I said I was almost raped...no, I *was* raped. First day it happened. The outbreak I mean. I was in the office working late. One of my male colleagues came back drunk and told me what was happening outside. He raped me.'

'Oh shit,' Heather says, seeing the dark look on Paula's face.

'I killed him,' Paula says. 'Then I killed every single one of the infected in my town...every man woman and child including my mother.'

Heather stares, listening closely as Paula talks so matter of fact about something so awful.

'I swore that I would never be near anyone ever again and I was fine with that. I could look after myself. I met Roy then this lot... Howie and the others I mean. Not all of them, some joined a bit later...but you know, not one of them have asked about my life before this and I don't ask them. We talk and sometimes things come out. Like I know Mo came from a bad estate and had a shit upbringing but I don't know the details. I don't know if any of them have brothers or sisters. I don't know what happened to their parents or families and they don't ask me. Like I said, things come out here and there but...it's too fresh, too soon and we're too busy to be completely honest. I saw my mother the day before it all happened. Then I saw her after. She'd turned. I didn't see her when I killed them but I knew she must have been there. Point is, the reason we're all together is because we've got nothing to go back for, no one to find or help. We've got each other and that's it and you know what? After everything I went through and swearing I wouldn't trust another human ever again? I wouldn't be anywhere else other than here with this lot and add to that we're probably all immune...' She trails off, exhaling into the silence with a flurry of thoughts rushing through her mind. 'Talk to Howie...give him a chance.'

'Howie?'

Paula nods, 'you'll see what I mean, just talk to him for a bit. They won't ask questions about anything. I promise you and if they knew, or even thought for a second they made you uncomfortable by looking at you they wouldn't do it. You're new. You're immune. You might be one of us so...'

'One of you? I'm not one of you.'

'No? Thirty nine was it? Over fifty during the night?'

'Paco killed most of them.'

'Still did it. Still walked away from it...no one else does. We do. We took on ten thousand that night in the square and walked away from it.'

'I'm not one of you.'

'Okay, that's fine. Just give us a bit of time...you can leave whenever you want but remember, those men that came down to the summer house were the ones that tried to save Paco and Meredith. They fought by his side. Right next to him.'

Heather stays silent, watching the woman talk. There's something comforting about Paula. The relaxed manner, the concern in her eyes and tone of voice that make it seem she really cares.

'Cream,' Paula says, lifting the tube up. 'You got bites on your back...want me to do it?'

'Er...'

'Ah,' Paula says, smiling gently. 'It's just cream, Heather. Can Paco do it?'

'He'll probably try and eat it.'

Paula chuckles, smiling at Paco still grinning in the bath. 'What's he grinning for?' She asks as Heather glances down with a wry smile and a blush spreading across her cheeks. 'Go on, turn round. I'll put the cream on then you can do Paco.' Heather turns, easing the towel down a few inches to expose her back. 'So, he doesn't speak then?' Paula asks, squeezing a dollop onto her finger-tips. 'Might be a bit cold, okay?'

'It's fine,' Heather says, facing towards Paco watching closely as another person touches Heather. 'He didn't at first...he couldn't do anything at first...but he's healing and...getting more intelligent every day. I can see it in his eyes. He gets frustrated that he can't make me understand what he wants.'

'Like most men,' Paula mutters. 'It's good that he's got you,' Paula says, rubbing the cream into the broken skin round the big bite on Heather's shoulder.

'He saved me.'

'Yeah?'

'Well, he tried to eat me then saved me.'

'Did he?'

'I got trapped at the top of a building. Paco found me first but then more came in. That was it. I was dead...but Paco attacked them instead of me. I ran...he found me then just followed me everywhere.'

'Seriously?'

'Then we just stayed together.'

'He can fight then?'

'God yes, never seen anything like it. Maybe you have but I haven't...he never gets tired, he doesn't feel pain and his strength is just...I can't explain it but...he can pick big men up and throw them like nothing but then he's so gentle with me. Like the way he touches me? So gentle...like he's afraid of hurting me. He snaps bones like they're twigs but when he looks at me it's like...I can't explain it...he's changed so much and he carried me one day. I jumped on his back playing and...and he can play too. He laughs sometimes, not like we laugh but you can see when he finds some-thing funny. And he's naughty, like mischievous? Like that. Like he refuses to do things sometimes to make me do them for him…' The words rush out in one solid stream of explanation from days spent watching him but being unable to talk to anyone else about it. 'And he carried Amna and let them poke him in the face. I didn't see that happen and I'd told the children not to touch him but they did and he was as gentle with them as he was with me but when he saw you in the square he got so weird…that's when he first spoke… he said dog and girl…' She trails off as if suddenly aware of speaking too much. A silence settles, awkward and heavy.

'Sorry,' Heather mumbles, withdrawing instantly.

'Don't be,' Paula says, trying not to think of Clarence while easing Heather's towel down a bit to reach a bite on her ribs and tutting at the sheer number of them. 'Like bloody Howie…'

'What is?' Heather asks.

'All these bites. He gets bitten more than anyone else…I swear he just shoves his body in their mouths when they attack him.'

'Who is that other woman?'

'Which one? Marcy?'

'Yeah, she's so beautiful,' Heather says quietly, turning to look at Paula then blinking as though realising she just made eye contact with another human being and looking away quickly.

'She is. She adores Howie too. Never seen someone more in love…until now,' she adds with a glance at Paco. 'She was infected but turned back…'

'They said,' Heather says, realising she is having a conversation with someone else after just having a shower with someone else. The world is weird.

'She sort of kept her mind when she was…infected or turned or whatever it is. Like a super zombie or something. Could speak, think…she turned hundreds…maybe more…'

'She killed them?'

'I guess,' Paula says, working on the next bite. 'But she was infected. The infection did it…not her. She turned Reggie but he kept his mind too, although it was Marcy that controlled him…until it wore off or they healed...I don't know but yes, there's two people with a worse history than all the rest of us together and we love them as much as the others...so we can't be that bad.'

'How did...I mean...if Marcy did that...why didn't they kill her?'

'We're all linked,' Paula says, wondering how far she should go in telling Heather while knowing they need Heather and Paco to stay with them for a while. 'The infection has a hive mind...that's how it controls all the people it turns. Like a collective consciousness or something. We've got that.'

'What?' Heather asks sharply, turning to look at Paula.

'We've got a hive mind,' Paula says simply. 'Not all the time... we can't read each other's thoughts or anything like that but...when Howie gets in a certain way we sort of...connect? It's only happened a couple of times.'

'Shit,' Heather mutters.

'And they're scared of Howie.'

'Who are?'

'The zombie things...they're scared of him. We've all seen it... they still attack but you can see it happen sometimes.'

'Why?'

'We don't know. We don't know anything. We don't know what you are either or Paco...but we've got Reggie,' she adds with a smile. 'All done on your back. I'll leave it with you...'

'Paula? You in there?' Marcy calls from outside.

'Yep.'

'Got clothes for Heather...Clarence has given a top and trousers for Paco and we found some underwear here, hopefully it'll fit.'

'Okay if Marcy comes in?' Paula asks.

'Er yeah, yeah I guess so,' Heather says, looking back to see Marcy leaning through the door before coming in.

'Oh you look much better. Did you get the cream?'

Heather lifts it up, looking at Marcy now knowing what Paula told her. She's never seen someone so perfect in appearance. Like someone from a movie. Heather glances at Paco with a sudden stab of jealousy but his eyes remain fixed staring back at her, tracking her every move. She looks at Marcy quickly who smiles as though she didn't see that look just happen. There's no trace on the woman. No red eyes, nothing.

'Hopefully they'll fit,' Marcy says, holding up the clothes. 'Went for black stuff...that okay? It hides the dirt and black is always flattering...not that you need flattering,' she adds with the expertise of someone highly skilled in the art of making casual conversation. 'Need anything else? Oh, hair bands...' she says, pulling a few from her wrist. 'Er...well, shout if you need anything. We're downstairs,' she adds, placing a hand on Paula's arm.

'I'll come down, see you in a minute?' Paula asks, moving towards the door.

'Yeah, minute...'

CHAPTER SEVEN

A sea of corpses from the house to the vehicles now brought down the driveway. An assault rifle rests across the crook of his arms. His feet planted. His eyes watching. A cigarette between his fingers on his left hand.

'Marine,' Clarence says, nodding as he stops at Blowers side.

'Para,' Blowers says, nodding back. 'Do you say para or something else?'

'Airborne sky gods? Maroon machine? World's best regiment? Any of those will do.'

'What was that song?' Blowers asks, pretending to be thinking.

'Oh here it is,' Clarence says, chuckling in his deep voice.

'Can't remember how it goes now...oh I got it...para para in the sky living proof shit can fly...' Blowers says, taking a big step away with a grin.

Clarence rolls his eyes, pulls a face and plants his feet to rest his assault rifle across the crook of his arms. 'Marine marine in a boat...living proof shit can float...'

'Buttfucker,' Cookey says, strolling over to plant his feet and rest his assault rifle across the crook of his arms.

'He just called you a buttfucker,' Blowers whispers at Clarence, nodding at Cookey.

'I didn't,' Cookey says, lighting his cigarette. 'I called *you* a buttfucker...buttfucker...'

'Who is?' Blinky asks, planting her feet to rest her rifle across the crook of her elbows.

'Blowers,' Cookey says.

'Fact,' Blinky says.

'What is?' Nick asks, going through the same as he lights a smoke.

'Blowers is a buttfucker,' Cookey explains.

'Ah,' Nick says, exhaling his smoke. 'Fact.' He adds, staring hard at Maddox who walks over but doesn't plant his feet or rest his rifle across the crook of his elbows.

'So what's happening now?' Cookey asks after a few seconds of silence.

'No idea,' Nick says, looking at Clarence.

'Same,' the big man says, shrugging casually which is still a monumental movement of bones, muscles and sinew lifting to plummet back down.

'Can't believe she said spastic,' Nick says, chuckling at the thought.

'Fucking funny,' Cookey says.

'Can't believe you sprayed your coffee on Nick,' Blowers says.

'Can't believe it's not butter,' Cookey says.

'Can't believe you're so ugly,' Blowers says.

'Can't believe you put that penis in your pocket yesterday.'

'Can't believe you...' Blowers pauses, thinking hard. 'Nah I'm out.'

'Already?' Cookey asks, disappointed. 'Blinky?'

'Fist me.'

'Okay, Nick? You got one?'

'One what?'

'One I can't believe.'

'I can't believe you just asked me.'

'Ah, good one...I can't believe...'

'So is that Paco Maguire?' Blinky asks, cutting across Cookey.

'You serious?' Blowers asks.

'Yeah. Is it then?'

'Fuck me, Blinky.'

'I don't do cocks.'

'Yes, it's Paco Maguire.'

'Oh. He's famous.'

'Yeah?' Cookey asks.

'He's famous as fuck...'

Maddox hides the irritation at the mindless conversation and watches the front of the house closely.

Inside Roy's van, Reginald shakes his head as the conversation outside rolls forever and always gently on. It's comforting though, in a strange way. Knowing they are there. Knowing that nothing can get through them, even if all they talk about is bottoms, genitals and faeces.

New things have happened that impact on the never-ending thoughts in his mind. He opens his bag, finds his notepad and spreads it open on the desk to read over his last entry.

Minutes pass with his mind absorbed from the soothing background noise of the mindless banter outside. His pen scribbles. Notes and observations. Connections made. Strengths of arguments increasing as other weaken. Objective, subjective and conjecture. Fact, opinion and guesses. He frowns, pauses frequently then scribbles on with the pen scratching over the paper.

He stops writing, reads it back and clicks the pen. *Safety off.* He smiles again and even adds a little chuckle at his new joke that he really rather likes. The others have all got big heavy guns they can click and make noises with. He has a pen. It also clicks. He clicks it again, feeling the tool vibrate within his hand. He clicks it off then back on. His eyes narrow, his jaw sets. He clicks the pen on and nods manfully as though staring down the enemy that all quake in fear at his mighty penmanship before fleeing in all directions.

'Right, listen up,' Paula says outside. Clearly addressing everyone. 'Heather doesn't like people staring at her. So don't stare at her. But be subtle. Not too subtle. Be subtle but not too subtle. Just don't stare at her. But then don't all look away at the same time either because that will be really obvious...'

He stops playing with his pen and puts his notepad back in his bag before going to the back door to idly look out and round at the others. His gaze rests on Maddox for a few seconds.

'...so just be nice but normal, but not too normal or weirdly nice. Just don't stare...I mean, not all of you stare but don't start whistling at the same time or checking fingernails...'

Reginald looks round from his perch. Everyone else is here. Howie is here. An idea comes to mind. Will it work? Will they see any difference? Will Paco pick up on everyone else's reaction and do the same. He'll need to be isolated.

'One or two can stare, more like casually looking but not staring...right, Blowers, you look over with Nick...er...Clarence, you glance but then glance away as though looking at the trees...'

'Mr Howie?'

'Yes, Reggie?' Howie exclaims, glad of the distraction from Paula's increasingly detailed instructions

'Am I free to speak?'

'Er...yes?' Howie says carefully.

'About Paco and Heather. Can they hear me?'

'Not from this distance if you keep your voice down,' Howie says.

'How do we know Paco is not a Trojan Horse?'

'A do what now?' Howie asks.

'A Trojan Horse? A spy.'

'Oh...oh I see...I was thinking of condoms then for some reason.'

'Ah yeah,' Marcy says, clicking her fingers and nodding at Howie. 'So was I.'

'Yeah?' Howie asks. 'Makes me feel better.'

'I was too,' Paula says.

'And me,' Nick says. 'What you tutting at?' He asks Maddox.

'Nothing,' Maddox says, looking away.

'Blowers was thinking of condoms too,' Cookey says, 'on men's will...'

'Good lord,' Reginald says, huffing loudly. 'Paco may be a spy.'

'Oh...er...and that's a bad thing?' Howie asks as Nick glares at Maddox rolling his eyes with the frustration now evident in his expression.

'Yes! Yes it is a bad thing.'

'Roger that. Paco being a spy is a bad thing. Got it.'

'We must be sure he is not a Trojan...stop sniggering. We must be sure he is not a spy.'

'Righto, Paula?'

'What?'

'Find out if Paco is a spy.'

'How?'

'Ask Reggie.'

'Reggie?'

'Gosh you are all insufferable. Completely insufferable.'

'Sorry, Reggie,' Howie says.

'Sorry, Reggie,' Paula adds.

'Sorry, Reggie,' Blowers takes it up.

'Sorry, Reggie,' Cookey passes it along.

'Stop it!'

'Sorry, Reggie,' Nick says.

'I mean it. I really do mean it. Stop that...'

'Sorry, Reggie,' Blinky says.

'Good gosh! Someone stop them. Clarence?'

'Stop it,' Clarence rumbles.

'Thank you,' Reginald snaps.

'Welcome...sorry, Reggie.'

'You are all damned idiots!'

'They're only playing,' Marcy says, waving at her hand at him. 'So go on then brainache?'

'We may have a spy in our midst and you are making blasted jokes again.'

'Want me to say sorry again?' Howie asks.

'No I do not. I do not wish that. I wish you to bring on that hive mind thing when he comes out so...'

'Oh no,' Marcy groans. Everyone groans apart from Maddox who looks round with fresh interest.

'It's the only way,' Reginald says firmly.

'For fuck's sake,' Marcy sighs.

'Mr Howie, we have to know if Paco is within our hive mind.'

'Hive mind?' Maddox asks, looking at Howie.

'Tell you later...I'm lost, Reggie. How does that prove anything? He doesn't speak.'

'We shall be able to tell from his reaction,' Reginald says. 'I will go inside the hallway with Dave and Mohammed to monitor him. You commence the hive mind and I will gauge his reaction.'

'You sure?' Howie asks reluctantly. 'I can only do it by thinking bad things...'

'We will be attacked imminently. We need to know if...'

'Eh? We're being attacked?'

'Yes! That's the whole point of knowing now...'

'When? Which way? How...'

'Whatever they have left in this area of course.'

'Fucking hang on. We're going to be attacked here?'

'Yes, Mr Howie. Did I not just make that clear?'

'Maybe you could have opened with that?'

'Opened with what?'

'Being attacked. Right...so you want me to...I can't hear anything.'

'Oh well I am sure they have changed their mind and gone somewhere else then based on your astute sense of hearing.'

'Meredith isn't reacting.'

'Good Lord. They are going to attack. I would attack if I had resources here. They will attack. You will kill them then we can get on with our jobs...now, please wait until Paco and Heather are in... what now?'

'I didn't say anything,' Howie says.

'It looked like you were going to say something.'

'Nope.'

'Wait until they are in the hallway then commence the hive mind...'

'What if I can't?'

'You must. You did it last night.'

'Yeah but I'm all chilled out now. Had a coffee a few minutes ago and...'

'I am sure Marcy can do something to prompt you. Now, wait until we are in the hallway. We will pass a message when we are ready. Dave? Mohammed?'

'Yes, Reginald.'

'Did you hear all of that?'

'Yes, Reginald.'

'Good good. Good stuff. Now, you must wait, Mr Howie. Do not commence it until we are ready.'

'Fuck...do I have to?'

'Yes. Yes you must. We must know. Paco is a big man and very strong and anything he hears or sees will be known by the other player if he is a spy.'

'It does make sense,' Paula says.

'Does it?' Howie asks. 'None of this makes sense. Nothing makes sense anymore. We're outside a big old house somewhere near the fort surrounded by bodies waiting for a world famous actor and his shy girlfriend to come down so we can see if we're all fucking telepathically linked. Yeah that's so normal that is.'

'Stop ranting,' Marcy says.

'Keep ranting,' Paula adds quickly.

'Good point. Keep ranting,' Marcy says. 'Think bad things.'

'Not yet,' Paula says. 'Reggie isn't ready.'

'Think nice things,' Marcy says.

'Not too nice though,' Clarence adds helpfully.

'Think medium things...like in the middle,' Marcy says.

'What the fuck?' Howie says slowly. 'What the actual fuck?'

'You know, things in the middle...build up slowly...er...think of...think of...'

'Stepping in dog shit,' Cookey says.

'Good one,' Marcy says. 'How annoying is that? Stepping in dog shit?'

'Oh my god,' Howie states. 'This is fucked up.'

'What's up from dog shit?' Marcy asks.

'Ooh,' Paula says thinking hard.

'Getting dog shit on your fingers,' Nick says.

'Imagine,' Marcy says, staring at Howie, 'getting dog shit on your fingers.'

'And you burnt your dinner,' Cookey says.

'And your dinner is burning,' Marcy adds.

'And you ran out of milk and can't have a cuppa,' Paula says.

'Oh that's so annoying,' Marcy says. 'Yeah, imagine you've got dog shit on your hands and your dinner is burning and you ran out of milk...'

'It's the fucking apocalypse,' Howie mutters. 'There is no milk...'

'Late for work?' Clarence asks.

'Alarm didn't go off,' Nick says.

'Slept in,' Cookey says.

'Shit the bed,' Blinky says.

'Slept in, shit the bed and the alarm didn't go off and now you're late for work,' Marcy says.

'I don't have a job. It's the apocalypse.'

'And and...your girlfriend just dumped you,' Paula adds, nodding eagerly.

'I don't have a girlfriend.'

'Excuse me?'

'I meant...'

'You don't have a girlfriend?'

'No, I meant...'

'You don't have a girlfriend?'

'I meant...'

'Did you really just say that?'

'Fuck's sake...'

'What the hell am I then?'

'I meant before. I meant...'

'Oh we just have sex do we? Fuck buddies are we?'

'Awkward,' Cookey mutters.

'Is that it? Fuck buddies? Just a fling? Just a fling am I?'

'No...I meant before.'

'Before what? Paula said your girlfriend just dumped you and you said...*I don't have a girlfriend cos I'm Howie and I'm single and like to shag everyone...*'

'What?'

'You are not bloody single.'

'Okay! I am not single. I have a girlfriend...'

'You did, Pal. I'm dumping you. Be single and shag everyone.'

'What? Grow up...I said...'

'Grow up? Grow up?'

'Stop repeating everything I said...'

'*Now, Mr Howie...*'

'I can't,' Howie says, flinging his hands up. 'I'm more worried I upset you now. I never meant I don't have a girl...'

'Get angry...'

'I can't...I...'

'Go on...wind yourself up with something.'

'Argh I can't...I didn't mean I didn't have a girlfriend. I meant before, like before all this happened...'

'Yeah forget that. Get angry and do the...'

'Now, Mr Howie.'

'Fuck's sake...*Reggie, I can't...*'

'You must. Marcy...you must provoke him.'

'Er...sex is shit,' she blurts.

'Eh?' Howie says, the hurt and shock clear on his face.

'Oh no, honey. It's not. It's beautiful,' Marcy adds quickly.

'What the...'

'NOW...make Howie angry...'

'I can't,' Marcy says, flapping her hands at her sides.

Good lord, if you want something done properly...Reginald smiles at Heather and Paco standing at the bottom of the steps. His hand comes up, motioning for them to wait a minute. His fingers press the button to open the radio channel. He draws breath and he speaks. *'Howie, you failed that girl in the square.'*

'No,' Paula gasps to the intakes of breath going through the group.

'You failed her. She died because you were too slow...'

'Hey,' Howie says, stepping back with his hands moving towards his radio.

'She screamed for help...where were you?'

'Please...' Howie whispers.

'STOP IT,' Marcy shouts.

'Where were you, Howie? You were crying on the floor weeping while she was tortured. A little girl, Howie. You heard her. You cried while she was...'

'Stop,' Howie backs away, his face changing with each step.

'She cried for her mother. Where were you? Where were you, Howie?'

'No...Stop it...' Howie swallows, breathing harder, his heart thumping stronger in his chest. Paula turns towards the house. Blowers too. Charlie's mouth opens to tell Reginald to stop.

'She cried for her mother while you wept and you failed because the infection is stronger...'

In that instant the whole of them know a mistake has been made. Howie changes. He becomes. His eyes darken to blaze with energy. A split second of life that passes normally until the energy comes but it comes provoked by a woman who took life and made them suffer and for that Howie knows no mercy. He explodes out, moving faster than any man has a right to move. As one they run in. As one they go to stop him knowing he will tear Reginald limb from limb because the monster inside has been fully unleashed. Every one of them fills with incandescent rage that surges through guts and muscles that makes hearts thunder in chests and eyes grow wild with fury but towards Howie they go. A mistake made. A provocation too great. A monster let loose that will destroy everything if it is not stopped but not just one. Two monsters unleashed. Two that turn with utter violence to charge towards the house.

Reginald feels it and it's good. Very good. His dark eyes furtive, cunning and filling with the rage surging up. It's stronger than yesterday. Far stronger. He braces against the tide and focusses on Paco and Heather at the base of the stairs. Paco instantly tense, his hands balling into hard fists. Heather staggers back as though gut punched but comes back snarling with her eyes blazing.

It thunders inside Mo. An instant change of absolute pure hatred and blind pulsing anger that demands to be spent. A hand on his throat. His feet leave the floor. Dave in his face glaring deep into his eyes. Dave dragging Mo at his side towards the door. Dave seeing everything. Dave knowing everything. Mo sees it. With that rage inside. With that pulsing sickening surge he sees Dave as never before. He sees Dave standing beside Howie at the bitter end while everyone else lies dead. He sees Dave's coldness of life and thoughts and lack of love for anything apart from one man that will fix this.

'Swallow it,' Dave's voice passing through Mo. Dave's voice

demanding a thing be done. 'Swallow it. We are not them. We stand apart. Swallow it...'

Mo swallows it because Dave demands this be done. Anger does not aid them unless anger is needed. They are control. They are cold. They are dispassionate. They stand apart and not with the others. This is what Dave meant. Dave sees the control coming back in Mo and with the smallest of motions from one arm he rights Mo to walk at his side instead of being dragged. Mo lands on his feet and in that first step he gains control to view the world as Dave views it. At what is a threat and what is not. As every person as a piece on a board from a game to which they know all the moves. He will kill them all if that's what it takes. He will stand by Dave apart from the others because that is what they are and that is what Dave demands.

Howie will kill Reginald. Marcy will kill Reginald. Two monsters. Two demons that have to be stopped. The rest feel the both of them, as organic and as natural as before.

Paula screams out, running in. Blowers goes hard, screaming Howie's name. Nick, Cookey, Charlie, Blinky, Roy, Reginald...the whole of them running to stop the two reaching Reginald.

As Howie goes so does one other. One other that is faster than he. One other that has only instinct and purity of heart and knows pack does not fight pack unless for the dominance of leading and only the small man that trains the pup could challenge the pack leader.

That one other stops him. She launches from the ground to slam into his side to take him off his feet. She clamps her jaws on his shirt and yanks him side to side, tearing the material but with enough force to rag Howie across the ground. The man is fast. The man reacts to fight her but she is instinct. She is power and control of motion. She twitches to grip his trouser leg to spin him round as he rages to gain traction. She grips his boot, ragging hard with enough power to lift Howie from the ground.

Mo and Dave run in. Streaking like the wind over the fallen

bodies. Running without expression to view it all and see everything. They see Meredith take Howie down. They see Meredith grip his shirt then his trousers then his boot to keep Howie from reaching Reginald. They see the dog holding the line against a demon that was never expected to be released. They see Clarence diving forward to pin Howie. They see Paula slamming into Marcy's side to take the woman down. They see Cookey and Nick behind Blowers. They see Blinky run past them, faster and harder than they to dive in with Clarence to pin Howie. They see Charlie impact into Marcy as she flails against Paula. They see Roy diving after the lads. They see these things and negate each as a threat. Each is a piece on a board from a game to which they know the moves.

Mo sees this. He sees this all in the blink of an eye. He sees Maddox moving backwards with a look of absolute fear in his face. He feels every single one of the others apart from Maddox. He feels the essence of all of them apart from that man who is lifting a rifle in fear of a thing he is seeing that he cannot comprehend. He sees Maddox's right hand move towards the trigger of that rifle and veers off. *A threat is anything that poses risk to Mr Howie.* His right hand blurs. His upper body twists. His pistol gripped in his hand as Maddox runs away from a thing everyone else is running towards. *We negate that threat.* As Maddox lifts the rifle so Mo takes him from the side. Slamming him down and away with his pistol rammed in Maddox's face. Maddox goes down hard. The assault rifle yanked from his hands so hard it snaps the buckle fastening it to the weapon. Speed, impact and overwhelming shock see Maddox staring up into the cold eyes of Mo holding his pistol at Maddox's forehead with a hard kneecap pushing into his throat.

As Maddox is taken down so Dave turns in a circle with his pistols held out either side. Mo draws his other to aim up the driveway then round to the house as he detects Dave aiming at Heather and Paco running from the house.

'SAFE DAVE SAFE DAVE,' he shouts, digging his knee in harder to choke Maddox.

Dave eases the pressure already applied to the triggers but holds the aim true and straight.

'ENOUGH,' Paula screams out again. Her heart thundering as Marcy fights to get on her feet. 'ENOUGH...Marcy, Marcy you have to stop him...Marcy...Marcy listen to me!'

'Can't hold him,' Clarence roars, staggered at the strength of the man winning against the weight of him, Roy, Blowers, Nick, Cookey, Roy and Blinky. Still Howie fights. Still he rises for nothing will hold him back. Nothing will stop him. He is death. He is power that rises to fight back against the darkness.

'Marcy please,' Paula begs through the rage still inside her. Tears coursing down her face. 'Marcy...stop him...please...Marcy...'

'PAULA...' Clarence bellows. 'DO SOMETHING...'

'Get her over there,' Paula grunts the words out to Charlie. The pair of them fighting Marcy to drag her screaming towards Howie. Marcy fights back. Her mind gone. Her senses vanished.

'Help us...' Paula flails from a hand striking her face. Her eyes find Heather. 'Help us damn you...'

Heather goes in. She goes fast with Paco at her side. Dave and Mo move back, pistols still drawn to assess every moving creature within sight.

'Hold her,' a female voice followed by a sensation of utter strength from two hands that grip Marcy to lift her up off the floor. Paco holds her with ease. His red eyes staring into her soul. His arms stretched in front. Marcy held tight, unable to move.

'Listen to me...' Paula grabs her face, forcing her to look. 'Howie will kill him...stop him...you have to stop him...'

The fight drains. The fury sinks to the realisation of what has been caused. Marcy nods, small and scared at first but firmer and deeper as her sense comes back.

'Let her go,' Paula says.

'Let go, Paco.'

Paco lets go. Marcy drops inches to the floor to be held by Charlie, Paula and Heather. She turns to go before balance is gained and trips to stumble across the ground to the pile of bodies holding him down. She goes to his head and drops flat to place her hands on his face. He headbutts up, slamming into her mouth. She shakes it off, spits blood and goes back down as the mound lifts from the strength in him.

'I'LL FUCKING KILL YOU...'

'Stop,' a simple word spoken simply. Her hands in his hair. Her voice in his ear. 'Howie...stop...'

He cannot stop. He will not stop. He will kill and kill until there is nothing left alive.

'Howie...stop now...you have to stop. I love you. I love you. Stop now. I love you...'

He will not stop. He will never stop. Reginald watches on. His body trembling from the surge of emotions but still his mind takes it in and works furiously to understand what he is seeing.

'Stop. Howie, stop...Reggie didn't mean it...he needed to make you angry. Stop, Howie...'

Her voice in his ear.

Stop now. Howie, you have to stop now.

Her voice in his head.

Soothing.

The darkness recedes. A tide pulling back but one that will remain watchful and ready to come again.

He feels the others there. He feels the essence of them and in turn they feel that acceptance flow into him. The hive mind as they knew it descends. Meredith urging him to stop. *Pack don't fight pack. Pack don't fight pack.* Clarence's strength. Blowers' pure loyalty. Cookey's love. Nick's integrity. Charlie's intelligence and passion. Blinky's bravey. Roy's terrified spirit that summons the strength to keep going. Paula's leadership. Marcy's love. Lilly's immense brutality to protect those she loves. Dave and Mo with them but not part of them. Two more. Two more that are new.

Heather who watches on, feeling them as they feel her. Paco. They feel him too. His absolute devotion to Heather and hers to him. They are as one but within the whole. They sense Paco as a soul repairing. They feel the frustration of his own limits.

Howie opens his eyes to feel Marcy's tears streaming down to land on his cheeks. Her face flushed red. Sweat on her skin.He rises as they draw back to twist and take her into his arms. She falls into him. None of them could know what would happen. Paula places her hand on Marcy. Clarence reaches forward, drawing the two of them in.

Paula sinks down. Her arms wrapping round them. Her forehead rests on the back of Marcy's head. Feeling the closeness of Clarence. Feeling the closeness of them all.

'Clear,' Dave says, holstering his pistols. He looks over to Mo still holding Maddox down. Eye contact held between the student and the teacher. Mo holsters one pistol but keeps the other pressing into Maddox's forehead. Another dig from his kneecap. Maddox coughs, trying to draw air. Mo holsters the other pistol. His face dispassionate. His eyes cold but there is pain inside. Hurt too. He idolised Maddox. They all did. They worshipped him. The man could do no wrong. Now he looks down and sees only Jagger and being forced away from the others while Lani was left alone.

He looks back to see Dave still watching him. Mo Mo's life is at a junction with one foot on either path and now is the time to choose. Be like Dave and be cold, be dispassionate and see the moves of the game, or, be like he was. He looks down at Maddox and chooses Dave. He chooses that path knowing it means more hardship than he can ever imagine. He chooses to be hit and struck by Dave because of the honour and privilege of what he is being taught. The choice is made but one foot still hovers on the old path for a few more seconds. He smiles. The old Mo smiles and looks down.

'You's fucked up innit bruv,' he says, revelling in the taste of his old voice and knowing there is no greater insult to be given to someone like Maddox than what he is about to do. He slaps him. He slaps him once with an open hand across the cheek and rises to look down in glorious distaste while he sucks his teeth. 'For Jagger, you get me?'

He turns his back and takes the other path. Walking from Maddox to his team that hold one of their own while Dave watches Maddox. Watching for reprisal. Watching his students back.

CHAPTER EIGHT

L illy smiles. She can't help it. The man is funny, the way he speaks, the lilt of his voice and the twinkle in his eye. He sees her smile and frowns lightly. She's what, sixteen? Seventeen? Eighteen at a push but clearly not intimidated at all. He looks round at the others with her. An old woman with short grey hair looking distinctly unamused. A man with his shirtsleeves folded neatly over his elbows in a way that screams squaddie. Two women, one mixed race with dark frizzy hair and the other a redhead. A few more nearby but not many, a couple of old soldiers further down perhaps but not nearly as many as he has. Still, it doesn't seem to bother the young woman though.

'Ah now,' he says, smiling again. 'We'll be at that impasse again,' his accent thick but light, something nice about it, a sort of Irish twang that lilts like he's speaking a poem with everything he says.

'It appears so,' Lilly says politely, returning his smile with one eyebrow lifting slightly.

'You see now,' the man says, shifting in his seat, 'may I get out? Would that be okay now would it? It's a hot day so it is.'

'Of course,' Lilly says, stepping back from the front passenger door. 'But your people will remain in the vehicle.'

'A few moments won't hurt 'em so it won't,' the man says, opening the door of his extra-long wheel base white van.

Lilly flicks her gaze to the open sliding door and the dozen or so men inside and smiles that polite smile. They smile back. Eyes twinkling. Heads nodding.

'How are you now?'

'Hello, Miss.'

'She's a lovely smile.'

'How you do now?'

'Hello, Miss.'

She chuckles at the responses, shaking her head as the man comes out of the front to stretch his weary limbs with a big satisfying groan.

'Is that a Stengun?' Joan asks from the roadside behind Lilly.

'So it is now,' one of the men inside the van says, holding the distinctive weapon up with the long magazine shoved in the side.

'Where on earth did you get?'

'Stole it so I did...well now I say I stole it, my granddaddy stole it if I be honest with you.'

'I see,' Joan says.

Tattoos on every arm and nearly every neck. Sun-tanned leathery skin. Thick limbed, thick necked, strong and fit looking men. Soldiers but of a different kind and ones that hold allegiance only to their mothers. Rifles in hands. Pump action shotguns. Pistols. Lugers. Old things, new things. Well used cleaned things held by men who know how to hold them. Magazines in bags at their feet. Knives on belts. Bats, swords and clubs within reach.

'As I said,' Lilly says once the man finishes his stretching. 'Weapons are not permitted to be carried inside the fort and you will allow us to search you and your vehicle so we know exactly what is taken in.'

The man smiles again, showing that puzzled expression. 'You know who we are?'

'I do,' Lilly says.

'Are you sure now?' He asks, glancing to Joan then back to Lilly.

'I believe the correct term to be used is travellers but please do say if that is wrong.'

'No no, travellers is fine,' the man says, winking to the men in the back of his van.

'She's a lovely girl.'

'Lovely smile she has.'

'Aye she does,' the man says, turning back to Lilly. 'That's the fort?' he asks, pointing a thick arm across the sea.

'It is,' Lilly says, standing politely with her hands behind her back, leaving the rifle hanging from the chest strap across her front. 'Forgive me, I never asked your name. I'm Lilly. That is Joan, Pea, Sam and that man is Gary.'

'Soldier?' The man asks, looking at Gary.

'Was,' Gary says, his weapon held ready with the safety off while he wonders what the hell Lilly is thinking. They're Pikeys. Gypsies. They shouldn't be here. She should not be letting them in. Tension in his arms and his bearing. The man notices it and offers a smile that Gary does not return. They're outnumbered too. The men inside the van look relaxed but Gary can see the way they hold those weapons. If it goes bent he'll open up in the van and hope the others do the same.

'Is that an accent I hear there?' Kyle calls out, walking round the back of the van to look down in surprise. 'Ah now, what have we got here?' The craggy faced man smiles as he looks inside the van. 'Hello, son...what on God's green Earth is that thing?'

'Stengun, Father.'

'I know what it is. Where you getting that from now?'

'Granddady stole it so he did, Father.'

'You got all manner of hardware in here,' Kyle says, smiling his genial toothy smile.

Lilly doesn't show reaction to the Irish accent Kyle slipped into within a couple of words. She doesn't show reaction to the men inside the van calling him Father either but stands politely with her hands behind her back.

'You the man in charge are you now, Father?' The man from the front passenger seat asks.

'No, Lilly is in charge here now so she is,' Kyle replies, sharing a quick glance to Joan who lifts a warning eyebrow at him.

Gary watches closely. Unblinking but listening and hoping Kyle will see sense and get Lilly to send them away. Even that is a worry though. They've seen the fort now. They could come back and try and take over. That's the problem with Gypsies, they never fuck off completely.

'Kyle,' Kyle says, holding a hand out to the man.

'Peter,' the man says, shaking Kyle's hand. 'Nice to meet you, Father.'

'Not a priest,' Kyle says.

Peter pulls his head back slightly, 'are you sure, now?'

'Quite sure.'

'Ach, as you say,' Peter says. 'We're at an impasse so we are, Father...Kyle.'

'An impasse you say?' Kyle asks, stepping back to look at Lilly, his eyes flicking to the lack of grip on her rifle and the way she stands so politely with her hands held behind her back. Those same eyes take in Pea and Sam stood a few feet behind her and Joan and Gary both further down at Lilly's side.

'The young lady says no weapons in the fort,' Peter says. 'But I said, politely I did, I said we got the right to defend ourselves so we do...'

'That is correct,' Lilly says, fielding the comments. 'On both accounts. No weapons will be carried in the fort, and you do have the right to defend yourselves which you can do with your weapons outside the fort by going elsewhere.'

'But see now,' Peter says, still smiling, his tone relaxed and easy. 'We can help you so we can. We've got weapons and can provide the security.'

'We have weapons and security,' Lilly says.

'So I can see,' Peter says, smiling wider. 'But you'll forgive me for mentioning this now and not be taking it as a threat because a threat is not what it is, but you only have a few here.'

'Indeed,' Lilly says, smiling back at him.

Peter shakes his head with a comical overt show of confusion that makes Lilly chuckle. 'You'll be forgiving me asking another question now but what happens to our weapons?'

'Your weapons will be stored in the armoury. Which is a small room at the back of the fort that is *not* locked...' Peter overplays the double take, glancing to his men in the van all of whom lean forward to listen.

'You are free to come and go as you please. If you leave the fort for any reason you may take your weapons with you but of course you will place them back in the armoury should you go back in.'

'Place them back?' Peter asks, unsure of what he just heard.

'Indeed. You will place them in the armoury when you enter and take them when you leave. It is an honour based system.'

'Honour based you say,' Peter says, scratching his chin.

'We have doctors, medicines, food and clothing but we also have a great deal of work to do. We need strong people to work.'

'So now, let me get this right. We walk in with our weapons and place them into this armoury.'

'Yes.'

'And this armoury is not locked.'

'No.'

'And we can take them back if we want to leave...and you say we can leave when we want?'

'Apart from during the hours of darkness you are free to come and go as you see fit.'

Peter goes to reply but stops. His mouth forms words again but again he stops and scratches his chin again. He's missing something. He looks at the men in the van who stare back, shaking heads and shrugging. He looks at the young mesmerising young woman standing with her hands behind her back. She's not even holding her rifle but there is something in what she just said. A prickle of something. A weird sensation that settles in his gut.

'You know we're Gypsies right, love?' The tattooed man holding the Stengun in the van asks.

'I do,' Lilly says, looking at him so directly he can't help but smile and ease back in his seat with a glance to Peter.

'Gypsies,' Peter says to her. 'Pikeys...'

Lilly frowns. 'I dislike that word.'

Peter blinks. The world is a strange place so it is. He expected opposition but not like this. He expected men with guns to be standing guard refusing entry. Everyone distrusts his kind. He rallies and smiles, bringing back his masterful charm and warm wit. His brown eyes twinkle once again.

'Now, I have to ask,' Peter says.

'Of course you do,' Lilly says, her mind always five steps ahead.

'Ach now,' Peter grins ruefully. 'What say, hypothetically of course, that people decide to keep their weapons with them inside your fort?'

'Why would they?' Lilly asks.

Peter looks inside the van then back at Lilly. 'Why wouldn't they, love?'

'My name is Lilly. Not love.'

'I mean no offence there,' Peter says, smiling a charm offensive. 'You're young...'

'We have lots of children in the fort. We do not need people with guns walking around. If we are attacked then of course, we expect every person that can handle a firearm to assist...'

'But what if they are inside your fort and do not put their guns in your armoury?'

'Oh,' Lilly says. 'In that case I would kill them.'

'You'll do what now there my love?'

'Kill them. I would kill them. In the same way I killed the last people that did such a thing. It would not be tolerated. It would be resolved. Do I make myself clear?'

'You did now,' Peter says.

'But of course,' Lilly says. 'We are only a few and you outnumber us already. You have more weapons than we do...' she brings her hands round to the front knowing every pair of eyes are glued to her. 'But if I don't kill you others will. You have heard of Mr Howie? This is his fort. This the fort he returns to. He has only a dozen or so people that fight with him but those dozen kill without hesitation. As do I,' she says, opening her hands to show the grenade in each that hangs from the pins looped on her fingers.

'Holy fuck she's got grenades...'

'What the...'

'Look at her hands...'

'I will kill you now and sleep soundly tonight if it means my brother and the children in that fort are safe.'

'Shit,' Gary mutters, blinking at the sight of the grenades in her hands and realising that's why she's in charge.

'Jesus...'

'Father, the wee girl has grenades in her hands.'

'Gentlemen,' Lilly says, bringing the attention back to her. Rapt attention too. All of them staring open mouthed but she also knows that surprise will not last. 'As I have made clear. We have honour here...' she stops at the feeling inside. The same feeling she had before and the same as last night when Howie got angry. It's stronger now. Much stronger. She breathes in, her eyes hardening instantly.

'Lilly?' Kyle asks, turning to look down the road.

'Take over,' she snaps, striding away to gain privacy. The rage is incredible. A pulsating anger inside and she can feel them too. The others. Howie most of all.

'What's happening there, Father?' Peter asks, staring after Lilly.

'Is the girl okay, Father?' One of the men in the van asks.

'She had grenades in her wee hands, Father...'

'Lilly? What's wrong?' Pea asks, walking after the girl.

Lilly's heart thunders. Her breathing coming hard and fast. Her eyes set to stare in the distance. She could roll the grenades under that van and walk away without blinking such is the feeling inside. Her face twitches. Her knuckles turn white.

'Lilly?' Pea says again, stopping just behind her.

The rage subsides mere seconds after it came. A feeling of calm descends. A strange sensation that makes her exhale slowly. What it was she has no clue. What caused it is unknown only that it was Howie. She doesn't know where they are but only that something just happened that was a hundred times more powerful than the feeling last night.

As she stares so her eyes gain focus to see the heat haze shimmering over the road at the far end. The sea on the left, glittering and inviting. On the right the remains of the houses already flattened and the plant machines working away to bulldoze everything else. The tarmac stretches off to disappear in the distance beyond the high hedges. The heat is intense. The humidity is staggering. She goes to turn and head back to the van but stops and stares at the road. Someone there? Looks like someone running down the road towards them. That in itself causes no surprise. People are turning up all the time now and most of them tend to speed up once the fort is in sight, almost as though they have rush before it closes or gets full. Another one comes into view. Then another. Then more. Hundreds. Thick lines that suddenly fill the view at the far end of the road and even from this distance she can see the uniform motion of people running together.

She swaps the grenade from her right hand to her left and pulls the pistol from the holster on her hip while pushing the safety off all in one smooth movement. She aims out to sea and plucks the trigger to send the booming retort of the gun across the bay. An intake of air that she expends with one word as she turns to every man and woman now looking at her.

'INCOMING...'

CHAPTER NINE

'Oh my. Oh my oh my that was really rather unexpected.' Blowers sticks his head up from the bundle of bodies. Blinking hard and trying to shove Blinky's arse from his face.

'Gracious...yes indeed,' Reginald says excitedly.

'Blinky...Blinky...' Blowers says.

'What?' she says, her voice muffled.

'Arse...get it out my face.'

'Get Cookey's knob out of my eye then.'

'That's my knob.'

'Get Nick's knob out of my eye then.'

'Indeed. This is most interesting,' Reginald says, rocking forwards and back on his feet. He looks at Heather and grins. He looks at Paco and grins wider. 'Hive mind eh? Well, and that was a strong one wasn't it. Most strong. And from two I might add.'

'Blowers?' Cookey shouts from somewhere in the pile.

'What?' Blowers grunts, still trying to shove Blinky's arse from his face.

'Did you see it?'

'See what?'

'See what he asks,' Cookey says, popping his head free from

under one of Clarence's legs. 'Charlie, Marcy and Paula were sex wrestling...'

'We were doing no such thing,' Paula says, easing back from Marcy.

'Did anyone else see it?' Cookey asks, looking round. 'Oh you lame bastards...seriously it was like the best thing ever.'

'You think everything is the best thing ever,' Nick's muffled voice shouts.

'No but this was, like it actually was,' Cookey says. 'Er...can I get out now please, Clarence?'

'Why you asking me?'

'I'm under your leg.'

'Are you? What you doing down there?'

'Haha!' Reginald says. Still grinning at Heather and Paco. 'Most interesting. Indeed. Yes that was very strong wasn't it?'

'Right, everyone sod off,' Howie shouts. 'Someone's on my leg.'

'That's me,' Marcy says.

'My other leg.'

'Still me.'

'What the hell was that anyway?' Paula asks. 'Nick, you got any cigarettes, honey?'

'Er...bit stuck at the moment, Paula.'

'No idea,' Howie grunts, trying to work out if it really is Marcy on his legs. 'You're not moving...'

'I can't,' she says, 'Blinky's on my legs.'

'Blinky's arse is in my face,' Blowers says.

'I'm under Clarence's leg,' Cookey says. 'But I saw Charlie, Marcy and Paula sex wrestling so...so I don't really mind.'

'We were not sex wrestling,' Paula says, shoving a hand into the bodies. 'Nick? Where are you?'

'Here.'

'Where? Where are the cigarettes?'

'Pocket.'

'Which one?'

'We could get everyone off first,' Howie says.

'This pocket?'

'That's...whoa! That's not my pocket.'

'Oh shit...I am so sorry...that wasn't your...'

'No it's fine...'

'I'm telling Lilly Paula was sex wrestling then groping Nick's willy.'

'Cookey! Which pocket then?'

'Over a bit.'

'Seriously, can't we all just get up first?' Howie says.

'That's my pocket,' Clarence says.

'Fuck's sake,' Paula says, pulling her arm free. 'Right, everyone get up. Blinky, come on...' she grabs a leg to pull which elicits groans and yelps.

'Hive mind eh?' Reginald says, still holding that grin at Heather and Paco.

'Reggie, stop it,' Paula says, holding Blinky's leg. 'You'll scare them off...just give us a minute,' she adds with a polite smile to Heather. 'Blinky, pull your other bloody leg out.'

'Yes, Miss Paula.'

'I say,' Reginald says, peering at the bundle of bodies. 'You really should get up now.'

'We're bloody trying,' Howie says.

'Well do hurry up. The fort is most likely being attacked...'

That does it. A massed disintegrating of limbs pulling apart and bodies popping free that stand with wild hair and wild eyes.

'You said they'll attack here,' Howie says, sending Marcy flying a few feet to the side.

'Well they are not so I would surmise they are attacking the fort instead.'

'Load up...' Howie says. 'We'll discuss this later.'

'Too bloody right we will,' Paula says, running past Heather then stopping to smile awkwardly. 'Er...so we think the fort is being attacked...'

'That man just said that,' Heather says, pointing at Reginald.

'Reggie,' Paula says. 'So we...we need to go...er...jump in Roy's van.'

'What?' Heather asks.

'The blue van. Jump in...we'll figure everything out in a minute.'

'You expecting a big attack?' Howie shouts, running past Roy's van.

'Not excessively so,' Reginald says. 'Perhaps a few hundred...'

'Righto...Maddox? You coming?'

'Or you can stay here,' Cookey mutters.

'Seriously, jump in Roy's van. It's only Reggie in the back,' Paula says, dropping her voice a notch. 'And he doesn't stare... much...he doesn't stare much.'

'Er...' Heather says.

'Come on, we've got to go...' Paula says, grabbing Heather's hand then reaching for Paco but stopping at the last second. 'He won't kill me will he?'

'No!' Heather says, glaring at Paula for a second before glancing at Paco. 'No!'

'Paula!'

'I'll jump in with Roy...come on, the fort's being attacked.'

'How do you know that?' Heather asks, allowing herself to be dragged towards the blue van.

'Reggie said and he's never wrong with that sort of thing.'

'I am never wrong with any sort of thing...oh, are they coming in here?'

'They are, shift your arse and let Heather sit down.'

'I'm fine,' Heather says.

'Reggie, move your backside.'

'I said I'm fine,' Heather says.

'Fine,' Paula says, heading for the front as Roy clambers into the driver's seat. 'Right...bloody hell that was something else that was...'

'Wasn't it,' Roy says, starting the engine.

'Roy, you got Charlie with you?'

'Howie, it's Paula...she not with you?'

'I'm in the trailer with Jess, Mr Howie.'

'...er...why?'

'For rapid exit. I just need someone to open the door when we arrive.'

'Are you on the horse now?'

'Yes, Mr Howie.'

'How the fuck...you're sitting on Jess in the back of the horsebox trailer thing?'

'Yes, Mr Howie. Just need the door opening when we get there.'

'Now that is dedication,' Paula says into the radio.

'Bloody is,' Clarence replies, his deep voice booming through the speaker in the back of Roy's van.

'Wish I was Jess...'

'You got Heather and Paco with you?' Howie asks.

'Yep, with Reggie...they can hear you by the way.'

'Can they? Oh...er...so Heather and er...Paco...sorry about all that. We'll explain later. We're moving out...'

Heather stares at the speaker then to the front to see Paula shaking her hair out before pulling it back into a ponytail. She looks round to Reginald pulling a notepad from his bag then to Paco watching her intently. Every instinct is still to run and go away but it's like a huge wave pulling her along so fast she can't even think to try and swim for freedom. *Go with it.* That's the voice in her head. Not that she has much choice seeing as the van is now steaming behind the army truck with a horse trailer bouncing behind it. She edges closer to Paco, her hand finding his.

'You said a few hundred,' she says to Reginald, swallowing before speaking to get moisture in her dry mouth.

'Water on the floor, love,' Paula says, still fiddling with her hair. 'By your feet, help yourself.'

She looks at Paula then down at the case of water bottles

feeling jarred and too slow to react. Water. She's thirsty. She grabs two bottles, one for herself, one for Paco.

'Thirsty?' Paula asks.

'Yeah I am actually,' Roy says.

'Chuck two up please,' Paula asks.

Heather hands them over and gets two more. One for herself and one for Paco. Again she pauses, thinking fast with a feeling she needs to catch up with the speed everyone else is working at. 'Water?'

'Hmmm?' Reginald asks, glancing up from his notepad. 'Oh yes, yes please. It is rather hot again today.'

They drink water. In the back of an armoured van she drinks water with a woman on the back of a horse in a trailer behind them while driving to a fort that is being attacked.

'You said a few hundred,' she says again.

'I did,' Reginald says, lowering his bottle from the tiny sips he was taking. 'It's very hard to calculate the precise number as I have not had sufficient time to analyse the surrounding geographical area but yes, I would estimate the opposition to be anywhere from three hundred to a thousand.'

'A thousand?'

'That is the most I think the other player will field but yes.'

'A thousand?' Heather says again.

'More likely a few hundred,' Reginald says as though to give re-assurance.

'Don't worry,' Paula says, leaning round to look back at Heather. 'Seems a lot but...well, you'll see. Listen, on that point... Paco can fight?'

'He can but not against three hundred or a thousand...'

'It's fine. Honestly,' Paula says. 'You'll see what I mean. What about you? Can you fight? Marcy and I will probably stay here with Reginald unless it goes completely tits up then we'll go in... actually, having said that, it's probably best if you stay with us for the first one until you get an idea of how it works. Can you fire an assault rifle?'

'No...I...'

'It's okay. Honestly,' Paula says, exuding confidence from every pore of her body. 'Pistol?'

'No...I mean I can probably...'

'Okay, at the back with me and Marcy then. Blowers will run you through the basics when we get a chance....what about Paco?'

'What?'

'Will Paco stay back or...'

'No, if he sees them he'll attack...he always does.'

'Okay...*Howie, it's Paula. Heather will stay with me and Marcy at Roy's van. Heather said Paco attacks when he sees them so he'll most likely go in with you.*'

'*Roger, got it.*'

'*It's Roy. Want me in with you or overwatch?*'

'*Overwatch please mate. Everyone listen in, we secure Lilly first...Dave and Mo, go straight for Lilly. Nick...don't do a Cookey and run in blind. We go together, we stay together and we push to Lilly together. Clear?*'

'*Boss.*'

'*Sir.*'

'*Clear.*'

'*Understood.*'

'*Yes, Mr Howie.*'

'*I'll put overwatch on Lilly.*'

'They know what they're doing,' Paula tells Heather. 'You'll see...'

'WE HAVEN'T GOT A FUCKING clue what we're doing,' Howie says, shaking his head as he pushes his foot harder on the accelerator.

'Say that again.'

'We haven't got a fucking clue...'

Clarence looks over, his face deadpan for a second before the grin breaks. He shifts to look back at the others. 'She'll be fine, Nick. She's immune.'

'Yep,' Nick says tightly as Marcy reaches out to rest a hand on his shoulder.

'She's nails, mate,' Blowers says.

'Hard as,' Cookey adds.

'Probably won't be any left for us,' Blowers says.

Nick smiles but the worry is there in his eyes. He swallows and looks down to the back to Dave and Mo.

Dave stares back. His eyes unblinking. His whole bearing devoid of expression. 'I will not allow any harm to befall Lilly, Nicholas.'

Nick blinks and looks away sharply. A sudden lump in his throat. Cookey widens his eyes. Blowers coughs and swallows. Clarence looks at Howie. Marcy exhales slowly. A feeling amongst them. The air thick around them. Howie drives faster.

CHAPTER TEN

The word repeats, mutates and spreads fast. The drivers of the plant machines jump to run down the road. Men and women carrying stacks of goods drop their loads to flee for the beach. Every boat available aims for the shore with engines opened to gain what speed they can. The seeds of panic are sowed, watered and grow roots to drive minds wild as heads turn to see the solid dense wall of human forms running at them.

At the shore side, Doctors Anne Carlton and Andrew Stone try and hold nerve to complete the medical checks of the new arrivals but the panic grips. The threat of the infected coming towards them makes them flee with everyone else towards the boats.

Lilly doesn't feel panic. The icy determination settles as her cold blue eyes stare at the coming darkness. This is what it feels like then. This is what Nick faces every day. This is what Mr Howie leads them against.

'Wait there,' Peter says to his men before walking behind Kyle to fall in next to Lilly. Joan comes forward with Pea and Sam. Gary follows suit. The very few left holding weapons stand back, unsure if they should be running for the boats or waiting here.

Lilly turns to view behind them and the people still running for the shore. She looks out to the sea and the boats trying to get back while the others disgorge the goods they loaded to take on people.

'You've not enough boats there,' Peter says quietly.

'Some will have to do two trips,' Lilly replies. 'We'll fight from here,' she adds, looking to her group. 'We need to buy time for the boats to get back.'

'There's a few hundred coming down that road there,' Peter says.

'I can see that,' Lilly says. 'We'll need more magazines,' she adds to Joan before turning to the older men stood further back. 'Go down and cover the beach...go back with the last boat and make sure the gates are secured.'

'You staying here?' one of them asks, his voice breaking with fear.

'Now, please,' Lilly says coldly, turning back to face down the road. The grenades go into her pockets. She draws the spare magazines that are placed on the road at her feet. Every movement is calm. Her hands steady. Her eyes flick up gauging distance to the thick mass coming towards them. This is what Nick has to see every day. This is what the others do. She is one of them. She will hold the line.

'Nuts,' Gary mutters, taking a knee next to Lilly to place his magazines on the ground.

'Is a bit,' Lilly says. 'Go back to the fort if you want.'

'Yeah right' he says, yanking the bolt back on his rifle.

'Sam, Pea? You two go back with the others.'

'Okay,' Sam says, dropping to take a knee.

'We'll do that,' Pea says, doing the same on the other side.

'Single shot at first, aim well,' Joan says, walking in front of them handing out full magazines from a thick black duffel bag.

'Thank you,' Lilly says, taking the spares.

'Thank you,' Gary says, taking the spares.

'Thank you,' Sam says, taking the spares.

'Thank you,' Pea says, taking the spares.

Kyle looks at Peter. Peter looks at the coming darkness then down to the five holding the line. Just five. One old woman. One ex-squaddie that should know better and two other women clearly terrified. All of them forming up on an ice-cold young woman staring death in the face without a flicker of fear. That spirit extends with an aura that reaches back to send a pulse of energy into the hard man. He turns and nods once to twelve strong men that stride from the van to take the line. Tattoos on arms and necks. Leathery skin and twinkling eyes that smile down to the old woman, the ex-squaddie, the two women and the ice-cold girl holding them all in place. They take knees. Weapons held. All manner of weapons.

'You'll not be kneeling there now, Miss,' Peter says quietly, resting a hand on Lilly's shoulder. She rises smoothly to step back as he takes her place, handed an assault rifle by one of his men.

Peter looks left and right up and down the line. 'Ladies, maybe you'll be going back to your fort.'

'And maybe we shall stay right here,' Joan says, arching an eyebrow.

'Soldier boy,' Peter says, lifting his rifle into his shoulder. 'You'll be marking the distance now.'

'Roger that...' Gary says, rolling his eyes. They get closer. So many of them and sickening in the way they run so perfectly together. The sound reaches them. The crunch of feet hitting the road together. Like a drumbeat that grows. They spread out wider across the road but maintain perfect form. Hearts beat harder. Hands tremble. Nerves fray. Voices in heads tell them to go, to run and never look back.

'HOLD,' Gary shouts, sensing the fear rippling down the line. He holds ano.her few seconds. 'TAKE AIM...' weapons lift. Some shake from the hands holding them. A ripple of motion from the line extending across the road. Less than twenty against hundreds. 'Ready, Lilly.'

'FIRE,' Lilly shouts.

That small line fires. A booming crescendo of noise that makes every person on the shore spin round to stare in abject terror.

Infected drop. They drop to get trampled and lost from view as that thick snake keeps charging towards them. The weapons fire. Assault rifles. Single shot bolt action rifles, shotguns, pistols and old army issued weapons stolen, pilfered and bought over the years. The sound is immense. The smell of cordite and shot hanging in the air. Ears ring. Shoulders recoil. Infected drop time and again. Lilly fires with them. Single shots but taken fast. Her finger plucking the trigger again and again. They kill many. They see it happen but it seems to make no difference. Every infected that drops is instantly replaced.

'KEEP GOING,' Kyle's voice booms, the power of him resonates as he stands taller, glowering with energy.

Magazines are changed. Bolts yanked back. They fire weapons as fast as they can. Joan gets headshots. Bursting skulls apart one after the other. Pea fires into the mass. Her senses deafened and gone. There is just here. There is just this moment now. Sam changes magazines, knocking the old one out to ram the new one in. She glances at Pea then faces back to do what must be done.

The boats load on the beach to carry the people away to the fort. The drivers fight and argue to stop the people clamouring to get in for fear of capsizing. Shouts sound out. Angry scared people desperate to find safety while the guns fire and the infected charge.

They fire faster. Gary, Joan and some of the men give burst fire from weapons to fell as many as they can. Pea keeps single shots but goes as fast. Sam spits to the side to clear the shit from her mouth.

'FASTER NOW,' Kyle thunders. Pacing up and down behind them. 'FIRE QUICKLY...'

'We're trying, Father,' the man with the Stengun says, the vicious weapon booming louder than all the rest.

Too close now. Too many and no sign of their numbers reducing. 'We have to dress back,' Gary shouts, twisting to get Lilly's attention.

'DO IT...BACK...GO BACK,' Lilly shouts. The line rises, staggered and broken to slowly start easing back. Peter glances to the van then forward to the horde and that awful synchronised running. They still get kills and the ones they don't kill still fall to be trampled underfoot but that sight is worst of all. The merciless nature of the beasts coming at them. The sheer disregard for their fallen kind. The hunger they project. They start screeching too. High pitched and primeval. A solid wall of noise that tightens the balls of fear in the guts of those few. Screams from the beach come back. People running into the sea to try and swim instead of waiting for the boats. Others sob and fall to knees to weep in terror.

'BACK...' Lilly changes magazine, ditching the used one to push the new one in. They fall back slowly towards the van. Peter glances again, his face a mask of aggression as he gauges distance.

'GO BACK NOW,' he shouts at Lilly then turns to Sam and Pea. 'GO BACK...TO THE BEACH WITH YOU...FOR THE LOVE OF GOD,' Peter thunders the words out. 'FATHER...GET THE WOMEN AWAY NOW...'

The horde breaks uniformity to charge screaming and wild. The pure hatred clear on the fetid twisted faces rushing towards them. The fastest sprint out from the horde. Arms pumping with poise and balance but with lips pulled back showing teeth. The least human yet and another step taken from the species from which they originate.

'Sam, Pea, Joan...to the beach....NOW!' Lilly sees how it will end. She can see the numbers coming at them and knows she will stand and fight and die here. The men around her burst for the van, ditching firearms, rifles and shotguns to grab clubs, bats, sticks, swords and bladed weapons.

Chaos on both sides of her. The beach is still too full. The first boats are on their way back. Heads in the sea as people try and swim away. The wild splashes as yet more run into the water. The heat of it. The sheer frenzied last few seconds before that impact comes. In that instance she knows truly what Nick faces and gives honour for knowing him and those he fights with. How so few hold against so many is beyond her. They can't do that here. They don't have Howie and in him she knows the power lies. On Howie they form. On Howie they fight.

Something else happens though. Something of a power that is staggering to behold. Kyle walking backwards dragging Sam and Pea with him to force them away. His eyes furious and Lilly sees what the others saw in the kitchen of the golf hotel. She sees that power resonating as the man seems to grow with fire blazing in his eyes. Time slows. Everything in pin sharp clarity. Every noise. Every sight. She can feel the heat bearing down. She can see the faces of the infected and that most terrible of hunger that drives them on. She can see the wild fear fuelled aggression in the faces of the twelve strong men led by Peter who choose to hold a line that means nothing to them except for the honour of a girl who would have stood alone. She sees all of that and more. She sees Nick's face. The tenderness in his eyes. The love he gave her that was so pure. She sees Paula smiling at her and feels the strength of Clarence when he hugged her like a father. Like her father should have done except he was weak and he failed. She will not fail. She will not allow it. As that snarl comes so she sees Kyle's face raging as he sweeps between Sam and Pea drawing the pistols from the holsters on their hips as he goes. Those pistols rise in hands that are used to holding such things and forward he goes. Striding with glory and righteous power.

'BACK YE HEATHENS…' The voice rolls. The voice booms above all else. The man grows and fires the left then the right. In that instant she tracks the line of the bullets to the heads blowing apart from the perfectly placed shots. **'GET BACK…**

STAY BACK…YE WILL NOT WIN…'** Every shot hits. Every shot counts. Lilly ditches her rifle to throw it aside. The thing is useless now. She draws the pistol to stand side on, aiming with a hand made steady by the ice running through her veins.

'See me,' she murmurs and fires. One more drops.

'HEATHENS…FOUL BEASTS THAT YE ARE…'

'See me…'

'GO BACK TO SATAN…GO BACK WITH YE TAILS BETWEEN YOUR CLOVEN FEET…'

'The Father's a gun toting badass so he is, Peter.'

'SEE ME…'

Lilly's arm holds rigid and each new aim is a twitch of ruthless calculation. Kyle's arms cycle back and forward. The pistols held almost tenderly as he fires and takes the recoil into his arms with a speed that is both stunning and effortless.

'BACK I TELL YE…' he fires the left, shooting the arm forward to pluck the trigger. **'BACK…AWAY FROM HERE…'** the right hand goes forward to fire then drops back as he goes on.

The words he shouts become a weapon as much as the pistols in his hands. Belief grows. That's what it is. It's the belief to stand and hold against something you know is evil. To spite the fear inside and do the right thing for the right reasons. To hold while everyone else runs away. To be steady and keep your nerve. She fires with Kyle. Sending every last bullet they can before the horde impact. The sound of their feet thunders towards her. A seething broiling mass of once human form but now of clawed hands and wild red eyes that drool strands of filthy tainted saliva. Animals. Worse than animals. Unclean beasts that do not belong.

The pressure of it. The pureness of that second. Her eyes steady and holding, knowing they see her unafraid. Without fear. She is one of Howie's. They know this. She sees the wilt and the sudden fear in their eyes at the sight of her and the words thundered by Kyle. She smiles cold and glorious without regret and without remorse for the lives of their kind she takes.

The horde closes in, pumped and charged despite the prickle of fear. The bullets run out. It's done. Over. Howie will come and sweep them aside and the big gates of the fort will lock to keep her brother safe but she will die here. As the impact comes so a thick tattooed arm loops round her waist to lift her from her feet. She goes back in Peter's arms as he twists to pass her on to the next who holds his arm around her waist to pass her back. She gets passed one to the other as the rest rush forward to brace the impact of the horde hitting. A rippling crash of meat against meat. Voices screaming loud. Men roaring as they swing weapons to cleave, hack and butcher. She fights to go back in. Screaming to be let go. Screaming as she sees Kyle with a blade in his hand gripping the hair of a woman as he slits her throat from behind. She's thrown away. Pushed far to stagger and trip but rallies to go back in. Seeing Gary swinging a machete into the neck of one while Peter swings a sword into the head of another. She draws her knife, goes low and runs hard to rise to fight to stab to kill and feel the hot blood of her enemy on her hands.

Outside the last house on the bay, she fights and leads those men who see a young woman with blue eyes slaying them with a speed that isn't right to see. Lilly's army forms. Lilly's army is formed there at that point.

Boudicca reborn. Joan of Arc rising to rally for there is no more a nobler cause for warriors to fight for than what she is now. On her they form. On her they fight. For her they will die. For what she is and what she means. All of them to the last is consumed by the pure emotion within them to hold and fight for her.

As strong as they are. As fierce as their sudden devotion is. They cannot hold against so many. It cannot be done. Hundreds pour down the road. Hundreds swarming into the fray. Hundreds that screech and don't feel pain or fatigue. They fell many. Those few kill more than they should but the pressure against them increases. The frenzied rage of those who attack beat them back towards the beach and the people still screaming in fear.

She slices deep, scoring the blade through the flesh to let the innards fall to snag the legs of the one coming at her. She dances back and feints left but goes right to drive the point into a throat of a woman that is hacked down by a tattooed man wielding a huge meat cleaver. Blood sprays, coating her arms and body. Teeth on her leg. She grunts and stamps down, booting the thing in the face. Back she goes with the line. Slashing left and right and knowing that each body taken down is an obstacle formed for the rest to clamber over. The road becomes slick. The stench of shit and blood fills their noses. Grunts sound all around her. Fighting is hard work. She glances back, seeing the shore still too full. Seeing the boats moving as fast as they can. Just a few more minutes. They'll come. She knows it. She can feel it. Gary goes down. Ripped from his feet to be raked deep by dirty jagged nails. One of Peter's men goes in after him. Fighting them back as more rush to drag Gary free but the soldier knows the damage is done. With the lust of the battle in his eyes he drops his weapon, pulls a grenade, bites the pin out and runs deep into the ranks of undead with a wild scream.

'DOWN,' Lilly screams. The men turn away as the muffled whump blows metres away. Blood and body parts fly overhead. A hole formed. A sensation of pressure easing. The men flood back in to hold the line as Lilly grabs the machete dropped by Gary to swing and kill.

'Go love...' Peter hisses next to her.

'They'll come,' she snarls, lowering for the next.

'There's too many, will you see sense now will you?'

'Fight. They'll come...'

CHAPTER ELEVEN

H e holds the wheel with both hands. The pressure is back. The pressure to be there now. The pressure to be moving faster. The Saxon feels alive beneath him. The engine as deep and throaty as ever as she gives what she can to gain speed down the road. Past hedges they fly. The sea on one side. Glittering and inviting. Silence inside save for the vibration of the chassis.

Through the last corner they go to gain the view ahead. Hundreds laying siege to a fight taking place next to the last house on the bay. Their house. The one Lilly saved for them. She's in there. She's in that fight now. They know it. They feel it.

'Fishtail?' Clarence asks, glaring at the back of the solid horde.

'Yeah?' Howie asks, gripping the wheel harder.

'Fishtail,' Clarence says.

'Fishtail,' Howie says, nodding once.

'Worked before,' Clarence says, turning to face the back. 'FISHTAIL…'

'Fishtail,' Blowers shouts. Legs shoot out to brace on seats opposite.

'Fishtail,' Cookey shouts down to Mo and Dave.

'Fishtail,' Dave says, pushing his legs out to brace.

Nick leans forward, wrapping his arms round the dog. Cookey loops one arm under Nick's shoulder. Blowers the other. Marcy leans forward to brace Nick and the dog as Blinky stretches to hold Marcy and Maddox, her hand grabbing his arm. He stares round seeing everyone else bracing as though they're about to crash. He grabs Blinky's arm. His feet going out to push against the seat opposite.

'Ready,' Clarence says.

'Give 'em some warning...'

'Roger that,' Clarence says, taking up the microphone for the loudspeaker. He thumbs the switch and inhales. **'COMING IN HARD...MOVE BACK MOVE BACK...COMING IN HARD...'**

'Fishtail,' Howie says, straightening his arms to lock his body in place.

'Fishtail,' Clarence says, pushing his hands against the front.

'FISHTAIL,' Howie shouts, steaming towards the horde.

'Fucking fishtail,' Cookey mutters.

'NOW,' Howie says. The Saxon hits the horde. The solid metal front slamming the bodies aside and under the wheels. The horde reacts faster than ever before. Turning to fling into the arches above the tyres. Howie slams the wheel over, his foot hitting the brake to bring the big rear end out sliding sideways into the human wall. Outside they pop apart. Explosions of bodies bursting from the immense impact. Huge bangs from hard bone versus solid metal. Inside they feel the vibrations and hear the dinks and donks of the bodies popping but feel the sensation of the big vehicle spinning to slew wildly. Maddox slides off his seat. Blinky grabs him, Nick holds the dog. Everyone else holds Nick. Mo and Dave braced at the back with their hands on the door handles waiting for the motion to stop.

'FISHTAILING,' Howie shouts, seeing the world outside spinning round.

'Fishtailing,' Clarence mutters, his eyes squeezed shut until the vehicle stops moving.

'Fucking fishtailing,' Cookey mouths.

'They're fishtailing,' Roy says, pointing ahead through the windscreen of his van. 'We're not doing that.'

'Thank fuck,' Paula lets the breath go.

Roy slows his van knowing he can't anchor the brakes on for fear of the trailer sliding out. Charlie remains low on Jess, her head buried in the horses mane. She feels the vehicle slowing and her own heart rate increasing. She rotates her wrist to make sure the axe tether is on tight.

'Ready, girl?' she whispers and hears the sounds of the Saxon slamming into the bodies. 'They're fishtailing,' she tells Jess.

A dull metallic noise outside. Light floods in. The doors open. Jess pushes out to dance into the road as Charlie rises in the saddle to gain the view of the world around her.

'COME ON, JESS,' she screams, Jess rallies, surging to bunch and explode out with awesome power towards the horde.

The Saxon slides deep. The weight of the vehicle and the speed generated travelling her deep into the battle. Finally it stops. A second of silence as heads shake to feel where they are in time and space.

'NOW,' Howie roars. Doors open. Mo and Dave leap to drop and land easy to twist on the spot and run.

Roy is out of his door, twisting to grab the handle to pull himself up onto the roof. His bow in his hand. His bag thrown up ahead. On his feet. Bow righted. Arrow out, nocked, he lifts as he exhales and settles his gaze on the battle taking place. His eyes searching for blond hair amidst the carnage. Calm inside now. All thoughts of ill health vanish. All worries ease away. He is centred within the world. There. He finds her and looses the first that flies true and straight while the next is nocked.

Lilly smiled at the sound of Clarence's voice. She knew they'd come. She knew it in her heart. 'GO BACK,' she screamed. The men didn't need telling twice. They fell back and away but the infected went after them. Chasing to keep the pressure of the attack on.

The Saxon hit with a sickening crunch and never in her life did she ever think to see such a thing. A huge army vehicle coming in front first at a speed that made her think it would go right through to the other side. Then it turned to slide and the back end slammed through the horde as the vehicle went side into them. As one the infected turned to fight into it. She saw the change. The split second reaction of the horde switching to attack the new arrival.

In the second of silence after the Saxon stopped so the sound of hoof beats filled the air. Heavy and solid and with a woman screaming on the top of the great horse swinging an axe to ride into the lines.

That sparked the fight back on. The sensation of rage increased as the hundreds left screeched to fight and take what they can.

Lilly spins to take the one down coming at her but finds it taken by an arrow embedding into the back of its head, sending it flying past her. She looks up, seeing Roy on his van nodding as he fires the next. A split second later another one is taken down an inch from her body.

This is what Nick does. This is why Nick walks away each time. Because of this. Because of those doors opening to disgorge the lads screaming to join the fight. Howie diving from the driver's door deep into the undead as Clarence launches after him. She spots Marcy jumping from the back doors to run towards Roy's van firing her assault rifle into the infected as she goes. Another gun joins in. Paula firing from the back by the horse trailer as another big man comes running round to sprint towards the fight. She knows him. Everyone knows him. Paco Maguire.

The pulse hits. The surge of energy that flows from each to the other. It fuels Paco. Days of fighting have honed his skills. His strength is staggering. His speed immense. He has the good of the evil, he does not feel pain, he has no voice in his head telling him a thing is too heavy or too hard to do and so he goes in snarling to slam three down in one sickening crunch of human forms being compressed. His feet start working. Stamping to break heads and necks. He picks one up, an adult female and flings her one handed into three more. He grabs another. A big man that finds his head wrenched to the side before he's thrown through the air.

Howie rises to his feet in the midst. His axe gripped and already swinging as they wilt back from him. He cleaves deep, swinging fast to clear them away. As he turns to the left so Clarence runs past his right shoulder to barrel into them.

Mo and Dave do as their mission dictates. Side by side through the horde that fall sudden and quick from Achilles tendons and hamstrings cut by surgically sharp blades. Lilly blinks once, blinks twice and they are there. The pair of them turning as one with their backs to her to face anything that comes. They lower stances to flick blades up against their forearms as another arrow swooshes a foot away.

'Heaven be Jesus,' a thick accent mutters near her.

'**LILLY SAFE,**' Dave roars through the battle.

'YE'LL DIE NOW YE HEATHEN BASTARDS… THE LIGHT IS HERE…DO YE SEE IT?'

'Is that Kyle?' Mo asks as they both look towards the booming voice.

'It is,' Lilly says from behind them.

'JUST A COOK YEAH?' Howie shouts, grinning like a fiend as the ground around him runs thick with blood.

'BACK TO SATAN YE BASTARDS…'

'That Father's a maniac, Peter.'

The lads steam in. An arrow head formation with Blowers at the lead, forcing a path through the infected to Howie and Clarence. Meredith ahead of them ragging bodies aside and launching to rip throats out. So many things happening. So many things to see. With Mo and Dave in front and a dozen strong men at her sides she views the thing Nick has told her about. The way

Charlie and Jess ride through the lines slamming them aside only to stop and rear up as the horse spins round on her back legs. The size of the beast. The sheer aggression on what should be a gentle herding creature. Those front feet come down hard into soft bodies that burst open. Jess's rear end doing a smaller version of what the Saxon did and knocking them away like dominoes as she spins round in an ever widening circle and all the time with Charlie swinging the axe.

'LILLY IS SAFE...' Howie's voice, a flicker of reaction in every one of the team. 'FIGHT OUT...'

'Shit,' Lilly never swears. She loves it when Nick swears because it is a part of him and never done with malice but to swear now is the only response to give. Seeing them come from the Saxon was one thing. Seeing them launch the attack was something else but to see them turn and fight simply to kill is a wholly new level of brutality.

Nick! She sees him wield the double-headed axe with a strange wry smile on his face. The speed of him. The strength in his arms. The cleanness and purity of him glows amidst the darkness of the ugly beasts around them, she watches him with adoration and love showing through the icy composure. Something catches her eye. A body rising up high to be taken back down and even from this distance and with so many other sounds in her ears she hears the body hit the ground. A space forms. A circle of death around Clarence as he spins while gripping that same ruined body to wither the infected around him. A human battering ram. A corpse as a weapon. A heavy adult too. He goes faster. The genial loving man changes to a berserker that destroys with a crazed roar coming from his huge chest. He stamps and flings them aside to die. He rages and thumps and breaks anything near him. Another body lifts in the air. Her eyes flick to see Paco launching one away then turning to boot one in the guts that goes back knocking more over. He runs into them, grabbing one that is used to beat the others with then throws it away when it becomes too broken and soggy.

'You see that?' Cookey gasps.

'Huh?' Blowers asks, taking a head off.

'Paco.'

'Where?'

'Behind us.'

'Hang on,' Blowers lashes out hard, clearing space to turn. 'Fuck me...'

'We got two Clarence's now,' Cookey says, jumping back as one goes flying past him with an arrow stuck in her head. *Cheers, Roy.*'

'Welcome.'

'Cunt cunt...cunty cunt...you're a cunt and you can cunt off you cunt...'

'You swear more than I do,' Nick mutters from behind her.

'FUCK YOURSELF...cunt...oh you dirty cunt...give me my fucking axe back...FUCK IT,' she screams, trying to yank the blade from sternum in which it is currently embedded. She tugs harder. An arrow flits past her head taking one out. She tugs again. Another arrow flies under her chin. She stamps down to add leverage. Another arrow flies. 'CUNT IT...' she stamps and tugs, heaving the body about the ground while Roy kills everything around her. 'HA!' She staggers back with the axe now back in her hands. Roy tuts mildly, twitches his aim and looses the next.

'Running low on arrows,' Roy calls down.

'I'll add it to the list,' Paula calls up, her rifle still held into her shoulder.

'Who do you think those men are?' Marcy asks.

'Don't know, Marce,' Paula says.

'Did you just call me Marce?'

'Yep. Problem?'

'Nope. My friends used to call me Marce.'

'Yeah? So it's okay then? Paco's doing well, Heather.'

'Oh very,' Marcy says. 'Reminds me of Clarence.'

'Er...yeah, yeah I guess he does,' Paula says lightly in a tone that earns a quick glance from Marcy. 'What?'

'What?' Marcy asks.

'Why you looking at me like that?'

'No reason,' Marcy says, narrowing her eyes before looking away.

Reginald watches the monitor on the desk showing the high-definition camera feeds from the lenses fitted in the van's light clusters. He watches Paco, examining the way the man moves. He tries to spot all of them in turn but only catches glimpses here and there. Clarence is easy to see because of his size. He wants to watch Maddox but can't find him. He waits for a while longer, hoping the numbers reducing will give him a better view but the tuts of frustration come closer together. He just can't see it all from here. He would launch the drone but the speed of the fight tells him it will be mostly over before he can get the thing launched and operated.

There's nothing for it. He stands quickly, huffing with irritation as he opens the back door and tuts again at the connecting bar of the horse trailer that he has to navigate. The heat hits him first. That solid wall of humidity. The noise comes next. It was muffled in the van but now he can hear every awful squishy squashy sound of wet flesh being torn and bones snapping. He peers from the back end, leaning further and further out before taking that first step into the road. Still no good. He still can't see properly. He goes out wider, frowning and blinking and still bending forward.

'Damnation,' he mutters, huffs and walks across the road to gain a proper view. 'Where is Maddox?'

'FUCK!' Paula snaps, turning quickly to aim her rifle at him. 'Don't bloody do that...'

'Maddox? Where is he? He's not dead is he?'

'With Blowers in the middle,' Marcy says.

'I say, Roy. Can you see him from up there?'

'Yep,' Roy says, loosing a shot. 'Come up.'

'Up there? Gosh I think not. How ungainly. What is he doing?'

'Who?' Roy asks.

'Reggie, what are you doing?' Marcy asks.

'Maddox of course, what is he doing?'

'Fighting,' Roy says.

'Well yes I assumed he was fighting but how? Do you see a difference?'

'He's bloody lost it,' Marcy mutters.

'He never had it to start with,' Paula replies.

'Difference in what?' Roy asks, glancing down while he pulls another arrow from his bag.

'Oh yes of course you don't know. I mean...' Reginald says.

'Know what?' Roy asks, nocking the arrow as he lifts to aim.

'Never mind that for now. Is there a difference?'

'Difference in what, Reginald?' Roy asks.

'His er...ability I think is probably the right way of saying it. In comparison to everyone else I mean.'

'Ability?' Marcy asks.

'Fighting ability,' Reginald says. 'The way he fights. Is it different?'

'Oh...hang on...' Roy lowers his bow and peers at the battle, spotting Maddox slashing wildly left and right. 'Well he's using a knife instead of an axe...is that what you mean?'

'No. Gosh I really need to see for myself.'

'Go up with Roy and have a look,' Paula says.

Reginald balks at the very suggestion. The mere thought of clambering up the side of a vehicle is simply abhorrent. The indignity of it. The embarrassment. Gosh no. No indeed. He stiffens and pushes his hands behind his back.

'Want a boost?' Marcy asks.

'A boost? No I do not want a boost. I most certainly would not like to be boosted anywhere...'

'Was only asking, Reg.'

'Reginald! Or Reggie if you must.'

'Paula just called me Marce.'

'That is simply divine and I for one am most happy for you but my name is...'

'Friends abbreviate friends names, Reggie,' Marcy says with a sigh. 'Sign of endearment.'

'Good Lord, Marcy. Can we focus on the matter at hand? Roy, I really need to know if there is a visible difference between Maddox and the others. Is he slower? Faster? Of equal speed?'

'Er...slower,' Roy says.

'Noticeably so or marginally so?'

'Noticeably.'

'Gosh indeed. Yes indeed. I really do need to see. I do. Indeed I do. Tally forth then I say. What must be done shall be done. Yes, Heather would you oblige me?'

'Sorry what?'

'I said I'd give you a boost, Reggie,' Marcy says.

'I do not wish a boost,' Reginald says stiffly. 'And Heather has kindly volunteered to assist me.'

'Have I?'

'Up we go. I say, is the best route from the wheel to the bonnet then up the windscreen?'

'For you yes,' Roy says.

'You want to go up there?' Heather asks the strange little man in the glasses.

'Oh yes, I need to see. I really do,' Reginald says, waiting expectantly.

'Er...' Heather says, unsure of what he's waiting for.

'He's incompetent at anything that doesn't involve a pen, Heather,' Marcy says.

'Just tell him what to do, love,' Paula adds.

Heather blinks and blows air with a slight pause before forming a cradle with her hands and lowering down to stare at Reginald.

Reginald stares back, down at her hands then back up to her. 'And what do I do now exactly?' He asks politely.

'You put your foot in my hands and I lift you up.'

'All the way up there?' Reginald asks, looking up at Roy.

'No. To the bonnet then you go up the next bit.'

'Oh. Oh yes. Yes I see. How wonderful. You are very good at this, Heather I must say. Righto, so my foot goes in there does it? Which foot? Does it make a difference?'

'Er…any foot will do.'

'Ah yes, right so I shall use my right foot. Gosh your hands are very high, do you think you can lower them a bit, perhaps a bit more? Yes, just a bit more…and again?'

Heather drops and drops until her hands are inches from the floor so Reginald can step in with a smile.

'Up we go,' he says.

'You need to hold on….no not me…the van.'

'Oh I am dreadfully sorry,' Reginald says, pulling his hands from her head. 'On the van you say.'

'Yes, ready…' she surges up, expecting more weight. Reginald yelps, falling into the side of the van as Marcy snorts a laugh.

'Just push him up,' Paula says, slinging her rifle for a second to help shove Reginald onto the bonnet. 'Go on…pull yourself then…'

'I am trying I am,' Reginald yelps again, flailing his limbs in an effort to try and swim through the solid metal sides.

'Fuck's sake,' Marcy laughs again. 'Roy, keep an eye.'

'I am.'

Marcy grabs the handle as Roy did and pulls up to get a foot on the bonnet. A deft twist and a shift of weight and she steps over Reginald while still laughing. 'Come here you bloody idiot,' she grabs his shoulders, heaving him up while Paula and Heather push his feet.

'Gosh! Oh my…I'm falling off…'

'Just stand up,' Marcy says, still laughing.

'I cannot! I am falling.'

'Reggie…Reggie…you're on the bonnet…just stand up.'

'I'm falling. Hold onto me…'

'Get off my legs for fuck's sake...oh you...right, just stand up. There, now see?'

'Oh,' Reginald says, rolling onto his backside. 'Indeed. Yes. That worked. Well done, Heather.'

He stands carefully as though the van will suddenly throw him off like a bucking horse. Clinging to Marcy he turns to the battle and goes up on tiptoes but tuts and huffs again.

'Go on then,' Marcy says, nodding at the windscreen. 'Roy, grab his hand?'

'Yep, be quick then,' Roy says, reaching down.

'Gosh. Will it hurt?' Reginald asks, tentatively reaching for his hand.

'Will if you don't hurry up,' Marcy says.

'Ready?' Roy asks, not giving him time to reply but heaving the man up the windscreen while Marcy pushes his legs.

Reginald screams. He screams for the fear of it. Heads turns and look.

'Stand up,' Roy says, dragging him back further onto the roof.

Reginald stops screaming and finally opens his eyes to look down at the solid roof of the van. He stands slowly again. Still convinced the roof will cave in or the van will start rolling with him on it.

'Ah now...yes. Yes I can see now,' Reginald says, staring round at the battle for several long seconds. 'And where exactly am I looking?'

'There,' Roy says, pointing towards the middle.

'Indeed,' Reginald says, nodding while narrowing his eyes. 'Er no. Cannot see a thing there, Roy. We're looking for Maddox.'

'Yes. He is right there.'

'Yes. Where?'

'Right there.'

'Where?'

Roy grits his teeth, aims and fires an arrow that flies an inch from the back of Maddox's head to hit an infected further back. 'There...see him.'

'Oh yes, yes I have him now. Indeed.'

Reginald watches the young man and marks the position before seeking out the others. He finds Clarence first and works from the big man to the others before trying to spot Maddox again. 'Ah, afraid I lost him again, Roy.'

Roy fires again. Another arrow goes in inch past Maddox's head making the man look round with a confused glance.

'Ah yes, I have him now,' Reginald says, his hands once again behind his back. It really does give a commanding view from up here. He can see the whole fight taking place. There's Howie doing his thing right there. Very fast. Very fast indeed. Blowers and his team right there. Again very fast. Yes, very fluid. Organic almost. Now where was Maddox again? There he is. Oh yes. The difference is most noticeable. Maddox can fight and fight well but his speed is noticeably different to the rest. He spots Lilly at the far edge of the battle being protected by Dave and Mo. Something in that view sparks his interest. A large built male stands close to Lilly. Tanned and weathered, tough looking and covered in tattoos. A similarity to the other man nearby, then another and another. He counts them quickly, his eyes absorbing details that his brain breaks down to component parts in order to fully grasp the situation. He takes a step forward with sudden interest. Twelve men all of the same kind. All tanned. All weathered. All thick limbed and just ever so slightly different in a way that sets them apart. Some are fighting, some gather round Lilly and are clearly ready to do harm should the need arise. Those that fight are like Maddox. Tough and competent but they are not the same as Mr Howie and his group.

He stands and watches closely. The intense danger of climbing the van now forgotten as his mind whirls with a hundred or more strands of thoughts. He takes it all in. The hosts. The changes in them. Maddox. The men near Lilly. All of it. The whole of it. The game at hand. He nods to himself as the plan forms and the way ahead starts to show itself.

'Indeed,' he mutters. 'We shall be busy.'

As the fight ends so Paco prowls the battlefield, staring down at his kills as though wishing they would rise so he can kill them again. His eyes as red as the infected but the intelligence and spark of life within him sets him apart. A groan sounds out. An infected male lifts his head. His body broken and ruined but his mind still filled with the urge to bite. He's a big man too. Thick limbs and a solid torso that give weight to his form that is lifted with ease by a man that has no voice in his head telling him a thing cannot be done.

The rest freeze. Staring over at Paco holding a fully-grown adult above his head with the power of his arms alone. A second frozen in time. An image seared into minds the same as when Charlie walked down the ruined street on Jess. An image that marks another twist in the journey.

'I could do that,' Clarence's deep voice rumbles out.

Paco stiffens, his upper lip curling back. Meredith runs, cantering at first then powering on as Paco hefts and sends the body sailing through the air to land in the space directly in front of the dog who launches in with a viciously deep snarl. A bite. A rag. The head is torn from the body.

'Would have thrown him further,' Clarence mutters.

'Gosh I need to get down now...'

They all turn from Paco to Reginald dropping to his backside to stare down the windscreen with a look of abject fear. He goes to slide then stops. Goes again and stops. He whimpers, closes his eyes and turns to lie on his belly then slides down the screen with a yelp. He lands on the bonnet, rolling and flailing about until Marcy and Paula reach up to drag him over to the edge then lift him down to the ground.

'Is that little man alright there, Peter?' A thick accent mutters behind Lilly.

'Thank you,' Reginald says primly, pulling the wedgy out of his backside and plucking his collar back to where it should be. He sets off towards the sea of corpses, tutting and holding his hands away from his body as he gingerly threads a route through the corpses.

'Well done one and all,' Reginald calls out. 'Most satisfying. Indeed. Several hundred here. Yes. Well. Gosh, they are a mess aren't they? OH MY GOODNESS LOOK OUT...that one moved...someone get him...'

A blur. A shot. A head explodes.

'Well done, Dave,' Reginald exclaims, breathless with fright as though he just faced certain death once again. The bluster and pomp hide the eyes flicking to absorb and process. He takes in the men stood round Lilly. The blood on their bodies, the blood on their arms and hands, the blood smeared across their faces from where they wiped those hands across their heads. The same as Maddox. Blood on his hands. Blood everywhere that would have sprayed and landed in tiny droplets that would have gone unnoticed in the midst of the fight. Notions form. Objective. Subjective. Conjecture.

'Indeed. Yes so well done to all of you for your splendid achievements and so forth but shall we press on? We have much to do. Ah, young Lilly. I watched you from afar but yes, very well done there and gosh, they are some rogues surrounding you aren't they? Oh my, tattoos on tattoos. Are you Gypsies by any chance?'

'Reggie!' Paula whispers.

'One of yours is he now?' Peter asks quietly.

'That's Reginald,' Lilly says. 'He is an exceptionally intelligent man.'

'Gypsies?' Reginald asks again, wincing and tutting as he works to avoid treading on anything bleeding, broken or organic in nature.

'That we are,' Peter says warily.

'Indeed. I gathered as much. Related are you? My understanding of your community is that you all tend to be related. Is that true?'

'Reggie,' Paula whispers again, trying to stare daggers.

'There or thereabouts,' Peter says.

'Oh gosh they are a filthy bunch aren't they,' Reginald says, looking round with distaste at the bodies as he comes to a stop in a carefully selected central position in which everyone can see and hear him. He blusters with pomp, tutting and pushing his glasses up his nose before looking once more to the men with Lilly.

'I understand your reluctance to impart any information after witnessing such a thing. Truly I do. But I must say I did wonder on the reaction to sub-cultures such as yourselves. Isolated as it were from mainstream society and of course, your propensity for violence and repellent natures...'

'Stop it,' Marcy snaps, glaring at him.

'Now then,' Reginald says with a wide grin as he nods at the men, then round at the corpses, at Howie, at Clarence, tuts at Marcy then looks at Maddox for several seconds then back to the men standing with Lilly. 'Now I must ask. Did you lose any before we arrived?'

'The soldier boy went down so he did,' Peter says.

'Gary?' Howie asks.

'No I meant any of your kind?' Reginald asks.

'Reggie,' Marcy snaps again.

'Gary died?' Howie asks again.

'He did, Mr Howie,' Lilly says, knowing she should feel bad but the coldness is still there preventing any other emotion coming forth.

'The brave bastard ran into them so he did...had a grenade in his hands,' the man who formerly held the Stengun says. 'Blew 'em sky high...bodies flying everywhere...'

'Good lad,' Clarence says quietly. 'That's brave that is.'

'Is,' Blowers says, nodding firmly.

'Ah yes very sad,' Reginald says, trying to show a sad face for a split second before carrying on as he was before. 'Now, were any of the Gypsy men killed?'

'Oh my god...' Marcy groans. 'I am so sorry...'

'None lost,' Peter says, inclining his head at Marcy as his men all start smiling and nodding at her.

'Truly?' Reginald asks. 'Well that is interesting. Most interesting. You see I did wonder. I truly did. As I said, your kind tend to be isolated from society and, despite popular opinion that you are all dirty and diseased and have those wild weddings, the truth is actually the polar opposite. Indeed. I am given to understand that the travelling communities have absurdly high standards of hygiene. Brought about of course by residing within the confines of a small habitat and often denied water and cleaning materials by the local residents so yes, yes indeed. I believe you developed very high standards of hygiene with the least waste generated as possible. And of course you have remained remarkably undiluted, one might say inbred, but I believe that is the key here. Is that true?'

Peter doesn't answer but stares at Reginald as everyone else looks to Charlie.

'Er, I think what Reginald is saying is that the travelling community are very clean people,' Charlie says from atop Jess. '...and that, by nature of your enclosed community you live separated from everyone else which means the infection would not have spread to you as fast as it did everyone else.'

'Ah got that now,' Peter says as his men mutter and nod.

'She's a lovely girl so she is.'

'Lovely horse there.'

'The other one is a cracker so she is, Peter.'

'They're all crackers so they are.'

'What a smile she has and a wee cut down her face there.'

'Still a lovely girl though.'

'That one there is a feisty one now.'

'Get fucked,' Blinky says bluntly.

'Ah now, did you hear that? What a girl!'

'Patrick is single…Patrick where are you now?'

'I'm here, Michael. She's a lovely girl so she is.'

'I'm gay fucktards,' Blinky says, holding her middle finger up at them.

'Have you seen the dog? That's a big dog that is.'

'Indeed yes,' Reginald says benignly, nodding and smiling at the men. 'Well that is most interesting. Indeed it is. Yes,' he adds slowly. 'Well, we must be off. Nice to meet you hearty chaps.'

Howie blinks and looks at Clarence who shrugs. Paula shakes her head as Marcy groans and the others look on. Reginald smiles at the men, nods his head and turns to walk off before stopping and turning back. 'Oh just one more thing. When did you find out you were immune?'

CHAPTER TWELVE

So it turns out, after Reginald did his *Columbo* impression of *oh just one more thing*, that the gypsy men knew quite early on they were immune. Peter was bitten on the calf. He went home, got a shotgun, put the end in his mouth and waited. The other men also got their shotguns, machine guns, pistols, rifles, sub-machine guns and general assorted weaponry, aimed them at Peter, and waited. He didn't turn. A day or so later another man got bit. Again they took to their arms and waited and again he didn't turn. A woman was bitten. She didn't turn. One of their kids was bit and didn't turn. They waited it out for a while then decided, after hearing rumours, to head for the fort.

Now here is where it gets interesting. Maddox is also immune. Maddox Doku is on the list Neal had. The list of people believed to have immunity. We are not on that list. We started to ask questions but Reginald clammed up and said he wouldn't discuss it right now, then he said a bunch of other stuff with really big words. Charlie translated and said our presence would attract the other side. Which takes us back to the original problem. We have a fort but we can't sodding well use it. Now we are preparing to leave. Which means Paula is making lists and haranguing everyone and

I'm sure I heard the words *shopping* and *we need to go* somewhere amongst the shouts while I stand outside the front door and drink my bottle of Lucozade.

'Mr Howie,' Dave says from behind me in that way that makes me flinch, wince, jerk jump and spray Lucozade with the fright of having a small man with a flat voice say your name without any hint that he is there in the first place.

'Stop doing that,' I say with drink dribbling down my chin.

'Doing what?'

'That.'

'What?'

'Creeping up...you scared the shit out of me.'

'Okay, Mr Howie.'

'You alright then?'

'Yes, Mr Howie. Nicholas and Lilly are upstairs.'

'Right,' I say, resuming my Lucozade drinking.

'I think they are having sex.'

The drink leaves my mouth for the second time.

'I asked him if he needed my protection.'

'What?'

'For his safe sex.'

'What?'

'His safe sex. I read it. You should have protection for safe sex. I am trained at close protection...'

'Not that bloody close...'

'He said no.'

'I bet he did.'

'I told Mohammed to wait outside the door.'

'You did what? Is Mo still there?'

'No.'

'Eh? Why not?'

'Nicholas asked Mohammed not to wait outside the door.'

'Did you tell Mo in front of Nick and Lilly?'

'Yes.'

'Shit, Dave.'

'Their sex is not safe now.'

'It doesn't mean that, Dave. It means...hang on. What about when me and Marcy had sex?'

'You had safe sex.'

'How did we have safe sex?'

'I gave you protection.'

'You...seriously? How close were you? Actually, don't answer that. It means using a condom, Dave.'

'What does?'

'Safe sex means using a condom. The condom gives protection...'

He stares at me, his face as devoid of expression as ever.

'From diseases...' I add.

He stares at me, his face as devoid of expression as ever.

'And babies.'

He stares at me, his face as devoid of expression as ever.

'Dave? Er...forgive me asking but have you ever er...you know...'

'What, Mr Howie?'

'Done it.'

'Done what?'

'You know.'

'What?'

'It.'

'It?'

'Yeah. You know...have you ever done it?'

'Done what?'

'Fuck's sake. The subject we were talking about...'

'Yes.'

'Really?'

'Many times, Mr Howie. I am highly experienced.'

'Are you?'

'I am an instructor, Mr Howie. I am teaching Mohammed now.'

'Eh?'

'Every morning I give Mohammed a hard time in order to...'

'What?'

'He did have red cheeks this morning.'

'What the...'

'It does get rough but only ever for the principles of instruction and never to harm.'

'Oh my fucking god...'

'I pinned him down when he became angry but he needs to...'

'You can't do that!'

'He needs to learn, Mr Howie.'

'Fuck! Does he let you?'

'I think he enjoys it, Mr Howie.'

'But...but...' I shake my head and blink.

'Mohammed is good at it, Mr Howie.'

'Jesus Dave! You can't...I mean...you have sex with Mo?'

He looks at me like I just shit in his mouth.

'What the...but...oh my god you mean close protection?'

'Yes, Mr Howie.'

'Oh fuck. I am so sorry...fuck...thank fuck...I mean...'

'Howie, can you come in here please.'

'Miss Paula is calling you.'

'Er yeah I heard...fuck I can't believe we just...you thought and...fuck...'

I walk into chaos but the word chaos tends to suggest a lack of organisation and a wayward haphazard manner but this isn't. It's just big is all. It's a machine that is gathering pace to roll on and now it's going it won't stop, and at the centre, in all her glory of power and might is Paula with pen and notepad looking happier than ever before.

'Jess needs cleaning, feeding and watering. Meredith too. Weapons need cleaning. The Saxon definitely needs cleaning. We need cleaning...everything needs cleaning. Magazines need to be re-filled which means we need more crates of ammunition bringing over from the fort. Charlie? You need a new saddle.'

'Yes please.'

'Roy is desperate for more arrows.' She scribbles on the pad, frowning with focus.

We're all skirting round the issue of what Reginald *didn't* tell us. He said Maddox is on the list and immune. The traveller men are immune too but only a few are on the list but Peter explained that was because they actively avoided away being on any national databases.

None of us are on the list and most of us either donated blood, have been arrested, had operations or gave DNA samples in some form. Certainly, the lads in the military gave DNA samples and both Blinky and Charlie had to give specimens for anti-doping measures.

It doesn't need a rocket scientist to work out what *we are*. Not that we didn't suspect before. We've talked about it loads of times but always concluded that we didn't know what we were. I guess that lack of certainty meant there was always a chance we *could* be immune instead of infected. I think we were clinging to that hope despite the overwhelming facts staring us in the face. We heal fast. We don't feel pain like we should. We need very little sleep to keep going. Our energy levels are stupidly high. We have a hive mind. Marcy was a zombie and I had sex with her. Lani was a zombie, then not a zombie, then a zombie again and I had sex with her while she was a zombie, which is actually really gross when I think about it like that. Anyway, so, it kinda all adds up when you look back at it like that. We don't give it voice though. At least not here and not yet. We are too dignified.

'So do zombies sleep then?' Cookey asks, following Marcy down the hallway.

'I have no idea,' Marcy says, waving her hands at him.

'Did you sleep?'

'Er...yeah, I must have I guess...'

'What about weeing?'

'Cookey, I don't know...'

'What about periods?' He asks, following her into the kitchen.

'Howie!'

Arse. 'Yes, Paula?'

She comes out from the front room with her hands on her hips. 'Are those men staying here with Lilly and what about Maddox? Is he coming with us? Charlie needs a new saddle and Roy is desperate for more arrows...we're nearly out of underwear and... where are you going?'

'For a poo.'

'I don't wish to know that,' she shouts up the stairs behind me.

'You asked,' I stop and smile down.

'I'll follow you up,' she says, mounting the stairs.

'I'm going for a poo,' I tell her again.

'We'll talk through the door.'

'What? That's fucking gross...'

'Why? We're sharing aren't we?'

'Urgh that's fucked up...'

'I am joking,' she says with a huff, stopping halfway up the stairs to frown. 'I forgot what I was thinking now.'

'Have a think while I have a poo.'

'Men are so gross. Hurry up we're going shopping when we leave.'

'Supply run.'

'What is?' she asks, stopping as she starts back down the stairs.

'We're the living army. We don't do shopping. We do supply runs.'

'SHOPPING!' Marcy shouts from somewhere.

'SUPPLY RUN,' Clarence shouts from somewhere.

'What the fuck...' I back out of the bathroom wafting the air under my nose. 'Jesus...' it smells like a badger died in the pipes. A badger covered in shit that rolled in manure and ate garlic for dinner before smearing itself with peanut butter. 'Dirty badger,' I go in. There isn't much choice. Who builds such a nice house and only puts one toilet in it? Oh no, there is one downstairs but I can't go for a poo with so many other people so close. What if it smells? I'd be mortified. At least whoever made this smell has anonymity, which is within the accepted boundaries of toilet etiquette. Does smell like Blinky though, or Clarence. One of those two. Christ, how close are we all now? I can match the smell of the bathroom to the user.

It doesn't take long. It can't due to the fact I hold my breathe from start to finish and rush to wipe, wash my hands and get out before the badger gets me.

Feet on the stairs. The heavy tread of assault boots. I run away and hide in a bedroom. The leader of the living army too afraid to be connected to the smell of dead badgers coming from the bathroom.

'What the fuck,' Blowers backs out, no doubt wafting the air under his nose. I hear him draw breathe and charge in while I make my escape down the landing to the stairs.

'Toilet free?' Clarence asks, standing at the bottom.

'Blowers is in there, mate.'

It was Blinky then.

'So what about erections?'

'Cookey, I don't bloody know,' Marcy says, walking back through the hallway with Cookey behind her. 'I think you'll be fine.'

'With what?'

'With getting an erection.'

'Eh? My erections are fine.'

'Then why did you ask?'

Fuck me. Only here would catch that snippet of conversation between two people that hardly know each other yet feel absolutely no sense of shame in discussing such a thing.

Blowers comes down. Clarence goes up. Paula steps outside and tries lighting the end of her pen with a lighter.

'BLOWERS,' Clarence bellows, no doubt backing out the bathroom while wafting the air under his nose and trying to kick the dead badger back into the pipes.

'PROBABLY ME,' Blinky shouts from the kitchen. 'I HAD A BIG SHIT.'

'Coffee in here, Mr Howie.'

That'll do for me. I start in that direction to see Kyle surrounded by about a hundred mugs. Blowers follows me in. Blinky is already there stuffing a bread roll in her mouth.

'So I could have had sex with April then,' Cookey says, still following Marcy about as they come into the kitchen.

'Er,' she stops to think, 'yeah probably,' she says with a shrug.

'Not a cook,' I cough into my hand while looking at Kyle. 'Sorry, had something in my throat...might need someone holding two pistols to come and get it out...'

'Two pistols?' Cookey asks.

'Yeah, someone with two pistols that isn't a cook,' Blowers says.

'Who's that then?'

'You dumb twat.'

'Dave has two pistols...'

'Not Dave,' Blowers says.

'Mo? He's got two pistols.'

'Not Mo,' Blowers says.

'Fuck knows what you're on about then.'

'Kyle you bloody idiot.'

'What about him?'

'Fuck me backwards,' Blowers sighs. 'He was holding two pistols.'

'Was he? Where?'

'In his hands you...fuck's sake...seriously, Cookey?' Blowers gives up, shaking his head and looking away.

'Coffee,' Kyle says, pushing one of the hundred cups towards me.

'Ta. Back to being a cook then.'

'That I am.'

'Where did you learn to shoot?'

'Drink your coffee before it gets cold now.'

'Dave said firing two pistols is really difficult.'

'Did I?'

'Fuck it...how did you get behind me?'

'I walked, Mr Howie.'

'Is firing two pistols difficult?'

'Yes, Mr Howie.'

'Dave said firing two pistols is difficult.'

'Coffee, Dave?' Kyle asks, sliding a cup towards him.

'Howie? We really need to go shopping,' Paula shouts from the front room.

'Supply run,' me, Blowers, Cookey and Clarence all say the same time.

'Whatever,' she adds, walking into the kitchen. 'We need tops, trousers, socks, pants, knickers, bras...'

'Coffee, Paula?'

'Thanks.'

'Did he fire the pistols together at the same time or one after the other?'

'Dunno, Dave. I was with you in the Saxon.'

'Can zombies grow beards?' Cookey asks.

'What?' Marcy asks, turning to blink at him as Kyle hands her a cup of coffee.

'Can zombies grow beards?'

'How would I know that?' Marcy asks.

'Do your legs need shaving?'

'What right now?'

'No I mean generally...'

'Yes I'm still shaving my legs.'

'Cool. I can grow a beard then.'

'Firing two pistols is difficult unless the person is ambidextrous.'

'Wish I could grow a beard,' Blinky says.

'You'd look good with a beard,' Cookey says.

'Fact,' she says. 'I should be a man but I don't like cocks...I'll stay a woman.'

'Zombies can grow beards,' Cookey tells Blowers.

'Yeah?'

'And get erections.'

'You'd know,' Blowers says.

'I would...' Cookey says proudly then frowns quickly as Blowers starts grinning. 'No...I meant you would...you'd know.'

I chuckle at the expression on his face and glance over to see Heather and Paco stood outside the back door. I head over and spot Maddox and Reginald deep in conversation at the patio table. Reginald says something. Maddox shakes his head, leans back in his chair then abruptly stands up before marching over to me.

'I want answers,' he says firmly.

'I want a day off...or at least a...'

'He won't tell me anything,' Maddox snaps, coming to a stop in front of me. I lift an eyebrow and sip my coffee at the petulant tone that he realises he just used. He stiffens, stands straighter and visibly alters his manner by composing his features and bearing. 'I think, given the circumstances, that I am entitled to know what...'

'Nope,' I cut him off, knowing Heather is standing only a few feet away.

'Howie...'

'MR HOWIE,' Dave bellows from the kitchen.

Maddox hides the wince, draws breath and once again composes himself. 'Mr Howie, it is not...'

'Nope,' I cut him off again.

'Is this because of Lani?' he asks politely.

'Nope.'

'Is this because I locked you in that room with dog shit?'

'Nope.'

He shakes his head as though to invoke a greater reply from me.

I shrug and sip my coffee. 'You asked Reggie?'

'He did, Mr Howie,' Reginald says from the table.

'What did you tell him?' I ask, glancing over to Reggie.

'I said it would be a strategic and tactical mistake to impart any further information at this time.'

'What he said,' I say, motioning towards Reggie with my coffee mug.

'If I am immune then…'

'Not if, Maddox,' I say, cutting him off again.

'*If* I am immune then I have a right to know exactly what that means.'

'You have no rights,' I say mildly. 'This is greater than any of us, Maddox. It's bigger than all of us. If Reggie says he can't explain then that's the answer. None of have asked him and we won't until he is ready and you know why? Because whatever we know the infection will know if we turn and that is the tactical…'

'I understand that…'

'Then why ask, mate?'

He thinks to say something but stops himself. The battle in his face keeps replaying. His intelligence is clear, his bravery is staggering but unfortunately, his ego is bigger than both.

'What now?' he asks instead, which was the question I suspected he would ask. Now comes the really difficult bit.

'You are coming with us again,' I say to him.

He shows no reaction but looks at me for several long seconds and within that gaze I know he understands why. He is holding a grudge right now. I know that and he knows that. So there is no way I will leave him behind with Lilly. He also knows I don't trust him. He also knows *I* won't kill him in cold blood but that Dave will. So that leaves two options really. I can either exile him and make him leave, but again, he knows I won't do that in case the grudge grows and festers. So the only option left is for him to stay with us. He inclines his head and takes a deep breath.

'You know why,' I say quietly.

He doesn't reply but gives a tiny nod of his head.

'Go see Lenski. Do what you need to do but be back here in one hour.' He moves off towards the door. 'Maddox...you fought well today...'

I don't get to finish the sentence before he walks off through the kitchen that falls to an awkward silence. Everyone watches him as he heads down the hallway and out the front door.

'He coming with us again?' Clarence asks, looming in the doorway that connects to the dining room.

'Aye,' I say quietly and notice the looks between Blowers, Cookey and Mo. 'Do I need to explain?'

'No, Boss,' Blowers says quickly.

'Cookey?' I ask.

'Lilly?' Cookey asks, his voice low and thankfully serious for once.

I nod, 'yep, he stays with us. Go a bit easier on him. We'll be moving out in one hour.'

'We're not staying.'

'Huh?' I turn back to see Heather staring at me.

'I said we're not staying,' she says bluntly.

'Okay, can we talk about it?' I ask politely.

'No.'

'Right, er...'

'We went through the towns you destroyed,' she says.

'What towns?'

'Day before yesterday.'

'Oh right, yeah that was when Reggie realised we were being played.'

'Played?' she recoils in disgust and looks over at Reginald. 'This is a game to you.'

'No I meant...'

'The other player yeah? I saw those towns. I saw the people in them...I saw Subi, Rajesh and Amna in that shop...'

'Tesco? Yeah Dave did that before I arrived.'

'Why don't you stop and get the people out? Why don't you go from town to town and get people to come here? Why don't you put signs up? Posters? Why don't you look for survivors or give out weapons or tell them how to barricade and defend themselves? Why don't you open lines of communication and organise more people into fighting back? All you do is drive about and kill them... here and there...a few at a time...'

'Christ,' I mutter and drop my gaze down from the truthful sting in her words that suddenly makes everything she said so obvious. The kitchen falls quiet. Everyone listening intently. 'That's er...that's a good point...'

'How many did you kill in that square?'

'Few thousand...Reggie thinks it was about ten thousand.'

'We were in the buildings opposite,' she says, still staring hard at me with emotion trembling in her voice that makes Paco stiffen . 'You didn't stop. You didn't call out. You didn't shout for survivors to come now and go with you...we had to run after you through the countryside to find the fort...'

'I'm sorry...'

'A child died...'

'I'm so sorry.'

'No no no,' Marcy snaps, striding out through the door to stare at Heather. 'You have no idea what they've had to do...'

'They didn't stop...'

'Why didn't you call out? Why didn't other survivors call out? How is that our fault?'

'You should have stopped. You don't see what you leave behind...'

'No we don't,' Marcy fires back. 'They see what's in front of them...and I'll tell you this right now. If they hadn't have done what they had none of the people in that fort would be here now. They've killed tens of thousands…maybe hundreds of thousands… look what just happened outside.'

'No,' Heather says, taking her turn to stay simple and all the more blunt for it. She shakes her head and steps back as though disgusted at us. 'Put posters up. Put signs up. Tell people they can come here…'

'Have you done that?' Marcy asks so quickly it makes Heather flinch and stop mid-sentence. 'Have you? What have you done? You got six children here and that's fucking awesome but what else did you do?'

'Enough,' I say quietly.

'Pick up a gun, Heather,' Marcy says, clearly furious. 'Pick up a gun, go kill a few thousand then come back and criticise…'

'Can you go back inside please,' I say to Marcy.

'Marcy, come in,' Paula calls out.

'And those towns…' Marcy says, ignoring me and Paula, 'now don't have hundreds of infected in them…they have corpses which don't bite…'

Heather blinks and looks away. Her cheeks blushing but I can't tell if it's shame, anger or a mixture of both. I nod at Marcy to go inside and get a glare in response. *Please* I mouth. She tuts, gives me another glare and walks off to stand with her arms folded just inside the door.

'Paco can fight,' I say after a few seconds of uncomfortable silence. 'We need that…'

'He needs to recover,' she replies without looking at me.

'Heather…this only happened twenty days ago. Fuck me, I was working in that Tesco you were in. Marcy was a waitress. Paula was an accountant. Reginald was…I don't know what the fuck Reginald was but the point is…'

'I know. I get it,' she cuts across me again which makes Marcy bristle inside the door.

'You're one of us,' I say quietly. 'You have what we have.'

'I'm not one of you.'

'We met a scientist that was there when this virus thing was developed. He died but Reggie has his records. There is a list...a list of people with immunity. Maddox is on that list. We're not. I bet you're not either.'

'Heather is not on the list,' Reginald says from the patio table.

'There you go,' I say.

'What?' Heather asks, looking up sharply. 'I heard what you said to that man...Maddox? He's on the list. I'm not. Who cares? What difference does it make? We can't get infected...'

'Um,' I say, wincing.

'I think the issue here,' Reginald says quickly, rising from the table and casting me a warning look. 'Is that we are somehow connected and...'

'We're not staying.'

'Heather, may I speak?' Reginald asks.

'Don't bother. We're not staying here. Can I see the children?'

'Yeah sure,' I reply. 'Come and go as you want but listen, Paco is...'

'Paco needs to heal.'

'Yep, okay you said that but he just lifted a fat fucker above his head and last night he was throwing other fat fuckers through a hedge...we need that.'

'No.'

'Maybe he wants to stay...'

'What?' she flares at me, fury etched on her face. 'He doesn't know what he wants. I have to wipe his arse for him. He has no mind to know anything and you think it's okay to make him fight because he's strong?'

'Fuck's sake. I didn't mean it like that.'

'He will heal. He will get better and if...*if* he wants to fight then that's *his* choice.'

'That's fine,' Paula says, coming out from the door to stand next to me. 'That's totally fine. Whatever you want we will do.'

Heather nods, just once and in that movement I can see how hard it is for her to talk to people.

'Listen,' Paula says then tuts with a smile as Heather bristles at being told to listen. 'Hang on, don't fire off yet. Let Blowers show you how to use a rifle and pistol okay? We'll give you weapons and ammunition so...you know...that helps doesn't it? Blowers? You okay with that?'

'Yeah course,' he calls out from the kitchen.

'Okay,' Paula smiles at her then up at Paco.

'I've got another idea,' I say. 'Reggie? That list of people...'

Now Reggie takes his turn to look guarded and suspicious. He even pulls his notepads and papers towards him across the table as though worried I'll make a desperate lunge for them.

'Fuck's sake,' I groan. 'Pack it in right now. Heather, we're not deviant bastards doing er...doing devious things and Reggie stop hiding those pads.'

'I'm not,' he says while frantically shoving the books into his bag.

'Heather got six kids safely through utter chaos. The people on that list should be here. Heather, if we give you the list can you find them and get them here?'

'What?' Reginald says, aghast.

'What?' Heather says, aghast.

'Ooh,' Paula says in admiration, turning the corners of her mouth down while looking at me. 'Good idea that.'

'Was wasn't it.'

'No,' Reginald says.

'No,' Heather says.

'Why not?' I say to both of them.

'We cannot allow a list of that importance to simply be taken away and...' Reginald blusters.

'Copy it. Charlie and the others will help,' I say.

'But. Mr Howie. That list is of supreme importance.'

'Yes it is, mate. It is for the people on it too and Heather was right. We should be doing something except *we* can't do it cos we're busy killing 'em. So Heather and Paco can do it. Right?'

'But...' Reggie says.

'Heather's already proven she can move about with relative ease,' I look at her and see the cogs turning in her head. 'Do it quietly. Sneak about, find who you can and get them here. If they don't want to come then tell them what they are...and while you're at it you can tell others about the fort too. Actually, fuck it. Reggie, get that list copied...focus on the people closest to here. Heather, to be honest I ain't asking. You were right. We need to do more so step up and do it.'

'Could split the list and give some to Maddox,' Paula says quietly, dipping her head in towards my shoulder so her voice doesn't carry. 'He's more than capable.'

'He needs to stay with us,' I reply.

CHAPTER THIRTEEN

He walks down the road to the beach. His head high. His emotions masked. Nerves and tension in the air. The people still shaken and scared from the attack. Everyone looking towards the last house as the traveller men use the plant machinery to stack the bodies further down the shore. More men work to pile wood into the mound of corpses ready to set it alight.

Maddox walks on. His rifle held in one hand. A pistol on his hip. His bag on his back. He scans round noticing how people avert their eyes, dropping heads or simply looking away. A few stare with barely concealed dislike. A few more with open hatred.

People need someone to blame for what happened. He carries that blame and knows he has fault within the mess but he still stares back with defiance and an almost open challenge in his eyes. They look away, but then he is armed with an assault rifle and pistol and his clothes are stained from the battle.

Thoughts whirl in his mind. He is immune. He is on the list. He has natural immunity to the infection. Darius is dead. Sierra is dead. Zayden, Liam and so many more. Those left are acting the same as the others and distancing themselves from him. They've sniffed the wind and know they are being scrutinised and watched for every move. Now they work. Now they smile and wear clothes that aren't just black.

A conflicting sense of emotions run through him. Emotions that previously he wouldn't have allowed anywhere near the surface. He never allows feelings to overrule his intelligence. The Bossman taught him those valuable lessons. Now those emotions are coming up. Too many things have happened in too short a space of time.

Was it a mistake to leave the compound? Was it a mistake to come here? He casts that thought aside. Life is life. It's done and nothing will undo it. Besides, life at the compound would always have been finite.

He wants to get Lenski and leave. They could go somewhere else. Just the two of them. Howie was right in that Maddox's bravery is beyond question. Maddox knows he can fight. He knows he can keep them both safe. He also knows this world just became very small and there is no place he can go that Dave will not find him. How would he even get out? The idea sounds simple. Get Lenski and leave but that means using a boat which means people will see. The fort is an island now. Even if he took a boat and went the other way out to sea they will still come after him.

Maddox aims for a boat filling with people to be carried to the fort. The animated conversation ends as he steps in. The talk of the fight finishes. The discussions, the opinions and the men passing judgement on what they *would have done* simply stops as he takes position on the prow of the small vessel.

As the boat moves out he suppresses the urge to tell them he was in that fight. He was right there. He was part of it. He helped defend the fort. He doesn't say that. His pride refuses it. His ego denies it. Instead he stares ahead to the fort steadily coming closer. Small conversations start up again. He lifts an arm to wipe the sweat from his brow. The heat is incredible. He squints to stop the glare from the water hurting his eyes.

As the boat grinds gently on the beach so he jumps off and

pauses at hearing someone mutter *scum.* Everyone holds still. He looks back at the faces and smiles politely before turning to trudge across the beach and through the open gates as the armed guards both make a point of looking away.

He goes through and blinks at the sight that Howie and the others saw yesterday and that dent of his pride comes again. The interior looks so different now. It's chaotic but it's not filled with corpses or burnt debris or kids with guns. He walks on towards the police offices and imagines what it must have been like for Lilly. A surge of anger at Sierra, Skyla and the crews for doing what they did. Grief too. Mourning and loss. He feels ashamed at losing control. He feels ashamed that a sixteen year old girl is doing what he failed to achieve. Too many feelings. Too many things happening in too short a space of time.

'You back,' Lenski looks up at the door as he steps inside. The air still smells of cleaning materials. Pine and lemon. Chunks in the wall from the grenade detonations.

'We need to talk,' he says to Lenski while looking round at people he does not know. Men and women who have come forward to help stare at him silently. The atmosphere changes. The conversations that were underway as he entered the room end.

He walks back out the room. Unable to think of how to respond or what to say. The conflicting emotions render him mute.

'What wrong?' Lenski asks, stepping out from the offices.

'Not here,' he says, looking at her. She is impossible to read. Her features naturally mask whatever thoughts are in her mind.

'We go,' she goes to walk past him. He falls in at her side, glancing across and noticing she looks different. Colour in her cheeks. Her skin has taken the sun. He looks down with surprise at her legs and only then realises she is wearing cut off jean shorts and open toed sandals. A simple vest top completes her outfit but the change is noticeable and for the first time in his life he feels a prickle of worry and insecurity. She is a beautiful woman. She smells nice too. Is that from shampoo or perfume? He wants to ask but stays quiet.

She glances across when he looks forward. His clothes are blood stained. His boots are dirty. His skin shines from sweat. That utter supreme aura of confidence has slipped too. She also stays quiet. Neither of them are people who discuss things in public.

She shoulders the door open to an empty room and waits for him to pass inside before closing the door. A grime-encrusted window lets enough light in. She stays quiet, watching him closely. He stops in the middle of the small room and turns back to face her. An urge inside to cry that he suppresses and swallows with barely a flicker showing.

'What happen?' she asks, her tone as hard as ever. 'They attack yes? They die now? You kill them? You work with Howie now yes? They accept you? Did this work? How many come here? What Howie say to you?'

A barrage of questions. He blinks and tries to find focus to reply and explain.

'I'm going back out with them,' he says instead.

'What? Why do this? Howie ask you yes? He want you fight with them?'

'Yeah,' Maddox whispers.

'He see you good at the fight. He see this yes?'

'Yeah.'

'This good yes? Howie see you good man. He see you no do the bad things.'

Maddox nods and looks down at the floor. He knows it's pride preventing him being open but he cannot overcome the obstacle in his head and admit a weakness or that something is not working the way he wanted.

'When go?'

'One hour.'

She blanches and lifts her eyebrows. 'One hour? Why?'

'The er...'

'You bring them yes? Howie say this before. They attack if Howie here. Howie not here they no attack. This reason yes?'

'Yeah.'

'When come back?'

'I don't know, Lenski.'

She blanches again and stares hard at him. He never uses her name. He never says her name in conversation like that. 'What wrong?'

'S'nuffin...' he clears his throat, instantly ashamed at the street slang in his voice. 'I mean nothing...'

She frowns, narrows her eyes and cocks her head over. 'One hour yes?'

'Yeah,' he says, still looking at the ground.

'Take clothes off.'

'What?' he looks up quickly.

She nods at him and steps forward while pulling her top over her head. 'We sex yes? One hour...your clothes have the blood. I get clean clothes after. We sex now...' She wedges her top over the window, making an improvised curtain to prevent any idle eyes glancing in. Maddox looks at her. The rifle still in his hand. The bag still on his back. The sweat still shining on his face. She turns and smiles a warm grin that chases the iciness from her features. He tries to smile back but it's slow, weak, wan and full of pain, hurt and pride all at the same time.

She takes the rifle from him. He slides the bag off. She takes that too. He pulls his top off.

'You wash yes?'

'Yeah.'

'With anti-bac yes?'

'All over,' he says.

'This good,' she says, undoing the button on her jeans shorts that she tugs down. 'You fight them?'

'Yeah,' he says, working at his belt then remembering his boots are still done up. He drops down to work the laces.

'What like?' she asks, toeing her sandals off.

He shrugs, 'like fighting...hot...'

'You kill them? I mean you? *You* kill them?'

'Yeah.'

'The blood. It go on clothes...it go in mouth?'

He stands up from pulling his boots off and drops his trousers that fall quickly from the weight of the pistol. 'I'm immune.'

Lenski pulls her head back in a very slight show of surprise, 'like Howie yes?'

He shrugs and pulls his boxers down, still unable to summon the words to explain. 'Yeah...like Howie...'

They stand naked in front of each other in an empty room in the wall of the fort. Too many emotions. Too many feelings. Too many things happening in too short a space of time. At that second, he wants only to hold her. To feel someone close. He has to go back out with Howie and be with more people that hate him. Right now, he wants tenderness and compassion. He wants love and under-standing.

'We sex now,' she says.

He shrugs, 'yeah.'

They kiss. The kissing invokes the natural reactions within him but the floor is dirty and there is no bed or chair. Instead, she turns round and places her hands on the wall. The act between them becomes almost sterile. An act for the sake of it. Sex for no other reason than he is going away to fight so they *should* have sex. He doesn't want it. She's not that bothered. They do it anyway because neither can communicate the feelings inside to tell the other. Too many things have happened. Too many emotions and feelings. She breathes harder. He does too. She moves into him. He moves into her. Thoughts whirl in his mind that threaten to over-come any shred of lust and the folly of man once again shows. He becomes more afraid of wilting, of losing his erection and not finishing than he does about expressing the true worry in his mind. She senses it and turns to look over her shoulder. That look makes him more afraid so he tries harder. She frowns. He sees that frown and the sweat runs down his face.

He finishes quickly and for the most fleeting of seconds the endorphins take away everything else. He bends forward, draping over her back to kiss her warm skin. Barely a few seconds pass and she moves to ease the cramp in her legs. He stands back. She turns and smiles, her face flushed and sweaty. She kisses him. He takes the kiss. The post-coital chemicals fade and again he wants to hold her, to just hold her and be close. She pulls away and starts to dress.

'I need toilet now.'

'Yeah,' he says, bending to pick his boxers up.

'Is good yes?' she asks him, smiling.

'Good,' he says, smiling back.

She dresses quickly and moves to the door. 'I get new clothes for you.'

'Thanks.'

She pulls her top from the window, puts it on and moves to the door without another word spoken. In the space of a few minutes it feels as though he just lost her. They just had sex but it was cold and empty. It was the physical act and nothing more. She goes out and walks past the window. She doesn't look in and smile but walks on and never before has he felt so crushed and alone.

CHAPTER FOURTEEN

Everyone does something. Everyone sweats from the crushing heat and feels the bloom of headaches in the backs of skulls that signals the pressure building for another storm.

'...and it's really important to keep it clean, especially in this weather. The moisture in the air from the humidity and the dust and grime in the air can mess it up...' Blowers and Heather both turn to see the funeral pyre ignite with thick black smoke curling up into the sky.

Half an hour is all it took for the traveller men to get the bodies stacked with dry wood, douse the lot in petrol and set it on fire. More of them scrub the road with stiff brushes and detergent, or *soapy water* as they call it.

Nick washes the Saxon. Clarence cleans the GPMG. Blinky and Mo take the ammunition cases brought over from the fort to stack inside the vehicles. Howie loads rifle magazines in the rear garden. Cookey loads pistol magazines. Dave and Roy work to put new edges on their bladed weapons.

The rest work at the patio table, going through the list to pick out the people closest to the south coast to give Heather and Paco the best chance at finding them.

Reginald watches Lilly while holding the secrets of the world in his head. It was the way Pea, Sam and Joan made straight for her when they got back. It caught his attention. People do that with Howie. They have that thing that makes other people want to follow them no matter where they are going. They are both aloof and they both have easy smiles and polite tones but underneath the surface they also have a vicious power that subliminally or subconsciously transmits to those around them. It makes you want to be on their side as opposing them is a step into something you will not survive. Howie is dark and brooding. Lilly is cold, almost clinically so. Howie has dark hair and dark features. Lilly has blond hair and blue eyes. The difference in their physical appearance is stark but the similarities in their manners are striking. The way Howie looks up and follows the conversation. Passive and laid back. The way Lilly smiles at the conversations going on and smiles politely.

Reginald realises, at that very second, that if Howie falls it won't be Clarence, Paula or Blowers who take his position. It will be Lilly. That realisation brings forth a fresh worry. He is about to take the strongest pieces on his half of the board and leave the queen undefended.

Perhaps Mohammed should stay behind and be to Lilly what Dave is to Howie. Reginald deliberates for a fraction of a second then concedes that leaving Lilly at the fort is the right thing tactically. If Howie's group are killed then she will remain to continue the game against the other player so why risk both Generals?

It raises another question and set of problems. Reginald will guide *his* team in the direction he surmises is the right one, but *if* Howie's team does fail then Reginald will fail with them and Lilly will be left here not knowing what to do.

Reginald also accepts that Howie's idea for Heather and Paco to gather the immunes and bring them here is a good one. He had already considered it. His reaction, at the time, was simply because someone else suggested it before he did. Which irritated him a little.

The plan forms. The way ahead starts to show clear. Howie and his team will move out to be seen and play the game. Heather will find the immunes and bring them here but Lilly must also play her part. Reginald thinks. He thinks a hundred or more thoughts at the same time and takes each single concept and applies it to every other concept. Everything is linked now. Every strand is woven like a tapestry.

A decision made from an intellect that grows more confident by the hour. Howie is the leader but to do this, to win the game and play at this level means Reginald *has* to be able to make decisions without seeking consent from Howie. He sighs heavily and closes the notepad open in front of him as though to signal he has finished reading. He rises from his chair, taking his mug with him as he goes.

'I shall make a peppermint tea,' he informs everyone.

'Reggie's brewing up,' Cookey says brightly.

'Coffee please,' Paula says.

'Coffee for me,' Marcy adds, holding her mug out.

'Cheers, Reggie,' Howie says.

'Indeed,' Reginald says, pausing to look round with a comical expression. He breathes in and shows a build up to replying. 'No,' he says flatly and walks off. The others chuckle. Cookey nods with respect at the timing of the subtle joke.

'Kyle,' Reginald says, nodding in greeting.

'Reginald,' Kyle says, returning the greeting as he takes in the casual way Reginald looks round to make sure no one else can hear them.

'I er,' Reginald says politely, dropping his voice to a low muted tone.

Kyle inclines head sharply as he places the pan on the hob and sets the gas jets to flame. *Not now.* He twists the valve to increase the flow, filling the room with the hiss of the burners. He pauses, looking at Reginald. A second later, the downstairs toilet flushes. The toilet door opens. Sam comes out and turns briefly to smile at Reginald before making her way down the hallway to the front door. Kyle nods. Reginald pushes his glasses up his nose and begins to explain.

'Boss? It's Blowers, we're test firing out the front...repeat...test firing weapons out the front...'

'Yep, got it, mate,' Howie replies into his radio.

'Lilly here, there will be test firing of weapons,' Lilly relays the message.

Heather fires the assault rifle. Surprised at the lack of recoil from the weapon. Single shots fired out to sea. Blowers watches her closely.

'Good, very good. Don't keep your feet together though...that's better. Squeeze the trigger...good. How many shots have you fired?'

'Seven.'

'How many in the magazine?'

'Thirty.'

'How many do you have left?'

'Twenty three.'

'Good. When I say, sling the rifle like I showed you and draw the pistol. Okay?'

'Yep.'

He waits, letting her fire off a few more shots before reaching out to place a hand on her shoulder. 'Weapon is jammed...'

She stops firing and goes to sling the rifle, 'do I put the safety on?'

'Always...I mean, like if they are right in front of you and that second of pause will get you killed then no...but remember it means you have a live weapon dangling down your back.'

She switches the safety, slings the rifle and draws the pistol to hold two handed. Her thumb finds the safety and flicks it over. She fires the first round, wincing at the power of the recoil.

'Yeah it's a bitch,' Blowers says.

'Hurts my ears,' she says, shaking her head.

Clarence watches for a few minutes then goes back to fitting the GPMG. Cases of ammunition are stacked. Magazines are distributed. Bags are checked. Hand weapons are taken back. Jess is loaded. Peter and a few of his men stand talking to Pea and Sam. Joan bustles here and there giving orders and chiding anyone not working.

Fifty minutes after he left the house, Maddox steps off the boat onto the beach and makes his way through the people working to stack and sort goods ready for ferrying to the fort. Again they show the same distaste at the sight of him. He trudges on but keeps his head high and looks only ahead.

Fifty nine minutes after Maddox left the house Howie walks out the front door and stops to take a cigarette from the packet offered by Nick. He bends his head to light the smoke then steps back with a muttered *thanks*. Clarence walks over to join them. Charlie and Blinky come from the house. Blowers walks down from the road with Heather and Paco. Lilly walks out to stand and talk to Nick. Reginald watches her and the way the twelve men, Pea, Sam and Joan all watch her. The same way Howie's team always know where he is. Reginald joins the group. Paula comes out the house, mid-way through a conversation with Roy. They both stop. Roy turns to lift his top. Paula frowns and looks at his back then says something. Roy pulls his top down. A toilet flushes. Dave and Mo Mo stand slightly apart from the main group. Watching. Scanning. Always watching. Always scanning. Meredith sits in the middle of group. Blissfully happy at the whole of the pack being in one place. Marcy walks from the house and up the path as Cookey notices Maddox walking towards them. Muttered words spoken. Everyone turns to watch Maddox approaching who inwardly braces in readiness for the insults. It stings more when they don't come as it means Howie has said something that everyone is now abiding by. He stops a few feet away and looks at the faces without a flicker of emotion showing on his face.

Paula gives him magazines for his rifle and pistol. She gives him a knife with a new edge. She gives him water bottles and shows the same level of attention to his kit as everyone else's. He says thank you and takes the items. Howie smokes. Nick and Lilly talk quietly with soft words.

Paula turns from Maddox and spots Heather. She smiles at the woman fidgeting with the heavy holster now on her hip and the rifle slung across her chest.

'You get used to it,' Paula says, taking the new list from Charlie. 'We've done what we can to check for the people closest to here.'

Heather takes the list but doesn't speak. There are too many people around her. The discomfort is obvious.

'We'll be going in a minute,' Paula says kindly.

'Heather, if I may?' Reginald says, easing through the crowd. 'Please do stay as covert as possible and do nothing to draw attention to your task. The other side cannot, they really must not know what you are doing.'

Heather nods at him. The list in her hand. Paula placing a bag at her feet and hands another to Paco who stares at it before she places it at his feet.

'Water bottles, magazines, toiletries but you'll need more as you go…if you run low or anything happens then head straight back here. The armoury in the fort has more ammunition…'

'Reginald?' Lilly asks, transforming from the girl talking to her boyfriend to the woman in charge as she moves a step away from Nick. 'Are there any instructions for us regarding the people with immunity?'

'Gosh,' Reginald says, blinking a few times as he thinks. 'Well it goes without saying they need to be kept safe…do try to stop them leaving…' he smiles as he finishes, a glance to Kyle at the back who nods once and discrete.

'Of course,' Lilly says, 'Pea? Did we arrange transport for Heather?'

'Coming now, Lilly,' Pea replies, walking over with Sam and

Joan. The traveller men follow them a few metres behind. The group growing thicker in number. An engine sounds from the road. A black four-wheel drive Toyota with big wheels and an oversized set of bull bars on the front. Rugged and tough looking. 'That do?' Pea asks, evidently pleased at the perfect timing.

Heather nods but still doesn't speak. As with everyone else she feels the conflict inside. The thrill at being a part of this. At being involved in the fight back and her role has suddenly become very bloody important too. Find the immunes. Bring them back. That's it. Have some guns. Have some bullets for your guns. Have a big machete. Have a bag filled with stuff and go do it. The lack of structure is awful. The lack of organisation and the haphazard manner but they are so few and this is all they can do. She can see it now. She understands why everything is so rushed and frantic. The pace these people move at is frightening. She looks up at Paco who immediately smiles at the eye contact and suddenly everything is okay. She has him. They have a big vehicle. They can go off alone and do their task their own way. That changes the perception in her head just enough to look round at the group.

'Thank you,' she says suddenly, everyone looks at her. The discomfort is intense. The instinct to shy away almost overwhelms her but she holds her ground. 'We'll try...I promise...'

'That's enough for me,' Howie says, giving her that easy smile.

'All we can ask,' Clarence adds, his deep voice so re-assuring.

'Well,' Paula says after a second of silence. 'That's it then...I think we're ready for our shopping trip.'

'Supply run,' the men of the group say together. Smiles all round. The awkward tension easing. The British stiffness of a group now ready to break up without knowing how to do so with etiquette and dignity.

'Come here,' Paula says, pulling Lilly into a hug. 'You'll be fine, keep doing what you are doing,' she whispers into Lilly's ear.

'Lilly,' Clarence says, taking his turn. He bends down and pulls the girl into his huge arms. Lost from sight she even closes her eyes for the briefest of seconds at the feeling of comfort that should have been given by her father. 'We'll come back,' Clarence rumbles, his voice loud enough to carry, which was exactly what he intended. He pulls away and lets his eyes flow over the twelve men. A message passed and understood as they nod back at him.

Howie steps towards her. Lilly smiles and accepts the hug that is given almost awkwardly. They are not the types to give public affection. They are not the types that either seek to give, or need re-assurance from one another in this way. A nod would have done it. A simple holding of eye contact for a second but this is a show of unity. This is the continuance of the message Clarence just passed. Lilly is one of us. Be warned.

'Stay alive,' Howie says quietly. 'Kill quickly...don't hesitate and trust your instincts.'

'I will,' she says. She wanted to say *you too* but saying such a thing to Howie doesn't feel right.

The rest take their turns. Apart from Maddox and Dave. Dave nods and Maddox tactfully moves away and offers a curt smile and head dip instead.

The goodbyes are said. The vehicles await. They move off to load up. Nick and Lilly share a few last stolen words. Three words each. Short but enough and said with meaning and heart.

Heather dumps her bags in the back of the Toyota and climbs into the driver's seat. Paco moves to the passenger side. Roy goes for his van. Reginald takes his seat in the back. Paula moves to sit next to Roy. Everyone else clambers into the Saxon. Doors close. Engines start.

The Saxon pulls away. Clarence in the front waving as they go. The rear doors open. The lads leaning out to wave, shout and grin in such a way it makes those left smile and shout back while waving. Roy's van pulls behind the Saxon. Jess shifts inside the horsebox, creaking the axles.

The Toyota brings up the rear. Paco staring only at Heather who stares only at the road ahead.

'Good people so they are, Father,' the man who formerly held the Stengun breaks the silence.

'That they are,' Kyle replies, his accent once more coming back as he straightens up, smiles at Pea and winks at Joan.

CHAPTER FIFTEEN

Eleven people. One dog. Ammunition crates. Bags. Cases of water and Lucozade. Assault rifles. Axes. Knees to knees. Shoulders to shoulders. The air is hot, close and silent. Meredith lies by the open back doors panting heavily. Mo's and Dave's legs either side of her.

'And the living army moves out,' Cookey mutters looking round. Blowers nods. Blinky lifts her eyebrows. Nick shifts position. Maddox stares down at the ground. Cookey sighs and looks towards the front. 'Where we going, Mr Howie?'

'Waiting for Reggie to tell us,' Howie calls back.

'Oh,' Cookey says, settling back and staring at Blowers. 'Bit sweaty there mate.'

'Yep,' Blowers says, wiping his head with the back of his arm.

Cookey thinks. He ponders. He frowns and shows a pensive outlook at the thoughts in his mind. Charlie starts smiling. Blowers tuts with a grin.

'What?' Nick asks, leaning past Blowers.

'What?' Cookey asks innocently.

'Twat,' Nick says, sitting back.

Cookey nods and sighs heavily. 'At first I was afraid,' he tells everyone.

'Eh?' Marcy asks, looking up.

Maddox stares at the floor.

'I was petrified,' Cookey says, nodding seriously at Charlie.

'What the fuck?' Blowers asks.

'You alright mate?' Nick asks.

Cookey smiles and sighs again. He starts humming. A tuneless noise that slowly gets louder. Blowers frowns. Nick looks round at everyone else. Mo and Dave stare out the back doors.

'You did me wrong, Blowers,' Cookey says, breaking from his humming to look at his mate.

'What?' Blowers asks.

'Just saying,' Cookey says mildly.

'Saying what?'

'That I grew strong,' Cookey says.

'What?' Blowers asks, clearly confused.

'I spent so many nights,' Cookey says.

'Mate, you alright?' Blowers asks.

'Nights?' Nick asks.

Cookey shrugs, wipes the end of his nose and looks towards the back doors with another heavy sigh as he starts humming again. The humming gets louder. Tuneless as first but changing to something that hints at recognition. Blinky and Nick exchange looks. Mo turns to look down to Cookey. Maddox stares at the floor.

Cookey stops humming, a sudden motion as he stares again at Blowers. 'I couldn't live without you by my side,' he says with that serious dip of his head.

'What?' Blowers asks again but Cookey looks away and carries on the humming with a tune growing more melodic by the second. His foot starts tapping. His head moving side to side. Charlie covers her mouth. Maddox stares at the floor. Clarence turns to look down the Saxon with a puzzled look.

Cookey starts drumming his hands on his thighs. The

humming grows louder. The foot tapping more a beat that holds the tune. Blowers glares. Nick leans forward to watch Cookey. Blinky stares at him with a look of confusion.

'Just no need for it,' Cookey says quickly, shooting Blowers another look.

'What?!' Blowers asks.

'You think that's alright yeah?' Cookey asks.

'What? What is?' Blowers groans.

'Well,' Cookey tells him, tossing his head to look away dramatically. 'I learnt to get along.'

The grin comes quickly to Blowers. The realisation showing in his eyes that crinkle with humour and delight. Cookey looks back and bursts out laughing at Blowers' grin, knowing he gets it.

'You deserved it,' Blowers tells him.

'Didn't,' Cookey says, tossing his head to look away again as Charlie laughs harder just at the sight of him.

'Well guess what?' Blowers asks darkly.

'What?' Cookey asks but starts humming quickly. Blowers joins in. Both of them holding the tune that slowly connects in the minds of the others. It goes on for a few seconds with both tapping feet and swaying heads before Cookey suddenly stops and looks at Blowers. Blowers stops and stares back.

'Where were you?' Cookey asks, breathless with worry.

'You know where,' Blowers says.

They hold, they pause, they wait and try not to smile at the sight of each other. A slight nod from Cookey.

'And so you're back...from outer space....I just walked in to find you here....'

They sing together. Swaying heads. Tapping feet. Hands drumming on thighs. Gloria Gaynor's *I will survive* sung by two young men in the back of a packed armoured personnel carrier. Clarence bursts out laughing, braying like a donkey. Charlie is already off, her own smaller bray joining the noise.

Nick grins as Blowers nudges him in the ribs. A second later and he's in with them. Singing along. Marcy laughs. Blinky nods her head in time to the tune. Mo chuckles at the sight then laughs without shame at the sight of the three swaying in time side to side. Maddox stares at the floor. Grim and depressed but the humour reaches him too. His mouth twitches. It's impossible not to.

Marcy joins in. Her voice giving a lighter vocal to the male dominated chorus.

'...Go on now go...walk out the door...'

Everyone knows the song. Even Mo knows the words.

'...Did you think I'd crumble...'

It gets louder. Howie laughs in the front. Clarence beats a drum on his thighs. Marcy presses the talk switch on her radio to fill Roy's van with the occupants of the Saxon blasting the song.

'...Now I'm saving all my lovin'...'

They sing together. Spirits lift. Maddox smiles and shakes his head as he gets a dig in the side from Marcy to join in.

'...Oh no not I...'

Paula sings to Roy who groans and shakes his head while Reggie tuts, huffs and tries to focus on the maps open on his desk as his hands start tapping and his foot lifts to drop in time to the tune.

The transmission reaches to Heather and Paco in the Toyota who stare at the radio in surprise at the voices singing in unison. That same transmission carries down to the last house on the bay too and it makes those who hear it stop to smile and look back at the road. Lilly laughs with delight at the noise as Sam and Pea crowd round her to listen. They activate their own radios to carry that transmission into their own network that gets blasted to the people in the fort who stop to listen.

In the Saxon they sing to the very end and suddenly the words die away and the singing ends. Cookey sighs. Blowers sighs. Cookey looks at Blowers. Blowers stares back.

'At first I was afraid,' Cookey tells him in a flat voice, speaking the first lines that carry through the radios to the fort. A second later the song is going again. Voices booming in an awful cacophony of noise but Heather sings to Paco and Paula sings to Roy. Pea and Sam sing to each other and the people in the fort burst to tune a split second after them. Men and women holding tools. The cooks at the fires. The twelve traveller men near Lilly. The children come out of the tents to smile in delight at the fort suddenly filling with noise. Old men and women, young men and women.

In the Saxon they hear the transmission from Lilly's radio network and hear the others singing. The noise is awful. A static filled barrage of voices but it matters not what it sounds like for the feeling it gives is the thing at play.

The distance grows. The transmission to the fort and back interrupts, breaks then drops away as the signal fails to make contact. The singing dies down but the sullen mood infesting the Saxon is banished as conversations pick up and turn to the job at hand and the things they need on the supply run.

Blowers listens in. His mood lifted at the song and now turning his head left and right to catch the topics of discussion underway. Marcy leaning past Maddox to talk with Charlie before deciding it'll be much easier if she was actually sitting next to Charlie. Maddox moves politely. His manner now different and subdued. The eye contact is less and his head doesn't hold so high and that arrogance seems to have eased. Blowers watches him. Hating him. Detesting him completely and wishing the prick wasn't here. His mere presence is an irritation but orders are orders and discipline is discipline. Mr Howie said to go easy and that was enough to stop the digs and jibes.

Blowers knows that Maddox must have had it hard when he was growing up but that mitigation holds no sway for Blowers. Maddox lifts his head to look round and in so doing, he catches Blowers eye. The two hold contact for seconds. Blowers barely hiding his contempt and that very reaction invokes the pride in Maddox who lifts his chin and refuses to show he is cowed.

A dig in Blowers leg. Cookey jabbing him, reminding him

without the need for words to stop it. Blowers nods and looks down to the back. Maddox looks to the front and feels that strange sense of jealousy again. Not jealousy but something else. The way Blowers and Cookey are so close. The way Cookey was speaking the song lyrics and Blowers made the connection before anyone else. Kindred spirits who know what the other is thinking and feeling. Maddox has never had that. His best mate was Darius but in truth, they were never close.

On the streets he was a somebody. He was smart, tough and ruthless. He was a heavy for the Bossman. He was a runner. A messenger. An enforcer. A debt-collector. He was a businessman and a drug-dealer. He was many things to many people but he was never cowed or fearful of anyone. He refused the stereotype of being a young black male growing up on a hard estate. He knew the perceptions of others. Just another black kid selling drugs but to Maddox it was a way out. It was money to save and get somewhere other than where he was. He never used the drugs. He never drank booze or smoked cigarettes. He ate healthy. He exercised and was careful who his associations were. He had a plan.

Now he has no plan. Now there is no plan. He is a grunt with a rifle and a pistol and being sent to be cannon fodder. He isn't a soldier. Soldiers don't think for themselves. They follow blind orders. He is better than that. He is more than that. Except right now, he is nothing other than exactly that.

Irritation inside. Frustration grows. Loss and grief. Pain and anguish all denied a voice. It was okay for people like Blowers. They had families and structure. They had support and decent educations. He casts a look down to Mo and thinks back to how easily Mo took him out. The speed of him. The strength in his body too. The ease in which Mo held him down and the utter belief that Mo would not hesitate in pulling the trigger.

'Mr Howie, it's Reginald.'

The Saxon falls quiet as the voice comes through earpieces and echoes from the main-set at the front.

'*Yep, go ahead mate,*' Howie transmits.

Blowers holds a hand out, signalling the others to stay quiet. Maddox waits, focussing on the voice in his ear.

'*Indeed, you said you required a location in which to gather the necessary supplies. Equestrian was a priority. Is that correct?*'

'*Charlie needs a new saddle if that's what you just said.*'

'*...Yes. Yes I did just say that. I have identified two locations which I believe, from this awful local guide-book literature...really, these are truly awful publications of very low quality. I mean to say, who exactly wants a ten percent discount on a full English at Bert's café?*'

'I do,' Nick says, quickly reaching for his radio, '*Yep, I do.*'

'*Reggie? Where are we going?*' Howie asks.

'*Ah yes, please do forgive me. We have two locations which I believe will serve our...*'

'Fuck me he does goes on,' Marcy mutters.

'*...and Roy assures me both have adequately stocked sports shops in order to replenish arrows and associated archery equipment...*'

'*Yep. Where we going?*' Howie asks again.

'*Now then. I am most interested to see if the other player has yet reached a level whereby it can predict our necessary re-supply and whether or not it will seek to mass in such locations. I believe one location will pose less of a risk at opposition but the commercial resources will be more limited as the town is smaller. The second has a greater risk but of course with greater risk comes greater reward and so the question is...*'

'Oh my fucking god,' Marcy exclaims, jabbing at her radio trying to cut in.

'*...having already fought one skirmish today do you wish to take the lesser risk, although obviously my advice is guidance only and there may well be things I cannot predict...or of course we can go for the larger location but...*'

'Stop fucking talking...stop it...stop...fuck's sake he just goes on...seriously, I've had days and days of his voice and....*Reggie! Fuck's sake you talk so much...*'

'Marcy? Good Lord woman. I was merely outlining the information so a tactical and strategic decision can be made.'

'Bigger one,' Howie cuts in.

'Yes I rather predicted you would say that. In which case you will need to take the motorway. I will guide from there but please do understand I am not able, at this time, to predict what level, if any, of opposition. As I made clear, it depends on the intellectual evolution of the other player and if it has...'

'I'm going to shoot him,' Marcy mutters. 'With a gun...in the arse...then run him over...ooh, *Reggie, it's Marcy, honey. Do they have a Boots in the bigger town?'*

'A boots? I am not sure I understand. Do you require footwear?'

'No. Boots. Boots the Chemist. The shop. Do they have a Boots? I need make-up remover and some moisturiser. This heat is making me sweat which means I am washing my face like so much more than normal and I'm getting dry skin. Shall I tell you about that? In long sentences? I wash my face with soap to rinse the sweat off but the soap residue dries my skin out which...'

'Oh my. Good gosh she is so infuriating,' Reginald exclaims as Paula laughs to herself in the front of Roy's van.

'And of course a lady still needs to look like lady even in the apocalypse. Shall I tell you about that too? In long sentences?'

'I hate her,' Reginald says emphatically.

CHAPTER SIXTEEN

'*Half mile warning.*'

'*Cheers, pulling over,*' Howie says, thumbing his radio. He smiles to himself at the curt tone Reginald used to give the last transmission. 'I think you pissed him off, Marcy.'

'Yeah?' Marcy says hopefully. 'Good.'

Heather frowns and looks at Paco next to her in the front of the Toyota. 'What's a half mile warning for?'

Paco does not know what the half mile warning is for.

'They're stopping,' Heather tells Paco, seeing the brake lights coming on at the back of the horsebox and the slowdown of the vehicles in front of her. She steers out to see ahead and looks down the long wide empty motorway. Fields on both sides. Rolling meadows and trees bordering copses. A heat haze shimmers over the road but the air-conditioning in the Toyota blasts out a beautifully ice cold breeze that makes her shiver with delight.

'Why are they stopping?' she asks Paco.

Paco does not know why they're stopping.

The Saxon glides to a halt. Roy eases the speed down to stop a few metres back as the Toyota, operated by a frowning Heather, also stops.

They file out from the Saxon. Dave and Mo drop down and away from the back as Blowers gives the order for his team to range out and watch the sides.

'Stay with me,' he tells Maddox dully. Maddox follows the corporal as they jump from the Saxon into a wall of heat made worse by the bare concrete of the motorway.

'What are we doing?' Maddox asks as Howie and Clarence head down towards Roy van.

'Drone,' Blowers says, giving a one-word answer that hangs in the hot air for a second. He nods in the direction of the town they are heading for, 'get some eyes up to see what's there.'

Maddox stares in the same direction then looks down towards Roy's van. He wants to see the drone and what it looks like. He wants to see the feed to the monitor and know how it works.

'Rifle!' Blowers calls out with a grin. Maddox turns to see Heather stop mid-step as she walks from the Toyota then darts back to pull her assault rifle from the back seat with a wave towards Blowers. 'We'll go down, Blinky, Charlie...you keep eyes on the front.'

He leads Maddox towards the armoured van as Roy steps out into the middle of carriageway to set the drone down.

'What's happening?' Heather asks Blowers, feeling comfortable to talk with him away from the others. They only spent an hour together but it was enough for Heather to see he was a professional soldier, polite, decent and committed to his role.

'We've got a drone,' Blowers explains, his tone markedly more friendly towards Heather than it was to Maddox. 'We try and stop half mile away from anything like a town...so we have an idea what we're going in against and the layout, the roads...that sort of thing.'

'I saw that,' Heather says, staring at the drone on the ground. 'In that square that day.'

'Yeah we used it there,' Blowers says. 'And er...don't forget your rifle when you get out the vehicle next time.'

'Yeah sorry, Blowers,' she says casually, staring at the way he stands with his feet planted apart and the rifle held over the crook of his elbows. She frowns and copies him, widening her feet then resting the rifle over her bent arms. 'Like this?' she asks.

'Yep,' Blowers says, just as casually. They both look at Maddox who stands with his rifle held in one hand down at his side.

'Heather?' Paula calls out. 'You coming with us to the town?'

'Er no, we're going through it,' Heather says, not knowing where she was going but thinking to stop somewhere and look through the list and maps.

'Ah okay,' Paula says easily, 'Reggie said we might get some opposition so...you know...might be an idea to go round or another direction.'

'Okay.'

'I'm not saying you *can't* go in the town but...if we're firing and bullets are going all over the place and...'

'Rounds,' Blowers says.

'Eh?' Paula asks.

'We'll go round,' Heather says.

'Rounds not bullets,' Blowers says.

'Is there a difference?' Paula asks.

'Yeah, they're called rounds not bullets. That's the difference... er...Miss Paula.'

'Cheeky sod,' she laughs at seeing his grin.

'How many rounds in the magazine?' Blowers asks, looking at Heather.

'Thirty, well...I guess twenty-nine if one is in that bit there,' she says, pointing to the chamber.

'Good enough,' Blowers says, leaning down to see if the safety is on then peering across her front to the pistol on her hip.

'Loaded, made ready, safety on,' Heather tells him, turning so he can see the holster on her hip.

'Cool,' Blowers says, glancing over to see Paco's pistol safely holstered.

'His is the same,' she says.

'Fair one,' Blowers says, inclining his head at Paco. 'Alright mate?' Paco doesn't reply but then he doesn't try and kill him either which Blowers takes as a good sign. 'So he does speak then? I mean, we heard him saying your name back at that house.'

'He does when he wants to,' Heather says. 'He will get better,' she asserts quickly.

'Fair one,' Blowers says again.

'Did you know him before?' Heather asks, hating having to talk about Paco like he isn't present.

'Only for like...half hour or something, actually it might have been longer but we were scrapping at the time. I mean fighting the...'

'I understand,' she says.

'We didn't really speak or anything like that,' Blowers says.

'Are we infected?'

Blowers looks at her carefully, seeing the change in her and the sensing there is a deep intelligence behind the shyness and projected dislike for people.

'Probably,' he says, tilting his head as though *what can you do.*

'Oh,' she says, looking from Blowers to Maddox. 'What about you?'

'Immune,' Maddox says.

'So...' Heather says and stops, looking from Maddox to Paco. 'What's the difference?'

'We're infected and he's immune,' Blowers says, nodding at Maddox with a grin. She smiles back. Showing she got the joke and hasn't take offence.

'I'm not tired or anything,' she blurts, 'and my bites don't hurt... is that normal for us?'

'Yep. Totally,' Blowers says, exuding so much competence it makes Maddox look away with a scowl. 'See the bosses wounds... got so many. Covered in bites and Charlie? The girl with the cut face? That only happened yesterday.'

'So it's normal? Like...normal for us I mean? What about not being tired?'

'Same for us. We don't get that tired...not like before...you know. We get knackered when we been fighting and running all day but...we rest and have a kip then we're good to go again.' He tenses his legs and shifts on the spot. 'My legs ache a bit and my shoulders but...nothing like they should be.'

'So...is anything different with us? I mean anything bad?'

'Dunno, mate. I don't think so...Reggie hasn't said anything and Marcy was fully turned and she hasn't said anything either...'

Heather nods, 'Paula's lovely.'

'They all are,' Blowers says, casting a quick glance at Maddox.

'And Charlie seems really nice too,' Heather says. 'Blinky's a bit strange but...'

'Hard as nails,' Blowers says.

'Hmmm, so...have any of you turned back into...like...those things...I guess not if...oh,' she says, seeing the troubled look on Blowers face and wincing. 'Sorry, did I...I mean...I'm not good at small talk and...'

'Nah it's fine,' Blowers says as Maddox looks away again. 'Er, like one of ours was turned but she came back...she er...she got hurt though and...we don't really know what happened but she er... turned back...'

Tension between them. Even Heather, with her non-existent experience of conversation detects the sudden darkening of mood between Blowers and Maddox. She goes to speak but dries up and suddenly feels very awkward.

'It was probably a one off,' Maddox says after a pause, finding voice in an effort to fill the silence. Blowers just stares at him.

'Er,' Heather says, wanting to just walk off. She walks off. Paco follows her. Heedless to any sense of awkwardness hanging in the air.

'One off?' Blowers whispers, glaring hard.

Maddox shrugs and glares back with challenge in his eyes.

'You two okay?' Clarence calls over.

'Yep,' Blowers says.

Maddox holds Clarence's eye contact for a few seconds longer than necessary as even the big man starts to think keeping Maddox with them might be the wrong move.

The drone comes to life. The electric motor whirring loudly as the four sets of propellers go from static to spinning faster than the eye can see. Roy stands at the back of his van talking to Reginald inside holding the controller for the camera. A nod from Reginald. Roy pushes the stick to give lift. The drone rises, the motor whines louder as the object rises slowly.

'That's not right,' Nick says as Roy frowns.

'What's up?' Howie asks, staring up at the drone.

'Too slow,' Roy says, thumbing the stick. 'Not responding either...'

'Battery,' Nick says, 'bring it back we'll swap over.'

'That *is* the charged battery,' Roy says.

'Can't be, you can hear it's fucked,' Nick says, cocking his head to listen. Blowers watches the drone and hears the whirring dropping in pitch and tone as it starts to descend back to the road.

'It is,' Roy says, 'I had it on charge.'

Nick goes forward as it lands and waits for the propellers to stop spinning before checking the battery. 'You getting a camera feed, Reggie?'

'There was for a second' Reginald says. 'The screen has gone blank.'

'It was on charge,' Roy says, moving to Nick's side as he disconnects the battery from the drone.

'Try the other one,' Nick says. 'Boss? It's right next to Reggie's desk...can you...'

'This it?' Howie asks, holding the other battery up.

'Yep, cheers,' Nick says running to swap over before going back to the drone. He slides the new battery into place and checks the connections. 'Try it now.'

'Nothing,' Roy says, fiddling with the controls.

'Seriously? They're both flat?'

'The one you took out was on charge,' Roy says. 'Must be the charging unit or...maybe a loose connection. Plug the other one in and see if it...'

'Doing it now,' Howie says, in the back of the van pushing the battery into the charger. 'The lights are on...green lights right?'

'Yep,' Nick says, sharing a shrug with Roy. 'S'fucked then...I can have a look later but...'

'No drone,' Roy says as Howie comes out the van.

'Shame,' Howie tuts, looking in the direction of the town. 'Reggie? How far to the other town?'

'Oh gosh...let me see...we are here,' Reginald says, finding their current location and tracing a fingertip over the map to the place he noted earlier. 'I would estimate we are...perhaps...yes just over one hour driving time.'

'Cock it,' Howie mutters.

'We went in plenty of places before we had the drone,' Clarence says.

'Yeah true,' Howie says. 'Right. Fine. Heather, you coming in with us?'

'No.'

'Okay,' Howie says after waiting for a second for the rest of conversation he expected to hear. 'Er...so...guess we'll see you at some point...at the fort probably.'

'Probably,' Heather says, retreating back to the car and wishing she could say something else.

'Reggie, what's closest? The horse place or the bows and arrows place?'

'The equestrian centre requires a slight deviation before we reach the town centre. I would advise we do that first in case we find heavy opposition within the town.'

'Righto mate.'

They load back up into the hot vehicles. The Saxon the worst of all. Cramped and sweltering even with the back doors left open. Roy's van and the Toyota pump air-conditioned breezes through vents that reduce the temperature and suck the crushing humidity from the air.

This time Heather waits for them to pull away and sits with Paco in the car idling the engine and letting the other two vehicles pull away to avoid any more awkward instances. She feels a strange desire to stay with them. That thrill is still there. They are the heart of the resistance to fight back. She smiles at Paco and remembers the golden days of just being with him but then she has a radio and the plastic object seems to magnify the connection to the others. She could press the button and simply say she wants to go with them. They'll be cool too. Easy-going and chilled out. They won't ask stupid questions but will respect her difference of manner.

She picks the radio up and holds it ready to press the button on the side but hesitates with her thumb touching but not pressing.

Go with them. Stay with them. Work together to find the immunes and do what needs to be done. Press the button and say something.

Still the fears linger. The fear that all people are bad.

CHAPTER SEVENTEEN

'Turn right...'

'Yep I see it, Reggie.'

'This is the access lane that runs for approximately six hundred yards to the car park which borders the premises.'

'Yep. Big sign we just passed says the same thing,' Howie says into his radio. 'Layout?'

'From studying the topography I can see we have open fields on all sides. There are several smaller buildings and what appears to be one very large structure.'

'That will be a sand school, Mr Howie,' Charlie calls forward.

'A what?' Howie asks.

'Sand school.'

'What the fuck is a sand school?'

'A school for sand,' Blowers says.

'Really?' Howie asks.

'No it's an area used for schooling horses...the surface is sand,' Charlie says.

'Ah...why isn't it called a horse school then?'

'I don't know, Mr Howie.'

'Should be called a horse school...*Reggie, why isn't it called a horse school?*'

'*I beg your pardon? Oh I see. I gather Charlie informed you the large structure is a sand school and you are now questioning the name of it. Is that correct?*'

'*Should be called a horse school.*'

'*Indeed. I am sure it should.*'

'*I'm hot.*'

'*I see. Well. Thank-you for informing me of that.*'

'*Hot as fuck.*'

'*Indeed. Again thank you, Mr Howie.*'

'*S*tupid name for a school. Should be a horse school...we're here, looks empty. Everyone out.'

The Saxon shuffle commences. Dave and Mo drop out. The first to gain the ground. They turn with rifles raised as they move out and create space for the others. The rest shuffle bums down the bench seats to reach the back doors and drop out. Meredith bounds out to land and sprint with excitement at seeing Paula coming from Roy's van. She hasn't seen Paula for at least ten minutes and needs to show that by whining, snaking and licking while her tail swishes and sways. Paula fusses her head. Calling her a good girl before Meredith decides the time for re-connecting is now over and she must run about sniffing things and have a piddle. Everyone watches the dog for reaction. Rifles up and voices hushed as they move quietly away from the vehicles with boots crunching over the unmade surface of the big car park.

Blowers walks out to the middle turning a full 360 to see the view. No vehicles in the car park. The doors and windows to the buildings look closed and secure. No noises. No signs of infected. He spots rabbits in the fields bordering the car park, which re-assure him that nothing has gone through recently and scared them off. He takes in the big structure of the sand school. The size of an airplane hangar with two huge sliding doors and a curved old stained corrugated iron roof. He spots normal sized doors and signs that welcome visitors to the café, the reception and urging them to shop in the outlets.

His team turn to view but keep a close eye on him. Waiting for instruction. Blowers signals to Blinky first, pointing at his own eyes then to the lane they just came up, *watch that lane.* Blinky nods and is off, jogging lightly. She drops to one knee and locks on with her rifle up and ready. To Mo and Charlie, *you two, watch those buildings and the fields beyond. That is your side.* To Cookey and Nick, *the sand school and the sides.* He drops his head to talk quietly into his radio.

'Reggie, it's Blowers. You got cameras on?'

'Indeed I have.'

'Roger that. Big area to cover. Watch all four please.'

'Yes, yes of course, Simon.'

'Overwatch on.'

Blowers glances up to see Roy in position on top of his van. He looks round to Meredith, double-checking for signs of aggression from the dog.

Two sides have open ground. One side is blocked by the sand school building but the last side where all the smaller buildings are give him concern. Too many places they can come from. Lots of little lanes and walkways. Lots of buildings, sheds and stables.

'Watch that side,' he whispers to Maddox, 'too many rat runs...' Blowers looks up to Roy and waves a flat hand in the same direction, showing the bowman his concerns. Roy nods once and turns to hold that side in the centre of his view. When Blowers looks again he spots Howie, Clarence and Dave heading towards the smaller structures. Rifles up. Feet placed carefully. Paula and Marcy right behind them. He holds his team in the middle while the elders clear the rat runs.

The tension mounts. The continual life and death pressure to watch, to scan, to stay alert and use every sense at your disposal.

Maddox wipes his forehead then dries his hand on the back of his trousers. He looks over to Blinky then over to the others.

'Eyes back on your side, Maddox' Blowers whispers.

'*Stinks of death through here,*' Howie's whispered voice comes through the radio. Eyes sharpen. Mouths open to hear better. Senses buzz with awareness. Blowers feels his heart rate raise slightly as his body, now experienced in such things, prepares to dump adrenalin in case of a fight. His hard eyes snatch glimpses from Cookey and Nick to Mo and Charlie then round to Blinky. To the van. To Roy. To Maddox. To Paula and Marcy just going out of view following the elders. He strains to hear, to listen for any such sound that will give awareness to something going wrong.

Minutes pass. Long minutes of heightened senses. Sweat drips. They breathe the hot air and wait.

'*Horses,*' Howie's voice again. Sad and angry at the same time. '*Left in the stables...*'

Blowers closes his eyes for a split second at the concept of the suffering that must have taken place. Pure anger follows a second after. Hatred for his kind that worried only about themselves and gave no care for anything else. That manifests to a pinpoint focus of something more than hatred for the infection. They caused it. They made this happen. A second after that and the professional soldier returns with hard eyes staring out to do the job at hand.

'You okay?' Cookey mutters across the car park to Charlie.

Charlie doesn't say anything but stares ahead to her side. Her own head fills with the too unwelcome images of horses trapped in stables without water or food. She knows it's unusual to put horses in stables this time of year. Most are out in warmer weather and they would have stood a chance at survival. Horses left in stables were most likely sick, injured or in foal. Which just makes it even worse.

Mo reaches out to her. Just a touch of a hand on her arm with a fleeting act of re-assurance that signifies the communal respect and decency. Charlie likes horses. Mr Howie just said some horses are dead, therefore the manifestation of the pity and grief they feel is directed to Charlie.

'You okay?'

Blowers turns in surprise at hearing Blinky using the radio. Her tone soft and worried for her best mate.

'Yes,' Charlie transmits back.

The elders come back. Grim faced with barely concealed fury showing. Rifles lowered. Only Dave looks the same as ever and in that they all see his coldness of life and that nothing touches him save his love for the boss.

'How many?' Charlie asks, her polite tone so eerie in the otherwise silent air.

'Too many,' Paula says, dropping her eyes as Marcy strides across the car park towards the Saxon with tears streaming down her cheeks.

'Couple looked like they bust out,' Clarence's deep voice only adds gravitas to the emotion of the moment. 'That's something I suppose...' he adds darkly.

'Let's get what we need and get out,' Howie says, 'Nick, you got a smoke mate? Mo? You getting anything?'

'Nothing, Mr Howie.'

'Meredith seems fine,' Blowers calls out.

'Okay, Charlie, any idea which building we need?'

'That one, Mr Howie,' Charlie says, her voice still clipped and raw as she points to a central structure. Blowers looks at the building and notices the difference. That one has bars on the windows, the door looks thicker, more solid and there is an alarm box on the wall. He thinks back to Salisbury when Dave told them which one the armoury building was. It seems so long ago now. Like months, years even.

'Mo, you fancy backing the Saxon up. We'll rip the door off.'

'On it, Mr Howie' Mo says. He goes to turn then stops and again reaches out to touch Charlie's arm again, 'you's okay yeah?'

'I'm fine, thank you, Mo.'

'Blowers, Maddox...' Howie calls out, taking a smoke from Nick. 'See if you can get into that big building.'

'What for?'

'MR HOWIE DOES NOT NEED TO EXPLAIN HIS ORDERS,' Dave roars, striding across the car park at Maddox. 'MR HOWIE GIVES ORDERS. YOU FOLLOW THE ORDERS...ARE WE CLEAR?' The voice is huge. Enormous. A drill sergeants depth and volume roaring as the small man stops nose to nose with Maddox. 'DO WE HAVE A PROBLEM, MR DOKU?'

Maddox tries staring him down but staring Dave down is like trying to take an arm from Meredith. There is only one outcome and that is pain. Lots of pain. Maddox sees it. He sees the complete lack of emotion and the void in Dave's eyes where even the hardest men would have a flicker of something. He blinks and looks away, showing submission from a simple instinct telling him this man will kill him.

'No...'

'NO, DAVE,' Dave roars, taking a step forward that makes Maddox take a step back.

'No, Dave,' Maddox says, louder this time, humiliation showing in his face.

'Someone coming out,' Nick cuts in.

Blowers spins from the enjoyable spectacle of watching Maddox being balled out to see the wooden side door of the hangar now open with a man standing halfway across the threshold. He's big too. Six four at least with wide shoulders and a fleshy strip of fat gut shows between his t shirt and jeans. Days of growth on his jaw. His hair wild and greasy. He lifts a thick arm as though to offer greeting while squinting at the sunlight hurting his eyes.

'Thank God,' the man says, the relief evident as he comes out further from the doorway. He shows his hands are empty as he walks slowly towards them. 'Been here since it started...'

'You've been here for twenty days?' Paula asks.

'Yeah...s'mine...I own it...I'm Frank,' he says, twitching his head to the hangar behind him. 'What's happening then? Government back are they?' Frank walks towards them. Comfortable in his environment and relieved at the sight of what he perceives are uniformed armed personnel in army trucks. He shields his eyes from the sun showing a meaty forearm smeared with dirt.

'How many of you in there?' Howie asks in such a tone it makes Marcy drop from the Saxon to walk quickly towards him.

Frank spots Marcy with a flicker of appreciation at the sight of her showing in his eyes. A wet tongue pokes out to lick his lips as he clears his throat and makes an effort to suck his gut in. 'We've got...'

'What the fuck was that?' Howie asks, staring at the man.

'Howie,' Marcy says, speeding up at hearing the dangerous low edge to his voice.

'What?' Frank asks, still flicking his eyes to Marcy's chest.

'Stop it.'

'Stop what?' Frank asks, unable to compute or understand what he's being asked to stop as he smiles and winks at Marcy.

'Fuck me. Stop it. Stop fucking looking at her...' Howie snaps.

'Eh?' Frank asks, blinking hard a few times before offering a knowing smile. 'Sorry, she yours is she?'

'What the fuck?' Howie says, stunned at the response.

'Yeah so you the army right? Who's in charge? That you is it? We got people inside. Food ran out a few days ago but we got a foal in but that's almost gone now and...'

'Do what?' Howie asks, taking a step close to the man despite Marcy's hand on his arm.

'So what's happening? Where you putting everyone? My lot want to stay here but we'll need supplies, beds and...of course I don't mind using my business but there'll have to be compensation cos...'

'You did what with a foal?' Howie asks.

'Got one in didn't we. Food ran out so...well they're tender and...'

'You ate it?' Howie asks, stunned again.

'Yeah,' Frank scoffs, 'I just said that. Food ran out...Christ, mate, you in charge are you? Ran out of officers did they? What are you, like a sergeant or something?'

'You ate a foal?'

'Yes. We ate a foal,' Frank says, opening his hands to emphasise his point.

'A baby horse?'

'Listen, mate. You got an officer I can talk with?'

'No. What about...I mean...okay,' Howie says, exhaling noisily as he struggles to understand what his brain is telling him. 'Okay, er...have you seen any infected here?'

'What's that? The things? Nah they stayed in the town I think. We been alright but...'

'Stop,' Howie says, holding a hand out. 'They haven't come here? Is that right?'

'I just...'

'And you ate a baby horse? Is that right?'

'Listen mate...'

'And you let the other horses die in the stables for what reason now?'

'Eh? What you on about? We couldn't go outside could we?'

'What about the baby horse you got? Where did that come from?'

'That was later. I ain't arguing with you, son...'

'Don't call me son. Where did the baby horse come from?'

'I want to talk with an officer. Someone in charge. This is out of order this is. We been cooped for twenty days waiting and you turn up being aggressive and...'

'Did you go outside to get the baby horse?'

'FOAL. It's a foal not a baby horse. I want whoever is in charge. This is outrageous. This is my business. I own it...'

'Okay, fair enough,' Howie says, 'but did you go outside to get the baby horse?'

'This is preposterous...'

'Ah because like, if you went outside to get the baby horse then you could have gone outside to let the other horses out of their FUCKING STABLES...'

'Right. You,' Frank says, ignoring Howie and pointing at Clarence. 'Get me someone in charge.'

Clarence stares back. Paula stares back. Everyone stares back at him, showing no reaction, unsmiling, unmoving and Frank fails to read the danger signs.

Instead, Frank glowers and seethes with righteous fury. He has spent twenty days not being able to consume his ten thousand calories a day that he needs *just to survive*. He's been cooped up seeing his profits being eaten by greedy survivors. He's spent that time rationing them, controlling what they eat, drink and do and only when *he* got hungry did he send two go out to grab the foal from the field to bring in for slaughter. Horses are profit to Frank. Horse people have money, they buy horse things, equipment, feed and clothing. They go to horse shows and pay money in his café and bar. His temper flashes. He sees the army in front of him. Men and women in uniform with army vehicles. This is Britain. This is a country with order and discipline. He is a business owner. He pays his taxes, sometimes, and he will demand for a senior official to be brought here. He looks round and spots Charlie. A young woman who even with a cut down her face still looks polite and educated. He steps towards her with his hand out waggling a finger at her face.

'Get me an officer right now. I will not stand for this. I want someone in charge. We have barely survived here...I will not be treated like this...'

Charlie stares at him. At the way he rages and the spittle flying from his lips. He stinks too. She can smell him. He stinks of stale body odour and filth. She spots that even while he plays his outraged sense of entitlement out his eyes still stare down to her chest. As she notices that movement so she becomes aware of his fat filthy finger waggling at her. Jabbing the air in front as he shouts and makes demands while horses lie dead from thirst and starvation not a stones throw away.

She breaks his finger.

'Holy fuck,' Cookey mumbles, stunned at the sight of her hand lashing out to grab and twist as the air fills with the dull crack of bone. The blood drains from Frank's face as he falls to instant silence.

'I make no apology to you,' Charlie says curtly, 'you let horses die.' She walks off towards the Saxon as Frank stares at his finger now pointing the wrong way. He gibbers with his mouth opening and closing.

'Mo, get that Saxon backed up,' Howie says.

'You...' Frank says, gasping the word out.

The Saxon starts up as Mo pulls out wide to reverse back towards the building Charlie pointed out.

'But...my...' Frank gibbers.

The Saxon stops. Clarence drags a chain out and with Nick's help gets a hook wedged into the door. A shout from Nick. The Saxon pulls away slowly. The chain goes taut, a wrench and a dull clang sees the door pulled from the frame.

'Whoa,' Nick shouts, 'that's it.'

'My finger...'

'You had that coming,' Clarence tells him, putting the chain back in the Saxon.

'But...'

'Blowers, Maddox,' Howie says, 'go down and see what the state is inside that building. Tell them to head for the fort.'

'Sir,' Blowers says, motioning for Maddox to go with him.

'Roy, you go with them in case they need a medic,' Howie adds.

'I'm not a doctor,' Roy grumbles, climbing down from his van.

'I need a medic,' Frank says weakly.

'You don't get a medic,' Howie says.

'But...'

'Charlie, get what you need.'

'Yes, Mr Howie.'

'But...that's mine,' Frank says, staring in horror at his finger then staring in more horror at his expensive tack store now wide open.

'Requisitioned for the war effort,' Paula says, following Charlie inside the building.

'It'll need re-setting,' Roy says, walking past Frank with his red medic's bag over one shoulder.

'Huh?' Frank gibbers.

'The finger,' Roy says, turning to walk backwards, 'you'll need to re-set it. Want me to do it now?'

'Huh?'

Roy stops going backwards then starts going forwards towards Frank. 'Your finger,' he says, nodding at Frank's hand still held up in the same position it was when Charlie grabbed it.

'Huh?' Frank says, staring at his hand.

'Can't leave it like that,' Roy tells him.

'But...'

'Just put it back in...grab it and push down...'

'But...'

'Are you deaf?'

'Deaf?'

'Just stupid clearly, right, stand still,' Roy says, dropping his medic's bag and reaching out to Frank who jerks his hand away in fright. 'Up to you, leave it like that and infection will set in, gangrene will spread up your arm...you'll turn green and die in a week.'

'Die?'

'Slowly,' Roy tells him in a serious manner.

'Slowly?'

'It won't hurt,' Roy says kindly, motioning for Frank to give him his hand. 'Come on, best get it done now. I'll just grab it and pull down okay? You'll hear a crack but that's fine...ready?'

'No,' Frank mumbles, watching Roy grab his broken finger.

'One...two...' A twist. A yank. Another dull crack.

'OH MY GOD.'

'All done,' Roy says, watching Frank stagger back. 'Get it splinted...and don't leave horses locked in stables again.' He grabs his medic bag and strolls on behind Blowers and Maddox.

'Wow,' Howie says, walking into the shop to stare round at the packed shelves, clothes rails, saddles on the wall, boots, whips, chains, ropes, leather things and shiny black things. He spots Charlie by the saddles talking quietly to Paula. 'You okay?'

'I am so sorry,' Charlie says quickly, turning to look at him with genuine remorse showing. 'I will of course apologise to...'

'Will you fuck,' Howie says.

'Fuck who?' Marcy asks, walking into the shop and stopping dead with a wince. 'I can't believe I just said that. I didn't mean it like...wow, that is so cool,' she picks up a riding crop to swish through the air. 'I'm keeping this...' she says to Howie.

'Dirty cow,' Paula laughs.

'Charlie should have one for when Cookey gets out of line,' Marcy says, swishing it side to side.

'I'm never out of line,' Cookey says, walking in after Clarence. 'What the...' he stops to look round, showing the same reaction as Howie and Marcy at the things on display. 'S'like a bondage club... Nick? You got to see this...'

'Oh Christ,' Paula groans, 'it's too hot for this.'

'THAT WAS WRONG.'

'Shut up.'

'We're armed.' Maddox tuts and shakes his head, 'a soldier would be court martialled for that.'

Blowers purses his lips and walks on towards the door into the hangar building. It was wrong but then it was right. The bloke had it coming but soldiers don't break fingers. Soldiers show discipline in the face of provocation by unarmed non-combatants.

'Focus on this,' Blowers says instead.

'Do the right thing yeah?' Maddox asks.

'We need to focus. Switch on...' he gets to the door first and goes through to an inner hallway stinking of burnt meat, stale body odour, cigarette smoke and alcohol. Signs on the wall welcome visitors and urge them to *take a look at our great menu*. Posters of upcoming events, dressage and jumping shows, winners of past events and all manner of stained peeling old sheets of paper pinned up to be left for years.

'Are we breaking fingers, Corporal?' Maddox asks politely, following Blowers down to the set of double doors.

Blowers pushes through to a long room filled with chairs and tables. An old style counter on one side with an empty hot-food cabinet and equally empty baskets that once held snack food. Food wrappers and drink cans litter the tables. Ashtrays filled and more butts on the floor. Stains on the table tops, the air stinks. The curtains drawn too giving the room a gloomy ambience.

'Will I be court martialled if I don't break fingers?'

'Fuck off, Maddox.'

The wall on the left is set to windows overlooking the large open sand school that has the appearance of a very old football pitch bordered by faded boards advertising local goods, produce and garage services. They see the people in the middle, gathered together as they wait for Frank to come back. Chairs and sofas in the middle of the sand ranged round an open fire pit and the air stinks of burnt meat.

Blowers goes through the door at the end to see one side has been set apart for people to watch the sand school. Wooden bench seats bolted to the ground now covered with more litter, food wrappers, clothes, empty cans and bottles of beer. It looks filthy, unclean and uncared for.

The people turn to look over, instantly falling silent at the sight of the two armed men walking towards them through an opening in the side panel. Blowers counts heads, getting to eighteen with a mixture of men, women and children. They all look as filthy as Frank too which he struggles to understand. There must be running water here.

'Hi,' Blowers calls out, coming to a stop a few metres away. 'We're with Mr Howie...' he pauses to wait for reaction. None shows.

'Not as famous as he thinks,' Maddox mutters. 'Hi, my name is Maddox. This is Simon. We're not the army or the government but we're not here to hurt you,' the charm comes instant and easy. The big smile Maddox reserves for special use only. His tone carefully delivered that immediately starts putting people at rest. Blowers hides the irritation and goes to speak but Maddox carries on quickly.

'We're from Fort Spitbank? Have you heard of it?' Maddox asks, smiling at a few of the adults nodding. 'On the coast. Not that far from here, it's a safe place. You should head there...we just stopped for equipment and so one of our people could break Frank's...'

'Maddox,' Blowers cuts in, glaring at him. 'Is anyone hurt? We've got a medic if...'

'Broken fingers?' Maddox asks.

'Blowers?' Roy calls out, spotting them through the windows from the café area. He heads for the door and comes through into the sand school. 'Anyone hurt?'

'They seem okay,' Maddox says, 'can't see any broken fingers anyway.'

'I've re-set it,' Roy says, either ignoring or ignorant to the meaning of the comment. 'Right, what have we got here? Anyone hurt? Any illnesses? You all look terrible...have you been outside? You need vitamins and sunshine. Good God the stench! Why aren't you washing?'

'Where's Frank?' someone asks.

'Outside with his broken finger,' Maddox calls back.

'Eh?'

'What broken finger?'

'Is he alright?'

Blowers takes in the worry coming from only a few while the majority seem to hang back and stay silent. The more he watches the more he notices the quiet ones look worse too. Hungrier, more drawn and sunken eyed with greasy matted hair. He clocks the hierarchy showing from the formation of the seats, and the way sofas and comfortable chairs are grouped together while rugs on the ground show where others have been sitting. He moves forward with his rifle held across the crook of his elbows as the vocal ones throw questions at Maddox and Roy.

'Hey,' Blowers says to a young woman standing stock still with her hands over the shoulders of two small children clinging to her legs. 'You okay?'

She nods but looks past Blowers to the small group of men and women trying to get answers from the other two. Fear on her face and in her eyes.

'Miss?' Blowers asks softly. She blinks and looks at him then down to the rifle in his arms. It's hot. Too hot. Sweat beads down Blowers' face and trickles down his jaw but the woman wears a long sleeve top covering her arms. He takes her in with a quick scan that she doesn't notice. A bruise on her neck covered by the strands of her hair hanging down.

'Are you okay?' Blowers asks, moving a step closer.

'She's fine,' a man says quickly, too quickly. Blowers looks round, seeing other young women looking cowed and terrified. He spots grip marks on the sallow skin of a young woman's upper arms. A child, a boy no more than ten with a fading black eye.

'Who hurt you?' Blowers asks the boy. Silence falls. Suddenly heavy and weighted with tension ramping through the ceiling.

Maddox sees the separation a second later. The people closest to him were the ones asking about Frank. They're more confident, more vocal. The others are sullen with the air of a beaten look.

'Now look here,' the man who tried speaking to Blowers says. 'Are you from the army? Where's Frank? What is going on? Are those things…'

'Shush,' Maddox says, whispering the word out with such a sinister look the man falls instantly quiet.

'He fell,' a woman says, finally answering Blowers question.

'What about you, Miss?' Blowers asks, looking back to the woman. He points at his own neck to the same place she has the mark. She swallows. Terrified and worried sick as she draws the children in closer to her legs. 'You're safe now,' Blowers says.

'They raped her…' the woman with the grip marks on her arms blurts.

'Shut up,' a man hisses, low and urgent.

'And me…and Sarah…they made us work for food…' the woman with the grip marks states.

'LIAR,' the man booms as the others with him exclaim shock and horror at the accusations.

'You,' Blowers says, pointing at the girl who spoke out. 'What's your name?'

'SHE'S A LIAR…We didn't do anything…'

'Carol,' the girl says.

'Carol, point out the ones who did it…' Blowers says, turning as he thumbs the switch on his radio. '…*Mr Howie, got a situation, assistance please…*'

'*On way…*'

'Everyone stay still,' Roy says, backing away from the group as he draws his pistol.

'SHE'S A LIAR,' the man screams, glaring at Carol.

'Don't look at her,' Maddox tells him calmly.

'Him,' Carol says, pointing a trembling hand at the man protesting loudly.

'You fucking whore…'

'We had to fuck for food,' Carol says, breathing harder as the rage suppressed for so many days comes out. 'All of them...' she says, still holding that arm towards the small group. 'Frank...his kid, Frankie..'

'Did I fuck!' A young replica of Frank shouts, his face ruddy and flushed. Wide shoulders like his dad and the same big gut hanging over his jeans.

'Simon...Colin...'

'YOU LIAR,' Simon screeches, the same man trying to dominate the group.

'Yeah?' Carol asks, bending over to grab the bottom hem of her filthy summer skirt she wore for the first time on the Friday evening it happened. She hoists it up, showing dirt encrusted legs covered in bruises and livid welts on the inside of her upper thighs. Blowers glimpses but looks away from instinct. 'WHERE DID THESE COME FROM?' Carol screams, holding her skirt up. 'GO ON SIMON...TELL THEM...'

'She's a lying whore,' Simon says, changing tact to wave a disdainful hand.

Carol snaps and rushes at him. Rage exploding as she scratches at his face. Simon goes back into his group. Frankie grabs at Carol trying to pull her back but finds a rifle butt slamming into his back as Maddox wades in.

The woman with the bruise on her neck flies past Blowers. Silent with tears streaming down her cheeks but she goes for Frankie as he drops from being hit by Maddox. Hard hits delivered by bunched fists that slam into Frankie's head who roars and pushes out, sending her flying. Blowers goes in, booting him down to the ground. Chaos breaks out. Women rushing in to swing hits and punches at the men and women who abused them. Children scream in fear. Women screech. Men bellow.

Dave and Mo arrive first. Both of them sprinting past the windows in the café to turn hard through the doorway and through the terrace to the soft sand.

'ENOUGH,' Blowers shouts, grabbing people to pull them away.

'Cunt,' Carol seethes. She and Sarah vent their rage on Simon and Frankie. Kicking, hitting, spitting and raking faces with sharp nails. A woman tries hitting at Carol but gets pulled back by Maddox.

Dave and Mo come to a stop. Both unsure of what to do and seeing Maddox, Blowers and Roy trying to stop a big fight already clearly underway.

'BLOWERS?' Howie's voice as he runs ahead of the others through the café. He double takes through the windows and comes out after Dave and Mo to plough in with the instinct to stop anyone throwing punches.

The rest come through. The whole team pouring into the sand school as they work to split the group and separate people attacking each other.

'I'LL KILL YOU,' Carol's rage increases, pushing past Marcy to kick at Simon.

'Enough,' Marcy shouts, trying to push her away. 'Blinky...give me a hand...'

'HE RAPED ME...HE RAPED ME...' Carol screams the words over and again, becoming wilder in her fury but within that rage she spots the pistol on Marcy's hip. A gun. A gun right there. Without thinking and without thought she snatches to pull it out. Marcy screams out to grab her hands.

'DOWN DOWN DOWN,' Dave spots the gun in the woman's hands.

A desperate struggle. The pistol held by Carol as Marcy tries to stay away from the front but wrestle it back. Fingers and thumbs yanking at the pistol that knock the safety from on to off. Carol gets to the trigger and yanks hard with a gunshot that booms to roll round under the corrugated iron roof.

Simon screams out from the bullet slamming into his stomach. Blinky grabs Carol's hair to yank her back as Marcy plucks the gun from her hands. Everyone else falls silent. Clarence moves in. Dave and Mo with both pistols drawn at seeing the woman holding the gun and hearing the shot.

Control is gained in that instant. Chests heaving for air. Sweat pouring down faces. Frank shakes from head to toe. Foolishly having followed the others as they ran in response to Blowers asking for help.

'What's going on?' Howie asks, staring round and trying to take it in.

'That woman,' Blowers says, pointing at Carol still pinned down by Blinky, 'and...the other one...'

'This one,' Maddox says, standing a few metres away with Sarah, the girl with the bruise on her neck. 'They said they were raped for food,' Maddox says.

'THEY DID,' Carol screams from under Blinky. 'THEY-DIDTHEYDIDTHEYDID...' she thrashes wildly, bucking and fighting to get free.

Simon shouts out, writhing in agony from the gunshot in his stomach. Frankie sits up nursing a broken nose. Others clutch heads or stay down with wild eyes now full of fear and terror.

'Jesus,' Howie mutters, 'right...so who did what to who?'

'Shush,' Marcy tries calming the woman pinned down by Blinky. 'Please...stop shouting...we'll help you but you've got to calm down...'

'Don't listen to 'em,' Frankie says, his voice nasal and muffled through his hands dripping blood.

'They broke my finger,' Frank exclaims, trying to hold his hand out.

'Shut up, Frank...they shot Simon,' a woman shouts.

'We didn't shoot him,' Marcy says.

'And they broke my nose,' Frankie wails.

'What happened?' Maddox asks Sarah quietly, drawing her away to the side.

She gasps for air, breathless from attacking the others and worn out from lack of food, sunlight and living in abject fear for so many days.

'Hey,' Paula says, moving to Maddox's side. 'What happened?'

'I've got this,' Maddox tells Paula.

'They…' Sarah says, hesitant and quavering. 'They…we were all here when it happened…saw it on telly and…Frank…I mean this is his…I work here, like in the bar. Carol too…place was busy but… like people saw the news and went home but Frank said we had to stay and work then Simon got here and said it was everywhere and…and Frank made everyone stay…'

'Okay,' Paula and Maddox say at the same time.

'Fucking liars,' Frankie mutters, 'FUCKING LIARS…'

'Shut up,' Howie tells him.

'Like…like we stayed and…' Sarah swallows and draws breath, her voice settling as she speaks. 'Like Frank's mates, that lot and their wives were eating and drinking…the rest of just hung round cos we couldn't go nowhere. Simon said they were in the town… Frank wouldn't let anyone go out and…it went on for days and…we said about the horses but Frank wouldn't let anyone open a door or…or even like move a curtain. We heard the horses. It was…so bad…and…'

'Don't listen to her,' Frank says weakly. 'Lying bitch…'

'Keep going,' Paula says.

'What happened?' Maddox asks.

Sarah straightens, emboldened by talking and having people with guns listen and speak calmly. Like the police are here, the army, the authorities.

'They got drunk,' she says, louder and firmer now. 'Every night. Got pissed up…played games and…' she swallows. 'Got worse. We was hungry. Kids needed food but Frank said we had to work for it. Frankie said it was his food and we had to clean and make meals… me and Carol had to stand behind the bar…got the kids doing it too. Made the kids pull pints when they should be sleepin'. Woke the kids up when they got pissed…started groping us…laughing like a joke. Carol got angry and slapped Frankie for touchin' her up. Frankie walloped her didn't he. He smacked her in the mouth... then he fucked her...'

'LIAR...'

'Raped her,' Sarah says, glaring at Frankie. 'In the bar in front of everyone...made me watch...then Simon had a go...' the words carry dull and clear through the open space of the sand school. Every pair of ears listening. Even Carol goes silent to hang off the words.

'Kept doing it,' Sarah continues. 'Had to do it for food. Had to do it for a drink. Wouldn't let us wash. Wouldn't let us go out...food ran out but they were too scared to go outside...made me and Carol go out for the foal and told us they'd kill the kids if we didn't come back...'

Silence. An absence of noise save for sound of breathing. Sarah shuffles to smooth her hair back with an act that shows the bruise on her neck.

'Love bites,' she says to Paula and Maddox. 'Frankie likes biting...' she tugs her arms free from the long sleeves to show her inner arms covered in the same marks then turns round as she pulls her top up to show red gauge marks up her back. 'Frank's wife with a crop...'

'You ungrateful little bitch,' a woman with once bleached blond hair screeches.

Sarah pulls her top down and faces the group. Silent and watchful, hurt and afraid yet with courage starting to show. 'Can I have a gun please?'

Paula swallows and looks away. Howie blinks and looks round.

'I'd like a gun please,' Sarah says politely, forcing her tone to stay calm but the tremble shows in her body. 'You can have it back...I won't nick it or anything...'

'Point them out,' Howie says so darkly it makes everyone else stiffen.

'Frank, Frankie...Simon...' Sarah names then in turn. Each

shouting protests that she's a liar, that she's a bitch, that she stole money, food, made it up and was jealous.

Nineteen in the group including Frank. Six are pointed out, leaving thirteen sullen, filthy starving others.

'You got vehicles here?' Howie asks.

'Out the back,' Sarah says.

'Blinky, let her up now,' Paula calls over.

Carol rises to her feet. The rage vented enough for sense of mind to return. She stands shaken, pale and drawn. Blinky stays close, unobtrusive but watchful.

'Take the vehicles, head south to Fort Spitbank...do you know it?' Howie asks.

'I do,' another woman says, an older woman within the thirteen.

'Can you find it from here?' Paula asks.

'I can.'

'Is that true? What that woman said?' Howie asks her.

'All of it,' the older woman says. 'Sarah and Carol got it worse but...we all...' she breaks off with a choking sob.

'Paula, take these people outside. Find the vehicles and get them away. Everyone else outside apart from Dave...'

'Howie,' Marcy says.

'Now, Marcy...' Howie says quietly.

'Come on,' Paula says, 'get them out.'

Clarence pauses at the door with a pained look as he goes to say something then thinks better of it and walks out. The team glance back through the windows. Seeing Howie standing over the six with Marcy a few feet away and Dave behind them both.

As the sound of the others recedes, so the sand school goes quiet. The six look to each other. Four men. Two women. Each named. Each identified. Each highlighted for the acts they did.

'Go,' Howie says to Marcy.

'Let me,' she says, pulling her pistol from the holster. The six gibber and beg, they plead and cry. Marcy doesn't want to do it.

She doesn't want to be here but she's killed before. She's taken life. There is sin marking her soul and for that she will keep Howie's clean.

'You will leave,' Howie says with a cold finality. She holsters and walks to the door and through to the café with a glance through the window to see Howie drawing his pistol as the six cry out in fear.

Paula turns to see Marcy coming out and stopping to squint from the bright sun. The rest stop and look round. A second of silence that stretches forever. One shot rings out followed by five quick and precise and in that they all know Howie fired once and Dave the rest.

Tears stream down cheeks. Lips tremble. Cookey wipes his eyes and wishes they were back in the fort. Charlie at his side grim faced. Blowers and Maddox staring down at the ground. Clarence's great head bowed with a big hand on the back of his neck. Paula puts a hand on his shoulder knowing this is true torture for his pure morals.

Howie comes out. His face dark and unreadable. A mask. Someone they don't know but he is the man who leads them. Dave behind him. Devoid as ever.

'Get them away from here, Charlie, take what you need. Everyone else drink...it's hot...'

'Yes, Sir,' Charlie says, moving off.

'Sir,' Blowers says.

Clarence stands straight, his rifle brought over the crook of his elbows, 'yes, Sir,' he says deep and respectful.

Paula locks eyes on Howie. Unsure of what to say but knowing she could never have done what he just did. In the end she does as the others and nods as she walks on, 'yes, Sir.'

CHAPTER EIGHTEEN

Tension can be broken with jokes. A bad atmosphere can be lifted with a silly comment and a facial expression pulled in the right way. A mood can be changed.

Not this mood though. This mood is different. It is pensive, strained and even Cookey stays silent.

It didn't take long for the people to go. They couldn't get away fast enough. Some were immensely thankful to Paula, the lads, Roy and Clarence. Others were clearly shell-shocked, traumatised and rendered silent by everything that had happened. Some glanced at Howie and Dave with looks of fear. Howie stayed quiet too. He took a smoke from Nick and stood away. Darker and more brooding than ever.

Charlie got what she needed for Jess. A new saddle, reins, spares of everything, stirrups, bags of feed, and nets for hanging straw. The others helped carry and load.

Now they sit once more in the hot Saxon, knees to knees, shoulders to shoulders. Rifles between legs. Bags, axes and hand-weapons stashed wherever they will fit.

'New saddle looks good, Charlie,' Nick says, breaking the silence in the Saxon.

'Yes,' she says quickly, smiling down the Saxon at him, 'much better now. Far less painful on my posterior.'

'Wish I was a saddle,' Cookey quips, earning a few grateful smiles as Maddox tuts softly and looks up.

'Loads of different ones,' Nick says, 'Saddles I mean...in that shop.'

'There are, yes,' Charlie says. 'Some for jumping, riding, hacking...hunting then of course for dressage and yes, there are literally hundreds of different things that go on a horse.'

'Oh,' Nick says, nodding with interest as Marcy worries. She wants to say something and her connection with Howie is such that from all of them, she *can* say something. Except the feel of the air stops her. After Howie came out it was like he had changed. He wasn't her Howie. He was *Mr Howie.* The man in charge that was suddenly unapproachable with a distance between him and everyone else. She looks over at the strands of dark curly hair plastered to his scalp from the sweat they all suffer, and that doesn't help things either. The fucking heat. The incessant relentless pressure bearing down that makes the air that feel thick, hot and full of moisture. It has to break soon. Another storm will come. Maybe that's a good thing. Like cleansing.

'Do the right thing.' Maddox mutters as though talking to himself but clear enough for everyone to hear. Blowers glares at him, wanting more than ever to drag the twat out and smash his face in.

'S'hot,' Maddox says with wince, shifting in his seat. Tops cling to bodies. Heat builds in crevices. Feet are too hot in boots and socks. Hands feel greasy, hair the same. Like they'll never be clean again. 'You got everything you needed then, Charlie?' Maddox asks.

'I did, thank you,' Charlie says, knowing she has to reply but sensing, the same as everyone else, that something else is at play.

'That's good,' Maddox says casually, even adding a thoughtful nod. 'And we got those people away,' he adds, still nodding. 'That's good too.'

Blowers clenches his jaw. Nick stares down and across at Marcy's knee as she looks to Maddox then past him to Charlie and Blinky.

'Hey Mo,' Maddox says with a sudden smile, that easy smile too, his nice one, his charming relaxed smile that catches Mo off guard for a second. The lad turns in response to a voice he knows so well. 'Remember that girl?' Maddox asks then tuts, 'what was her name? Oh yes, Carla...remember her?'

Mo's face darkens. His eyes grow hard. His whole body stiffens as Dave watches him closely.

'That was a mess,' Maddox says, lifting his eyebrows as though reminiscing. 'You tell everyone what happened with her?'

'Do not talk to Mohammed,' Dave says dully.

'Fair enough,' Maddox says with his hands splayed open. 'Sorry, I forgot,' he turns to look at Charlie, then at Blinky. 'So this girl Carla right...'

'Stop,' Mo says.

'Nah it's funny,' Maddox says with charm dripping from his voice. 'This girl Clara fancied Mo like mad. Like really fancied him...this was about a year ago...'

They shouldn't listen. They can all see Mo is uncomfortable but Maddox, despite only being nineteen years old, is a master at this. He can adapt when he needs to, he can put people at ease.

'So she is *in love*,' Maddox says with a chuckle. 'Completely infatuated with Mo Mo. She was like fourteen or something? A couple of years younger than Mo anyway. Mo's nice to her, he's a good kid and doesn't flirt with her or anything but then Mo never struggled with girls,' he adds with a smile. 'So this Clara. She wants to be everywhere Mo is, at the park, at the places we hang out...and it get worse. She gets obsessed with him. The girl doesn't leave him alone...'

Mo goes to say something but the look from Dave instantly

reminds him of the path he chose. Composure is gained with cold control that centres the youth as he releases the anger and turns to look out the open back doors.

'So Clara really loses it but she can't be with Mo Mo because she's too young but she can't handle that rejection. She's pretty, get's loads of attention from boys but Mo doesn't want to know. She's thinking *what the fuck?*' Maddox even mimics a female voice, high-pitched and chavvy that makes Blinky smile as he continues. 'She tries everything to get his attention and in the end Mo starts avoiding her... so what does she do?' Maddox looks round with a smile that fades. 'She says he raped her...'

Mo stares out the back doors as Clarence stiffens in the front seat next to Howie. His huge hands balling into fists. That awful tension mounts. The mood so thick you could scoop it out.

'Mo didn't do that,' Maddox says quickly, holding his hands out to hold their attention. 'Anyone who knows Mo knows he would never do that...but she said it...she told her mate who believed her... whole estate went into meltdown. Gangs out looking for Mo...filth got involved but anyway, she retracted and it was all sorted before any damage was done...'

Silence again as Maddox sits back without a flicker of expression at the point he just scored.

'Point is, people lie,' Maddox says, blunt and hard as he rams that point home. 'What's that thing?' he looks round as though expecting an answer. 'That soldiers thing? The Geneva Code?'

'Stop,' Blowers says through gritted teeth.

'You gonna break my fingers if I don't?'

Maddox scores twice. Two nil with deft motion and perfect delivery. Every single one of them knows that to shout him down or threaten him is exactly what he wants. He's itching for it. Waiting for it. Wanting it.

'Brave man after the fact,' Clarence's voice rolls down the Saxon, full of depth and bass. The big man stares forward. His whole body still and poised.

Two one.

Maddox in the lead and he concedes the score with a shrug as though he's not bothered. Not bothered at all.

The front seat groans as Clarence twists round. His huge right arm stretching over the back of the seats to aid his movement. His enormous shoulders hindering his own motion. 'You think they lied?' he asks, looking at Maddox. 'Why didn't you say something?'

'I'm just a grunt. Not my place...'

'Then it's not your place now,' Clarence says the second Maddox replies. 'So shut up...'

Two all but it was a dirty goal and they all know it.

The silence comes back. A silence filled with the noise of the big tyres on the road. The chassis vibrating. The air rushing past outside. The engine from the front. The noise of Roy's engine behind them heard through the open doors. Noise everywhere but silent it remains with a lack of conversation. A day of days and it isn't over yet. Another town lies ahead.

'Hydrate,' Dave says.

They hydrate. They drink water and Lucozade. They drink water until their bellies slosh but knowing that water will soon leak from pores and leave them gasping with thirst. Skin becomes sore and irritated from constant wiping and chafing. Hair stays slick to heads. The day becomes merciless, unforgiving and just long. It's made worse by the memory of the night before and the fort as they saw it yesterday. Of the food they ate, of the people smiling and being nice. At being in the back garden laughing and joking. At feeling clean.

'*Mr Howie, Reginald here. Take the next junction off the motorway. That leads to a large roundabout. Stay on the main road ahead. It feeds into the town centre. The sports shop we need is on our way in...I believe it is on a side street full of specialist stores on our right side.*'

'*Yep, thanks.*'

Howie's curt voice transmits through the speakers into Roy's van. Reginald stares at the radio with his mind processing those hundreds of strands of thoughts. Paula told him what happened when she got back in. Reginald was shocked but did not show it. Instead, he asked questions to understand precisely what happened. Who said what? Who did what? How many people were there? What did they look like? What did the place look like? What did Howie say? What did Maddox say? Did anyone try and stop Mr Howie? Paula and Roy answered the questions, both of them familiar with Reginald and his need for the minutia of details.

'I bet the atmosphere in there is awful,' Paula mutters from the front.

Reginald raises questions in his mind while countering with answers that bring more questions. Two things stand out. No, three things. The first is Charlie breaking the finger. The second is the summary execution. The third, and the most worrying, is that Maddox will use those things to undermine the group from within. Mr Howie will not release Maddox. Maddox is here against his will so it is in Maddox's interests to be such a proverbial pain in the side the others want him gone. He lifts the radio back to his mouth and thinks as he hovers his thumb over the button. A second passes. Another goes spinning by to become part of the history of humanity. A decision made. This group must retain unity. Above all else they must be unified.

'*Reginald here chaps,*' a ripple in the Saxon from the unexpected transmission and the tone of Reginald's voice so carefully toned. '*How is everyone?*' Reginald asks the radio, his mind running clear. '*Now if I may, I would like to offer my opinion one what you may now be thinking was an act of assault and the summary execution of six people. One could be mistaken to assume the actions you took were beyond that of acceptance in normal society...I say, would you like me to pause here so Charlie can translate?*'

Humourless smiles in the Saxon as Charlie blushes lightly and rolls her eyes.

'Reginald said we might think we did something everyone else would say was wrong. Is that correct. Reginald?'

'Indeed, Charlie. Societies are bound by consequences of actions. From simply dropping litter to committing acts of murder. Our societies told us what was acceptable and what was not and we sought to punish those who broke our laws. But one must keep in mind that law and order are gone. Society as we knew it no longer exists. As I understand it, those people used their physical size to control others and in a very short space of time they were committing morally abhorrent crimes. That was a choice. Those people chose to do those actions. Frank and his associates chose to commit very serious and grave offences against others, rape, torture, starvation and forced servitude and they would only ever have been stopped when someone more powerful stopped him. In this case it was first Charlie who stood up to him by showing a woman is not merely a sexual object to be leered at, and then by Blowers, Maddox and Roy taking control and of course then the actions by Mr Howie. Indeed, it was the only appropriate course of action to take. It was necessary and proportionate to the situation. Thirteen people will now know someone stopped a very bad thing happening. Those thirteen will tell other people and in a way that brings back consequences to actions. It tells others there are good people who will step in and stop tyrants. I dislike trite clichés, you know I do, but I am proud of Charlie for what she did and I am equally proud for the actions of the others ...so come on now. Lift those heads eh? You've none of you done a thing wrong...Reginald out.'

Three two. Reginald wins.

'WHAT THE HELL,' Heather says, staring at the radio as she sits with a map spread open on her lap and Paco holding the list up for her to read. 'Did you hear that?'

Paco doesn't say if he heard it. He holds the list Heather told him to hold and watches her closely.

'Jesus,' Heather mutters. 'It's like every half hour with that lot,' she mutters then sips from her bottle of Lucozade.

'Zade...'

'Huh? Oh you want some?'

'Zade,' Paco says.

'It is nice isn't it? I'll hold that...have some of mine...what now?' she looks up at the flotilla of vehicles heading towards her. A liveried van advertising *Big Frank's Equestrian Centre* in the lead that slows on seeing the Toyota with the two front doors open.

The van slows to a crawl. An older woman staring out through the windscreen. Sarah sits next to her, looking across to Heather staring at them and a big man guzzling from a bottle of Lucozade, his head slowly tilting back as he necks the lot with big gulps.

The van stops. Heather stares up. The women stare down.

'Zade...'

'You've got one...Hi,' Heather says. 'I heard on the radio...'

'Eh?' the woman asks, showing immediate concern at the sight of the assault rifle on the back seat.

'Zade...'

'You've got one...Mr Howie?' Heather asks.

'I'm not Mr Howie,' the woman says. 'We just met him.'

'Zade...'

'Paco, you've got one...have you finished it? You greedy sod. Hang on I'll get another one in a minute,' she rolls her eyes and looks up at the women in the van. 'No I meant I heard on our radio...I'm with Mr Howie...' Heather says, holding her radio up to show them. 'They said thirteen of you got away?'

'Oh,' the woman says, clearly relieved. 'Er yeah...they said to head for the fort?'

'Yep, Fort Spitbank. You know where it is?'

'We do...'

'Zade.'

'In a minute, Paco.'

'Er, we'll be off then.'

'Yep, okay. Er...safe drive?' Heather suggests, unsure on how you end a conversation with people that have apparently been held in forced servitude in a horse place.

'Zade...'

'Is that Paco Maguire?' the woman asks, about to drive off but holding still for another second.

'No,' Heather says.

'Oh.'

'Yes it is,' Heather says, unsure of why she lied and now realising she looks really stupid for contradicting herself.

'Oh...er...bye then,' the woman pulls away.

'Zade...'

CHAPTER NINETEEN

They come to a stop at the edge of the town. The High Street stretches away before them. Long and straight for hundreds of metres. A wide road with broad pavements on both sides and the sleek fronted tinted plate glass offices give the impression of affluence and wealth. Wrought iron benches. Trees in bloom with raised flowerbeds set in brick built ornamental cubes dotted along the road.

This town had money. A direct train line into London placed it firmly on the commuter belt, which attracted wealthy city folk who demanded decent services, designer shops and boutique stores. A blend of urbanised rurality where the city meets the country.

Now it looks foreboding with windows like eyes that stare down and doors that hang open like mouths ready to spew the infected at them.

'On foot from here,' Howie says, staring through the windscreen to the buildings ahead. 'Marcy, you drive the Saxon. Charlie on Jess...' he pauses to press the button on his radio. *'Paula, we're on foot from here. You drive Roy's van...'*

So it begins. The venturing into another town seemingly empty and devoid of life. A place that holds the things they need but a place that holds the greatest threats too. Reginald activates his screen to get the camera feeds running, tutting at the horsebox blocking half the view. Marcy clambers over the seats to take Howie's vacated seat as everyone else jumps down and moves out.

Blowers switches into his role with a slow turn as he walks away from the Saxon and takes stock of the ground. The objective is to proceed up this road and find the side street then locate the archery sports place Roy needs. He looks up at the high buildings and the flats above the shops. He takes in the gaps between the buildings and the width of the road. A wide street like this is both good and bad. It gives greater room for manoeuvre but it also leaves them open to be flanked or encircled and that risk will only increase the deeper into the town they go.

Howie and Clarence take point while they wait for Charlie. Blowers motions to Nick and Blinky to take the offside of the vehicles. Cookey and Mo the nearside. He motions for Roy to go for the rear and cover Charlie while she leads Jess out already fitted with the new saddle.

'Windows, doors…those gaps…keep turning and watching,' he says to Maddox, his voice low and muted.

Jess comes out from the horsebox too fast. Her feet clanging the ramp dropped onto the road that sends a metallic thump echoing up the street. A slight rise in heart rates and a tensing of muscles in preparation from a noise that will signal where they are.

The great horse skitters and tosses her head. Glad to be free from the confines of the horsebox and now taking in the smells of this new place. Charlie soothes her long nose, reading the reactions as Jess starts to settle.

As Charlie mounts and settles into the new saddle so she smiles at the input Dave had during the saddle selection process. Which involved Dave staring for about ten seconds before telling her to use *that one*. She complied of course and quickly understood why. It was the D rings and straps that enabled pouches to be fitted behind the saddle that could be filled with magazines. It was the strap at the front too that Dave used to attach another pistol holster and the tethers, rings and hooks that were to be used to hold the axe in place. He even gave her another pistol.

'Your sidearm remains with you. This one remains with the saddle. You will service and take responsibility for both.'

'Yes, Dave,' she answered quickly, watching him work to get the saddle how he felt it should be.

Now she twitches the reins and turns in a wide circle to see how Jess moves on the surface of the road. Another twitch, a click of her tongue and she moves on past the horsebox and Roy's van to clip clop up past the Saxon and a grinning Marcy waving at her while feeling like a sheriff from a western.

'On point, not too far,' Howie says, his dark eyes still as brooding as before. Reginald's words settled everyone else and helped lift the awful tension but not for Howie who has stayed as quiet as before.

'Sir,' Charlie says, geeing on to gain distance out the front.

Blowers stands ready, his rifle now not in the crook of his arms but held ready to fire. His left hand on the underside handguard, his right hand on the pistol grip with the forefinger held across the trigger guard and the barrel aimed down.

Maddox stands next to him. Still sullen, still frustrated, angry, pissed off, hot, fed-up and hating every second of being with these people. His mind keeps flitting back to Lenski, the fort, the crews now dead, the crews still alive, the six people Howie killed and a hundred other things.

'Move out...Charlie, Meredith coming up to you.'

The procession starts. Charlie out front. Howie and Clarence behind her. Dave behind them. Nick and Blinky on one side. Cookey and Mo on the other. All of them staggered to give the best view. Rifles held tight. Bags on backs. Axes wedged down. Hand weapons ready to be drawn.

The signs of damage from the storms are almost non-existent. A few tiles lie broken in the road. A glass window cracked but held in place. Further they go into the town but slowly, carefully. A chimney stack from an old dwelling that survived the bombings raids of the Luftwaffe lies almost intact on the pavement. Nick cranes his neck trying to see where it came from.

'*Body here...looks old,*' Charlie's voice through the radio. They all look forward to see her indicating off to the right side before trotting on.

'*My team, go out wider from the vehicles,*' Blowers transmits, earning a look round from Clarence and Dave. '*Vehicles engines too loud this close,*' Blowers says in way of explanation. Clarence gives a thumbs up. Dave shows no reaction but walks on.

Minutes go by. Sweat drips down cheeks and foreheads. A heat shimmer rests above the road at an ever-steady distance. The sunlight gleams from the windows still intact. Blowers notices a lot of the windows at the this end are unbroken. A few doors smashed in here and there but the town looks good considering some of the hell-holes they've seen. This is obviously the commercial centre and he guesses that a Friday night wouldn't have that many people here. The night-life must be centred somewhere else and the residential dwellings with be further out too.

'*Mr Howie, the road bends to the right,*' Charlie says into their ears. '*I think that must be the side road Reginald saw on the map.*'

'*What's ahead?*' Howie asks through the radio.

'*Precinct area, Mr Howie...there is a small road going left that looks like it feeds to the back of the shops and away from the centre.*'

'*Understood, hold that junction until we get closer.*'

'*Reginald here, yes yes I do see that now. It had the appearance of a side road on the map but on checking the street atlas on a closer scale I can in fact see it is a continuation of the main High Street.*'

'*Roger,*' Howie says. No funny comments, no quip, no questions either. Just a dull hard voice that makes Nick and Cookey look to Blowers who stares stoically ahead.

Blowers sees the layout as described by Charlie. A service road to the left just wide enough for a delivery lorry. The main road bears right down a slight hill to the specialist stores while ahead lies a wide plaza with signs forbidding vehicular traffic. Brand names of stores over doors and windows. Strewn litter picked up by the rainwater then dumped in gulleys and dips.

'Charlie, go into that precinct, we'll go right down the road... Blowers, when we find the sports shop put one of your team at the rear to watch the road we came up and the precinct...'

'Roger, Roy's at the rear now, Boss,' Blowers transmits.

Charlie moves on and away at a steady pace. Her eyes scanning left, right and ahead. Her hearing straining to detect anything other than the engines and the sound of Jess's feet. Meredith runs ahead with her nose down to the ground following trails left by the infected as they moved about. They were here. The things moved here. Many of them but the tracks are too many and varied for even her nose to discern clearly.

Blowers scowls at the sensation of being watched. His hard eyes flick constantly to the windows above them as though ready to see someone pulling back or the motion of a figure moving.

The procession follows the sweep to the right, feeling the slight decline of the road. Clarence stays at Howie's side. Sensing the need to give comfort by closeness.

'There,' Howie says, pointing ahead to a double fronted store. A set of doors in the middle with huge plate glass windows either side. The right side window smashed in with a gaping hole, but then who wouldn't break into a place with posters of crossbows in the window when the world is falling down?

'Got it,' Clarence says, his manner all business as he matches Howie's curtness and solidity of tone.

'Hold,' Howie says into his radio, 'Dave and Mo upfront, building clearance.'

Blowers turns to see Mo running up from his position at the rear nearside. 'Take Mo's position,' he tells Maddox.

Maddox stares at him then at Mo. A roll of his eyes. A reluctance in his bearing as he strolls slowly down to Mo's position, giving Cookey a smirk as he passes.

'Charlie, you okay?'

'Fine, Mr Howie. All quiet.'

'Charlie, it's Paula. Is that shopping centre open?'

'Yes it is, doors are smashed in.'

'Howie, we can use that for supplies,' Paula says.

'Yep, we'll get this done first...'

'Boss, it's Blowers. You okay if we turn the engines off? Can't hear a thing over them.'

'You don't need to ask, Blowers. Do as you see fit.'

The engines stop. A silence settles broken by the ticks and clunks of vehicles cooling as they come to settle. Dave and Mo go forward. Rifles slung. Pistols drawn and held double handed as they work towards the front of the shop. Blowers wipes the sweat from his forehead and stretches his back from the uncomfortable sensation of his wet top clinging to his body. As he turns he spots Maddox reading a poster in a window. His rifle held in one hand at his side.

'Get your fucking eyes on,' Blowers hisses into his radio. Maddox turns his head slowly then goes back to reading the poster. 'Roy, you got the back?' Blowers asks, furious at the gap in the defences.

'I have...Maddox, stop staring at that window...' Roy says.

Maddox stares at the window. Refusing to budge or turn. Refusing the order. Blowers seethes but stays where he is and denies the urge to run over and batter the twat up the street. He glances down to Clarence whose face shows exactly what he thinks. Howie watches the building as Dave and Mo test the door then start climbing through the window.

Blowers scans and watches, turning infrequently to see Maddox staring about as though bored. He knows Maddox is smart and knows this is just a show but the irritation is there. The refusal to do what everyone else is doing. They only stay alive by everyone doing their part. That's what soldiering is. It's a machine where the total is greater than the sum of it's parts.

Everyone else feels the same irritation. Cookey watches his mate. Nick, on the other side of the vehicle, tuts softly and wishes for a few minutes alone with Maddox. Blinky scowls. She wasn't part of whatever Maddox did before but she can see the effect he's having on the team and that's shit. He needs a kicking. She'll do it with pleasure.

'Silly boy,' Paula mutters, wincing at the look of fury on Blowers' face.

'Maddox?' Reginald enquires softly.

'Yep,' she replies. 'Only one way this will end if he keeps pushing Blowers like that.'

'Indeed,' Reginald says, mopping his brown with a handkerchief despite the air-conditioning only having been off for a few minutes.

'Sooner the better too if you ask me,' she adds.

'Ground floor clear, Mr Howie,' Mo says through the radio.

'Okay. Both of you come out.'

Only then does Howie turn to look down past Blowers to Maddox still reading posters in windows and looking everywhere but where he should be. Clarence looks too but whereas Howie hides any reaction Clarence's face says it all with an expression of utter distaste.

'Pah,' Mo sputters coming out the window brushing his hands over his face as he gets over the sill into the street. 'Cobwebs,' he says, trying to pluck invisible strands from his skin.

'Blowers, your team up to Charlie. Have a look at that shopping centre...Roy? Get what you need. Marcy, Paula, you hang on here until Blowers reports back. Mo, back in your team.'

'Sir,' Mo says, still pulling webs from his face. 'They get you?' he asks Dave coming out the window behind him.

'No,' Dave says.

'Why not?' Mo asks as Blowers stares on wondering how the hell Mo can talk so casually to Dave.

'Spiders are scared of me,' Dave says as flat and dull as ever.

'Really?' Mo asks, a deadly killer in training and a gifted soldier but still as gullible as he is young.

'Dave just made a joke,' Cookey whispers.

'I know,' Nick whispers from the other side of the Saxon.

'My team on me,' Blowers orders. 'Maddox, you too.'

The team filter off to re-group behind the horse-box as Roy walks down tutting and shaking his head at Maddox then sharing a pained look with Blowers. 'Long day,' he mutters.

'Say that again,' Blowers replies, unaware that is the first small talk he has exchanged with Roy.

'You're giving them more freedom,' Clarence says quietly once Blowers' team is out of earshot.

'Blowers knows what he's doing,' Howie says.

'You okay?' Clarence asks.

Howie nods then shrugs and nods again, 'yeah...'

'Enjoy your new crossbow, Roy,' Blinky says through the radio.

'It's not a bloody cross...' Roy snaps as he realises the joke within the words and looks up to see Blinky walking backwards grinning widely while showing him a middle finger. *'Very funny... Patricia,'* Roy transmits, smiling back at her.

Clarence tracks the joke shared then looks again at Howie as he senses there is a smarter plan underway. None of them ever make jokes with Roy but Blinky just did and the conversations between Roy and Blowers have been better today too. Maddox has become a common problem. A difficulty they can all share and in that the unity grows tighter. Is Howie intending that or is it by accident?

'I'll be as quick as I can,' Roy says, rushing towards the broken window as Marcy and Paula climb out from their vehicles and walk down.

'Take your time,' Howie says.

BLINKY TURNS BACK, grinning and chuckling as she falls in with the others. She chuckles again, sighs, looks round and then over at Maddox. 'You're a cunt.'

'What?' Maddox says, surprised at the suddenness and the way she said it.

'Selfish cunt...like a total fucking chopper. You're letting the team down, stop being a cunt.'

'Well said,' Cookey says.

'Fact,' Nick says.

'I'm not in your team.'

'You are. You're here,' Blinky says. 'This is the team and you're in it...I swear, Maddox. If someone gets hurts cos you're being a bellend I'll fuck you up...'

'I'll keep that in mind,' Maddox replies

'These are my mates,' Blinky says, staring past Cookey and Nick to Maddox. 'You don't fuck about out here, Maddox. You got an issue then deal with it off the pitch...'

'Pitch?' Maddox sneers.

'I'll fuck you up you snotty cunt...'

'Enough, focus,' Blowers says.

Blinky faces forward. The team captain just gave an order and orders are followed. She'll dig him later when no one is looking.

They reach the end of the building line and move across into the pedestrian area bordered by the brand name stores. Charlie waits in the middle on Jess. Smiling at them walking towards her with her rifle butt resting on her right thigh.

'Hey sexy lady,' Cookey calls out.

'Hello, Cookey,' Charlie says, already grinning at him.

'I was talking to Jess but hey, Charlie, you okay?'

'You fancy my horse?'

'Your horse is fit,' Cookey says.

'How's Mr Howie?' Charlie asks, the smile easing a little as she speaks.

'Quiet,' Nick says, looking back towards the road. 'Anything here?'

'Nothing, Meredith keeps sniffing but...I've got that horrible sensation of being watched,' she whispers with a shudder. 'Most unsettling.'

'Most unsettling,' Cookey says.

'It is,' Charlie says.

'I know,' Cookey says, nodding seriously, 'it is most unsettling... anyway, so...' he looks round the street then at Maddox. 'Mate, seriously...you got to stop being like that.'

'Like what?'

'All awkward and sulky and shit. Grow up...we're here, we've got to do it so...'

'I do not want to be here. I do not like you. I do not like any of you.'

'Maddox,' Cookey says, looking at him earnestly, 'speak your mind and let it out...'

'What?'

'Do you want a hug?'

'What?'

'You are a very angry man aren't you, yes? An angry man? Are you an angry man?' Cookey asks, his voice getting higher in tone. 'Bit angry yes? Little bit angry?'

Maddox sneers, shakes his head and looks away with cool disdain.

'Wanna hug? Wanna huggy poos? Wanna man cuddle? Wanna a reacharound from Blowers?'

'Twat,' Blowers laughs as the others chuckle and grin.

'Wanna do bumming? Wanna do manhugging? Wanna do...'

'Fuck off,' Maddox snaps.

'Ah,' Cookey cheers, seeing the twitch at the corner of Maddox mouth. 'Made you smile made you care made you lose your underwear...'

'What the fuck?' Nick asks, laughing at him.

'I ain't smiling,' Maddox says, suppressing the smile.

'You did smile.'

'I did not smile.'

'You did. I saw it. You smiled...you smiled when I said bumming which means you want some willy...ooh you look all angry now...'

'Keep going,' Maddox says quietly, staring hard with a tone that Mo knows is his pre-cursor to fighting. Mo stiffens, sliding his right foot back as his head cocks an inch to the side.

'He's getting all naughty,' Cookey says, sensing the mood drop and seeing the threat but having precisely no concern at either. 'Mr Howie is a good man and he's having a bad day...you say anything to him again and...'

'You all keep making threats,' Maddox says, looking round at them all. 'Someone do it then...someone beat me...give me a kicking...come on? I'm right here?' his tone stays calm and controlled as he deflects the subtle aggression back at them.

'Maddox,' Charlie says, as frustrated as everyone else but her voice as respectful and polite as ever. 'Please stop, this is hard enough without...'

'Just get on with it,' Maddox cuts across her words while making a point of looking away as the tension and frustration continue to grow in all of them.

***

'WHAT A SODDING AWFUL HORRIBLE DAY,' Marcy says, walking down to join Howie, Dave and Clarence.

'Isn't it just,' Paula calls out, marching down from the van. 'We've got to do something about Maddox...'

'We are doing something,' Howie says.

'Are we?' Paula asks curtly coming to a stop next to Marcy. 'What's that then?' she demands with a glare at Howie. 'He's disobeying constantly...Blowers is like this far from snapping,' she adds, holding her thumb and forefinger a fraction of an inch apart.

'Like I said, we are doing something,' Howie says.

'What? What are we doing? It's not fair on Blowers to let it get so bad he snaps.'

'What do you suggest then, Paula?' Howie asks with an edge to his voice.

'I don't know, Howie,' Paula retorts.

'Christ,' Clarence groans, rubbing the back of his neck.

'Look I'm sorry,' Paula says, still terse but clearly trying to back-pedal, 'but I hate him...'

'Try sitting in the Saxon with him,' Marcy says. 'Should have heard what he said before Reggie...'

'What?' Paula asks quickly. 'What did he say?'

'Some shit about Mo being accused of rape by a girl that fancied him...' Marcy explains, 'he was making a point that people lie...'

'That's it,' Paula fumes, folding her arms as the steam plumes from her ears. 'Seriously? He actually said that? What did you say? I hope to God one of you told him to shut up.'

'What could we say?' Marcy asks, as bewildered as everyone else. 'Blowers tried but then Maddox asked if they'd break his fingers?'

Paula doesn't reply but lifts her eyebrows in that gesture of hers that suggests she really is not very happy right now.

'I am really not very happy right now,' she tells them.

'It'll come to a head one way or another,' Clarence says heavily after a few seconds of silence.

'We can't leave him at the fort,' Howie says.

'Er, mind if I?' Roy asks, hovering a hand towards the sports shop.

'Yeah carry on mate,' Howie says. 'Listen, we've just got to stick it out with him...' he tells everyone else.

'Yes,' Paula states pointedly.

'Argh,' Roy calls out from inside the sports shop.

'You alright?' Clarence asks as they all turn.

'Cobwebs,' Roy calls out.

'So what next?' Marcy asks, sagging on the spot.

'You look hot,' Howie says.

'I am hot. I'm very hot. I stink and my skin is sore...' she wipes her hand across her forehead to show Howie her glistening hand. 'See that? I'm sweating...I'm hot...my skin is sore and getting dry and we're running about all over the place again...' she stops suddenly with the sudden memory of what Howie did back at the equestrian centre and closes her eyes with a pained look, 'I'm sorry...'

'What for?' Howie asks.

'Moaning...you okay? I mean...you know...after that.'

He shrugs, nonchalant and casual but the flash of darkness is there in his eyes. 'Is what it is.'

'Don't let Maddox get to you...ask Dave to beat the shit out of him. Dave? Will you please beat the shit out of Maddox...'

'No,' Howie says quickly before Dave runs off and commences beating the shit out of Maddox.

'This sounds weird but it's like we all did it,' Paula says quietly, looking at Howie then over at Clarence.

'Did what?' Clarence asks.

'What Howie did...back there...like it feels like I did it but Marcy did it too...like we all did it. Ah, doesn't make any sense.'

'No that's how it feels,' Marcy says before looking back to Howie.

'It's done,' Howie says blasting air out his nose and thereby showing he wishes the conversation to end. 'Reggie? What's next? Why aren't they attacking?'

'I have no idea,' Reginald replies, his hands clasped behind his back as he stares round at the street. 'Truly,' he mutters to himself.

'You think they're here?' Marcy asks.

'Oh undoubtedly. We are under observation as we speak...but by how many and where from I am unable to say. As I explained before I wanted to see if the other side made the connection to our gathering of essential supplies but the lack of opposition at the equestrian centre already disproves that theory.'

'BLOODY COBWEBS,' Roy shouts from inside the shop.

Paula shudders at the thought, glancing at the shop with distaste.

'What's after here then?' Marcy asks, looking at Reginald.

'I would suggest we locate somewhere remote to spend the night while I plan ahead...'

'That is exactly what we need,' Marcy says wistfully. 'Somewhere with a bath so I can lie in cold water for a few hours...'

'Now that,' Paula says. 'is the best idea all day.'

'Boss, it's Blowers, looks all clear up here...'

'BLOODY COBWEBS,' Roy shouts, plucking the strand from his face as he looks up and round for the offending spider that's no doubt growing fat from all the flies also growing fat from all the bodies lying everywhere. An image swims into his mind of an obese fly trapped in a web huffing and puffing with red cheeks as a fat spider waddles towards it. Roy's mind works differently to other peoples. What bothers them does not bother Roy. Zombies do not bother him. He can handle the heat too. He is fit, lean and blessed with an ability to withstand the changes in temperature. He's irritated by Maddox but not to the extent of the others. He feels bad for what Howie did but also knows it was the right thing to do so therefore there is no need to keep thinking about it.

Instead he hovers between that state of utter calm where

nothing in this world affects him, and a state of near on blind panic of knowing he is dying right this second from being infected with the virus.

Of all of them, Roy absorbed the understanding the deepest of all. He never said anything because to give it voice would have seen him drawing his pistol and blowing his own brains out.

Long years of therapy kicked in. The cognitive behaviour therapy asserted itself from the hundreds of hours and many well-meaning therapists that tried, and mostly failed, to ease his fears and obsessions of imminent death. He takes stock of the facts he knows. He uses those facts to reassure himself and just about stave off that panic attack bubbling away under his skin.

It's Marcy that prevents the fear manifesting. Marcy's hair, Marcy's nails, Marcy's skin tone and complexion. Roy doesn't fancy Marcy. Roy can see the attraction for Marcy, who wouldn't? She's stunning but what Roy sees is beyond that. What Roy sees is a woman that has the thing he now apparently has and that woman looks absurdly healthy. Reginald too, in a geeky, stay-indoors and never do any exercise kind of way. Marcy was taken early too which means she's had it for a while, and not only is she not dead but she looks great, and seems perfectly well.

That's it. Just that. That is the dam holding the waters back. The simple fact of Marcy's appearance.

It's a funny world and it's made up of funny people. People who all feel fears and have hopes and dreams the same as everyone else so whatever it takes to get through the day is all that matters.

He nods to himself, takes a deep breath and pushes the panic away. Besides, there is nothing he can do about it and also, there is strength in numbers. Whatever he has got, the others have got too. Clarence, Howie, Dave, Blowers...all of them. And they all look healthy too. Really healthy.

Yep. Keep that dam in place. Stay calm and carry on. Anyway, this is a nice thing, a good thing, he is in a sports shop that specialises in archery supplies.

He looks round the gloomy interior and tuts at the display stands knocked over then tuts again at the cash-register lying open on the floor. Looting a sports shop at the end of the world is fine, it's to be expected in fact, but there's no need to make a mess and why get the till open? For what? To steal money you can't use?

He spots the now empty crossbow section and smiles at the memory of the joke Blinky made. That was nice. Being included in the banter like that. He wouldn't want it all the time. That would be annoying and besides, some people can say the most awful abusive comments and get away with it. Like Cookey and Blinky. If Roy told anyone to go fist themselves it would sound like a real sexual request.

He tuts again at the wire cutters left on the floor that must have been used to snip the security wire holding the crossbows to the display wall. Why leave decent wire cutters behind? He crosses over to pick them up, nodding at the weight and decent craftsmanship of the tool. He'll keep these. You never know when you'll need wire cutters. Actually, they should get more tools, and that hot water idea from earlier too. They should do that. Roy likes working with Nick when they tinker and fix things.

He moves further into the store, spotting the football team shirts and clothing racks. The cricket supplies and then the empty sections where the cricket and baseball bats would have been stored.

'Ah,' he says, seeing the untouched bows left on the display wall. 'Urgh,' he says at the cobweb brushing his face as he walks forward. 'Oh,' he says on seeing within one glance that the bows are all mid-priced low-end quality things.

He picks the first compound bow up and adds another tut at whoever left it strung. Why do that? Just so idiots can come in and pluck the thing a few times and feel like Robin Hood probably.

He picks the next one up, a recurve bow and barely adult sized. Weak and lacking power. Another compound bow. Another recurve. All cheap and no good for the demands of the apocalypse.

Still, it's nice to pick them up and have a few minutes of examination and study. The compounds operate with pulleys and wheels to lessen the effects of the draw and increase the power but these are too cheap. The pulleys snap, the wheels jam up. The recurves are the best out of this lot and look like an old-fashioned gentleman's moustache with that curved shape. They do look nice. Very artful and pleasant but oh no, no no no, too light and this one has awful balance. Probably mass-produced from cheap materials.

'Boss, it's Blowers, looks all clear up here...'

Roy pauses for a second at the voice in his ear and for a second he wonders why they aren't being attacked yet. Maybe the things aren't here. Ah now what's this one like? He reaches up to grab the recurve bow on the top plinth and has a second's worth of hope that is dashed the second his fingers brush the cheap wood.

'Sod it,' he mutters, looking round with another tut. He'll get some arrows from the stock-room and bugger off. He's got his current compound which is functioning. It's not great but it does the job. He thinks back to his van that he ditched when he saved Paula. Maybe it's still there? They could go and see. He had everything in that van, plus his Kindle was in there and he does miss having a book to read. Not that they have any time to read now.

He wanders through the store, idly musing on this and that while avoiding the thought that he has a deadly, awful, filthy disgusting disease in his body. A second of panic hits. A thudding in his heart. Think of Marcy and Reggie. Think of the lads and how healthy they all are. Think of how his bow use, aim and rate of fire have all got better since he started fighting with Mr Howie. Think of how much stronger he feels. Think of those things. Ah but the magical thinking is there too, the worry that if he doesn't worry enough he will die. Okay, so have *some* worry but not too much. Enough worry to keep the bad things away but not too much worry that you can't do anything.

'Argh,' he yacks again at the light graze gliding over his nose then the sensation of a sticky strand on his cheek. 'Fat spiders,' he mutters, reaching for the light in the stock-room before remembering there is no electricity. 'Arse,' he carries on muttering, pulling his pocket torch out to flash the beam over the shelves.

He finds the arrows. The distinctive packets stacked up neatly and gives thanks they are the bigger two-dozen packs instead of the smaller dozen sized ones. He drops his bag, opens the top and starts ripping packets open to slide the shafts in. These are pre-fletched too. He prefers fletching his own but that takes time and his skill is such that he can adapt to a slightly imbalanced arrow. In fact, that makes it more interesting sometimes.

He shoves a few dozen in and grunts in approval at having his ammunition now restored. The rest of the packets he will take into the van for re-supply.

The shelf empties and in the gloom he spies more on the next section that he reaches for without paying close attention. Only when the first packet is lifted does his mind snap to the contents in his hand. He pauses, standing stock still while staring. The packet is too long for recurve or compound arrows. He draws it closer, feeling the weight and balance even within the packaging material. Longbow arrows. These are longbow arrows and bloody good ones too. He pushes the torch into his mouth and uses both hands to open the pack and draw an arrow out. An oak arrow. A perfectly balanced beautifully straight thirty inch oak arrow with threaded and glued fletches. Steel tipped with a wicked barbed point. Hunting arrows without a doubt. Longbow arrows are fired by longbows. There must be a longbow. He rushes out back into the store and over to the bow section. No longbows. Just the cheap thing he casted aside.

'Roy? We're going up to Blowers,' Paula calls through.

'Longbow,' Roy shouts back.

'You what?'

'Longbow arrows...'

'Right, okay...er...'

'They've got longbow arrows.'

'That's nice. We'll be up with Blowers if...'

'I can't find the longbow though.'

'You've got a bow.'

'I've got a compound but...'

'Okay, listen we're going up the road. Howie, Clarence and Dave are here.'

'Where is it?' he mutters, rushing through the aisles. Why stock so many arrows if not the bow to go with them? He comes to a stop at realising it's what he used to do. He used his local archery shop to order and stock his longbow arrows for him. They never had any actual longbows, just the arrows. 'Bugger,' he huffs, sags and walks back to the storeroom and underneath the glass fronted display cabinet holding the handmade longbow fixed to the wall over the counter.

'Longbow,' he whispers frantic, excited and running backwards to trip and stagger over the till on the floor. He doesn't care for falling or tripping but keeps his head turned and fixed up at the cabinet. 'Longbow...bloody longbow,' he reaches up but his finger-tips only brush the underside of the cabinet. A yelp and he rushes behind the counter looking for a chair or stool. Nothing. He goes into the store room, spots a chair, grabs it and runs back out. Chair down and he jumps up to stare at the cabinet with eyes full of hope.

Hinges at the top of the cabinet and with almost reverential poise he lifts the front up to reveal the bow resting on two big hooks. It looks good. It looks great. Must be yew. Has to be yew. Is it yew? It looks like yew. He almost doesn't want to touch it for fear of ruining the hope but touch it he must and so, with the caress of a lover, the tips of his fingers brush the warm dry wood and the world is full of calm. All the noise vanishes. All the panic fades. All the fear and worry simply is not there. Instead, there is a yew longbow lifted carefully from the cabinet as he drops lightly from the chair.

He holds it one handed in the middle, feeling the weight and balance which are just...just...well, not even perfect because to be perfect suggests a thing manufactured or made and a bow is neither of those. A bow is crafted and a yew bow is born from the yew tree.

He turns it over and brings one end down to the ground. Six feet. An inch taller than he. A great thing. A long thing that holds power far beyond the appearance of the slender wood that, unslung, is almost straight with only a hint of a curve.

While the sweat slides down his face he finds string and commences, quietly and with laser focussed attention, to string the bow. The calm radiates from his core. A quietness within his soul. One end attached. He braces the bow and flexes the bend to fit the other end and in so doing he feels the suppleness of the wood and the resistance being offered to his hands. Like a living thing that gives consent to bend and allows the string to be fitted. He even murmurs a thanks when the stringing is finished and the bow takes shape.

Then he stands and looks at it. Just looks. Just looks for the sake of looking and as the heat builds and the tension rises and the pressure grows so he smiles and feels warm inside.

———

'HAVE YOU BEEN INSIDE?' Paula asks, coming to a stop with Marcy at the entrance to the shopping centre. Glass fronted, with multiple sets of doors all smashed through with small chunks littered across the entranceway. A corpse lies twenty feet in. Old and rotten. Dust, leaves, litter and filth all blown in by the wind and rain. Past that initial section the floor and windows look clean.

'Went to the end of this section,' Blowers says, staring through the doors. 'Meredith hasn't reacted...she's sniffing like crazy but...' he looks round for the dog still trying to discern the tracks of the things she can smell. 'Did see that though,' Blowers says, pointing to the first shop on the right inside the doors.

'What?' Paula asks, trying to see what he's pointing at. 'Oh…oh I see…a coffee shop.'

'If we get the vehicles up here I could run a power supply in from Roy's van,' Nick says as Paula realises they've already discussed it, 'if we find an extension cable,' he adds.

'Think Howie would like a coffee?' Paula asks Marcy.

'After today?' Marcy says as though the question caught her off-guard, 'I think he'd attach a drip if he could.'

'Okay,' Paula says, 'get someone down to bring Roy's van up…'

'Roger,' Blowers says, nodding at Nick who sets off back towards the road at a steady jog.

'We'll go in and start getting supplies,' Paula says, sighing with discomfort at the same feeling they all suffer of wet clothes soaked through from sweat and hot feet, sore skin and irritation levels rising.

'Mo, stay with them,' Blowers says, 'Blinky, in the main aisle with line of sight on Mo and the door. Cookey on the door with line of sight on Blinky and Charlie…Charlie, you head up that end away from the road…if anything happens we all fall back to this doorway first then down to the others. Everyone got it?'

'Sir,' Marcy says, grinning at him.

He smiles that easy grin, brushing the compliment off. 'Maddox, we'll float…'

'I don't care,' Maddox replies.

'Listen you…' Marcy flares up, her face twisting up as Blowers cuts in.

'Don't bother, we've tried,' he says.

'Yeah don't bother, they've tried,' Maddox says, offering her a humourless smile.

'Come on,' Paula says through gritted teeth. It's only been one day with him and already everything feels disjointed and off-centre. The moral they always have is plunging. They've had heat like this before and long days of hard gruelling work but they had each other all pulling in the same direction. One slight alteration, one different character in the group and it shows. She hates herself for thinking it but her mind is turning to ways to be rid of him. What they are doing is too important. That single thought stops her dead in her tracks. That's all there is to it. They are the line between the infected and their species being wiped out and right now Maddox is threatening their ability to deal with that. If this was a work place Maddox would be dealt with under strict procedures. He would be advised to change his conduct. He would then be served with a warning and told he can have a union rep present when that happens. That warning would be issued with a time limit. *Improve within fourteen days or you may face dismissal.* Industry doesn't suffer fools, not when there is money to be made so why are they suffering it now?

That takes her back to the initial problem. Maddox cannot be left at the fort with Lilly. He cannot be exiled either and nor can he simply be allowed to go off now for the same reasons. That leaves execution. Which put bluntly means Dave shooting him. Could she do it? Could she walk over right now and shoot him dead? She knows she couldn't which then begs the question that to use Dave now would be taking advantage of his autism and lack of attachment.

'You thinking what I'm thinking?' Marcy asks quietly, making Paula realise they are both staring down the aisle at Maddox leaning against the front doors with his rifle held one handed at his side.

Paula sighs heavily, wearily and suddenly feeling drained as the tiredness of a hundred fights shows. 'Come on,' she turns to walk on and smiles warmly at the sight of Mo waiting patiently. A man but a boy. A highly capable man but still a boy and the contrast from Maddox makes her realise just how bloody good he really is. 'You okay, honey?'

'Fine,' he says, smiling back at her and Marcy.

'Know what,' Paula says, going to his right side and looping her arm through his as Marcy takes his left and does the same. 'We've got our Mo Mo and that's all we need,' she leans in to kiss the side of his head. A crimson blush starts in his cheeks that grows deeper as Marcy kisses him from the other side.

'Our Mo Mo,' Marcy says.

'WHAT THE FUCK IS THAT?' Howie asks.

'This...this is a *longbow*,' Roy says, standing proudly with the new bow held out so they can see it.

'We invading France or something?' Clarence asks.

'Ah very good,' Roy says, smiling over at him.

'France?' Howie asks.

'Agincourt,' Clarence says.

'Oh right,' Howie says then looks at Dave. 'What's Agincourt?'

'Famous battle, Mr Howie,' Dave says in that dull tone but somehow implying that anyone that doesn't know what Agincourt is must be an idiot. 'And gentlemen in England now a-bed shall think themselves accurs'd they were not here and hold their manhoods cheap whiles any speaks that fought with us upon Saint Crispin's day...' he tails off in that way that suggests there might be more coming, but there isn't, just silence as he looks round and up and resumes being Dave.

'Was that Shakespeare?' Howie asks the stunned silence.

'Yes,' Dave says.

'You just quoted Shakespeare?'

'Yes, Mr Howie.'

'Course you did. Why wouldn't you...'

'Why wouldn't I what, Mr Howie?'

'Quote Shakespeare.'

'I did.'

'From the movie right? With that bloke...the actor man... what's his name?' Howie asks, clicking his fingers as tries to remember.

'Kenneth Brannagh,' Roy says, staring at his longbow while Howie and Clarence stare at Dave.

'Him,' Howie says.

'Who, Mr Howie?'

'Kenneth Bummer...'

'Brannagh,' Roy says.

'Brannagh,' Howie says.

'Who is that?' Dave asks.

'The bloke from the movie.'

'What movie?'

'The bloody Shakespeare movie...it had that thing you just said. That bloke said it.'

'What bloke?'

'Oh my fucking God, Dave...you do this on purpose.'

'Do what, Mr Howie?'

'I've got a longbow.'

'We can see,' Clarence says. 'Is that good?' he ventures to ask.

'Is that good?' Roy asks, blinking at Clarence.

'Yes, is it good?' Clarence asks.

'Is it good,' Roy mutters, shaking his head in disbelief that such a question need be asked. 'I shall show you...where's Reggie?'

'In the van,' Howie says. 'Said it was too hot out here and he wanted to sharpen his pencils.'

'I am reading important information, Mr Howie,' Reginald calls through the open door. 'And trying to discern why we are not currently being attacked...and it was Henry the fifth.'

'What was?' Howie asks.

'The surprising quotation from Dave. It was from Henry the fifth.'

'It was Ken Bummer,' Howie says.

'Kenneth Brannagh,' Roy says.

'Kenneth Brannagh was in the motion picture version of Henry the fifth,' Reginald calls back.

'Reggie, I've got a longbow,' Roy says.

'Yes, yes indeed I heard.'

'I'm going to test it.'

'Er, that's marvellous, Roy. I shall await the result with baited breath.'

'Right,' Roy says, staring at his van and not understanding why none of them are as excited as he is. 'So...I'll fire the compound first and then the longbow...if you wanted to see that taking place?'

Howie coughs. Clarence clears his throat. Reginald tuts softly, places his maps down on the desk and rises from his chair. 'Indeed, I shall come forthwith and witness the testing processes of your new bow.'

'Longbow,' Roy says.

'Yes, longbow,' Reginald says, appearing from the van with a wince at the heat.

'Get comfy,' Howie says, sliding along the front of the Saxon he and Clarence are resting against.

'Boss?' Nick calls down, jogging from the precinct. 'Alright if I take the van up?'

'Yeah sure,' Howie says, 'what for?' he adds.

'Er...' Nick falters, unwilling to lie for anyone but not wanting to ruin the surprise of making a hot fresh coffee for the boss. 'We need a power supply plus we'll need to start putting kit inside.'

'Yeah no worries,' Howie says. 'Everything okay?'

'Yep fine, keys in it?'

'In the ignition,' Roy says.

'Is that a longbow?' Nick asks, coming to a stop as he turns to run round the front of the van.

'HA!' Roy exclaims, 'there is a man with taste and knowledge...'

'We invading France or something? It looks old as fuck.'

'France?' Howie asks, looking back at Nick in surprise.

'Yeah, Agincourt...Henry the fifth...hold your manhoods cheap?' Nick says.

'What the fuck?' Howie mutters.

'I'll take the van then,' Nick says.

'Yeah...yeah you take the van while I find a book on Kenny Banana...and don't accidentally run Maddox over or anything.'

'That would be bad,' Clarence says seriously. 'Go over him with both sets of wheels if you do.'

'Twice,' Roy adds. 'Anyway, so...this is my compound bow,' he presents his compound bow to Dave, Howie, Clarence and Reginald. 'It's a modern design that has much stiffer limbs. So much in fact that you can see the resistance if I try and move them manually,' he grunts and tugs at the limbs of his compound bow as Clarence, Howie and Reginald make observant noise and Dave stares on. 'So the use of the pulleys, cams and cables makes for an energy efficient movement when the user draws while still maintaining a relatively high power output. Let me show you...'

They have all seen Roy fire a bow many, many times but to say that now would be rude, so they don't. Instead, they watch as he selects an arrow, nocks it within the string and prepares to draw.

'Okay, see the sign at the bottom of the road? Not the speed sign but the directional sign fixed at a right angle to the metal post which is coloured brown and has the words *town centre* on it. See that sign?'

'Er yep, yep I can see the sign,' Howie says.

'Got it,' Clarence says.

'Reginald? Can you see that sign?' Roy asks.

'Indeed I can,' Reginald says, easing down to rest between Howie and Clarence.

'The compound allows the use of slow or fast drawing techniques to achieve peak draw-weight. In this case, I shall use a slow draw with a full extension which maximises the power output... when I loose you will see the arrow move and strike the target...ready?'

'Yep,' Howie says.

'Yes,' Clarence says.

'Indeed,' Reginald says as the van behind them starts the

mammoth task of reversing up the road with a horsebox attached to the rear.

Roy looses. The arrow flies off and slams into the target sign with a loud metallic clang. Which is what they all expected to happen.

'That's good,' Howie says.

'Very good,' Clarence rumbles.

'Indeed,' Reginald says.

'The sign is so rigidly fixed it has absorbed the impact of the arrow but you heard the noise?'

'I heard it,' Howie says.

'Heard it,' Clarence says.

'Indeed,' Reginald says.

'Ah now, so here we have the longbow,' Roy says, placing his compound down and picking the newly strung longbow up with that same reverential manner. 'The compound manipulates mechanics to gain the power output whereas the longbow...and in particular, this longbow is crafted from one piece of wood. Yew, to be exact. It is six feet in length and as you can see it does not have any pulleys, cams or...well anything at all. It is just one piece of wood...' he shows them the bow again and again they nod and make the serious noises of menfolk who are socially required to make such noises.

'Now, the arrows are wooden shafted so...one is nocked and the draw can begin but the strength required is immense. They say the archers of medieval times were deformed due to the constant stresses placed on their bodies oh, this is an interesting fact...'

He places the longbow back down and picks the compound back up.

'With a compound you pull the string to fire, see? The bow is held and the string is pulled...' he pulls the string a few times to which they nod and make noises.

'But with the longbow, and especially when drawing fully, the technique is to lean into the bow as it were, so in effect the bow becomes part of the motion. It is not merely a static item but an extension of the movement. I couldn't simply pull the string back due to the strength required and to repeat that again and again would seriously hamper your strength and ability.'

He shows them what he means by nocking the arrow and pulling the string back as he did with the compound. The string moves and the bow flexes but the degree is far less. Roy does it again, pulling further back each time but still using just the string to pull on. Slowly, he increases the way he pushes into the bow which in turn allows a greater draw.

'I'm stronger,' he says dully in the way of observation. He goes quiet as the others watch him drawing, relaxing and seemingly building up to a full draw. 'I am much stronger,' he remarks again.

It happens quickly. Roy draws properly, lifting to hold the bow that he leans into as he pulls the string fully back. The yew bends, flexing with him. The whole of the bow becomes a part of Roy and the arrow is merely within that encapsulation. A slight pause and he looses.

All four stare on. Stunned at the speed arrow flew at and the power of the strike which removed the rigidly fixed sign from the metal pole and sent it spinning away into the road beyond. The noise was hard too. Whereas the compound arrow struck solid, the longbow arrow smashed the shit out of it with a noise that tells the world what just happened.

'Fuck,' Howie says quietly, standing up to look down the road towards the sign.

'See?' Roy asks calmly, quietly.

'Very good,' Clarence says, genuinely meaning it as Reginald stares solely at Roy with that deeply interested expression adorning his face. Reginald knows what longbows are. Any history buff knows what longbows are and how they were used. He also knows the finding of a hundred or so longbows on the wreck *The Mary Rose* changed the view of what historians thought they knew of the longbow. He is aware of the power required to draw it and if asked, he would have asserted that someone with Roy's build would not be able to draw fully and repeat that action more than a few times. It would take someone with the strength of Clarence or Paco to use such a thing fully. But Roy just did it. Roy is fit and strong but his muscularity is lean rather than beefy. Interesting. Very interesting.

NICK BACKS the van up the road, his tongue poking out as he focusses to navigate the horsebox. He reaches the corner, feeding the wheel gently to go back into the bend before stopping and driving into the precinct.

He spots Maddox by the front doors and wishes he could do as the boss joked and run him over. Just an accidental slip of the accelerator then an accidental change of gear into reverse to go back over him, then maybe another accidental slip forward.

He slows the van, waiting for Maddox to move but the lad just looks round and stares dully at Nick. Nick motions him to move. Maddox stares. Nick holds both his hands up showing his frustration. Maddox shrugs and strolls away painfully slowly.

'Cunt,' Nick mutters drawing alongside the front doors. 'What was that for?' he asks, jumping down to move quickly round the front.

'What?' Maddox asks.

'Fuck me you are such a prick,' Nick strides past him, mindful of Mr Howie telling them all to go easy but now finding it very hard. 'Blowers, you got it open?' he calls down the corridor.

'I asked Maddox to do it.'

'Maddox?' Nick asks.

'What?' Maddox replies, having heard perfectly well what Blowers just said.

'Have you opened it?'

'I don't have a key.'

'Fuckstick,' Cookey mutters.

Nick holds the comments in and crosses to the glass door just inside the main corridor. He pushes the door first, doing what Clarence taught them to check where the locks are. This one is locked at the top middle and bottom which means it will be easier to smash through the glass rather than try and open the door. 'Mind out,' he steps back, swings his axe and slams through the glass that shatters to fall in tiny cubes.

'*What was that?*' Mo's voice in the radio.

'*You okay?*' Howie asks next.

'*Nick's breaking a window for entry,*' Cookey responds.

Maddox knows he could have got through in seconds without breaking the glass and feels a surge of self-loathing for refusing to help or join in. A part of him wants to be involved and to stop the act he is portraying. He has never behaved like this. It's childish, immature and beneath him, but he can't stop it. His pride has been dented massively. His ego is deflating by the second and he isn't *alph*a here. He isn't special. Everyone here is alpha. Everyone here is fit, strong and fast and some of them are more intelligent than him. Reginald and Charlie without doubt are both way ahead of him. He measures himself by comparison and in so doing, he starts to realise maybe it was easy to stand out on the estate. There was no expectation of achievement so therefore anything he actually did stood out. He also had the Bossman guiding him, the same way this lot have guidance. Except the similarity there ends. The support within this group is respectful, endearing and warm. That they really do care for each other is obvious, and not in a trite fake way either, but with real emotions that he isn't used to.

He stands outside in the shade of the doorway and looks up to Charlie trotting round the precinct. He looks at Meredith still sniffing the ground and thinks even the two animals are putting more effort in than he is. Lenski comes to mind with that stab of insecurity. Lenski has always been cold. She's just a cold person. She cares and she shows she cares in the things she does but she isn't warm or loving in the way that Paula or Marcy are. Maddox accepted that but her coldness stood out this time because he wanted and needed comfort, and it wasn't there.

'Fuck's sake...Maddox!'

'What?' Maddox spins as Nick storms past holding a huge extension reel found in a cleaning cupboard at the back of the coffee shop. 'I didn't hear you,' Maddox says, almost guiltily.

'Yeah right,' Nick says, going into the van to push the plug into the socket. He goes back out and into the coffee shop while pulling his multi-tool from his pocket. Maddox watches him go, wishing again to go after him to see if he can help. He watches Nick rip the wires from the coffee machine from the fixed electrical point on the wall then start splaying them out. Again an urge to start cutting the wires on the extension cable ready for them to be joined.

'*Maddox, eyes out,*' Blowers transmits.

'*Forget him,*' Cookey says back through the radio. '*I got eyes out and Charlie's out there.*'

'*Fair one,*' Blowers says.

Nick works fast. Stripping the coating to expose the wiring. It's a bodge job and not without a level of danger too. He doesn't know if the fuse in the extension plug will cope with the coffee machine but it's worth a go. He uses electrical tape to join them then props the joined section on the counter and covers it with trays and heavy pots so no one touches it.

Maddox knows the van needs turning on now to get the power flowing. He could offer to do that. He could take the first step to bridge that gap.

Nick walks past him, unable to even glance at Maddox as he goes into the van, starts the engine and gets the power into the cable before going back into the coffee shop. A nod of satisfaction at the lights coming on. He draws his fingertips over the buttons, murmuring softly as he works out what button does what. Like Roy with a bow, Nick feels a connection to things like this. The mystery of them is exciting and unique. The figuring out of systems, circuits and the mechanics of things. He susses it out and works a way to get the grinder going to grind the beans then where that goes to get the water through as Maddox watches on and Blowers shakes his head for the thousandth time.

'Is what it is,' Blowers murmurs.

'Yep,' Blinky says, making Blowers aware he spoke out loud.

Like Roy with a bow, like Nick with electrical things, like Charlie with Jess, like Dave with knives, soldiering is what Blowers does. The instinct of it. The feel of it. The hundreds of things that make up what soldiering actually means.

His mind is ever running. Mo is with Paula and Marcy as they source the supplies they need. Mo is highly competent and Dave Trained so that means they are safe. Blinky is midway between them and the door. Cookey on the door. Nick is close. Charlie is outside. The other elders are down the street. The angles are covered. The entry and exit points are within sight.

That same mind also works out where the weaknesses are. The back of the shopping centre will be accessed by the service road that runs from the bend in the main street. That back area will have entrances and exit points and as yet, it has not been checked. That cannot be helped. They do not have enough units to deploy to all points so line of sight is the next safest option.

'Blowers?' he turns at hearing Paula call his name.

'Here,' he calls back.

'Mo's got into the outdoors shop,' she says, walking into view at the end of the corridor. 'We'll get clothing and kit from there... there's a Boots on the other side. Mo can get into that next so we'll have wipes and a clean up here before we push on...that okay?'

'Yeah sure.'

'Howie still down the road?'

'Yeah I think so...he hasn't come up yet anyway.'

'Nick? You got that machine on?' She calls down.

'It's on,' Nick shouts back. 'Be ready in a minute...found long life milk too...I reckon I can make a proper cappuccino.'

'Yeah?' she smiles, 'have a go...'

'The spoke thing steams the milk right?'

'No idea,' Paula says.

'Yes it does,' Marcy shouts from further back, making Blowers wish they wouldn't shout out like that when so much of the area is still unchecked. 'Long metal bit, put the milk into a metal pot then turn the dial to get the steam going.'

'Yep, got it,' Nick shouts back.

'Sorted,' Paula says, walking back down the corridor to the outdoors shop. 'How you getting on?'

'Yeah fine,' Marcy says, pulling wicking tops from the display stands. 'We've got enough here for a few days...'

'I'll do underwear,' Paula says, moving off towards the socks and undergarments.

'Argh,' Marcy spits and pulls back with a hand rubbing her face.

'Cobweb?' Paula asks, coming to a sudden stop as she checks round, up and anywhere that could hide a spider.

'Third time now,' Marcy says.

'Lots of flies,' Paula says, shuddering again and suddenly wishing to be outside. 'You okay with spiders?'

'Me?' Marcy asks. 'I bloody hate them...'

'Same,' Paula mutters, steeling herself to continue to the underwear selection.

'I cannot wait to get changed,' Marcy says. 'Dry clothes, cold wet wipes and a bucket of moisturiser...and make-up remover, and cotton buds...and hairbands...my skin is sooo dry and sore right now...'

'Yep,' Paula says, working fast to shove packets of socks and underwear into a large basket. 'My thighs are chafing. Are yours?'

'Oh don't,' Marcy says. 'We should get those cycle shorts things...don't they stop chafing?'

'Probably.'

'Know what else I want?'

'What's that?' Paula asks.

'Perfume.'

'Perfume?'

'Yep, really really expensive perfume…couldn't afford it before…'

'Fair enough,' Paula says. 'Beats smelling of sweat I guess.'

'And a diamond necklace.'

'A what?' Paula laughs.

'With massive diamonds…and earrings…and a watch…'

'Bracelet?'

'Totally and rings too…proper blinged up.'

'Innit blud,' Mo quips from his position at the door, they both smile over at him, at the serious way he holds guard with his rifle slung and his pistol gripped in both hands lowered but ready.

'Think Howie will mind?' Marcy asks.

'What's that? Getting a diamond necklace?' Paula asks, moving to grab another basket she starts filling with more kit. 'We'll need trousers too.'

'Over there,' Marcy says, nodding over her armfuls of wicking tops. 'Think he'll mind if we rob a jewellers? Get some diamonds and…'

'Ha! Put a ring in his hand, stare for a few seconds then just walk off,' Paula jokes.

'Oh he'd shit himself,' Marcy laughs. 'Should do it for fun… when he's in a better mood though. But seriously, we're getting perfume. Nice perfume. And aftershave too. I love the lads but they stink…not you, Mo Mo, you don't smell.'

'Thanks,' Mo says. 'There's a jewellers over there,' he adds.

'Is there?' Marcy asks, walking over to peer out. 'Oh yeah, you think you could get inside it?'

'Yeah,' Mo scoffs then coughs to be more serious and grown up. 'I mean yes, yes I can.'

'You're so sweet,' she says, grinning at him. 'Paula, we're breaking into a jewellers when we've done this.'

'Okay, Marce,' Paula says, smiling as she works. 'We'll take everything from here into that Boots and get some wipes, cleaning stuff and get them up in two's and three's to get changed and cleaned up.'

'Roger,' Marcy says, staring at the trousers. 'What sizes?'

'Just grab loads...I'll sort them in a minute.'

'FUCK YES,' Nick says, holding the metal pot full of long life milk under the spout that spurts steam and churns the milk into a frothy pot of goodness. The first one was awful. The second was terrible, the third and fourth not fit for human consumption but this is the apocalypse, this is the end of days so it doesn't matter how many cups he uses.

Maddox has even moved inside to watch and as with all young men, he thinks he can do better and bites the urge to make suggestions.

'How's it going?' Blowers asks, walking in to burst out laughing at the sight of the used cups scattered all over the counter.

'Yep,' Nick says focussing on the milk in the pot. 'I'm a fucking barrister...'

'Barista,' Maddox says, unable to stop the correction coming from his mouth.

'Whatever,' Nick mutters. 'Is the boss coming up?'

'Not yet,' Blowers says.

'Give him a shout, I'll get four made up for him, Clarence, Roy and Dave...Cookey?'

'What?' Cookey shouts from outside the café by the main door.

'Come clear this counter.'

'I'm watching Charlie.'

'I can see Charlie from here,' Nick says, turning to look at Cookey then pointing at the windows at the front.

'Fair one,' Cookey says, walking through the busted in door.

'Latte frappuccino skinny sunny side up with a heaped serving of cunt for Maddox.'

Maddox could have cleared the side. Another chance comes and goes. Another shot of stubbornness mingled with an ever-growing sense of dislike for himself that he twists into a dislike for them.

'Boss? It's Blowers. You coming up?'

'Oi,' Nick blurts, 'not now for fuck's sake...'

'You just said to call him,' Blowers says.

'I haven't made the fucking coffees yet.'

'Yep, we'll come up now. Everyone okay?'

'Yeah fine, Boss. Er...no rush though...'

'Oh that was smooth,' Cookey says, shaking his head at Blowers.

'Fuck off,' Blowers sighs.

'No rush?' Howie asks through the radio. *'What's Cookey done?'*

'Eh?' Cookey says, *'I haven't done anything.'*

'I've got a longbow.'

'Oh Roy's got a longbow,' Nick says.

'Er...okay, Roy,' Blowers says, looking at Nick and Cookey with an expression of *what the fuck do I say?'*

'I'll show you when I get up there.'

'Er great, we'll er...look forward to that.'

'You sound almost excited there, Blowers,' Marcy quips through the radio.

'Wait till you see it firing,' Clarence says.

'Don't tell them that,' Roy says. *'I want them to see it without knowing.'*

'Right,' Clarence says. *'Ignore my last.'*

'Now that is a fucking coffee...' Nick says, pouring the frothy milk into the cup.

'Where's the chocolate shaker?' Cookey asks.

'Oh yeah, have a look...see if they got those things to make shapes...' Nick says.

'We should do a cock shape,' Cookey says.

'I'm not serving Dave a coffee with a cock on the top,' Nick says, pouring more milk into the pot for steaming and making frothy.

'Got it,' Cookey says, holding the chocolate powder shaker up. 'Blowers, put your dick over the cup so I can do a template.'

'You want me to put my cock on Dave's mug?'

'Er...yes?' Cookey asks.

'I'm not putting my cock on Dave's cup.'

'Use that one in your pocket.'

'What?'

'The one you took from Meredith...the one you kept...for stroking at night...that one...use that one...'

'No,' Blowers says. 'I'm keeping that one.'

'Use a bit of cardboard...' Nick says.

'Fucking good idea,' Cookey says.

'Fuck's sake, you can't put cocks on their coffees,' Blowers groans.

'Fucking can,' Cookey laughs, tearing a section of cardboard from a box under the counter. He pulls his knife and gets to work, slicing a template of a penis with an oversized head and two big balls at the base.

'Next one,' Nick says, pouring the frothy milk into the next cup. 'Hurry up, they'll be here in a minute.'

'I'm trying,' Cookey mutters with the upmost concentration.

'Blowers, get some hot water in that mug for Reggie.'

'Which one?'

'That one...got the peppermint teabag in it.'

'Got it...er...where's the hot water?'

'Put it under that nozzle and push the middle button.'

'This one?'

'Is that the middle one?'

'Yeah.'

'Then yes, that one you fuckstick.'

'Fuck you,' Blowers mumbles, pushing the middle button in and smiling as the hot water comes out.

'So cool,' Cookey says, holding his cut out willy and testicles up.

'What's that?' Nick asks.

'The cock and balls for the chocolate,' Cookey says.

'You need the other bit,' Nick says.

'What other bit?' Cookey asks.

'The fucking other bit...the bit you cut it out from...the chocolate goes through the hole you made not on the bit you cut out.'

'Oh,' Cookey says, nodding as he catches up. 'Oh yeah....so this bit then?' he asks, holding up the cardboard now with the hole in the shape of the willy and testicles showing.

'Yep, put it over the mug and shake the chocolate over.'

'Sorted,' Cookey says, doing as Nick said. He holds the cardboard over the top of the rapidly flattening once frothy milk and shakes the chocolate shaker with a fast frenzied action that sees chocolate power flying everywhere. 'Oh my god...look at that,' Cookey says, bursting out laughing at the perfect shape of the genitals on the cappuccino.

'Brilliant,' Nick says.

'Fucked up,' Blowers laughs. 'Do the next one.'

'I am,' Cookey says.

'Pouring,' Nick says, pouring the last lot of milk as the sound of the Saxon reaches them.

'They're coming,' Blinky calls through.

'Yep,' Blowers calls back.

'Ha!' Cookey says in triumph at the next perfectly formed chocolate powder genitals on the next mug.

'Quick,' Nick says.

'I am,' Cookey says, laughing as he shakes the shaker.

'They're here,' Blowers says, looking outside to see the Saxon pulling up behind Roy's van.

'Ah fuck,' Cookey says, shaking harder.

'They're out the Saxon,' Blowers says, watching Howie, Dave, Clarence, Roy and Reginald jump down. 'They're looking round... they're coming in!'

'Done it,' Cookey exclaims, stepping back to admire his handiwork as Nick bursts out laughing at the sight of the four cock adorned cappuccinos and one peppermint tea.

'What's this?' Howie asks, walking through the main doors then into the café as his eyes follow the power cable across the floor and up to the counter and the three lads standing guiltily behind it trying not to laugh. 'What the...is that coffee?' he asks, sniffing the air.

'You got power in here?' Clarence asks, stepping through behind Howie and Dave.

'Got a longbow,' Roy says, coming through to show them his longbow.

'Your coffees are served,' Nick says, grinning from ear to ear as Cookey turns away from laughing so hard and Blowers bites his bottom lip.

Reginald walks through, his keen eyes taking everything in. Seeing Maddox scowling and the lads behind the counter trying not to laugh. *Unity. At all costs there must be unity.*

The elders go forward, slowly advancing the line towards the counter with suspicious eyes and wary notions.

It's too much for Cookey. He laughs so hard he turns red and drops down as Blowers turns away and Nick starts to go.

'Twats,' Howie bursts out laughing as Clarence brays and Roy grins at being included in another joke. 'Fucking idiots,' Howie says, still laughing.

'Brilliant,' Clarence says, picking one of the mugs up to stare at the top.

'First time a penis has been in my mouth,' Roy says.

'Blowers said that once,' Cookey says from somewhere behind the counter.

Maddox turns away. It was stupid, childish and just immature. A waste of time. A waste of effort. All that stuff about pushing on and working hard and they spend more time fucking about than doing anything else but now more than ever he feels isolated and rejected from the main. The way they laugh and joke. The sight of Clarence chuckling as he takes a sip and Reginald smiling as he sniffs his tea and Dave staring as devoid as ever. Maddox doesn't know Dave well enough to see that within that expressionless stare there is a hint of amusement.

'Nicely done,' Howie says, lifting his mug. He takes a sip and groans audibly and long. 'Proper coffee...who made it?'

'Nick did,' Blowers says, still chuckling.

'Spot on, mate,' Howie says.

'Look at you lot,' Paula says, striding into the café. 'Smells nice though.'

'Tastes nice too,' Howie says.

'Right, well grab a chair and relax for a bit. We'll be here for while,' Paula says. 'Lads, got enough to make some more?'

'Loads,' Nick says.

'We'll be up the corridor getting kit sorted...'

'We'll come and help,' Howie says, turning from the counter with his mug of coffee.

'Nope, we're fine,' Paula says. 'Let us have a few minutes...is it okay if we get Charlie in?'

'We can sit at the front and keep watch,' Clarence says, walking to the big plate glass windows to look up and down. 'Yeah it's fine. Got a good view.'

'Charlie, you come inside, love,' Paula transmits.

'On way...are we here for a while? I'll leave Jess out if we are... it's too hot in the horsebox if we're not moving.'

*'That's fine. Grab a coffee and come up to me and Marcy...*Seri-

ously,' she says, looking at Howie, 'drink your coffee, relax for a few minutes.'

'You sure?' he asks.

'I'm sure, lads, grab a coffee, Blinky? You come down and grab a drink. It's already late so we won't get anything done today. We'll call you up for clean kit when we're ready.'

CHAPTER TWENTY

All the paths of your life lead to this point now.

This is where you are in time and space. This is the present so look back with reflection and see the route you took and feel the pain of each step be it right or wrong.

Days of fighting. Days of running. Days of heat and sufferance to do what must be done and achieve what must be achieved. Days of peril, anguish and strife that culminated in a return to the fort where they, for one brief evening, found peace.

Then they woke and fought and killed and ran and sweated and did all the things they did before. They did it without complaint too. They did what must be done. They achieved what must be achieved and so they will after this too. They will keep going until the bitter end.

Today though. Today has seen Howie execute six people based on the reactions to the emotions of a group of survivors. He took life that was *not* infected. He took life from people that posed no threat to him or his group and in so doing he took a step into a world none of them have ventured, and that brings a disquiet of mind, an unsettling of a mood that is only made worse by the presence of Maddox.

A strange thing happens. A strange feeling of melancholy, of distraction and complacency that are all born from the paths of their lives that lead to this point now. So now, they seek the company of men. The company of women. The company of their kin of soul, spirit and mind. They bring forth a break in the chase and a pause in the frenzied nature of their existence.

They are infected, not immune. This is not discussed.

What Howie did is not discussed.

Where they are or where they are going is not discussed.

Nothing of virtue or significance or importance is discussed because sometimes there is just the company of men, of women and of those that match your soul, spirit and mind.

Howie sits in the front of café with Clarence, Roy, Reginald and Dave. So positioned to see all the angles of the street outside. They drink coffee and talk quietly in the company of men. The quietness of elders who make decisions that affect the lives of every single person around them. What they do counts. What they say means something. Now they chat quietly of things that hold no importance, of bows, of famous battles, of history and places and peoples and they idly watch Jess drinking water from a bucket and eating oats from a bowl.

Paula, Marcy and Charlie move about the outdoors shop in the company of women. It gives them time and space to talk and move at a pace they are comfortable with. They have killed. They have taken life so many times. They are bloodied and hardened and do not know each other as women but as members of the group. Now is a time for the bond to grow and be strengthened on a level not born from the primeval instinct for survival. They do not talk men or clothes or fashion but they talk as people with lives and experiences that are shared and understood. They cross to the huge Boots pharmacy and make pleasant comments at Mo who blushes as he deftly breaks in. They pluck cobwebs from faces as they move inside and then wait patiently with warm wry smiles as Mo *advances* to *secure* the area.

Mo, for his part, needs this company of women. It is soothing in a way nothing else can be. He is sixteen. He is a boy transitioning to becoming a man. His life was hard before this. It was bitter and nasty. It was neglect and abandonment and a lack of nurture from either maternal or paternal care. Within this time now, he finds something that fills that gap within his soul. He adores Paula. He worships her in the way a son worships his mother so to gain a smile from her, a look, a hand on his arm, a kiss on his head or cheek is like when Dave praises him. They are entirely different but entirely the same in the product of the response within him.

The endearment he feels for Marcy and Charlie are less than Paula but still there and so, to be within them now means he can be a man to guard them. He is trusted. He is *Dave Trained*. He stays close, watches the angles and looks serious with his back straight. He smiles and blushes too when they say *our Mo Mo*. He likes that. He likes the meaning of it, the sense of belonging.

Outside the main doors, down a little into the precinct in the lee side of the Saxon so the rest stand. Each with feet planted apart. Each with a rifle over the crooks of their arms. Each with a giant *grande* coffee mug held in one hand that actually makes it hard to drink when holding the rifle like that but they look good so they won't change. They are squaddies. Soldiers. They are the matching of souls, spirits and minds. Blowers, Cookey, Nick and Blinky. A fearsome foursome whose bond strengthens in the ever-increasing vulgarity of the comments they say to one another. A spunk trumpet full of cunt means I will stand with you. I will hold the line with you. I will not leave you when the enemy grow so large in number it makes your insides go like jelly and the voice inside screams to run away and never look back.

They joke and talk. They turn to look too. Constantly watching, always watching, always scanning. The elders are inside. This is downtime. Blowers can relax his role for a few minutes and be with his mates. They swap stories and tell-tales of the things they saw and did in the fights they've had. They talk about Paco holding that big man above his head earlier. They talk about Mo's speed which turns into an awe-filled muted discussion about Dave. They talk about girls, cars, movies, songs, places, people and things. They talk as people talk and they call each other fucktard, fuckface, fuckstick, wankstain, cockbreath and a hundred other things that prove offence will not be taken nor given for they are brethren of spirit and soul and mind.

Meredith lies in the shade inside the back of the Saxon. She listens to the conversations of the pack and watches Maddox standing off alone and isolated. He is not pack. He is a visitor to the pack. His rights are different to the others. The way she sees him is different but she knows the distance is self-imposed. It is his choosing to maintain that separation. He does not want to be pack.

He bloody does. He is desperate to be pack but that is a truth too uncomfortable to give voice so he twists it to suit his own perception and labels it as something else. If he was in charge he would do everything differently. He would get what they need and get out. He wouldn't hang about chatting and drinking coffee. If he was in charge he wouldn't travel in the same vehicle as everyone else either. He'd be at the front with his lieutenants and let the grunts come behind. He would have a chain of command. He would have proper discipline and order. He would do everything differently, properly too. Not like this. This is a mess. Everything about these people is a mess. He doesn't understood how they're so relaxed either. Howie killed people and Maddox rammed the wedge into their peace of mind with a large dollop of spite to hurt them the way he is hurt. It hasn't worked though. Howie is drinking coffee and everyone else is pissing about being idiots.

That isolation from the group means there is no break to the internal voice that grows louder as the day wears on. His self-loathing increases. His projected loathing increases. The insecurity and awareness that he is suddenly not special, not the leader, not the best-person-here increases too.

Jess eats oats. Meredith stretches and groans softly then lifts her head to pant in the heat of the day. Nick appears, smiling and making noises while filling her bowl with more water. He rubs her head. She twitches her ears and tail to show she likes it.

'YOU JUST WAIT THERE, BABY,' Marcy tells the jewellery shop as she walks past carrying armfuls of clothing from the outdoor shop into Boots. Mo chuckles at the wink she gives him. 'And you wait there too,' she tells the long glass fronted perfume cabinet in the shop.

'Eh?' Paula asks, looking up from the mounds on the floor near the checkouts.

'Talking to the perfume,' Marcy says, dropping the clothes with a heavy huff as she wipes the sweat from her face.

'Right,' Paula says, stepping back to draw the back of her right arm across her forehead that comes away slick and wet.

Trousers, tops, socks and undergarments arranged in piles and each with a packet of cleansing wet wipes, toothbrush and tooth-paste. Marcy added the moisturiser and deodorant. Then Paula found the foot powder section and remembered about fungal prob-lems in hot weather so added a bottle of that to each. Charlie found the razors, shaving cream and flannels. Marcy added shampoo and shower gel. Charlie found gel nails. Marcy found teeth whitening paste. Charlie found dental floss. Marcy found condoms. Charlie found lube and so it went on as the mounds grew in size with just about every product available.

'Done?' Marcy asks.

Paula nods, 'yep, done.'

'Thank God,' Marcy says. 'Please say we can go first...actually, I'm not even waiting for an answer...Mo, honey?'

'Yep?' Mo asks, turning smartly from his position at the main door being a serious committed sentinel, and still with his pistol held double-gripped and down in front of his waist, heroic and brave with grit in his eye.

'We're stripping off so no peeking.'

He blushes instantly, blinking a few times while nodding quickly and trying to stop the mental image of a naked Marcy and Charlie popping into his head. All of this happens at the same time as he realises he is still staring in instead of staring out. 'Shnure,' he blurts, wincing at the strange sound that just came from his mouth as he snaps out the fastest about-turn ever known in the history of humanity. He even strides forward a few steps to position outside the door as though to show he really really won't peek while wondering what shnure means.

The three women share smiles, all of them having seen his cheeks blooming with colour.

'Poor lad,' Paula says quietly, 'he could have had something for his wankbank...'

'Paula!' Marcy exclaims with mock wide eyes and shock at the comment. 'That was a proper Cookey comment.'

'It was,' Charlie laughs, moving away a few steps to her pile of clothes and goodies.

'Mo Mo doesn't have a wankbank,' Marcy says, keeping her voice muted and quiet. 'He's too sweet for that...oh that's so nice,' she adds with a groan at pulling her sodden top up over her head. 'Either of you bothered if I strip off here?'

'Not fussed,' Paula says.

'Hockey player,' Charlie says.

'Fair enough,' Marcy says, reaching back to unclasp her bra fastening with another groan. 'Oh my god that's so nice...I've got underboob sweat.'

They strip off with groans as appreciative as Marcy's. Wet tops pulled and thrown into a pile. Bras taken off and packets of wipes opened to rub faces, arms, hands, necks, chests and stomachs. The used wipes are thrown into the pile of old tops as Mo stares ahead listening to the groans and moans coming from behind him. *Shnure?* He said shnure. What does that even mean?

Boots and socks off. Feet cleaned. Trousers off. Legs cleaned. They cool down and wipe the sweat from their skin then use new towels to dry off.

'If Cookey walked in now eh?' Marcy jokes, standing in just her knickers holding a brand new fluffy towel. 'Wankbank,' she says with a tut at Paula. 'Do you think they have?'

'What?' Paula asks.

'You know...had a wank,' Marcy says quietly, giggling as she says it.

'I don't know!' Paula says, wincing at the thought. 'I doubt it... where for a start? We're always together.'

'Hmmm,' Marcy says, thinking for a second, 'good point.'

New trousers. New socks. New tops. Deodorant sprayed in armpits. Faces cleansed with cream applied and slowly the feeling of being human is restored. A boost to moral. An ownership of an environment they have taken control of and now dominate with their mere presence. They drink coffee made in the café and chat until finally they are done and once more resplendent in the now assumed black uniform of their group.

'*Blinky, you come up and get changed,*' Paula says into the radio.

'*Yes, Miss Paula, Sir. On way now, Sir.*'

Paula blinks, shaking her head at the burst of speech firing through the radio. A few seconds later Blinky appears from sprinting down the length of the main shopping centre aisle and comes to a sudden stop with her hand hovering as though ready to salute.

'Here, Miss Paula, Sir.'

'Er, s'just Paula,' Paula says to no avail as Blinky blinks.

'Your pile,' Paula says brightly, dropping to a crouch to sort through Blinky's kit. 'Your top and spares, your trousers spares...underwear, socks...foot powder, wet wipes...ignore the condoms and lube Marcy and Charlie added...and the evening primrose oil capsules and the eye wash, tanning lotion and lipsticks...what the...' Paula stops at the grunt coming from Blinky standing topless with her trousers round her ankles trying to pull her right boot off. 'Er...so...we'll give you a minute?'

'Sir, Miss Paula, Sir...'

'Blinky isn't shy,' Charlie says.

'Get fucked posh bird,' Blinky grins, tugging her boot off then hopping to start work on the left. 'You all done?'

'I am,' Charlie says.

'Did you see Marcy naked?'

'Er,' Charlie says.

'Right here,' Marcy says, lifting her hand.

'Fit,' Blinky grunts, pulling her left boot off, 'ha, stupid cunt,' she tells the boot. 'Right, this mine then? What's this? Is this lube? Why have I got lube?'

'I just said...' Paula goes to say.

'And johnnies? Why you giving me rubber johnnies? I'm gay... these wet wipes?'

'Yes they are,' Paula says into the surreal environment as Blinky shreds the packet apart and starts cleaning herself.

'Hot as fuck,' Blinky tells Charlie as though it's safe to speak normally as long as she doesn't actually look at Paula or Marcy. 'Sweating like a fucker...did you have coffee?'

'We did yes,' Charlie says.

'Did Cookey put a cock on yours?'

'No,' Charlie laughs.

'He put them on Mr Howie's and the others....funny as fuck...'

'What was that?' Paula asks.

'Nothing, Miss Paula,' Blinky snaps.

'I'm only asking,' Paula says.

'Don't know anything, Miss Paula, Sir.'

'Blinky, I'm not asking you to snitch or anything...I just wondered...'

'Wasn't there, Miss Paula. Didn't see it.'

'Right, yep okay then,' Paula says.

'Maddox is being a right bellend,' Blinky says, resuming her *private* conversation with Charlie. 'Won't stand with us...won't say anything. Total fuckstick, like...not a team player at all.'

'It is awkward,' Charlie remarks.

'Do I have to put all this shit in my bag, Charlie?'

'Not the lube, Blinky...or the condoms...or the, okay yes you can put it all in your bag if you want.'

'I'm done,' Blinky says, now cleaned, dried, dressed and ready in the space of two minutes. 'Can I be excused, Miss Paula?'

'Er yes?'

'Thank you, Ma'am...fuck you Charles,' Blinky marches off, digging Mo in the arm for good luck as she goes. 'Tosser.'

'Gotta love that girl,' Paula muses into the void left from the whirling dervish force of nature that was Blinky. *'Blowers, the others can come up.'*

'Yep, cheers, Paula.'

Blowers releases his radio switch as he steps out wider to see Howie and the others still in the café chatting quietly. He gets Clarence's attention and motions first to his group then to Clarence. *You going next or us?*

Clarence nods at him. *You go next.*

'I'm clean and dry fucktards,' Blinky says, striding out the doors.

'You okay here for five?' Blowers asks her.

'No I'm scared. Can someone stay with me please,' Blinky says.

'Come on,' Blowers motions for the others to follow him through. Nick and Cookey fall in behind him as Cookey tries to shoulder barge Blinky who laughs and pushes back sending him into Nick who runs forward a step into Blowers. 'Twats...Maddox, you come up too.'

'I'm fine,' Maddox says curtly.

'Fuck's sake, Maddox,' Blowers says, unable to hide the irritation he feels. 'It's hot as...'

'I'll go after.'

'You'll go now. The Boss will go after. This isn't...'

Maddox shrugs, passive and unbothered. 'Whatever,' he falls in behind them. Following to the same destination but not part of them. He becomes aware of Howie, Clarence, Roy and Reginald turning in the café to watch him walk past the windows. The pressure grows. The feeling of isolation and loneliness magnify.

'Mo Mo!' Cookey says at seeing the sentry outside the entrance to the shop. 'You alright mate?'

'Yeah good,' Mo says, still wondering what the hell shnure means.

'Hey,' Blowers goes in first, nodding at the three women then blanching at the piles of kit on the floor. 'What's that?'

'Charlie! Miss you...'

'Miss you too, Cookey.'

'Oh my god...is that lube? Fucking brilliant. And condoms?' Cookey laughs, looking at the products on the piles.

'What's this?' Nick asks, holding up a set of eye-lash crimpers that resembles a thumb torture device.

'Blowers, that one is yours,' Paula says, pointing to a pile. 'Nick, yours...Cookey, yours is this one...Mo? You come and get changed, sweetie...'

'Come on, sweetie,' Nick calls out.

'Honeybun?' Blowers calls.

'Pickle chops?' Cookey joins in.

'Maddox,' Paula says, her tone dropping a discernible notch as she says his name. 'I guessed your size...there's more over there if I got it wrong.'

'Hey sweetie,' Cookey says as Mo walks in. 'You okay fluffy pumpkin?'

'Pack it in,' Paula says, her voice rising in pleasure at speaking to Cookey.

'He's an iccle bunny,' Nick says, cooing as he leans in to pinch Mo's cheek.

'Fuck off,' Mo laughs, leaning away.

'You leave my Mo Mo alone,' Paula says, waggling a finger at Nick.

'Sorry, Paula,' Nick says with a grin.

'Lube,' Cookey drops down to pick the tube up. 'It says strawberry...is it flavoured? Oh my god...best day ever...you can actually eat this? Fuck yes! Blowers, try the lube...'

'Fuck off!'

'Go on, try it...eat some lube...'

'You eat it.'

'I will if you will...Nick, lick the lube...'

'I'm not licking lube.'

'Ah go on, Blowers, try it...'

'We'll leave you to it,' Marcy says, laughing at Cookey urging the others to eat lube.

'Marcy,' Cookey blurts, 'you try it...'

'I'm not eating lube, Cookey.'

'Ah someone do it...Charlie? You fancy some lube?'

'Cookey,' Blowers groans, wincing as he looks away.

'I already have and it is very nice,' Charlie says politely, holding a poker face as the three women walk down towards the back of the store.

'Dick,' Nick mutters with a chuckle at Cookey's shocked expression.

'Charlie? Did you really try the lube?' Cookey asks.

'Maybe,' she calls back, now blocked from view behind the shelves.

'Wow,' Cookey mumbles, staring at his tube of lube. 'Was it nice?' he shouts.

'Very nice,' Charlie shouts back. 'You can really taste the strawberries'

'Yeah?'

'Yes. Try it.'

'Um…yeah, yeah fuck it…' Cookey says, twisting the top off.

'What the fuck you doing?' Blowers asks, pulling his top off.

'Trying it,' Cookey says, staring at the curved plastic plunger at the top of the bottle. He squints at the label then gingerly pushes the plunger down to squeeze a dollop of clear looking gel into his hand. 'Argh it's slimey…'

'It's lube you idiot,' Nick says, laughing at him.

'Smells nice,' Cookey says, sniffing the gel in his hand.

'Oh you are fucking gross,' Blowers says, pulling a face at Cookey moving closer to the pile of goo in his hand. 'Don't… Cookey don't…'

'What? It's flavoured…'

'Yeah but, oh mate don't…'

'You can eat it,' Cookey says, looking up at Blowers as he pokes his tongue out towards the goo.

'Don't look at me and lick it you fucking dick…' Blowers protests.

'Look at me,' Cookey says in a mock deep sensual voice. 'I am licking the lube Simon Blowers…'

'Argh stop…you dirty fucker…Cookey…fucking stop it…'

'Mmmmm,' Cookey says, licking the lube while staring at Blowers. 'It's slimey…'

'Oh you…something wrong with you…' Blowers grimaces and turns away but can't help looking back while Nick and Mo laugh in delight.

'You want the lube Simon Blowers,' Cookey purrs.

'Stop that voice…just…oh mate that's gross…'

Cookey licks the lube. A long languorous lick that brings a big dollop into his mouth with the sensation of oily goo. He gags, yacks and spits with his face screwing up in distaste.

'You twat,' Blowers says, bursting out laughing.

'S'fucking gross,' Cookey bleats. 'Argh so gross…Charlie! It's gross…'

'Can't believe you did that,' Nick says, wiping the tears from his cheeks.

'Well,' Cookey says dully, standing up to look down at the dropped tube of lube. 'I ain't licking that off your willy, Blowers...'

'Fuck's sake, Cookey,' Blowers groans.

The three women laugh at the sound of Cookey, smiling and shaking heads as they reach an open chiller cabinet filled with bottles, cans, snack food and sealed packets of now mouldy sandwiches.

'Water?' Marcy asks at the sound of Cookey gagging.

'Yeah cheers,' Paula says.

'Charles?' Marcy asks, using the name Blinky called her with a smile.

'Thank you.'

Natural daylight fills the café and spills down the long aisle into the front of the store. The strength of light wanes over that distance but gives enough illumination for the lads to see what they are doing as they start stripping down and going through their kit. That light finds it harder to reach the back of the store. The display units, shelves and columns all work to block and prevent the spillage of that light which in turn, plunges the rear of the store into a darker area of shadows. Paula, Marcy and Charlie hardly notice it. It's entirely natural for them to move from light to shadow and they think nothing of it. Instead, they unscrew the lids from the bottles of water and take sips while wearing new dry clothes and with skin freshly cleansed and moisturised. Marcy lowers the bottle as a flash of a strobe effect of light crosses her eyes. She blinks and looks to see the end of the glass fronted perfume counter across the way. That reminds her of her desire to have perfume and so, while sipping, she looks down the row of perfumes on display with her eyes travelling the distance of the cabinet.

Movement catches her eye. She tenses, unsure of what she is seeing then instantly relaxing as she realises it's the reflection of the lads changing. Almost a mirror quality reflection too.

Paula sees Marcy staring and looks in the same direction to see what she is looking at. She too spots the perfumes and in an absent-minded manner of passing the time, she looks down the cabinet until the same movement catches her eye. A blink and her eyes process what the image she is seeing of the lads near the front changing.

Charlie sees both Marcy and Paula engrossed in staring at something so she shuffles a pace to follow the direction of their eyes to the perfume counter. She focusses to see what's on display and sips her water. The movement catches her eye. She frowns and looks further down to see the reflected image.

A moment in time is captured in seeing something through reflection rather than directly with the naked eye. And naked they are too. Well almost anyway.

Five young men with lean hard bodies who strip tops off to show flat defined stomachs and shoulders of muscularity and arms shaped just so. Of long legs defined with muscles and strong jaws.

It becomes like something from a soft drinks advert. Soldiers marked with grime and dirt stripped down to underwear as they laugh and joke and use wet wipes to rub those smudges away.

It's not the lads they watch. It's not Blowers, Cookey, Nick, Maddox and Mo. The identity of them is removed. The association of knowing them drops away. That none of them linger their eyes on Mo is left unspoken because they don't speak. They are each removed from the desperation of this time and taken to a place, for a few seconds, where the admiration can be taken without offence or perversion.

What they see is Blowers' strong arms packed with muscle from the years of boxing that have honed and shaped his biceps and triceps up to his shoulders and formed striations across his chest.

What they see is the bulge of the muscles in Maddox's defined stomach and the way those muscles bunch and stretch as he stretches and twists to clean himself with the wipes.

They see Cookey's frame, lean and hard without an ounce of fat showing and the contrast between his light skin tone to that of Maddox. Both defined, both hardened and so different but so similar in shape. That contrast of skin colour mesmerises them for a second, captivating and forgetting where they are and what they are doing.

As one, the three women glance to Nick. Taller than the others and that extra height brings a symmetry to his shape and frame. His wide shoulders just starting to bulk with muscle and so broad too. They take in his arms, chest and stomach and his easy quick smile that flashes as someone makes a joke. Nick *is* the Diet-Coke advert. Paula blinks, Marcy swallows and Charlie sighs all without knowing they do so.

'She's a lucky girl,' Marcy whispers with a voice giving sound to the thoughts in her head of Lilly.

'She is,' Paula whispers back, caught in the same thought process.

'Very,' Charlie whispers.

The bubble pops. The realisation of voyeurism as Marcy suddenly blushes and turns away. Paula blasts air and looks down to read the label on the bottle of water as Charlie shakes her head and turns on the spot to stare at the range of baby feed bowls.

They start chuckling. Low and embarrassed with glances to each other that set them off more as the laughing becomes louder at the way they caught themselves doing something naughty. Marcy makes a point of leaning to look down at the glass again and adds a sigh that sets the other two off.

'What they laughing at?' Cookey asks, pulling on his new trousers.

'Probably you eating that lube,' Nick says, fastening his belt then working to get the pistol holster in the right place.

Blowers turns to bend over. His frame clad only in boxers as he unknowingly presents his arse towards the perfume counter. A split second later the sound of three women laughing floats down.

'You alright?' Nick calls out.

'Fine! Yep fine,' someone shouts down, the voice somewhat strangled and choked from laughing.

Now is the time for Maddox to bridge that gap. He could make a comment, an observation or a simple passing remark on how nice it is to be clean and wearing new clothes. He could at least try and deep down he knows that first step will be rejected but in time he will be accepted. However, what he also notices is that he is now losing his identity even more than before. The clothes he wore were his own and he maintained a difference of appearance to the others. Now he is wearing the same as them. Black trousers and a black wicking top. He has uniformity which to him is a step into being what *they* are.

So he doesn't offer to bridge that gap. Instead, he scowls and feels the isolation growing more profound until finally, they are all dressed and his last shred of pride feels lost and gone.

The lads head back down the aisle, leaving Mo to resume his serious work of sentry and guard to the three inside the store. Blowers, Cookey and Nick each offered to take over for a bit but he stated he was happy enough to stay.

'We up?' Clarence calls out, seeing the lads stroll back down.

'Yep,' Blowers says, giving a thumbs up.

'Got lube,' Cookey says, showing them the tube in his hands.

'Got a longbow,' Roy says, still eager to show them what it can do.

Clarence looks at Howie and the worry shows in the big man's eyes. The energy is pouring off Howie. The disquiet of mind. The unsettled nerves that long to be running and fighting and doing anything instead of sitting still. Clarence knows Howie is doing this because everyone else needs the downtime to decompress and the day is already long. The afternoon has given way to evening and soon the twilight will come. They'll get their kit and move off to find somewhere for the night. He rises from his chair, thinking to find a time later to broach the subject of what happened, or ask

Paula or Marcy to do it tonight. Probably Marcy. She'll be the best one when they take first watch. One thought leads to another and he smiles at his bag now full of horse treats ready for the Second Watch Biscuit Club.

'We're going up,' Clarence calls out to the lads at the front. The five men walk up the aisle. One huge. One holding a longbow. One dark and brooding. One small and pushing his glasses up his nose and one other small man that shows no outward expression as he spots Mo standing sentry.

Mo spots Dave and almost comes to attention. Visibly straightening to stand taller at the sight of the five elders heading towards him. These men hold power. An aura of capability surrounds them. The lads are tough, Marcy and Paula are exceptional but these men are the core. Roy suits being with them. Reginald too. The five have a presence that seems to silence any noise save for the tread of their feet and the rustle of bags and kit. Nobody can kill Dave. Nobody can outthink Reginald. Nobody can match Clarence for strength. Nobody can fire a bow like Roy and nobody will ever come close to Mr Howie.

They nod and smile at Mo. A few gentle words spoken that lift him inches until Clarence pats him on the shoulder and drives him back down.

That aura goes with them into the store and the mood, that only a minute ago was jovial and child-like in humour, grows serious and meaningful.

'You okay?' Marcy asks, looking directly at Howie.

'Fine,' he says, 'you?'

'Yeah fine.'

'Roy,' Paula says, smiling at him then at Clarence then back at Roy and moving quickly to hide the slight fluster she suddenly feels inside.

'I fired my longbow,' Roy says, smiling happily.

'Oh,' Paula says. 'Er, any good?'

'Very good,' Clarence booms. 'Took a sign off at the fittings.'

'That's great,' Paula says.

'Perhaps I will go and check on Jess,' Charlie says, as polite as ever in the astute sensing of a feeling of imposition at the dynamics changing so quickly.

'You okay, Charlie?' Howie asks as the girl goes past.

'Yes, fine, thank you, Mr Howie.'

'Charlie?'

'Yes, Mr Howie.'

'Maddox was wrong in what he said...'

'I should not have broken that man's finger,' Charlie replies quickly, firmly and dipping her eyes in apology as she speaks.

'Not now,' Paula cuts in. 'We'll discuss it later but Charlie? Do not worry. You're fine, okay?'

'Thank you,' she says, nodding respectfully and seemingly hesitating as though waiting to see if Mr Howie is happy for her to go.

'Catch you in a minute,' Howie says. 'Right, we got new kit then? Is that lube?'

'Yeah it was er...just a joke for the lads,' Marcy says.

'Howie, this is yours,' Paula explains, 'Clarence...yours is the huge pile...Roy, this is yours, Dave...yours is right there next to Reggie's. We'll leave you to get changed...Marce, can you grab that empty bag please love, we'll empty that drinks cabinet while we're here.'

The two walk off back to the gloom at the rear as the five start dropping kit to undress and clean. Reginald, being a sensitive soul, takes his to the other side of a shelving unit for a degree of privacy while the others disrobe where they are without shame or worry.

'Tense,' Marcy whispers, holding the bag open for Paula to load with bottled drinks.

'Just a bit,' Paula whispers back. She glances up over Marcy's shoulder to the perfume section and the reflection of Clarence and Roy cleaning themselves with wipes. She pauses, growing still as Marcy clocks the way her eyes flick left and right. Marcy turns to look and spots the two men as Paula resumes loading the bag.

'You okay?' Marcy asks, glancing back at Paula.

'Fine,' Paula says.

Marcy stares at the reflection and finds Howie in the view but even with the intimacy of her relationship with him it somehow still feels wrong to be looking. 'Strange days,' she mumbles, turning back to look at Paula.

'You sound like Howie,' Paula remarks.

'Hmmm,' Marcy says. 'So you fancy Clarence then?'

Paula freezes again. Her left hand in the cabinet. Her right in the bag held by Marcy. A look of panic steals across her face. An imploring look up at Marcy who flinches and edges closer.

'Wow,' Marcy whispers, lowering down to make extra sure no one can hear them. 'I was only joking...'

'Yeah, yeah, haha, funny,' Paula tries to laugh it off but the words stumble out awkward and weird.

'Oh my god, Paula...you fancy Clarence?'

'I'm not thirteen, Marcy,' Paula says stiffly.

'Still a woman though,' Marcy retorts. 'Does he know?'

'Know what?'

'Paula,' Marcy says in such a way it tells Paula she thinks she is talking shit.

'No,' Paula groans, receiving the *stop talking shit* message loud and clear.

'Christ, Dave. You done already?' Howie's voice floats back to them.

'Yes, Mr Howie,' Dave's dull tone comes a second later.

Paula huffs and turns to plonk her arse down on the front ledge of the drinks cabinet. A can of Coke Cola in her hand. The full sugar one too. She pops the cap, lets the bubbles rise and takes a long drink before offering the can to Marcy.

'Share?'

'Ta,' Marcy says, taking the can as she plonks down next to Paula.

They share the can of coke, listening to the deep voice of Clarence and the others all making conversation as they change. Marcy goes to say something but Paula waves her hand.

'We're done,' Howie calls up.

'Okay,' Paula calls down. 'We'll be down in a minute…got a few more bits to get.'

'Need a hand?' Clarence asks making Marcy smile mischievously as Paula slaps her leg.

'No, we're fine, thanks, Clarence.'

'*Mo's still on the door*,' Howie transmits as he walks out with the others.

'*Yep, thanks*,' Paula radios back.

'So?' Marcy asks into the silence that follows. 'Wanna talk?'

CHAPTER TWENTY-ONE

'*Charlie, you come inside, love,*'
    '*On way...are we here for a while? I'll leave Jess out if we are...it's too hot in the horsebox if we're not moving.*'

She never imagined they would be like this and to hear them talk is weird. Nice but weird. She glances at the radio in the central console then across to Paco who, in the last few minutes, has suddenly discovered his fingertips are the perfect size for shoving up his nose.

'Stop it,' she says, reaching over to pull his right hand down as his left hand comes up to continue the exploration. 'Paco, stop it. You'll make it bleed.'

Paco leaves his nose alone and smiles at Heather. 'Ether.'

'What?' she asks, glancing ahead to the road then back at him.

'Ether.'

'Yes, what?'

'Ether.'

'Yep.'

She decided to drive round the town rather than going through it. She did consider driving through and *accidentally* bumping into them again, then maybe stopping for a bit and you know, just hang around and chat with Paula and stuff. Then she worried it would be obvious and weird so she navigated the Toyota off the slip road and into the country lanes that fed round the town towards the big hill on the far side. Now she drives steady with her left hand resting on the top of the steering wheel and her right hanging out the window to feel the air rushing by. She should close the windows to make the air-con work better but it's nice to feel the hot air blasting over her arm.

'Zade.'

'You've had loads.'

'Ether...'

'What?'

'Zade.'

'No. You've had too many.'

'Ether...zade...'

'Paco I said no...actually, know what? You're a grown adult so if you want Lucozade you can have Lucozade...' she reaches back to rummage through the bag as he grins widely with an expression that makes her chuckle.

She hands the bottle to him. He takes it but finds her holding on. He looks at the bottle then at her as she lifts an eyebrow.

'Zade...'

'Yep.'

He tries to pull it gently from her hand but she holds on. He frowns, puzzled and trying so hard to understand what he is required to do. That expression brings forth a rush of guilt that she's treating him like a child and he's not a child. His behaviour is sometimes child-like but he is a man. A grown adult and a very dangerous one at that. As she sends the signal from her brain to her hand to release the bottle so he suddenly grins.

'Ank-you,' he blurts, gravelly and broken but clear enough to be understood.

It makes her feel worse. The tiny nuances of emotions that lift and plummet and form the day of a human being.

'Welcome,' she says, slowing the Toyota to a stop at the edge of the junction. Right is towards the town. Left is away from the town but the direction she wants is ahead to go up that big hill and find somewhere to rest for the night. A nice barn or stables in a large field and with a sweeping view of the town below. The heat makes her think there will be a storm soon, which in turn sends a creeping sense of dread crawling up her spine. Astraphobia has dominated her life since childhood. A debilitating fear of thunder and lightning that stems from the realisation of a complete loss of control. That the forces of nature can make such noise and throw barbs of pure bright energy at the ground terrifies her. Her mother was a heroin-addicted prostitute that died when Heather was young. The system failed thereafter and Heather was left to suffer the awful circuit of foster homes where the foster carers were not allowed to hug or show physical affection, either that or they showed too much physical affection and in the wrong way. Those formative years shaped her life. She was intelligent but could never settle or make a decision on what she wanted from life. Only that whatever she chose had to be away from other people. All of those things manifested into a fear of a loss of control, and a storm is the biggest reminder of the insignificance of a mere mortal.

Now, for the first time in her adult life, she is making connections to people. Paco is a person, albeit an extremely strange one who is currently trying to pick his nose, drink Lucozade and stare at Heather all at the same time.

She heads left with an instinct telling her the road will lead up the hill. As she drives, and as Paco guzzles, picks, delves, fidgets and stares she thinks of the people down in the town and resumes the train of thought that Howie and the others are not what she expected.

She'd sort of tracked them for the last couple of days, and having seen what they leave behind, she assumed they would be hardened, cold, bloodthirsty bastards who didn't give a shit about anything other than killing the infected. As it turns out, only one of those presumptions has proven to be correct, that they are hardened. Yes, she admits to herself, there are degrees within them of being bloodthirsty cold bastards but through necessity rather than design. In fact, they appear to be incredibly caring and loyal, and while at the same time as being highly capable, they are ridiculously incompetent. Mind you, it has only been what, twenty days since it began?

'That's fair enough then,' she tells Paco then tuts as he quickly pulls his finger from his nose. She bursts out laughing at the sudden memory of the old woman shoving the coffee cup into him that was so wrong but so funny at the same time.

Paco goes still at her laughing but the sound is nice and even though he doesn't know what made her laugh he grins and laughs too. Broken and guttural but clearly a chuckle.

'Blinky, you come up and get changed,'

'Yes, Miss Paula, Sir. One way now, Sir.'

Heather's eyes flick to the radio with a puzzled expression at Blinky calling Paula sir. They are right there, in that town doing whatever it is they do. Again she gets that prickling feeling of weirdness at the connection and inclusion. She can hear them talking and they sound so normal and...well, *informal* she guesses is the right word.

'Anyway,' she tells Paco who looks over with deep interest. 'We've got our job to do haven't we?'

Paco doesn't say if he considers the question to be direct or rhetorical but holds his Lucozade bottle upside down to show Heather it is now empty.

'We'll chillax tonight then...oh my god...did I just say chillax? I said chillax. I hate myself right now...'

'Ether.'

'Yes, I know. I said chillax. I bet that's something you would say. *Hey there, I'm Paco Maguire and I've shagged a thousand women and I like to chillax...*' she mimics a deep American voice at him as he waggles the bottle upside down.

'Dirty bugger,' she tuts at him. 'Anyway, so...we'll find somewhere tonight then make a start in the morning. Yes? Agreed? Paco? Do you agree? Say yes I agree...Paco? Say yes...'

'Ess.'

'Agreed then...'

'Zade.'

'Eh? Already! No more, Paco. Seriously...so what do we do anyway? Like just knock on doors and tell people they're immune? *Oh hi, we're from the fort and this is the famous actor Paco Maguire that was bitten by a dog for being a zombie but he's totally fine now...so yeah, you're immune. Please go directly to the fort and do not tell anyone....especially the zombies...*what do you think? Do we say that?'

'Zade.'

'No more, Paco. I suppose that's all we can do really, isn't it? Just find them and tell them what they are. I mean, what else *can* we do? Oh, oh yeah, I guess we could actually take them to the fort...you know...to make sure they get there safely. Hmm, I think that's what Howie meant actually. What do you think?'

'Ess.'

'Yeah? You think so too? I think so too. Okay, we'll do that. So we find them *and* offer to escort them. Do we do one at a time or several all at once? I think there's a couple near here so we could do both...'

She drives and chats as the vehicle starts a gentle incline that grows steadily steeper as the road weaves up the side of the hill. High hedgerows on both sides block their view from anything but the immediate area.

Pure coincidence means they miss the infected pouring over the land towards the town they drive away from. They don't see the lines rushing down the hill and they drive through the gap between two hordes crossing the road from one footpath to the other with no knowledge of any such thing. The engine blots any sound of running feet. The restricted view blots any view of the forms running. Instead, they climb steadily as Heather chats on feeling an ever so strange sense of being just slightly at ease with the world. Like things are right and not wrong for once.

'Blowers, the others can come up.'

'Yep, cheers, Paula.'

Heather looks down at the radio once again musing on how normal they sound and idly wondering what they are doing right now. By looking at the radio she misses the glimpse of the infected man disappearing into the field as she navigates a bend in the road. Paco continues shaking his bottle and also misses the infected man.

On they drive without any knowledge of what they drive through. It's hot. The windows are open. They have things to do and a destination to aim for. They have guns and food and drinks. That air of complacency that infests the team in the town and makes them separate and relax their awareness extends to Heather now. They've had a battle today already. The team have had two in fact. The first in rescuing Paco and Heather and the second on returning to the fort. Those things, coupled with the heat, reduce the expectation of a fight.

The road winds on up the hill, snaking between the high thick hedges. At times she cranes to see through to search for the top of the hill but those times are fleeting and uncommitted in serious intent.

Paco asks for *zade*. She gives him water. He stares at the water and asks for *zade* and so they focus on the issue surrounding Paco having too much sugar and glucose, which serves to distract from the invasion underway.

They reach the crest of the hill. The pinnacle. The top. The summit. A plateau of land formed millions of years ago by the shifting of plates deep within the earth that made the peaks and dips. On this peak rests fields, meadows and glades of trees complete with stables, barns and all manner of gloriously rural outbuildings that promise an evening of quiet rustic shelter. They drive slowly so Heather can enjoy the decision making process. She reaches a five bar gate leading into a field that slopes down a little with a promise of a commanding view of the town below. A block of wooden framed outbuildings to one side. It looks good. She jumps out to open the gate as Paco jumps down to follow her opening the gate. She gets back in to drive through and waits for Paco to get back in so she can drive through.

She deliberates for a few seconds on whether to close the gate behind them or not and after weighing the options she concedes it is better to have an open escape route so leaves the gate open.

She looks ahead to the buildings and drives the Toyota bouncing over the pitted grass. A hose on the side is a good sign as it means they can have a decent wash and get changed. She sighs as she stops the vehicle and stares at the idyllic setting and that promise of a beautiful evening stretching out in front of them. Hopefully there will be bales of straw or hay they can split to make soft beds to rest on. Old blankets and a small fire to cast a flickering glow.

With the engine switched off, she clambers out and waits for Paco while remembering what Blowers said about taking her rifle with her. Does she need it here? They've got pistols and she's got Paco. She goes to walk on then stops, tuts and goes back to the vehicle to pull the heavy rifle out that she checks the way she was taught to do.

'Perfect,' she says a few minutes later after breaking the lock on the barn door to see the best inside-of-a-barn she has yet to see. A concrete floor. Bales of straw. Old blankets stacked up. A gas stove too. Matches and even a pan for boiling water. She stretches and sighs, suddenly feeling very tired. She didn't sleep last night but spent the previous day and night running and fighting. She should be exhausted and ready to drop. 'Looks nice eh?' she says to Paco.

'Ess,' Paco doesn't actually know what he is saying yes to, but he does know that giving a verbal response seems to make Heather happy.

'Can we see the town from here?' she asks him.

He doesn't know if they can see the town from here but follows as she walks on across the field that starts sloping down to that promised view of the land below. It takes a few minutes to get far enough into the field to allow the lay of the land to drop away enough and with the sun starting to set so she has to blink and squint and use her hand to shield her eyes.

'*Mo's still on the door.*'

'*Yep, thanks.*'

The transmission startles her. The unexpected hearing of voices from the radio now on her belt. She recognises Howie's and Paula's voices and again wonders what they are doing as her eyes adjust to the glare and she begins to make out the details of the town below.

Time stops. Her blood runs cold as her heart thunders from normal to frantic in the blink of an eye. Paco stiffens, growing in stature as his hands ball into fists at the sight of thousands of figures running into the town from all sides. So many. So so many. She blinks and stares harder, seeing thick dense hordes already in the town. Every street seems to be full. Every road is choked with them. She scans while her hands tremble and her legs suddenly grow rubbery and weak.

'Oh my god...oh my god...'

There, right in the middle of the town is the centre and the only place not filled with infected. One long road and right in the middle, even from this distance, are three distinctive vehicles. The Saxon. The van and the horsebox. They're trapped. Encircled on all sides and that mass of darkness is collapsing in towards the last remaining patch of light in the middle. She spots what must be Jess and Charlie, the shape blurred but just about recognisable. Two more figures further down at the opposite end of the street. She can see the infected are metres away as they disappear into the premises bordering the empty street.

Her hands move to grab the radio that is lifted as she presses the button, inhales and shouts.

'OUT...GET OUT...TRAP TRAP...GET OUT NOW...'

CHAPTER TWENTY-TWO

'Mate, I'm telling you...you have to fucking snap out of it...' Blowers says, staring at him. A last ditch effort. A last attempt as he patrols down the precinct towards the road that bends round to the specialist stores. He stops and looks round, seeing Nick leaning in the back of the van tinkering with the drone charging unit.

'This a pep talk?' Maddox asks, not bothering to hide the sneer. Blowers had decided to walk him down to the road as in patrolling the area but to buy distance and a few minutes to talk. He now bites the anger down and glares at Maddox wondering what he can do or say to make the situation better. Maddox looks round disdainfully in a way to show Blowers he's not interested in the conversation. He spots Charlie at the far end of the precinct on Jess and venturing further down the road. Cookey and Blinky someway back from Charlie and over to the left side.

'Maddox,' Blowers says, forcing a tone of calmness into his voice. 'What can I do?'

Maddox doesn't answer but watches as Howie, Clarence, Dave, Reginald and Roy walk from the shopping centre.

'Mate?' Blowers says in frustrated desperation. 'The boss won't leave you at the fort with Lilly...he won't let you go either in case you...'

'A lesson in addition to a pep talk then.'

'Fine,' Blowers says, thereby giving up. 'On you, mate...'

'SEEN WHAT'S OVER THERE,' Nick says on seeing Roy.

'What's that?' Roy asks, wanting nothing more than to show Nick his longbow. He follows Nick's gaze to the Halfords store, the vehicle audio, electrical and cycle parts shop so ubiquitous in every town centre.

'Ah,' Roy says, smiling back at Nick. 'We could get some tools...'

'I was thinking about rigging up the water thing,' Nick says.

'We'll have a look,' Roy says, falling into step with Nick as they walk across the road.

'WELL, I shall retire to my books,' Reginald says, nodding at Clarence, Dave and Howie.

'Yeah okay,' Howie says, 'er...so where are they?'

'I can only assume they are not here,' Reginald says, as equally stumped as to lack of show from the other player. 'I should imagine we have been seen...in fact I would guarantee we have been seen but as to why they are not attacking or showing I cannot, at this time, rightly say.'

He goes into his command unit. Now refreshed with tea and conversation that did not contain boobs, bums and willies as the main subjects. He rests down into his chair and starts opening his bag to take out his books while all the time feeling increasingly uneasy at the lack of contact from the other side.

'SO?' Marcy says, urging Paula to explain and give the gossip. Both of them sit perched on the edge of the drinks cabinet entirely unaware of the dark shapes moving above their heads that creep out from the gaps in the ceiling tiles. Hundreds. Thousands. All of them held in place by the single conscious will of an entity evolving with frightening speed. Small ones, big ones and each with eight legs that they use to start abseiling down on almost invisible strands of web.

'Oh nothing,' Paula groans, rubbing her face. 'Ignore me.'

'No no no...tell me about Clarence.'

'Tell you what?'

'Oh you so fancy him. I can tell...you keep looking at him then going all weird and flustered.'

'I do not!'

'You so do. Admit it...go on...'

'What's the point?'

'You do then?'

Mo stands sentinel. Idly staring round and wondering where they will stay tonight. He doesn't know where the feeling comes from or what causes it. He doesn't hear anything or see anything but the rush inside is so strong it cannot be denied. It comes now. That feeling rushes through him in the otherwise silent air of an empty shopping centre.

THE AIR IS LISTLESS with no breeze and that single thing prevents the smell of the infected reaching her until they are so close there is no room for evasion or preparatory manoeuvre. Now she locks on to the smell. The fetid rancid decay of tainted blood that pumps inside thousands of bodies that she now, at this instant knows are on all sides. She gives voice instant and strong. She barks with a huge sound to tell them to stay back and stay away. She tells them who she is. She tells them her pack are strong and they will die if they come here. She gives fair warning to them and to her own, all of whom snap to the voice of Heather screaming through their radios.

'*OUT...GET OUT...TRAP TRAP...GET OUT NOW...*'

A blink of an eye. A beat of a heart.

'*CONTACT CONTACT CONTACT...*' Mo's voice, bellowing from his position on the door.

Every window in the street explodes out in showers of glass as the infected, having crept unheard, unseen and undetected through the buildings, now charge forward while screeching to crash into the street.

The spectacle is staggering. The split second between calm and the detonation of utter chaos of every window on the ground and first floors smashing out with bodies surging into the street. Those that come through the first floor simply drop to snap bones or die from impacts with a sickening display of an intent to sacrifice host bodies for the goal in sight.

Mo releases his radio switch as the windows at the end of the shopping centre blow out in a huge crashing splintering cacophony of noise and motion. The rear doors to the shopping centre were left open by survivors who wished to have a discrete way into the mall. The infected took those survivors and knew about those doors. It crept through, staying low in shadows and barely inching forward as the mass grew from the hordes pouring across the land into the town.

That same blink of an eye. That same beat of a heart sees his pistols drawn, aimed and firing at the figures already recovering from smashing through the windows.

THE STRUCTURE of the Arachnid species differs between

types. Some have six eyes, others have eight, some only two. Some eat the webs of other spiders. Some eat other spiders. They don't have true blood either but an open circulatory system that pumps haemolymph from a heart through arteries into spaces surrounding their internal organs. It was this factor that either enabled or prevented the differing types of the species either taking or rejecting the virus.

As the infection gained the knowledge of the likely destination of Howie so it sent human hosts into lofts, sheds and garages to seek, find and pass the infection. Some bit into the spiders but that killed them. Others tried to bleed on the spiders but the creatures were too fast to flee. Others stuck their hands and appendages towards the arachnids and simply waited to be bitten. Spiders bite in attack and defence and so they bit to draw blood that was taken in. Some simply buggered off, heedless to the filth within the blood. Others turned and took the blood in that changed the composition of what they are. Those spiders became ramped, charged, pumped and frenzied, but like the rats from days before, their small bodies are unable to withstand the virus for any substantial length of time.

The infection does not need a substantial length of time. It needs this time now to create panic with the use of a host that causes more fear than any other creature on the planet.

It knows that spiders respond to pheromones. So it dumps pheromones. Lots of them, and it makes the spiders wild with aggression.

Garden spiders, house spiders, huge wolf spiders, daddy long legs, orb weavers, false widows, money spiders, spotted wolfs, spitting spiders and more that range from tiny to huge. Many were already hovering in the air above Paula and Marcy, hanging on strands of web while more clung by their claws to the ceiling tiles.

Now the pulse of an urge is sent through their tiny brains and the ceilings of the shops, buildings, flats and houses in the town centre broil with dark masses of eight legged creatures that become frenzied for food.

Paula and Marcy snap their heads up to look forward at first the sound of Heather's voice then Mo's. In that blink of an eye and a beat of a heart so the windows within the centre implode as the attack is launched. They both surge up to their feet as the spiders drop. They both flinch in confusion at the overwhelming assault to their senses of people screaming, Mo firing, windows breaking, infected screeching and the feel of hundreds of things landing in their hair, on their faces and down their bare arms.

At that second they gain awareness. At that second they feel the thousands of clawed feet scrabbling for purchase on their skin. At that second the true realisation hits home and as one they look up to a ceiling now alive and seething with spiders that drop in a deluge of spindly legs, sharp claws and sharper fangs that dig into whatever they can find. They both scream out with an instinctive revulsion that renders them unable to gain coherent thought. Some miss and hit the floor where they run hither and thither until they find feet to climb and legs to crawl up.

More land on Paula and Marcy. Burrowing into hair and dropping down backs to claw down their spines. Wild panic grips them. An utter disbelief of a thing happening. Spiders don't do this. Spiders are solitary creatures. It is happening. They can feel it. They can feel the mad scrabble of eight legged things crawling over their cheeks and the strands of silk formed in silk glands and pumped through their anus-like spinnerets. Fangs dig in. Some are too small to pierce the layers of human skin but they try. They bite and claw and dump pheromones that send the others wild and crazed. Others can bite and they do. They dig those sharp fangs into the skin to inject venom ready to liquefy the insides to be sucked out and consumed.

Paula screams the loudest she has ever screamed. A screech of pure terror from her worst nightmare now coming true. Marcy spins on the spot, beating herself with wild thumps and slaps. She plucks spiders from her arms as more crawl down over her face. She slaps and hits herself, thrashing wilder with every passing second.

Paula flails, spinning and screaming into a shelving unit that crashes over sending baby goods flying over the floor. Marcy stamps, slaps and shouts while outside Mo's pistols boom one after the other and overhead the sky splits with an almighty crack of thunder from the clouds that formed as unseen as the infected pouring into the town.

Spiders are crushed, squashed, flung away, booted, hit and slapped but for every single arachnid they kill so hundreds more continue to rain down from the ceiling tiles.

Mo hears their screams but he can't move. The attack is too strong and the infected are coming too fast. Training kicks in. The calmness of the moment. Aim and fire. One after the other. *Emotions do not aid us. Fear does not aid us. Anger does not aid us.* He takes that step into the world shown to him by Dave. Aim and fire. Aim and fire. Heads blow apart from the bullets sent spinning through. Bodies drop as Mo makes every shot count. Thunder overhead. Noises from the front. Marcy and Paula screaming behind him. He stays calm and denies the prickle of panic inside his gut.

IN THE STREET they are caught completely unprepared. Cookey and Blinky strolling up on the left side trading insults to score points freeze as Heather's voice shouts through the radio. They spin to look back, both already switching to focus as Mo shouts contact. A second in time passes then the windows go. An explosion of glass from what feels like every window in the street bursting out from human figures charging through. Bodies drop from windows. The sounds of bones snapping and the dull thuds of meat impacting from a drop. Screeches fill the air. Inhuman and wild. The whole street comes alive with hordes pouring to fill the spaces between them and the others. The infected charge. They both blanch in the second it takes to change the mind-set and prepare to fight. Shots ring out as the closest attackers spin away with heads blown apart.

CHARLIE HEARS Heather then Mo and twitches to bring Jess round as the street detonates. Glass showers down and all around her. Voices wild and primeval fill the air. Gunshots from the shopping centre. Everything happening in the blink of an eye and the beat of a heart. She flinches at a body dropping from a window above aiming straight at her but the thing is slammed away in mid-air. No time to look again or think. The gap between her and Cookey and Blinky is already filled, the same with the spaces between all of them.

NICK AND ROY hear the same thing. The burst transmission from Heather then Mo. They freeze, spinning on the spot as Roy reaches back to draw an arrow from the top of his bag. The windows go to the left, to the right and on the other side of the street. Glass fragments spray out as Nick lifts his rifle with an instinct telling him to make ready. The blink of an eye, the beat of a heart and the beasts come screeching and wild. Roy takes one step out and spots the street already seething. Further up he sees Charlie on Jess and a body bursting from a window above. He lifts, draws and fires to send the arrow shooting across the street that slams the falling male with such power it snaps the body away from Charlie who digs in to make Jess give flight and gain distance.

In that instant they can both see the street is lost.

IN THE DEAD centre of the street stand three men. Three men who cock heads at the transmission from Heather. Three men who turn at the transmission from Mo and three men who then look round to the windows of the street exploding out.

Here there is no panic. Their calmness is sublime. This is what they do. This is why they are here. For this. To do just this. Nothing else. Be as you are. Be as you were born to be and do not heed the worries of others or the small things of life that give concern for you are a warrior and this is your time.

Howie and Clarence lift rifles in the same second they realise neither of them are good enough to shoot without risk of missing and hitting their own. Dave *is* good enough. This is fact. His rifle lifts aims and commences with perfect single shots that buy Cookey and Blinky time to react. He saw the body plummeting from the window towards Charlie but he also saw Roy drawing back which told him which targets to choose.

Howie takes it all in. The noise is all around and in that blink of an eye and beat of a heart he knows there is no possible way to get everyone back to the vehicles. The numbers coming in are too many and moving too fast.

'Dave, cover Clarence...Clarence, get Reggie to Nick and Roy... both of you,' Howie shouts, snapping Nick and Roy's heads over as he points at the shop behind them. 'Get in...get up,' he points up as he shouts the order. 'Nick, protect Roy. Roy, overwatch. Reggie, go with them...'

Clarence runs to grab a terrified Reginald from the van and fills his arms with the bags of spare arrows taken from the sports shop. Nick smashes the window as Roy fires the bow at the infected coming close.

Howie hunkers down, dropping to a crouch to bend his body and shield the background noise from his radio. He presses the button to speak but the noise is too immense, drowning out his voice. 'Dave...orders...'

'Ready, Mr Howie,' Dave says between plucking shots.

'Tell everyone to leg it...'

'ORDERS...TEAM   WILL   SCATTER...IN   AN ORDERLY FASHION...' Dave's immense voice booms over the precinct. His words fast but clear as his mind works to track targets that he shoots down between the words.

'Tell 'em to stay calm...we'll be okay.'

'TEAM WILL REMAIN CALM...'

'Just hide until we call them back...'

'TEAM WILL GO TO GROUND AND WAIT ORDERS...'

'That includes Charlie cos she'll try and fight the lot on her own...'

'CHARLOTTE...THAT   INCLUDES   YOU... SCATTER AND WAIT ORDERS...'

That's it. That's all there is time for. The surge is so great that Clarence just about gets Reginald through the now smashed window to Nick and Roy before the ever growing horde closes in. Dave walks backwards firing burst shots to get as many as he can as Howie slings his rifle and pulls his axe overhead as the first one charges at him. He steps away, expecting to see the infected woman go past but her reactions are fast and she turns to close in. With nothing else to do he goes forward to slam his forehead into her face. Bones crunch. Blood sprays. She drops from the impact and finds the axe coming down to cleave through her neck.

Clarence turns from the window expecting to draw his axe but the ferocity and speed of the attack is staggering. The sheer over-whelming aggression is incredible. A cluster of men and women slam bodily into him driving the big man back through the window Nick broke. The window ledge snags Clarence's ankles making him topple backwards with mouths and nails coming in faster than he has time to react. He thrashes to fight, bunching his great fists that start whacking them aside like ragdolls. A glimpse through the bodies to Dave already with two knives drawn and spinning to fight and a flash of a view of Howie lashing out with his axe.

'CLARENCE STAY DOWN STAY DOWN.'

Clarence stays down. He really stays down. He really stays down to avoid the bullets firing inches above him as Nick goes to the side to strafe the bodies attacking him.

'CLEAR...'

Clarence surges to gain his feet and charge out into the fray but this time with his axe drawn and ready.

BLOWERS AND MADDOX glaring at each other with open hatred are caught as unawares as everyone else.

First the transmission from Heather. *'OUT...GET OUT... TRAP TRAP...GET OUT NOW...'*

Then the transmission from Mo. *'CONTACT CONTACT CONTACT.'*

A blink of an eye. A beat of a heart and the windows blow out down the length of the precinct. The sight is spectacular. An entrancing visual phenomenon as the final rays of sunlight pushing through the rapidly darkening clouds catch the chunks and shards of glass that twinkle and shine as they fall down. Both of them blink. Both stunned at the noise and sight. Both rooted to the spot as hundreds of infected pour through the ground level and first floor windows. They see bodies drop to die and the simple snuffing of lives gone for nothing other than a show of power from a side only too willing to sacrifice its own hosts.

'Fuck,' Blowers mouths, snapping to the now and the sudden change of events that his soldiers eyes process. He goes forward intending to run back to the vehicles but already the precinct is thick with too many. He stops to scan round, desperately seeking alternatives. He knows he cannot fire into the infected for fear of hitting his own team.

Maddox has no such worries and strides past Blowers with his rifle lifting to brace in his shoulder. Blowers reacts fast, lunging while shouting at him not to fire. A single pluck of the trigger sends a round through a window with the noise lost in the bedlam of the attack.

'What the fuck,' Maddox shouts, jerking away.

'Friendly fire you cunt,' Blowers snaps, glaring back at the already packed precinct then behind to empty street at the rear. 'Come on...'

'You joking?' Maddox asks in genuine shock as Blowers moves towards the precinct.

'Now, Maddox...we'll run through...'

'Fuck that,' Maddox booms, backing away while shaking his head. His eyes wide, his whole manner that of a man with a firm decision in mind.

'We can't leave them...' Blowers shouts, snapping from the sight of the hordes pouring in to Maddox backing away. In just seconds the street is gone and with it the chance of reaching the vehicles. He snarls, grimaces and thinks to go anyway. His mates are there.

'ORDERS...TEAM WILL SCATTER...IN AN ORDERLY FASHION...'

'Bollocks,' Blowers spits, seeing the sense of the orders.

'TEAM WILL REMAIN CALM...'

Blowers knows that it will be Howie telling Dave what to say and that single fact eases the grip of fear in his guts. For Howie to be so calm means he knows the others are all okay.

'TEAM WILL GO TO GROUND AND WAIT ORDERS...'

It makes sense. Everyone can starburst and work a way through later. They can regroup and come back to fight in formation.

'CHARLOTTE...THAT   INCLUDES   YOU... SCATTER AND WAIT ORDERS...'

'Come on,' Blowers turns to tell Maddox to move and spots the lad already running away. That Dave told them to run is one thing but Maddox *already* running is still fucking annoying. He legs it after him. Running hard to sprint away from the precinct. 'NO,' he shouts after Maddox heading down the street they came from. There's more shops down there and the buildings are high on both sides. To go that way is inviting to be trapped.

Maddox stops to see Blowers staring at him. The two men pause to stare at each other and the intent in Maddox's face to use this time to disappear is clear as day. So clear in fact that Blowers' face hardens as his rifle lifts an inch in preparation to aim and fire. Maddox glares back with an urge to tell Blowers to let him go. He even considers promising never to go near the fort again but he knows the soldier will shoot him down.

'On you,' Maddox says, running back towards Blowers who holds that poise for a second before moving on into the service road.

CHAPTER TWENTY-THREE

A cruel trick. The venerable gods in all their glory cast the die to rejoice with mirth at the hands played. It matters not for they are but mortals to be played with. They are but men and women who possess only the superficial qualities of sentient beings.

Yesterday they experienced goodness and what it feels like to be loved and respected and the warmth of a thing done right. They returned to the fort and ate good food in the company of good people. They slept soundly and woke without hunger gnawing in their bellies.

That was the good but as in all ways of life so the hand will be played that brings forth the suffering. And such suffering too for it gets worse.

Night comes. It comes early as the thick grey clouds blot the last remaining rays of the setting sun. Darkness pervades and creeps to steal over the once upmarket little town nestled in the countryside of southern England. It happens quickly too. Like a switch going off. One minute there was light. Now there is none.

They lose coherent thought. They lose all ability to form rational judgement to seek a resolution to the current situation but then one cannot blame them. Their worst fears pour down over them with thousands of spindly legs crawling upon their flesh while fangs sink and bite and silken sticky webs trace over their faces. If that wasn't bad enough, so the light goes and they are plunged into darkness.

That darkness makes the sensations only worse. They fight though. They fight and scream to pull creatures with bodies that crunch in their hands and spill hot goo over their fingers. They throw them aside and feel more all over them. They batter their own legs, faces and pull their own hair out. They run and smash into high shelving units that spill goods onto the floor that trip and snag their feet. They tumble, trip and fall only to feel the horror of being on a ground covered in more spiders.

Mo cannot get to them. He is as pinned to his place as Howie, Dave and Clarence are. The press of the attack is too great. The numbers coming are too vast. He fires his pistols until both magazines click empty. He re-holsters and tugs his rifle round to keep firing and fill the darkened interior main corridor of the shopping centre with bright muzzle flashes. The bodies mount up. The blood flies and he scores kills but still they keep coming. He changes magazine as quick as a flash and goes back to firing while behind him Paula and Marcy fight something they now cannot see and cannot stop.

Paula trips to sprawl out. Banging her knees and hands as she goes down. That impact on the ground makes several drop off her and with a pulse of instinct she drops to lie flat and rolls while feeling the crunch of spider bodies under her frame.

'ROLL MARCY...ROLL MARCY...' she screams the words twice and intends to scream more but a spider drops into her open mouth. She gags and cries out as legs and claws scrabble over her tongue and push into her cheeks. Her brain sends the signal to bite down faster than her mind can tell it to stop. She bites and chews. She chews fast before realising what it is she is doing. Goo explodes in her mouth. The legs crunch between her teeth. Her stomach heaves, flips and surges up her windpipe to spew out over the floor. She scrabbles back screaming and puking with hot tears burning her eyes and more things dropping into her hair and down her back.

Marcy slaps and slaps. She kills, squashes and crushes with a fleeting sensation of fighting back. Panic takes over. The thought of them. The mental image of the segmented legs, the shape, the swollen abdomens and the fangs biting and nipping. She screams as Paula screams. She cannot see the way out now. It's too dark. She runs backwards into a shelving unit and in that panic she grabs whatever her hands can find to throw. Sealed packets of toothbrushes fly across the shop. Boxes of toothpaste rain down and she gains kills as those boxes plummet to crush the smaller spiders but she may as well be pissing in the ocean for the good it does. Not that she computes that so she carries on throwing anything she can grasp. Her right foot steps down on a round can of deodorant that slides out in front of her. She goes to fall but throws herself back with a jarring impact into the shelving unit. A sudden jab of pain on her earlobe then the sensation of a thing crawling into her ear. She jabs her finger in and feels something pop and crunch. Another one scrabbles down her face. She snatches it to grip and squeeze. Another one on her other ear, more in her hair, more on her arms and she loses the last ounce of control to thrash on the spot with arms and legs flailing in an act of demented angst.

In that thrashing she kills more than since it began but still they drop. Still they come. Every house in the country has hundreds of spiders in it. Every acre of land has thousands. There are hundreds of millions of spiders and they have feasted to grow strong too from the flies that grew bloated on the corpses now littering the streets.

Mo remains the sentinel. He can hear them scream wild and terrified but he cannot move to help them. The attack coming against him is too strong. A flick of his eyes down the length of the corridor and the hordes outside the doors in the precinct tell him the others are also pinned down. He strafes a sustained burst of fire to buy a second of time in which he drops his bag and quickly opens the flap to grab the next magazine. He fires again with another burst and hears the click. His hands move fast to eject and re-load as something drops down his neck. He pays no heed but works on. Aiming and firing controlled burst shots. His ears ring from the percussive retorts in the enclosed space. His nostrils fill with the stenches made by gunfire and death. The heat closes in as fast as the infected and sweat pours down his face as something else lands on his head.

Still he shows no reaction. He saw a glimpse of spiders in the shop when he looked so figures a couple have crawled across the ceiling. Creepy crawlies do not bother Mo so he shakes his head to flick whatever it is away. Another drops. Then another. More rain down as they climb through the gaps in the ceiling tiles and crawl through the ruined doorway. He shakes and flinches, twitching at the sensation. Something runs down his left arm that holds the rifle. He flicks out sending it scooting off but keeps firing. It's dark now but he can see the shadows coming at him and the flashes of bare skin caught in the weak illumination coming from the main doors and windows.

A twinge of pain on his neck. He slaps at it and feels the crunch as he kills the creature. Another one on his left ear. Others crawling down his right arm. More going down his shirt to writhe and bite with fangs that puncture his skin. He grunts with minute flinches and fires to the left, then ahead, then back to the left. The bodies of those he has killed already are starting to impede the new ones coming through. That's good. It buys time. He braces and fires a whole magazine in one sustained burst as he strafes from left to right then back again. A quick drop to his bag and that move-ment makes the spiders burst to activity. He pulls a grenade, stands, pulls the pin and shouts. 'GRENADE OUT...'

That's all he has time for. To give one fair warning before he throws the bomb across the corridor into the shop where most of the infected are coming from. He drops flat, grimacing for the long seconds before the huge blast shatters more plate glass windows and sends debris flying into the corridor. The shockwave scorching through the corridor dislodges hundreds more spiders clinging to the ceiling who drop to engulf the lad as he rises. Creepy crawlies may not bother Mo but this is something else. This is a second sustained attack of things crawling up his face and biting into his flesh. He digs his torch from his pocket to bathe the area in the bright white light from the super-powered LED's. What he sees are bodies. Lots of dead bodies shot down from his own hands and hundreds of black spiders crawling fast towards him and yet more dangling from strands of web that glint in the light of the torch. More on the ceiling that seems to writhe like something alive with a seething mass of legs and web.

Movement in the shop opposite. Something heavy crashing about and tripping to land hard. Marcy and Paula screaming behind him. His senses threatening to become overwhelmed and only the hours of drill from Dave keep his mind cold and his brain calculating.

'GRENADE OUT...'

The second one goes into the shop. He goes flat and waits the few seconds that seem to stretch forever. The bang that comes is satisfyingly loud and accompanied by a wet splatter of what was once human form bursting apart.

On his feet. Fresh magazine into his rifle. Left pistol drawn and re-loaded. Right pistol drawn and re-loaded. He keeps the right pistol out and holds the torch with his left as he ducks to run into the shop behind him towards the screams of Paula and Marcy. His torch picks out the sheer mass of creatures plummeting from the ceiling. It looks like thousands of them. A solid broiling carpet of spiders that crawl over each other and drop down to fresh screams. Spiders on the floor too. Running frantic and pumped on the pheromones secreted.

His eyes scan to take in and assess while his own body is bitten and crawled over. A flash of a memory from a few years ago and seeing kids torturing insects in the local park. He watched mesmerised and somewhat sickened by the gleeful way the children killed and laughed but the method they used was effective. That's how his mind works now. To seek the most effective manner to kill the enemy and negate the threat. He spins to look and spots the thing he needs. A run across the store with the torch light bouncing and Marcy thrashing wildly while trying to scoot backwards into a shelving unit. He sees Paula rolling over and over across the width of an aisle and even with the coldness of Dave within him he feels a surge of revulsion at the masses of spiders crawling over her.

He gets to the section and re-holsters his pistol then grabs the two biggest he can find. He clunks the tops against each other to dislodge the lids and sprints hard towards Paula. At the last second he drops to his knees and slides the last few feet while pressing the triggers on his new weapons.

Both hiss as they discharge their contents and the air fills with the scented aroma of hairspray. He keeps the nozzles pressed down and reaches Paula to spray down over her body and round the sides. The spiders scurry back from the onslaught and a new furious battle commences. Motion outside. Cans down. Pistols out and he surges up to his feet to fire one after the other at the fresh wave coming through.

'Paula...use the cans...PAULA...'

She's gone. Lost to the panic of the knowledge that her body is covered in the thick hairy legs of spiders. All she can do is protect her mouth and ears. That's all she worries about, stopping them gaining entry to her body with twisted images in her mind that they'll lay eggs and hatch baby spiders in her brain.

The wave of infected is killed. Mo drops, holsters and takes up his secondary weapons to re-commence the other side of the battle. The air becomes thick with spray. Choking even. He coughs and sputters as the spiders cough and sputter and run back away from the vile chemical warfare being waged against them.

'Fuck yes,' Mo mutters at the new idea in his head. He drops one can, digs in his pocket for his lighter and thumbs the wheel to create flame. A quick cast round. The situation is critical. Heavy armaments are needed.

He pushes the nozzle to jet the contents at the flame that ignite with a foot long arc of pure burning fire.

'Yeah bitches,' Mo shouts his warrior's cry and drops to use his flamethrower, burning spiders to a crisp as he destroys their immediate environment. The bigger ones flame for a second and crawl on fire before curling up as the moisture is taken from their forms.

The effect is brilliant but not enough. The jet of flame can only be focussed in one place at one time. He grabs the other can, ignites the spray and revels in the glory of now having two flamethrowers.

He runs round Paula, burning the ground around her. She tries to roll and he shouts at her to remain still but she's still gripped by panic. If she rolls she'll get burnt. Mo drops on her, wedging his knees either side of her back to pin in her place while flexing round to send his jets of flame at the spiders. He aims up to kill the ones overhead. Hundreds drop instantly but they fall dead and crispy.

Movement outside again. Cans down and as he lifts his thumbs from the nozzles so the flames end and plunge the room back into a near pitch darkness. Torch in mouth. Pistols drawn and he rises to fire over the shelving and cuts down the infected charging in.

It's the combination of the sensation of Mo' voice, the light and heat of the flamethrowers and the booming retorts of the pistols that finally break through Marcy's mind. Like someone surging from freezing cold water she gasps and opens her eyes to see Mo firing and the air filled with the stench of hairspray. Hairspray? Why hairspray? A whole series of connections are made within the fluidity of the human thought process and as she reaches the conclusion so Mo ceases fire, drops and ignites one of the cans then takes up the other to ignite from the first and thus re-create his dual flamethrowers to recommence his genocide of the fuckers trying to eat his Paula.

She's in. Marcy is so in. She tries to surge up but trips and falls back down so instead goes for an ungainly half crabbing crawling motion as she uses the light from the flames to find the shelves filled with hairspray. She takes two and screams while shaking her head to rid the big one hanging off her nose and smashes the back of her hand into her face hard to kill the spider but also knocks herself staggering back. Blood streams from her nose as the Gods laugh at the new extra layer of misery she suffers.

'ME,' she says that one word to Mo and in that one word he sees she is armed and ready. She will hold the line and wield her flamethrowers with guts and courage. He ignites her cans and the darkness is pushed back another few inches. They go to work and four beats two any day of the week. Four jets of flame cause carnage to the enemy. They scorch the ground and the air and Marcy revels in the slaughter. She stamps and roars in defiance then starts coughing from breathing air now so thick with chemicals. Blood sprays from her mouth that had poured down from her bloody nose. She steps back while coughing and kicks Paula in the head.

'Ow,' Paula says, literally kicked back to her senses. She looks up with wide eyes to see four arcs of fire jetting around and above her. Heat too. Heat and light and it stinks something awful.

'Shit,' Mo drops his cans and yanks his rifle round to focus on the door and the infected still coming in. Paula goes for his cans and takes up the weapons.

'Light me,' she growls at Marcy.

'What?' Marcy coughs, spraying blood while spraying fire.

'LIGHT ME,' Paula demands, maddened with rage and ready to kick spider arses, or set them on fire instead.

'What?' Marcy coughs, her eyes watering from the fumes. 'I think I'm getting high...'

Paula lights herself by aiming her right can at one of Marcy's flames. She lights her second and grins with sadistic pleasure from a face covered in small sore lumps made by spider bites.

'ARSE IT,' her flamethrowers go out. The contents exhausted. 'MAGAZINE,' she bellows, running across to grab fresh rounds from the shelving unit. Lids off, nozzles depressed and she lights the spray to join in.

A battle of two fronts is waged. Mo holds the door. Marcy and Paula hold the rest as they slowly set fire to Boots the Chemist.

CHAPTER TWENTY-FOUR

Everything is okay. Everything will be fine. Breathe. Breathe in and breathe out. It will be today and that's fine because everything is okay. Everything is fine.

She has the towels. She has the water. She has the gas stove ready to boil the water. She has pain medication. She has sterilised surgical scissors ready for cutting and that's good because everything is okay. Everything will be fine.

She's scared. Terrified even. The fear of having to do something alone and without any help. What if it goes wrong? It won't go wrong. Everything is okay. Everything will be fine.

The fear comes again. The fear that brings the tears to her eyes and the deepest wish right now is to have her mum here. Her mum is dead. Everyone is dead. Her bottom lip trembles, the panic rises but she has to swallow it down.

'Everything's okay, everything's okay, everything's okay.'

The mantra helps soothe her nerves and eases the throb in her head that comes when she thinks about her mum and what it means to be a mother. Which is what she will become today.

She cradles her swollen belly and feels the life inside. The life of a child that she has grown from nothing to something. The life inside that today will come out and become part of this world in all its decaying broken filth.

The sob breaks from her mouth as the pain comes again. The contraction that signals the time is coming. She bends with a grunt to navigate past her stomach to feel between her legs for any signs of her waters breaking. They said she would know but what if she doesn't know? Her body is going through so many changes right now she could miss anything. It's dry. That's good.

Her spot is chosen. The kitchen floor that has been scrubbed and made cleaner than any operating table. Every side, every cupboard door and handle, every surface, every edge and well, just about everything in the room has been anti-bacced once, twice and thrice. The kitchen is at the back which means any sounds she makes will be muffled from being heard at the front.

Throughout the morning she paces the house, breathing in, breathing out, leaning, sitting, pacing and breathing. The contractions come but the space between them doesn't reduce. She checks between her legs periodically and keeps wondering into the kitchen to be absolutely sure her birthing area is ready.

As the day wears on so the contractions come marginally faster but the pace is painfully slow. She sweats from the heat and drinks water to replenish her fluids. She eats tinned fruit and sits on the toilet while tapping her feet nervously.

Her boyfriend is dead. He went out on the Friday night it happened to get Doritos and salsa dip. She was craving. She had to have them. She absolutely had to have them. She told him this. He laughed and teased until she threatened to waddle to the shop herself but he pulled his trainers on and kissed her on the belly and on the head before going out to the car.

He never came back. She waited and even tried calling him but her phone signal was gone. She mused for a while, paced about and started getting irritated because all she wanted was fucking cheesy snacks and salsa dip. He didn't know what it was like to have cravings and a body that was doing weird things.

After an hour she called her mum on the landline but it rang out. Her mum never went out on Friday nights. She tried again. Tried her boyfriend. Tried her friends. The lines were either jammed, engaged or ringing out.

After two hours she turned the television on and caught the last few minutes of the news anchors sobbing at their desks from a world breaking apart. It was everywhere.

Now, twenty days on and she has done everything she can to be ready. Her baby will come today. The contractions have started.

She is scared. She wants her mum, her boyfriend, a friend, anyone. To do this alone is too much. She breathes and calms. She thinks and panics and so the day goes as the pains come closer together.

Then, in the afternoon, she hears them. She hears the feet running outside and in a minute of mistaken hope that help has come she rushes to the window to pull the curtain back. Her hand clamping over her mouth prevents the scream of fright coming out at the street thick with those things. All of them running towards the town centre. So many. So so many. Men and women. Old and young. Elderly and children. All of them possessed by whatever the thing inside them is. All of them focussed on one task as they move with military precision.

The cramps come harder. The pains radiate through her body. She staggers back from the window as the tops of her thighs grow wet from the waters coming out. Shock hits. Her heart rate thunders. Her breath comes fast and shallow as her body and mind go into shock.

She gets into the kitchen, to her refuge, to her birthing area and lies down in the chosen spot surrounded by towels. She weeps. She weeps from pain and fear. She weeps silently for the horror of the things outside after near on twenty days with only glimpses of them in the distance.

There she stays. Silent and terrified as the cramps come and the natural stages of her body dictate the transition towards the birth.

She doesn't know anything about her neighbour from the top of her street going into his shed to shove his finger at the big spider in the corner. She doesn't know when that spider bites into that finger. Nor does she know when that spider rampages to infect the other spiders that rampage to infect the other spiders. She doesn't know that house by house the hundreds of arachnids become infected with a virus that drives them in one direction.

She only knows that she is lying on her back with her knees bent and her legs open while sobbing and trying to breathe through the contractions. She freezes at the sight of that wolf spider running across her ceiling and she remains frozen in absolute terror when the hundreds behind him run across.

She hears the scuttling claws and catches sight of more running across walls and across her kitchen worktops. She doesn't know they are infected. She doesn't know they are driven to go in one direction and do nothing other than that. All she knows is for a few minutes her kitchen and birthing space is thick with spiders and the panic rises until she's ready to scream.

Then they're gone and it's like it never happened. Five minutes later she convinces herself it was a delusion brought on by fear and panic. That makes her focus on breathing again. Breathe in. Breathe out. Cope. Deal with it. This is happening and everything is okay. There were no spiders. It was a trick of the mind.

Still those contractions come slowly and it takes hours for the pace to quicken. She sweats constantly, unaware of her body dehydrating rapidly in the intense heat. She focusses solely on the pain and the contractions.

The afternoon gives way to evening. The heat grows worse. She hears the running feet many times outside but there is nothing she can do and so as the breathing becomes panting so the urge to push starts to build.

CHAPTER TWENTY-FIVE

B lowers and Maddox fire as they run through commercial zones into the abyss of residential rural England where every front garden has either rose bushes or old sofas the council refused to come and collect.

It's dark now. Night is here. Not that they notice because they have to run and run and keep running. Hundreds of infected came after them. Far more than they realised and even with them stopping to fire thirty rounds at a time each they still don't drop enough to even hope to stand and fight but by drawing them on, Blowers knows they are giving the others a better chance.

'On,' he gasps, ejecting his used magazine to ram a new one home. Maddox complies because right now it suits him to run. It is the correct course of action to ensure his survival and his own survival is the primary objective. The thing he was waiting for is here. The night is his ally and a tool to be used. He can slip away when the time is right and disappear into the darkness while the confusion is highest. If he gets it right, Blowers will think he was taken and killed which will prevent any risk of Dave coming after him. This attack is a disaster for the others but a blessing for him.

They run hard through street after street. Blowers keeps his mind clear. He knows he can run for miles and that's exactly what he intends to do. He plans to run and draw the horde on and away enough so he can go back and join the others.

'Next corner,' Blowers says between sucking air in, 'we'll stop and fire then sprint away…'

Maddox doesn't reply. Not because he can't speak but because he doesn't like Blowers. He hates him. He detests the way the idiot switches between playing at corporal to being everyone's mate. He thinks he is something special, something unique because he has a smidge of authority and can tell a few other idiots which way to face when they point their guns.

Maddox started the day believing he would be at the top table with the leaders and would show them his ability to think tactically and strategize. Instead, he's been running about with stupid people all day. The insecurity over Lenski has been niggling too. The loss of his crews. The death of Darius. Finding out he is immune but being refused any more information. All of those things and of course the self-generated isolation.

'Now,' Blowers comes to a stop, turns and fires. Maddox does so too but his movements are not as sharp as Blowers. He slows a bit more gradually, turns a bit slower and fires when he is ready instead of when he is told.

The two rifles fire with bursts. Infected drop but more come. Sixty bullets are sent down the road in a matter of seconds and they score a handful of kills. Blowers pauses for a second, changing magazine while trying to see how many are left. Too many. Far too many. That's a good thing though. He smiles grim and determined. More here is less back there attacking his mates. Divide the enemy and whittle them down. It's a valid tactic.

'Come on…' his voice snaps off at the empty space next to him. He spins trying to see where he went but there's no sign. 'MAD-DOX?' he shouts and casts a worried look at the horde charging down the street. 'YOU FUCKING CUNT…' Blowers runs on. Fuming, seething and knowing without doubt that if he saw the prick now he'd shoot him dead without blinking. Sulking is one thing, being difficult is another but cowardice in the face of the enemy is unforgivable. There is no choice now. There is nothing else he can do but run. 'COWARD...HEAR ME? YOU'RE A COWARD...'

Maddox sprints hard. He saw the mouth to the alley as he turned when Blowers said to stop and fire. He duly fired and also knew that Blowers would change his magazine and do the same thing he's already done each time they've stopped and try to count his kills to see how many are left. That's when he went. Right then. He sprinted to the alley and the years of experience at running through estates show true. He changes his magazine as he goes, simply discarding the used one on the floor. The opportunity isn't as perfect as he hoped. Ideally he wanted them to think he had been killed but you can't always have the best of everything. He'll find a car, a fast one and head down to the fort. He'll get in quietly and see if Lenski wants to come with him. He knows he can get to the fort while these idiots are still here fighting. Lilly will ask him why and he already knows he will tell her he pissed Howie off so much he was sent back. The people from the equestrian centre will vouch for seeing him. The plans form as he runs. Get a car. Get to Lenski then go. Find somewhere far away and start again.

'YOU FUCKING COWARD...'

His lip twitches at hearing Blowers' raging into the night. He knew he would feel guilty at leaving him. Maddox is many things but he is very intelligent and he expected the rush of guilt but he also knew he would be able to ignore it. What they do is down to them. He is not one of them. Their way is not his way.

Blowers saves his breath for running. Maddox thinks he has a right to do as he pleases because he had a hard life. Everyone had a hard life. Cookey and Nick had hard lives. Marcy was broke. Paula was in a job she hated. Clarence felt abandoned and lonely after leaving the army. Roy was a social reject due to his mental health. Dave found work in a supermarket for fuck's sake. The hardest most dangerous man in the whole country stacked shelves in Tesco. Blowers was no exception. He joined the Marines and had his life planned out, then in the final week of training, he broke his leg. At the time, it was thought the injury was bad enough to end his military career so he was forced to leave but not once did he look back and feel someone owed him something. He was so close to earning the green beret of the commandos. The *green lid,* but that's what life is. It's hard and brutal but you get on with it. Even his life before the Marines was shit and he doesn't look back at that and think he is owed anything. That's not how his mind works. He grew up on the edge of an estate like the one Maddox and Mo come from. His mum had a succession of boyfriends, too many, far too many and she fell in love with each one as they moved in, took over then moved out a few months later. He can't remember how many times he was given a pack of sweets and told to *go wait outside.*

He found boxing, or rather, boxing found him. He was angry. He had a temper and was quick to fight. Too many different men in his house made him hostile to affection and weary of everyone. He got into a few scraps at school, was suspended, let back in, suspended again, let back in and on it went until he bust the jaw of another kid during lunchbreak. The other kid was the son of his mother's latest boyfriend and was bragging at how his dad *fucked* Blowers mum.

The police officer that dealt with the incident took Blowers to the local boxing club and made him promise he would complete a month of training in lieu of being prosecuted. Blowers didn't know the other kid wasn't making a complaint after being told not to by his father.

Blowers found a new home and one he was welcomed at. He was good too. He trained hard and had enough respect to listen and learn. He fought in competitions and won. He grew tough and bigger and soon the men in his house avoided him as much as he avoided them. It was the hard eyes that did it. The thousand yard stare he perfected in the ring to show his opponent he was not afraid.

Now he runs on his own to lead hundreds of chemically pumped infected humans away from his mates and his family. He runs on his own to draw them away and buy time.

CHAPTER TWENTY-SIX

The pain is too much. She'll die. It feels like she's being split in two. She pushes knowing she has to push but wishing she could do anything instead of push. The veins in her neck bulge. Her face flushes deep red. Her mouth open, teeth gritted, eyes bulging. She grunts and makes noises and wants to scream but she can't. Her fists ball. Her nails dig into her palms.

She breaks and breathes. Panting hard with sweat burning her eyes. Why hasn't it come out yet? Why is it taking so long? Something's wrong. She pants and makes ready as the next spasm hits with an urge to push.

It hurts more each time. A burning agonising pain that threatens to render her unconscious. It's dark in here. Too dark. On the floor of her kitchen in a near on pitch black room she tries to give birth but the baby won't come. It's been hours already and each time the urge comes so she pushes but it won't come out.

She pants again. Drawing energy before the next one comes. She weeps and sobs, she whimpers alone and terrified for her baby. She tries to look down but can't see past her bulging stomach and any attempt at moving sends waves of the wrong type of pain going through her. So she doesn't. She stays on her back without water while sweating and losing fluids. She's bleeding too. She can see the pool of darkening liquid spreading out round her body.

The next one is intense. She grits her teeth and pushes. She pushes until stars and lights bloom in her eyes. She pushes until her vision starts closing in and the pain increases to a whole new level. She cries out from the agony and tries to stifle the noises but it's so hard. She wants her mum. She wants her boyfriend. Please, someone, anyone. There is no one. There is nothing but here and now and pushing a thing that will not come out. She will die here. Her baby will die inside her. The utter hopelessness of it all crushes her soul and breaks her heart into a thousand pieces.

MADDOX AND BLOWERS RUN. They each run for their own purpose. One to make the things chase and the other to get away and hide.

Blowers sprints down the next road. He needs the magazines from his bag which means sliding the bag off while running. He'll have just seconds when he stops. Seconds to drop the bag, open the flap, grab a magazine and re-load. He runs it through in his mind, visualising each component move.

Now. He stops, drops the bag, takes a knee, opens the flap, grabs a fresh one and ejects the used one. Fresh one in. Bolt back, aim and fire. Sustained bursts under control. Several drop and he knows he gets kills but by fuck these bastards don't stop coming.

Another magazine goes into his pocket and he's up and running. Breathing hard. Sweating loads. He runs fast enough to keep ahead but steadily enough to get his bottle out and take a glug. Not much but enough to keep him hydrated and functioning. He glances up and fails to see any stars. That means clouds. Hopefully that means rain. Rain will be good right now. It'll mask noise and give him a chance to hide somewhere and fire into them from behind.

Maddox runs in the fashion he learnt. In a zig zag manner

instead of a straight line. It always worked when the police were chasing him. They were always too fat to go over fences and through gardens. Maddox wasn't then and he isn't now. He vaults fences and walls with ease and drops deftly to assess each new microenvironment before choosing his new path and running on. He weaves and takes hard lefts and rights while every now and then hearing the shots from Blowers assault rifle and others in the distance.

He needs water. He needs to catch his breath. He vaults a fence, runs through a garden and spies the next border is a six-foot high wall. He takes that with ease and drops down the other side onto a ceramic plant pot that smashes under his weight. He freezes at the noise, going still to listen. The garden is enclosed on all sides and the noise he made doesn't seem to have caused a reaction from anywhere. He takes the time to open his bag and drink water deep into his stomach. He pours more over his face, sluicing the sweat away while a smug sense of freedom steals over him. Conflict too. The dig in his soul at ditching Blowers to deal with that lot on his own. *Not my problem.* He goes to move then stops at the sound coming from the house.

She hears the pot in the garden smashing. The big one her mum got her from the garden centre that she was going to grow tomatoes in. She pants as silently as she can, staring at the closed back door and willing the next contraction not to come. *Not now, please not now.*

It comes. It comes because her body tells her the baby has to come out. She clamps a hand over her mouth to stifle the noise but the pain is growing and tearing her skin. It gets worse. It gets deeper and more searing. She shakes and trembles while pushing and desperately trying to stay quiet.

Maddox stares hard at the back door. Someone is inside it. Someone panting hard and moving about. He stays still. His rifle lifting to aim. His eyes twitching left to right to take in the dark windows. He looks at the fence ahead and mentally prepares for the run and leap to vault the top.

The pain. It's too much. Everything hurts now. She thrashes her head side to side to do something instead of scream. She has to push. She pushes and strains. Blood comes out. She can feel it hot and sticky on her legs. Blood like that isn't right. Her baby is dying inside her. Her baby.

'My baby...'

The words come out before she can stop them. The choking sob follows. She covers her own mouth then gasps as the pain intensifies as her body tells her things are going very badly wrong.

He edges towards the fence. He's not that bothered if there's an infected inside as he can outrun them and besides, he's got a big gun. What bothers him is being spotted and the signal being sent as to where he is. That will tell the others where he is too. Time to go. He bunches for the run up as the words come whispered and broken from the back of the house. His heart misses a beat. His blood runs cold. *My baby.* He heard that. He hears the sob that comes after and the rustle of someone moving about. He hears a person in pain and a voice gripped by terror and fear. It's not his problem. He runs for the fence.

The pain is so bad. It tears and burns like every nerve ending in her body is being jabbed with hot needles and cut with razors. She clamps her mouth and for a second she holds the noise back but it's too much and she cries out in a voice of pitiful agony that drops guttural and broken as the need to push takes over.

He vaults the fence and drops to the next garden as the scream comes. A mournful wail of absolute pain. Another human in agony. A person suffering. He goes to run, to get away and be free but he falters, glaring back at the fence he came from. The noises drop off as he tells himself this isn't his problem. Whoever it is will be fine. Whatever it is has nothing to do with him.

She screams again. She can't not scream. She is dying. Blood is coming out. Too much blood. The contractions threaten to become convulsions. The urge to push becomes a spasm.

Maddox's face twists as he fights the conscience inside. The voice of reason and goodness that tells him not to be an utter cunt and go help. He has his own life to lead. No one ever helped him so why should he help anyone now? Fuck whoever it is. Fuck everyone. The strong survive this world.

She claws back from the edge of the abyss that will pull her down to death. With the instinct of a mother she finds strength inside to do what must be done. She pushes. She growls wide eyed impervious to the pain. She strains and screams out. Blood sprays from her nose from the pressure bursting a vessel. Her head swims. Vision closes in but my god she pushes with one final immense urge to birth her baby. She can die. She doesn't care but give life to her child. Please god, *give my baby life.*

It's no good. As strong as she was in that second so her body weakens and the pain takes over. She breaks the push to sob as she starts slipping over the edge to plummet down into the dark abyss. It's over. Her mum is dead. Her boyfriend is dead. Her child is dead. Everyone is dead. Her body prepares to die too. The brain knows the end is here and so it dumps chemicals to ease the passing. It floods her with calm while it dampens the nerve endings but to do that creates a degree of delusion in her mind. Images of her life swim through her mind.

Maddox creeps quickly to the window while the voices in his head argue bitterly. He has to run and go but the encoded strands of DNA in his system recognise the sounds of another human in distress and that resonance draws him closer. He peeks through the gap in the curtain to see a kitchen. It looks normal. He doesn't see anyone. He frowns, ready to go as she moves on the floor and brings his eyes down as his vision adapts to the darkness inside the room. He spots the towels first. White fluffy towels stacked up. Then he spots her. A woman on her back with her legs bent and wide open. Blood on the floor. Blood on her thighs. Her stomach is swollen.

She murmurs softly. He'll be back in a minute with the Doritos and salsa dip. She'll phone her mum tomorrow and say how he sweet he was to go out and get them for her. She smiles and sighs. Her head lolling side to side as her brain receives another signal to push. She snaps back to reality. Surging from the delusion to the awful now and the pain radiating through her body.

Maddox sees it. He sees the sharpness come back to her eyes and the way she grits, heaves and strains as every vein in her neck and head pushes from her skin. The noise she makes is almost inhumanly low and guttural. Like an animal but she isn't an animal, she's a person in distress. A woman giving birth who is bleeding out.

A second in time. A choice to make. The hardness of his life and all the bitter experiences weighed off against the now and in that second his mind gives self-justification that millions have died and millions more will die. She is just one more, that's all. Just one worthless life that means nothing to him. She never helped him. She never did anything to make his life better. There is no connection. There is no reason to stay. Be cold. Be ruthless and live a life instead of dying here trying to help someone who will die anyway.

CHAPTER TWENTY-SEVEN

R eginald fights. He takes life. He is a warrior. He is strong and wields his weapon with true majesty. He strikes and moves. He dances and feints left then darts in from the right. He is here, in the battle, in the moment.

Roy stands in the gaping hole where the window used to be. The glass and frame kicked out so he can find angle and space to draw and fire to help the three below him. Clarence, Dave and Howie fight a battle on all sides. Compressed almost back to back and all they can do is hold their tiny space while Roy fires to do what he can.

At Roy's back stands Nick. Nick who holds the line on the upstairs landing at the top of the stairs as the infected charge up from pouring through the shop below. He lashes his axe left and right to hack through bone and limbs then boots them back down to trample the rest coming up. It's dirty and hot. His hands, arms and face are streaked with blood and gore. His voice is hoarse as he grunts but that wry smile twitches on his face.

In between Nick and Roy is where Reginald fights. He sweats too. His arms and hands are streaked with gore and filth and but he grips his weapon hard and screams out as he kills another one with a roar of righteous glory spilling from his lips. He is Dave. He is Clarence. He is a fighter and protects his team from the enemy.

'You alright mate?' Nick asks, turning in the second's pause while the infected gather themselves for the next charge up the stairs. Reginald blinks at him, his face a mask of rage and battle-lust. 'Righto,' Nick says, nodding at him. 'Good work...'

Reggie stiffens and slams his fly swatter down on the next spider coming at him. A big one too. A big body and thick legs but he kills it and dances back to spin and check the flanks. More come. More drop from the ceiling and charge out across the floor. Reginald roars and brings his mighty right foot down to kill. He swings his battle-swatter and sends another back to the spider-hell from whence it came.

'Reggie...one on my head,' Roy says calmly as he draws back and looses to strike one in the neck lunging at Howie who gives a curt nod of thanks before smashing the next two down.

'Not so hard eh, Reggie?' Roy mutters through gritted teeth at being swatted round the back of the head.

Reginald doesn't reply. He is gone. He's in the killing zone. The time to lay down his pen is here. It is time to take up a weapon and fight and so, as Nick takes the next dozen coming up, so Reginald takes on the money spider abseiling down.

'REGGIE...' Howie shouts between kills. The press coming in is too much. They're just about holding but not gaining ground and there is no hope of fighting out right now.

'He's killing spiders,' Roy shouts down.

'Eh?' Howie asks, risking a glance up as he swings his axe round taking a head off. 'Roll call...' he grunts.

'Pardon?' Roy asks, drawing back to fire.

'**ROLL CALL...**' Dave booms.

'Ah got it, Reggie, Mr Howie wants a roll call,' Roy says, turning his head a fraction to speak to the small man behind him.

'I am somewhat occupied,' Reginald snaps back, delivering the final blow to the brave little money spider who fought a good battle. Reginald even nods at it in respect of a duel well played. 'Gosh, this is hot work...' he spins to check, sees he has a chance and thumbs the radio under his shirt. *'Roll call for Mr Howie....Er... Paula, Marcy and Mo, how are you holding up?'*

'VERY FUCKING BUSY ACTUALLY,' Marcy bellows through the radio. *'BIT OF HELP WOULD BE NICE YOU KNOW...'*

'Yes yes, we're all busy my dear. We're all fighting you know. I'm sure someone will come when they can...' Reginald pauses, thinking of who is next, *'Charlotte? Roll call for Mr Howie...'*

'Fine...Cookey get that one...YES! Good shot...we're fine, Reggie. I'm with Cookey and Blinky...we've drawn a few hundred away from you...'

'Well done,' Reginald says gravely and wisely and full of gravitas as Nick calls a zombie a cunt and punches him back down the stairs. *'Roy? Roll call for Mr Howie...'*

'I'm right here,' Roy says.

'Oh gosh of course you are. My mistake. Heat of the moment. Right er...ah yes, Blowers and Maddox? Roll call for Mr Howie...'

'The fucking prick has ran off,' Blowers gasps through the radio.

'Who has?' Cookey asks, cutting in front of Reginald who tuts in irritation.

'Maddox the coward...HEAR THAT YOU FUCKING COWARD? I WILL HUNT YOU DOWN...'

'You okay?' Howie's voice blurts rushed and full of background noise of voices snarling and hissing.

'Yep,' Blowers voice comes back, *'got a few behind me...leading 'em away...I'm fine...you want me back to help Paula and Marcy?'*

'We're good, Blowers,' Mo's voice cuts in.

'WE'RE NOT BLOODY GOOD...I PUNCHED MYSELF IN THE NOSE,' Marcy shouts. *'AND THERE'S FUCKING SPIDERS EVERYWHERE AND PAULA ATE ONE...'*

'It's Charlie...we'll do what we can with ours then get back to Paula and Marcy...'

'*Paula ate a spider?*' Cookey asks.

'*If you's does get back,*' Mo says, '*go for the back doors into the shopping centre...cut the flow off...we's gotta get out in a bit as we got a small fire going on...*'

'*IT'S NOT A SMALL FIRE, IT'S A HUGE FUCKING FIRE...PAULA...ONE IN MY HAIR GETITGETITGETIT.*'

'*Er...It's Heather here...um, so like...do you want us to do the back doors?*'

A split second as everyone pauses to take in what they just heard.

'*Heather, it's Roy, everyone else is pinned down...they need help...do what you can...*'

'*We will.*'

CHAPTER TWENTY-EIGHT

Pride is a funny thing. Pride will see a person fail but pride will also see a person suffer the worst of times and hold their head high. Pride will bring a person down but pride will carry you through hell and high water.

Pride and nothing more. Ego and nothing else. That's all it is. That one thing from Blowers calling him out over the radio to the others. Calling him a coward. Maddox isn't a coward.

He stops and turns back. He walks then jogs and runs to vault the fences as the anger inside from the unfairness of his life bubbles up. He isn't a coward. He lands and runs to vault the next. It's not cowardice to want to be free. He jumps the next and lands softly to go back over the gardens. How is it cowardice to run away from those that will harm him? How is that cowardice? He isn't a coward.

Cowards don't go back to help other people. Cowards don't go to locked back doors in the middle of a town swamped with infected. Cowards don't shoulder the door open and step inside to look down on a woman and cowards don't suddenly stop and wonder what the hell they are meant to do now.

'Shit.'

He looks down at her. At the blood between her legs and her swollen stomach. He blanches at the smell of piss and shit that must have come out when she was straining to push. He reels at the wet heat, at the crushing humidity and at the realisation that his reaction to being called a coward brought him here but now he doesn't know what to do.

'Hey,' he drops to her side, propping his rifle against the side. She doesn't respond but murmurs softly, delirious and clearly bordering on losing consciousness. 'Hey,' he says louder, firmer. Still no response. His face twitches at the uncertainty of faced with a thing he knows nothing about.

She didn't hear the back door being forced in and she doesn't hear his voice either. The awareness only comes when he gently touches her hand. She smiles at him, weak and wan with a lack of focus in her eyes.

'Hey,' she says slowly, softly. 'Did you get them?'

'Get what?' he asks, looking round the room.

'The Doritos,' she chuckles.

'Er yeah, yeah I did,' he says. Her hand is sticky with drying blood. As his eyes adjust to the darkness so he takes in her features and the dryness of her mouth as she tries to talk.

'Salsa,' she says, licking her dry lips.

Water. Get water. He looks round for a cup or glass but finds nothing. How long has she been without a drink? He goes to move to rise for the sink as her hand shoots out to clamp on his wrist.

'Don't go,' she breathes the words fast and terrified.

'Get you water yeah,' he says, prising her hand off.

'Michael?'

'I'm Maddox...'

'Is Michael back?'

'I'll get you some water...' she won't let go but digs in with a grip that belies the slenderness of her wrists. He pulls at her fingers, easing them back to yank his arm free as her head lolls side to side with soft words uttered and missed.

He runs the tap, finds a cup and swills it out. Smells of cleaning detergents reach his nose. She prepared the room and got ready for this but she seems out of it. He avoids looking down at the area between her legs and focusses on filling the mug.

'Water,' he says. She murmurs and rolls her head side to side. 'Hey, water...you thirsty?'

'Huh?' she asks, blinking at him.

'Drink yeah,' he edges closer as she spots the cup and tries to rise but the movement sends a surge of fresh pain through her body. She cries out as his wavering hand tries to lift her up but he's too passive, too gentle. She writhes in agony, grunting from the pain.

'Leave it,' he says.

'Thirsty,' she grunts, reaching a hand for the mug that knocks it from his hand. The contents splash down over his legs, soaking his lap and her top. She scrabbles for the mug, her brain registering the offer of a drink and how thirsty she is. He fills the cup again and rushes back and this time is assertive in his movements of lifting her head and shoulders up. That it hurts her is obvious but she goes up and clutches at the cup that he guides to her lips. She downs it in one with water cascading down her chin.

'More,' she gasps.

He lowers her down, goes back, re-fills and guides the cup once more to her lips. She drinks deep and solid. She absorbs fluid into a body that has been too long without water. It rushes through her system giving an instant tiny lift to her energy that helps focus her mind.

'More,' she breathes, panting hard as she realises how hot she is.

Again he fills the cup and helps her drink. She guzzles it down while grimacing at the pain of having to lift her head.

Degrees of awareness come back. That she is giving birth. That she is bleeding. That there is a strange man in her kitchen. Maddox sees the transition as the focus comes back into her eyes.

She looks down at her belly then at the blood pooled out. The fear comes back. The pain intensifies. The comprehension of death and her baby inside her stomach. A contraction hits. Strong and pulsing that makes her drop her head with a thud as she locks out and stiffens from the agony.

Maddox watches, his eyes flicking over her body and the way she grunts with immense straining pressure. Her face flushes a deep red, the veins bulge, her hands curl into fists as she fights to push.

'What do I do?'

The pain renders her unable to respond or even hear him. She pushes and strains because that is what her body is telling her to do. It is the only thing she knows in those few seconds and so everything else, including the ego of Maddox Doku, becomes insignificant.

When it ends, it does so suddenly. A cessation of straining and an end to the effort as she slumps gasping for air. She breathes hard and fast, too fast. Maddox remembers something about women needing to breathe calmly through a contraction, or was it *with* a contraction?

'It's not coming out,' she says in a growl of a voice that breaks off in a sob, 'it won't come out...'

'What...' Maddox flounders, helpless and impotent.

'It won't come out...' she sobs and cries, tears streaming down her face. He thinks to offer more water, to mop her brow or hold her hand but instead he stares on unable to summon words. 'Get it out...'

'Wh..what?'

'Get it out...GET IT OUT...'

'Shush, don't shout. Don't shout...tell me what to do...'

'It's...' she swallows and breathes, 'it won't come out...get it out...'

'But...'

'It'll die. You got to get it out. Listen to me,' she fixes him a look, holding his eyes on hers. 'I'm bleeding too much…the baby,' she bites the sob down at voicing the word that means so much, 'the baby is stuck…you have…you have to get it out.'

'How?' he asks, his tone even, deep and re-assuring. She takes in the youthful look of his face but his eyes are older, wiser. Her senses come alive. She spots the rifle leaning against the side and the pistol on his belt but right now she doesn't care who he is. Just that he is here. 'How?' he asks again, asserting the question with intensity.

'Look,' she says.

He stares at her in response at what he assumes is the pre-cursor to a statement.

'Down there,' she says when he doesn't move.

'What?'

'Look…look at it…see if…'

'You want me to look down there?'

'Yes I bloody want you to look down there…LOOK!'

'I am! I will…don't shout, just…got a torch, you can't shout… don't shout…' he digs the torch from his bag and moves down through the blood to peer tentatively at the area between her legs. The blood is thick and glistening wet. Her thighs smeared with the same.

'What do you see?' she asks, her voice strangled with pain and fatigue.

'Er, blood yeah,' he says, 'like loads of it.'

'Can you see the baby?'

'The baby?'

'Can you see it?'

'Er…' Maddox twitches the torch beam towards her groin while a voice inside chastises him for looking at a ladies vagina in this way. The sight stuns him. Blood everywhere and the opening stretched wide and long.

'Can you see it?'

'Er...I'm...' he flounders, staggered, repulsed and mesmerised all at the same time. 'Your er...your vagina...it's big right? Like er...'

'The baby,' she growls, 'can you see the fucking baby?'

'What...what's it look like?'

'LIKE A FUCKING BABY!'

'Shush, please don't shout...I'm looking yeah,' he peers closer, trying to make sense of something he has never seen look like that before. He blinks, focusses and switches on. Her opening is stretched wide but there's blood everywhere, obscuring what he can see. 'I er...I gotta wash you...too much blood, you get me?' he slips into his normal voice in the panic of the moment.

'Do it...' she heaves as the contraction comes again. The urge to push building. He darts off to the tap, fills a cup and drops down to wince and grimace as he hesitantly pours the contents over her groin. Some of the blood runs away but it's not enough. She drops her head to strain with low grunts of pain and pressure. He fills again, pours again and finally thinks to fill something bigger than a mug. He uses the bowl on the side. While she writhes and pushes he pours the water down over her groin. The blood washes away pink and watery. More comes but the flow of water is faster than the fresh blood seeps out.

'Head,' he blurts, spotting a mass of black curls. Is it? He drops on his knees with the torch to go closer. 'I think it's the head...' he reaches out without thinking. His brain telling him the feel of the object will help his decision making process to determine of it is a head. He touches hot wet curls of hair and the density of bone that can only be a skull. 'It is...it's the head...'

She strains and pushes as the contraction goes on. The agony is searing and she drops back when it eases to pant and swim back to focus.

He pauses, unsure of what to do, but continually glancing at the head of the baby. He looks closer but can only see the crown and he has no idea which way the baby is facing.

'Got to...got to...' she pants and gasps for air.

'I can see the head,' he says again.

'Okay...can you see the face?'

'No...just like the top of the head...you's gonna push yeah?'

'Can't,' she gasps. 'It's not coming...'

'Gotta push it out...push hard...'

'I have been...' how she stays calm is beyond him but she does. His mere presence brings that calmness. The fast he isn't panicking or running away. He's worried and nervous but his voice is deep, his manner is strong too. 'I don't know what to do...' she pants and tries to think back to the classes and the information she was bombarded with. The stuff they said about what happens if things go wrong. She read about it online and in books but right now she can't bring the details back. Is the cord wrapped round its neck? Is the baby stuck? What does she do?

'Just push,' Maddox says, 'gotta push...push hard...'

'I've been trying,' the sob comes back into her voice.

'Try now...try...push...what's your name?'

'Juliette...Julie...'

'Julie...listen, Julie...push, you's got to push it out...yeah?'

'Okay.'

'Okay yeah? Push...'

'Okay. I will.'

'Push...'

She summons air, breathes deep and feels the contraction coming. She rides the wave until the urge hits then she pushes. She pushes harder than she has pushed before. She strains with everything she has got.

'Push...come on...push,' Maddox wills her on, staring at the head that doesn't move. Her whole body writhes, her pelvis lifts off the floor, blood comes out, piss jets but the head doesn't move, not one bit. 'Harder...push harder...'

She cries out with a scream that escapes her lips because there is a man with a gun here and he's telling her to push and it's safe to make noise now. She strains, grunts and heaves and the pain makes her want to die as it gets worse, harder, sharper until she flakes and breaks off panting and weeping.

'Didn't come,' Maddox says, his voice deep but the words blunt.

She sobs harder. The agony, the desperation and fatigue and the worst nightmare now confirmed. 'Cut me,' she gasps.

'What?'

'Cut me...get it out...it'll die...cut me...'

'I ain't cutting you...you's gotta push again.'

'I tried. Listen to me. Listen...I've been hours...it's not coming out...you got to cut me and get it out...'

Maddox glares at the top of the baby's skull. There is no way he can cut her. What if he cuts the baby? What if she dies? He thinks hard, desperate and worried and not knowing what to do. His hand goes for the radio. His thumb feels the switch under his shirt. They'll kill him. He knows they will. That they will help is without doubt but that they will execute him is also without doubt. Millions are dead. Millions more will die. What difference does one more make?

The room lights to something beyond the spectrum of daylight. A flash of lightening that sears the image of every single detail of the room into his mind. It makes the darkness deeper. A second later the windows rattle in the frames as the thunder rolls and booms across the sky. Static electricity seems to grow in the room. The air becomes heavier and charged. He has a knife. He can cut her. He has a radio. He can call for help.

Either way, someone dies.

'It's Maddox...I need help...'

He waits for the death threats to come from Blowers. He waits while his brain tries to work an angle of him leaving before the others get here. He waits but nothing happens.

'It's Maddox...I need help...'

Nothing. He presses the button a few times listening to the click in his ear. *'It's Maddox, anyone hearing me?'*

'You're Maddox?' Julie asks in a strangely soft tone.

'Yeah...*It's Maddox. Anyone there? Blowers?*'

'Maddox,' Julie says, lifting her head despite the pain. A flash of lightning comes. A blinding explosion of silent light that makes them both blink. The thunder seems to come the very instant the lightening goes. A huge rolling beat of drums that echoes across the sky. 'You have to cut me,' she shouts to be heard with a voice that carries on shouting as the thunder stops.

'Blowers, it's Maddox...you hearing me?'

Still nothing. He gets to his feet and heads for the back door while pressing the button over and again.

'Don't go...' Julie says in alarm.

'Blowers...you there? It's Maddox...anyone hear me?'

A crackle comes back. A burst hiss of static. He presses again, speaking again and waiting again. The same crackle comes through his ear. He goes further into the garden that switches for the blink of an eye to that light beyond daytime where the image is imprinted in his brain like a negative photo. Nothing comes back. Only a crackled hiss. He transmits again. He shouts over the boom of thunder and paces to the end while Julie screams his name in a voice that cuts off mid-way. He runs back in to see her straining in the grip of a contraction. Lightning strobes. Thunder booms. He goes back to watch that patch of hair but it still doesn't move.

'PUSH,' he shouts. She grunts, straining and trying. 'Come on...push...push...COME ON...'

Movement. Hardly noticeable but it moved. It turned but it hasn't come out. An instinct tells him the baby is stuck. The force of pressure of the woman straining to push it out that makes the baby turn but not move down. Something must be stopping it. Maybe that cord, the umbilical cord, maybe that is wrapped or trapping the baby. What does he do? What can he do? He can't cut her. Where would he cut? How deep? What if the knife nicks an artery?

She has to stop pushing. That instant fact follows the instinct.

'Stop. Julie...stop pushing...JULIE...'

'I can't,' she screams out in a voice broken and hoarse.

'Stop, stop it...you got to stop.'

She breaks off, panting and gasping for air. Sweat pours down her face. The raging thirst is back and the pain makes her mind feel like she's ready to pass out.

'It's Maddox...I need help...ROY? ROY?'

Still nothing save for the burst of static. He runs for the front door and starts slamming the bolts back and working the lock to get out into the deserted street. Gunfire in the distance. Several sets of automatic fire.

'It's Maddox...I need help...ROY?' he spins round on the spot. His face a mask of furious thinking.

'...fucking...ill you...ing prick...'

'Blowers. I need help...there's a woman...she's giving birth but the baby is stuck...'

'..dox..re you...'

'Who's that? It's Maddox here. A woman is giving birth. The baby is stuck...'

Static bursts of broken transmission. Voices saying something but mangled and incoherent. Sheet lightening scorches the sky raising the sensation of static electric in the air and he feels the thunder in his bones. So low, deep and powerful. He risks running further up the street, pushing the button to transmit but getting the same mangled voices back.

The desperation mounts. He thinks fast. The woman and the baby will die if he does nothing. If he cuts the woman he also risks killing them both. Is cutting the only option? The baby is stuck. What's making it be stuck? It could the cord thing. The head might be too big. Could an arm or leg be stuck somewhere preventing it coming out? Hospitals don't cut women they pull the baby out with forceps. Forceps! He needs those. What are they? Like tongs? Pliers? That won't work, he could kill the child. Hands then. He has to use his hands. He turns to run down the street back to the house as a chunk of brick on the wall behind blows out from the 5.56 mm round fired from the assault rifle further up the road.

'COWARD...'

'NO! Blowers no...' Maddox drops down as he launches to the side. More rounds pepper the space he was standing in as Blowers runs down aiming towards him.

'You fucking coward...' Blowers seethes, he fumes, his mates are in the shit. His family is struggling and this worthless scumbag ran off after causing them grief all day. If Maddox gets away he could get to the fort before anyone else. He fires again. Single shots aimed into the dark shadows where Maddox ran. He spots the lad running to vault a wall into a garden and fires a burst before checking behind him. On hearing the transmissions of the others he ran faster and started making distance between him and the horde with the idea of losing them and working back to the town centre.

'WOMAN'S GIVING...'

'You're a cunt but I never took you for a coward, Maddox...'

'GIVING BIR...' he cuts off as the rounds slam into the wall sending shards of brick flying past his face. He hunkers down and scrabbles further into the front garden as he looks to the locked front door of the dark house.

The lightening comes. Several individual sheets that strobe one after the other in a series of blinding bursts of energy. The thunder starts before the lightshow ends. Deep and furious as it matches the murderous intent on Blowers face. That he will kill Maddox is now fact. The man has been given every chance and he is too dangerous to be left.

'MADDOX...'

A woman screams the name. A terrified wail of agony in a voice breaking off. Blowers snatches his head round in the direction it came from.

'Who is that?'

'WOMAN GIVING BIRTH,' Maddox screams out.

'MADDOX...' Julie screams as the urges come back but Maddox said don't push but her body is telling her to push. She looks round for a knife, intending to cut herself and make Maddox take her baby. The knives are in the drawer. She tries to move but screams out as the pain sears through her body. Teeth gritted, tears rolling and she starts inching to slide over with a hand reaching up towards the drawer handle.

'What woman?' Blowers asks, turning to look behind him again.

'In there...in that house...the baby is stuck...won't come out...'

Blowers strides down the middle of the road with the rifle wedged into his shoulder as he holds the aim to where he knows Maddox is. The fury is palpable. The desire to kill is real but the soldier in him stops the finger from pressing down as Maddox stands up with his hands raised.

'Where's your rifle?'

'In the house with the woman...'

'MADDOX...'

'That's her,' Maddox says.

'Does she know you?'

'What?'

'She knows your name. How does she know you?'

'No! I told her my name...Blowers, the baby is stuck in her. It won't come out...she's bleeding to death...'

'MADDOX...PLEASE come back...' Julie screams out from the pain caused by reaching for the drawer. She almost got it but fell back from the surge of agony. She tries again, bracing and knowing her own pain means nothing.

Blowers thinks to shoot him now, check the woman and deal with whatever the situation is. A howl behind him. The infected still coming. His finger increases the pressure on the trigger. Maddox stiffens, sensing what's about to happen.

'Run...' Blowers says in a growl.

'What?'

'Run. Fuck off...'

'Blowers, she's dying...'

'I'll sort it. Fuck off...go on...run...'

'You's got the things coming...how you gonna help her? Get Roy...Blowers, get Roy here...'

'I said FUCK OFF NOW...'

'I'll cover you, Blowers. I'll lead them away...you help her. You know that shit yeah? You did combat triage? The baby is stuck...it might be the cord or or...I thought forceps but...have to use hands, she said to cut but she could die and the knife could cut the baby but she can't push cos the head turned but didn't come out and...'

Blowers can see the passion in him, the genuine worry and emotion playing out in his voice and facial expressions. Maddox implores him to help her. He's connected now. He saw the baby's head. He saw it move. He has to help it.

'I'll take them away,' Maddox urges. 'You's help her...get Roy yeah? Get Paula here, Blowers. She's dying...'

'Show me.'

'Ain't time,' Maddox states.

'Got about thirty seconds. Show me.'

'Blowers, we ain't got...'

'SHOW ME OR I WILL SHOOT YOU NOW.'

'Okay...in that house...look right there...I'll come over...' he scrabbles to clamber the wall with his hands still raised.

'Pistol off your belt on the floor, hold it by the top...point it this way and you will die.'

'WE DON'T HAVE TIME...'

'PISTOL. NOW...'

'Fuck it,' Maddox rarely swears. Swearing is a sign of low intelligence and a common trait used by people who cannot otherwise express themselves but right now swearing is the only vent he has. He slides the pistol out by the top and bends quickly to place it on the floor.

'Move,' Blowers says, stepping backwards to let Maddox go

past. The screeches and howls behind him sound closer. The horde closing the distance he created. The sound of feet running. Maddox moves fast. His hands away from his body as he runs to the door and stops to make sure Blowers is following him. Blowers does follow and he goes with a fast stride and his rifle still held aimed and ready.

'Down here,' Maddox says.

Blowers left hand drops to his pocket. He pulls his torch, pushes the end and brings his hand back under the rifle as he lights the path ahead of him. In through the front door and the metallic tang of blood hangs in the air. Other smells too. Sweat, urine and shit.

'No!' Maddox runs fast seeing Julie pull the drawer to the floor scattering knives. She grabs a handle and sinks back with the blade aimed at her belly as Maddox rushes to grip her wrists. 'No don't... Julie don't...my mate's here, he's a soldier yeah...he can help you... let go, let go, Julie...'

Blowers takes it in. A rapid assessment that clocks the rifle propped up against the side and the floor now littered with knives. He sees the woman's huge stomach and the blood between her legs. He sees her face in the torchlight and notices how dehydrated she looks. He sees it all quickly and calmly.

'Look,' Maddox says, ditching the knife taken from her hands and motioning to Blowers. 'See the head yeah? That's the head... she's pushing but it's not coming out...it's stuck...I saw it turn round so...so something is holding it in...'

'Hold,' Blowers cuts in and drops his left hand holding the torch to the radio switch under his shirt. '*It's Blowers. Receiving me?*'

'I tried that...it didn't work...'

'*Blowers? You okay?*' Howie's rushed voice, frantic and filled with background noise of death and war and infected screeching.

'*Got a woman. Giving birth. Baby stuck. Roy? Advice please...*'

'Can you see the baby?' Roy pauses between shots, his mind running fast as he summons the mental image.

'See the head...the top of it,' Blowers says, his voice calm, his manner calm, his whole bearing one of professionalism in the face of adversity.

'How long has she been in labour?'

'How long she been in labour?' Blowers asks.

'Hours...Julie? You said hours right?'

'Yeah...I gotta push, Maddox. I got to push...'

'Don't push...not yet...'

'Roy, she said hours.'

'Is there blood?'

'Loads.'

'Could be the cord wrapped round the baby holding it in...or the head could be too big to get through the birthing canal...could be that and the baby is facing down towards the mothers back which is the wrong way...'

'Orders?' Blowers asks.

'Christ,' Roy says, holding his bow in his left hand while trying to think. Nick grunts from somewhere behind him while fighting desperately against numbers that keep coming. Below Roy, the battle hasn't changed. The ground is thick with corpses. The air stinks of blood. The heat is awful. The whole of it is the closest they are to losing yet. Smoke is billowing from the shopping centre from the ceiling tiles that caught aflame from the cans of ignited hairspray. Mo fires and fires at the door. The waves of infected are relentless. Behind him, Marcy and Paula wage war on the spiders. There is no way out. The only exit is through the door that is jammed with infected. The closest they are to dying is now. The closest they are to losing is now. The complacency of their actions. The pride that they were undefeatable comes down as crushing as the pressure of the storm brewing overhead.

Charlie reins Jess in and looks down at Cookey and Blinky soaked with sweat and covered in grime. Jess's flanks gleam with sweat, blood and gore. Behind them the trail of corpses mark their passage but more are coming. More than three can deal with. All they can do is fight and run and try to keep them away from the middle.

Blowers closes his eyes for a second. The second's worth of pause from Roy tells him how desperate it is and the closest they are to losing is now.

Roy looks down at Howie, Clarence and Dave. That those three are still standing is beyond human comprehension. They've killed more than everyone else combined but the infection has resources that make his insides drop. He looks down the street to the solid ranks. He looks behind him to see Nick fighting at the stairs and makes eye contact with Reginald. They had a plan a few seconds ago. Heather and Paco were going to the back doors of the shopping centre to cut the flow. That would free Mo, Paula and Marcy to join the main fight. The lads would work back and they would, as they have always done, turn the battle and win but suddenly it doesn't look like that. Suddenly the hope dwindles but Howie kills the one in front, turns and locks eyes on Roy to give a single nod. 'DO IT...' Howie shouts and turns back into the fight.

Roy presses the button on his radio to do what must be done. Howie cannot give orders as Howie is busy. The same with Clarence. The same with Paula. Roy is older, therefore he takes the burden of responsibility and makes the order.

'Heather, Charlie...go to Blowers...Blowers, hands in and try to pull the baby out gently. If you have to cut her then go from the stomach down...the mother will die if you cut but the baby is the priority...'

It is the only option. Without Paco here the chances of winning are gone. Without Paco storming into that shopping centre they can't free the three inside but a baby is worth more than all of them. They all know it. It is their way. It is the right way. He releases the radio, draws an arrow and fires.

Cookey draws the back of a hand across his forehead, his chest heaving as he sucks air and looks up at Charlie. 'Take Blinky...get to Blowers...'

'But...' Charlie says, knowing Cookey doesn't stand a chance against so many.

'I'll be fine...I'll keep running,' Cookey says.

'I'll stay, you go,' Blinky says.

'Mate,' Cookey snaps.

'I'm fitter...I can run faster and further...you go...go with Charlie...'

'She is,' Charlie says quickly.

The thought of leaving Blinky alone is abhorrent but it makes sense, 'you got enough magazines?' Cookey asks.

'Yep now fuck off cuntbreath,' Blinky says, nodding at him, her own chest heaving as the sweat pours down her face.

'Just keep running,' Cookey says, locking eyes.

'I will...fuck off,' Blinky snorts, phlegms and spits to the side.

'Hate you,' Cookey says, his filthy face showing the grin.

'Hate you more,' Blinky grins back.

'Here,' Charlie offers a hand to help Cookey heave up behind. Jess skitters round at the extra weight. 'Hold on,' Charlie says. Cookey holds on without a joke and without a comment made.

'Run Blinky...don't try and fight them...' Cookey shouts.

'Yep,' Blinky says.

'ON JESS,' Charlie screams the horse to action.

'Mate, it's Cookey...where are you?'

'Blowers? It's Heather...we'll come to you...where are you?'

Heather grips the wheel with her right hand. The left holds the radio. Paco clenches his fists and readies to fight simply from sensing the tension in Heather. She drives fast through the lanes as the lightning and thunder drive fear deep into her gut but for the first time in her life she refuses to allow the panic to take over. The desperation is obvious. The energy she can feel is right there. The words, the way they were said, the honour of them, the sheer fucking integrity of a few that do something so vast it boggles the mind.

Blowers turns to look down the hallway. A soldier born. A soldier made. A soldier by definition of the core of steel running through his body. How do people find each other in a dark town in the middle of a war? Satnav? Maps? Directions? Fuck that. He'll do it the soldiers way. He'll go old school.

'Hands in...try and ease the baby out, it should be face up not face down but go gently though...Roy said gently. He said the cord could be wrapped and if you have to cut then do it from the stomach down...'

'Where you going?' Maddox asks as Blowers strides off down the hallway.

'The others are coming. You'll be fine.'

'Blowers,' Maddox shouts. 'Where you going?'

'To light a path for the others...I'll hold them back...ease the baby out or cut from the stomach down.'

He marches out into the street. Bag off. Flap open.

'Blowers, where the fuck are you?' Cookey shouts into his ear.

'Need directions,' Heather's tight voice follows.

Blowers pulls the grenades out as the horde reaches the corner at the end of the street. He stands and gauges distance, direction and the houses on the other side of the street.

'Gonna light a path...follow the explosions...'

'Roger that,' Cookey replies.

'What are you doing? What does that mean?' Heather asks.

Blowers pulls and throws. He pulls and throws. He pulls and throws and pulls and throws. He grunts with each and aims the hard metal bombs through windows of houses and down the street to the parked cars left on the side of the road. He pulls pins and throws grenades to light a path with sound and light.

Jess canters on. Cookey clinging to Charlie as they stare and listen. Heather grips the wheel and leans towards the windscreen, staring out at the blackness of the night.

'Holy fuck,' Cookey murmurs in Charlie's ear as the grenades detonate one after the other. Direction is gained instantly. Flames scorch up into the air. Bright flashes and dull thuds that sound one after the other as Howie stiffens with pride and Clarence growls. As Paula's upper lip pulls back as she takes up her rifle to join Mo. Roy glances to the booms and flashes of the grenades exploding as Nick nods at the fuckers coming up and growls the defiance of his few that kill so many.

Blowers pulls and throws. He explodes cars and houses. He makes it obvious for the others. He gives flame to a street. He gives sound and light as Jess bursts from a canter to a gallop, taking corners at speeds that ain't right while Charlie feels the horse beneath and Cookey holds on.

Blinky turns at the sounds. Grinning in awe of her utter devotion to Blowers. The man is a god to her. She would never have thought to do that. She turns back as the horde come steaming down the road towards her. She wipes her nose, lifts her rifle and fires a sustained burst that empties the magazine.

'RUN THEN,' she bellows, taunting them, goading them, 'FAT CUNTS...RUN...COME ON...' All day long. She flicks a finger at them and legs it.

'There,' Heather shouts, hearing and seeing the explosions. She speeds up. Pushing her foot down harder. Hedges flash by. Lightning joins the show. Thunder comes to play but the grenades are a different noise. Harder, duller, manmade and not organic.

The grenades are gone. Blowers takes up his rifle and fires the magazine. He changes and empties his magazine. He takes a knee in order to reduce the distance needed to travel to reach the spare magazines in his bag. Time for one more. He loads, yanks the bolt back, aims and fires. They drop dead. They drop injured. They drop to trip the ones that come after but they come all the same and they do so fast and pumped.

Blowers stands, leaving his rifle left on his bag as he takes his axe up and stares at the enemy. So many of them. Fuck there's a lot. He can't run now to lead them off as the others won't find the door. He has to hold them.

'Boss, Blowers...er...got a few coming at me right now...um...sorry for asking but if you could get angry I'd appreciate it...no worries if not...it's er...it's been an honour, Sir...'

'NOW HOWIE,' Clarence roars the second he hears the words in his ear.

'NOW HOWIE,' Roy echoes at the chilling calmness from Blowers.

'Shit shit...hold on, Blowers,' Marcy mutters.

'Hold on mate,' Nick says.

'Simon. You will hold that line. You will fight. Do you hear me?'

'Yes, Dave.'

'We do not yield, Simon. We do not surrender. We fight. YOU WILL FIGHT, SIMON.'

'Yes, Dave.'

'FIGHT SIMON. HOLD THAT LINE.'

'Yes, Dave.'

'Mr Howie...they took your sister. They hurt her. They took Jamie. They took your friends...'

'Fuck, Dave,' Howie growls.

'YOU WILL RAGE NOW, MR HOWIE. YOU WILL RAGE...'

Oh aye.

A pulse.

A surge.

Here there is no panic. Just a rage that grows instant and furious. This is what they do. This is why they are here. For this. To do just this. Nothing else.

Be as you are. Be as you were born to be and do not heed the worries of others or the small things of life that give concern for you are a warrior and this is your time.

'Let's fight...'

Blowers charges. He takes on a horde with an axe as a streak of black powers up the road behind him to overtake and slam the line ahead with a snarl and a flash of teeth that rags and destroys. It ain't one against many now. It's two. Two who are connected in mind and spirit who are connected to all the others as that pulse sweeps through them.

Knives out. Marcy, Paula and Mo charge the door as the shop behind them engulfs in fire.

Nick takes the stairs. He goes down one at a time to reach the bottom then turns righteous and glorious to drive them back from the shop with a speed that isn't right.

Reginald wages war. He grows wild and crazed in his desire to kill and around him the corpses of his foes lie splattered and broken.

Jess goes faster. She takes corners at an angle without guidance or steerage from Charlie who snarls unblinking and feels Cookey's energy at his displacement from Blowers pulsing through her back.

Blinky stops running. She dumps her bag and rifle, grips her axe and turns back towards the horde. There is a time for running. There is a time for legging it and it's not now. Blowers is fighting them on his own. She can feel it. Fuck it. She charges. She charges her horde with her axe gripped and lifting.

Mo goes faster. Spinning left and right to protect the flanks of both Marcy and Paula while dealing with what's in front of him. The rage in the others is different in him. It's channelled and focussed.

Blowers and Meredith take the horde on. They take it with a vicious urge to cause harm. Meredith takes one down. Blowers takes two. Meredith takes another. Blowers takes two more. They are fast. They are brutal in the violence they visit upon their common enemy.

Charlie and Cookey ride. Heather drives. Everyone fights.

CHAPTER TWENTY-NINE

Maddox stares down as Blowers strides from the house. His heart racing. He swallows then rushes to fill a cup with water that he hands down to Julie. She lifts up with a grunt of pain but takes the drink to gulp thirsty and deep.

'You heard him yeah?'

'Yeah,' she says, nodding at Maddox. She drops the empty mug to reach out for his hands. He tightens his grip on her. She squeezes as they stare with eyes locked.

'I gotta put my hands in you...'

She nods, tears spilling down her cheeks.

'It's gonna hurt,' he says as softly as he can. She chokes a sob and reaches up to smooth her hands down his face. 'I'm sorry,' he says.

'Do it,' she whispers.

'Don't push...'

'I won't...'

He strokes her cheek, smooth the hair from her forehead, 'I'll be with you yeah? I'll be right here, Julie...'

'Okay,' she whispers the word.

'You don't gotta whisper now...you can scream...'

'The other man? Where did…'

'He'll stop them coming in. We got more coming…they'll be here soon…'

'Okay…do it…'

She swallows and gulps air as he moves down to kneel in the sticky blood pooling between her legs. His torch shines, showing the head still in the same position. He puts the torch in his mouth, bites down and reaches out.

She feels hot. Too hot. The blood is sticky but he feels the tight curls on the scalp and the warmth coming through the skull. Something moves that makes her grunt with pain. A shift of the baby inside. A squirm. Sweat pours down his face as the grenades outside blow explosions that sound a hundred miles away.

Slowly, so slowly. Gently, so gently he feels the baby's head and moves out to the sides and her skin that is taut and unmoving. The tiniest of pressure exerted to stretch her wider sends a wave of agony. He freezes, looking up over her stomach.

'Do it,' she gasps.

He tries again to physically stretch her. She grunts but he tries more, straining against her skin.

The urge to push comes. The contraction of her muscles that send the signal to birth the child in her body. She resists with everything she has, fighting the urge as Blowers and Meredith charge the horde for the life of her unborn baby.

Maddox becomes engrossed in the tiny fractions of the thing he does. The scalp he can see is smaller than the palm of his hand but he can't tell how far it extends out. He knows he is being too gentle, too tentative but also knows that he is hurting her. It has to be done. He has to push inside and try. He draws his knife without a word said and hovers the blade as he tries to think where he should cut but then Roy said only to cut down from the stomach. What if he cuts her somewhere here to make the opening bigger? He can't do it. One slip and he could kill both.

He puts the knife down and goes back to try harder in pushing her skin aside. He needs to get his hand inside but without harming the baby. He goes for the top and starts pushing his fingers in while heaving upwards away from the baby. Her skin tears. Blood pumps down over his hand and wrist. She screams and slams her hands on the floor but he keeps going, pushing in and up. The force needed is huge. He grunts with the effort and strains to go further in. She tears again, more blood comes, she screams out and he can feel the quiver of agony searing through her body. He bends lower to shine the torch in the tiniest of gaps created between her body and the head of the baby. More dark curls of hair. More scalp and skull. He pushes harder, forcing the gap to widen. Her voice pierces his ears.

'Back of the head,' he tries to mutter, forgetting the torch is between his teeth. He can see the back of the head so that means the baby is facing down towards the mothers back. That's bad. The baby has to be the other way Can he turn it? There is nothing to grip. He looks for the cord but can't see past the baby's head. He has to go in further. He exerts force to stretch her skin, tearing it apart. The pain is indescribable and it gets worse. It goes on and will never end. It almost becomes too much, like it's torture but she holds in her mind the single thought of her baby living.

Still not enough. He has to go deeper. He has to see more. He grimaces, tenses and pushes as she screams shrill and agonised.

CHAPTER THIRTY

The will was there. The will is still there but willing a thing to happen is not the same as making a thing happen.

Two cannot hold so many back. It cannot be done. Blowers realises this as he makes the connection they are going for the door. He drops back with Meredith, slashing left and right to chop them down as they come at him and round him. Mangled corpses litter the ground and the gods play on to roll the die and score a double six as they laugh with mirth and let the storm begin.

The rain comes. Instant and sudden with a torrential downpour that simply commences as if it was always here and always happening. As the rain starts so the front ranks charge together. Blowers is taken down hard, slamming into the road as the axe spills from his hands. Meredith rags the one in her jaws and spins round to run and hit the few on Blowers. Her force makes them scatter as her teeth go to work. Blowers fights to get free, thrashing wild and demented to get his legs out so he can roll away and surge up. He goes for the knife on his belt but the next one is there. He lashes out with an instinct honed from years in the ring. A hammering right hook that sends the infected staggering away. The next one comes as he repositions and uppercuts with a power that smashes the jaw in several places.

That instinct kicks in and he drops with his feet positioned and his fists coming up to guard and work. The rain pours. His hair grows slick and wets his top tight against his frame but with his fists alone he holds them back.

A barrage of punches into the face of a man lunging to bite. Fists pulverise the nose, eye sockets and hold the beast back until he whips in with a vicious left hook that lifts the male and drops it dead.

Blowers is stronger than he was. Faster. He hits harder. He hits with enough power to kill and the skill shows now.

Jabs slam out. Jabs that fracture and knock heads back. He weaves and ducks, spinning to come in fast with another barrage that smashes them back. A hand lashes. He block, ducks and powers up with another uppercut. He goes back, feet dancing, upper body weaving to dodge and weave.

Three come. Three at once. Bang bang bang. Hits given to hold them back as he hooks and jabs then slams in the heavy right cross. Skulls fracture. Bones break. Bodies fall. He gets faster still. Speeding up to do a thing he has practised for what seems his entire life.

His hands become a blur. The jabs summon power that explodes out from his hips and core. An opening, a chance to take. The hook is nasty and vicious and drops the infected. The uppercut is brutal power. The heavy right is hard. All of them have their place and when used together they are devastating.

To Blowers, he is in the place fighting and cannot see himself. He cannot see the dance he weaves like Dave and Mo. He cannot see the ducks and jumps back to feint and fool as he slams his knuckles into faces and heads. He cannot see he kills with ease with a speed that is a blur. Left, right, left, right, hook. Left, left, right, hook. Right jab, left jab, huge power explosion of an uppercut.

He goes back towards the door but for a few glorious moments he holds a horde with nothing but his fists. They come harder, smelling the blood in the house, hearing the screams, sensing the fear. He fights harder. Hands rake his skin. His t-shirt rips. His skin is cut and bleeds. He hammers out, dancing to weave and duck and hit again. Several come in. Teeth find his arm. He screams out guttural and hard. Meredith grabs an ankle and pulls to remove the teeth on Blowers. Nails slash down his face, a heavy flailing arm slams into his face. His nose breaks. Blood pours but his nose has been broken before and he doesn't feel the pain now. He is bitten, raked, cut and battered as he is beaten back towards the door but the two hold the line. They fight in the rain as the lightning forks down with ragged scars that scorch the ground.

He boxes for his life and that of an unborn child. He boxes to keep them back. He reaches the short path to the house and feels the organic touch of the others. He feels Mo's coldness that is becoming more like Dave. He feels Nick slamming them back through the shop. He feels Paula and Marcy furious and in pain from so many bites. He feels Clarence's enormous strength and the worry the big man has for Blowers. He feels Roy and Reginald. He feels Blinky fighting and Charlie and Cookey racing towards him. He feels the closeness of Meredith and the will inserted that tells him *to hold on brother, hold on.* Above it all he feels the power of Howie radiating out that pulses through them and he knows, without knowing how, that in the time since Howie brought the hive mind hundreds of infected have died. In that turmoil of the fight, and along with every other nuance of connection he feels two more. He feels Heather's fear of the storm and the wall of rage that is Paco. A tsunami that comes in the form of a man that is half what they are and half something else.

He breaches the path and fights back to the door. He goes down but batters free. He falls into the house and calls himself a cunt for not locking the door when he came out. He goes into the hallway still fighting. Still boxing. The doorway reduces the numbers that can attack him at once. They still get through but he holds them from within while Meredith does what she can from outside.

Maddox looks up at the noise and Blowers fighting to hold the door with his bare hands. Maddox feels inside the woman who screams as she feels every single shred of pain. The baby is facing down. His fingertips feel the cord wrapped round the baby's legs. He pushes harder in, feeling the cord's tightness and works to the frantic conclusion that both of those things are preventing the baby coming out. He has to get the cord off and he has to turn the baby. It's so wet, so slippery, he cannot gain purchase or leverage and knows he is causing her untold pain. The knife is there. He glances at it, knowing it may come to doing what Roy said and cutting down her stomach.

Inch by inch Blowers loses ground. Inch by inch they come surging through. The front windows of the lounge on Blowers left go through with bodies falling hard to the floor. They come pouring in as Blowers braces to hold the front door and the ones coming from the lounge. It gets harder. It gets nastier. The compression increases. He pulls his knife from his belt and stabs out into soft flesh. Blood spills, innards hang, he cuts throats and stabs through eyes into brains.

Maddox pushes harder. His face a mask of focus and concentration. He feels the cord going round the legs and tries to work it free but his fingers slide off. He tries to hook and drag it but he can only do millimetres before again his fingers slip off. He tries to turn the baby but suffers the same problem and he doesn't notice when Julie grows quiet and still.

It comes to this. As Charlie did in the doorway to protect the three girls, so Blowers uses his body to shield them from breaching the kitchen. That he suffers is without question. That teeth find his flesh and nails slice his skin is apparent and obvious. He bleeds but he clots. He feels pain but he fights. He summons the darkest recesses of his soul for the last tiny bits of energy that is drip fed by the love of the others as they fight to get free to come and help him. The compression grows. Meredith rags them wild and fast but even she cannot stop them going in. She grips and kills. She launches again and again to tear throats out as she hears and feels Blowers roaring inside from the rigid thumb driving into his eye. He stabs and stabs. He thrashes but the thumb drives deeper, pushing his eye back so hard it feels like it will touch his brain. He screams out as it bursts and a searing burning agony goes through his head. He twists and bites into the wrist of the hand blinding him. His teeth open skin. Blood spurts. He thrashes again as the thumb goes but the vision in his left eye won't come.

As one the others scream out at the pain and fear rushing through Blowers. Charlie yells for Jess to go faster. The horse belts it down the roads, taking corners hard and fast. Every muscle in Cookey's body tensed. His face a mask.

Pack must come now.

A pulse from Meredith calling for the pack. C*ome now. Hold on Brother, hold on. I'll come to you.*

Hurts. Can't see.

HOLD ON BROTHER.

Too many.

I'm coming mate.

Too many, Cookey. Can't see. I can't see.

I'm coming, Blowers. I swear it.

The vision in his left eye gone. His right misted, blurred and the agony is searing. He stabs, braces and takes the pain for the voices of the pack willing him to hold on.

Maddox curses, his grip lost again. He tries and feels his way over the legs to the feet then back up as he tries to pull the cord down. He glances to the hallway and sees Blowers flailing blind and bleeding heavily. He sees how close they are and knows he has but seconds. Julie is silent. She isn't screaming. He looks again to see blood still seeping from her that tells him her heart still beats but slow and weak. It has to be now. From the stomach down. It has to be now.

In the precinct Howie, Dave and Clarence slay with frantic fear driven energy under a torrential rain that cools their skin and drips valuable fluids into their parched throats. Mo, Marcy and Paula scream as they fight out from the shopping centre and Nick batters a savage path from the shop front. The hive mind is upon them. The intrinsic connection to each that flows and tells them Blowers is going down. He can't see. Pain everywhere. Too many against him.

Meredith snarls and takes them down. Her body twisting, lunging and fighting to get through into the house but they press in harder, closing the gaps and preventing her getting through. They charge hard to push and strain with the goal of taking one of Howie's now so close.

Blowers braces and holds. His body battered and hurt. Blood pouring from his nose. The vision in his left eye gone. The knife held in his right hand puckers a throat as he flails out with his left fist.

Howie roars out as Roy fires his last arrow, drops his bow, draws his sword and drops from the window to land on the bodies beneath him. The pressure is immense. The sense of victory in their foe who can taste the death of one of theirs. He slashes out wild and frenzied. His face contorted to beat them back and break free so he can to Blowers. They all do it. They all fight to get free. The infected compress. Sacrificing so to feed the weapons of the living army to keep them pinned and held as it drives harder into the hallway and tastes the blood of Simon Blowers.

Blowers weakens. Blood streaming from wounds all over his body. He stabs with his right hand and pushes his open left hand into the face of an infected woman. The pain from his eye is agonising and burns. His head throbs, his legs start to shake and tremble. He holds them with everything he has. He grits to brace and not yield, to hold the line.

Maddox digs the point of the knife into her stomach. What must done will be done. He cuts her. The sharp blade peels the flesh apart so easily it sickens him. He is killing her. She will now never recover or have life. With the torch in his teeth, he operates on the blood soaked floor to cut through a human being to save the child within her.

Blowers feels more pain than he has ever felt in his life. His left hand on the face of the infected woman who thrashes faster than he can react. His fingers go into her mouth. He pulls back but she bites hard and deep with a crunch through the bone on his little finger. He screams and slams his forehead into hers. Skulls meet. Stars flash. She goes back, tearing his finger from his hand as she goes. He roars out, incensed. The final rage explodes as he batters the soft bodies in front of him. The stump where his finger was sprays blood but he rams that broken hand into their faces. He stabs, kicks, bites and headbutts as he goes back towards the kitchen. Voices in his head. Voices in his mind. Cookey screaming. Meredith exerting her will. Charlie riding Jess. He feels them all. He feels each and gives thanks for knowing them. He gives grace for the honour of serving with them. In the final seconds of his life he wishes them well and to carry the fight on.

Julie is dead. The blood has stopped coming from her. Her heart has stopped beating. The baby will die. The infected are coming. Blowers is losing. The others aren't fast enough. Maddox cuts down and pushes a hand in to feel the baby's feet. He cuts again and works to find the cord.

Blowers starts to fall. He has done what he can and no more can be asked. Power flows into him. A will exerted from the others driving their love into his heart. He grunts and fights to rise up to use his body to block them. His head swims, his legs buckle then stiffen as he snarls and digs in to hold.

Maddox cuts to see the legs and reaches in to pull the cord down and free from the tiny limbs.

Jess takes the corner and powers on with a burst of speed

towards the huge crowd pushing into the doorway of the house. They ride into a scene of hell. Of bodies strewn and more raging and snarling as one dog attacks them like a beast from a nightmare. The flames from the houses blown to light a path bathe a fiery glow. Smoke plumes thick and black. The rain pours. Cookey grips his axe as Charlie fixes the door in her eyes. A signal sent. A message received and it is to that point that Jess aims. Jess who flies on feet that bring thunder and doesn't flinch as she slams into them with a power unbeknown to mere humans. Only she can do this. Only Jess can move them away in such a way. Only Jess can hold this point and she does. By the goodness of God she smashes them back and turns on a sixpence to rear as Cookey slides back to land with his axe swinging.

A screech of tyres. Headlights sweep the street. The Toyota revs loud and solid as it drives hard with the wall of rage that is Paco. Heather was aiming for the door to do the same as Jess but sees the horse already there. She stamps on the brake and heaves the wheel round. The vehicle slews out with the passenger door already opening as the wall of rage comes out to join the fray.

Blowers cannot see. He cannot hear. The pain is gone and he barely feels the dull thuds of bodies slamming into him. That he still stands is from will power alone. From courage and an allegiance to duty before death, and he knows his death is here. He'll go as a soldier. He'll go as a warrior with discipline and dignity. One single sound penetrates his head. A new sound of a thing unheard for many days. A beautiful sound of a new born baby crying out as Maddox pulls it free, cuts the cord and blinks from the spray of blood hitting his face. The baby cries. A new-born boy who inflates his lungs to mark his place and right to live in this world. Blowers grins in a face battered and soaked with blood.

'By sea...by land' the words come mangled, broken and whispered. The motto of the Royal Marines. His biggest regret in life was that he failed his Commando course but now he has earned his badge. He has earned his beret. 'We win...' the final words whisper as his heart stops and he drops slumped and inert to be trampled by the feet of the infected who go over him into the kitchen.

To the last they feel it. To the last they feel his heart stopping and the loss of one from the pack of the hive mind. Where Blowers was there is a void. An emptiness that sees them falter and weaken. A sapping of energy that is sensed by the other side who screech out with the victory of taking one of Howie's. The infected becomes emboldened. It becomes stronger as though the taking has given it strength. It pushes harder, snarling louder, raking faster. They are mortal. They are not unkillable. It has proved this. It will take more. It will end it here in this shitty little town that burns with flames and runs red with blood.

Cookey staggers away. Rendered weak and dumb. Charlie launches from Jess to cover him. Running to get in front and fight them back to protect Cookey mouthing words that don't come. Heather runs in with her machete swinging to join Charlie as Cookey's legs go weak and he falls to his knees. Meredith barks loud and deep and with Paco and Jess clearing the door she pushes through the legs and bodies into the hallway to the body of Blowers. She drops on him. Her body covers his. The whole of her protects him. Her lips pulled back as she lashes out at anything coming close. In between each bite, she licks his face and whines with an instant change from raging wild beast to an animal consumed with grief.

CHAPTER THIRTY-ONE

He roars with defiance as he holds them back and it takes but a second for him to realise they are not there. He staggers back. Confused and raging. His chest heaving. His hands balled to fists to fight. This is not the hallway. Maddox is not behind him. He spins round, his hard eyes wild and still filled with the lust of battle but it fades away. All trace of the emotions he had ebb away and his breathing slows.

It's light now but grimy and grey. He's in a street so ruined and destroyed it looks like something from the Second World War. An old park lies in a square behind rusted railings. The slide has fallen down into a pile of rubble, rusted swing chains nestle amongst the yellowing grass. The sky is streaked blood red and the clouds look heavy and threatening. The place is unfamiliar. He looks round for the others but they aren't here. He's alone. A feeling of a presence. Something malevolent and evil that is coming closer. He can't see it but he can feel it.

Blowers starts walking. The feeling increases, like being watched and hunted. He starts jogging, then running then sprinting as fast as he can to be away from here.

His left eye feels weird. His vision blurs. He tries to call out but his voice is silent. He looks behind to see dark shadows flitting between the ruined walls. Dark shapes of things that are evil with intent. A laugh echoes round, rolling to bounce off walls and buildings. The laugh becomes a dry hacking cough. Twisted and not right. Like a taunt. The fear grows inside him. They are coming for him. A certainty. A fact. He makes himself stop running to face his death with bravery and courage. He is a soldier. He doesn't run away but faces the enemy. He stiffens to stand proud while wishing the others were with him. He wants a joke from Cookey. He wants to feel Clarence's size next to him. To have the boss lead the line. He wants Meredith to push her nose into his hand and lick his face that suddenly feels wet as a whine is heard that rolls round the buildings.

The fear inside grows but he stiffens and holds. His hands once more bunch to fists. His hard eyes glare. He twitches at the sensation again. A shooting pain in his left eye that loses vision for a second before swimming back.

Movement on his right side. He spins to see a flash of black fur and a long tail running behind the broken wall of a house down the street.

'Meredith?' he calls out, his voice hollow and strangely flat in this awful place.

A bark. It's Meredith. He knows that bark anywhere. He sets off running towards where the noise came from but when he gets there she is gone.

Another bark. He turns quickly to see her now standing in the middle of the road further down. She barks again. She barks to tell him to move. To get away. She spins to go, turns back and barks.

He starts after her, calling her name. Whispers from the sides ripple down the street. Predatory inhuman sounds. Meredith barks, louder now, more urgent. That feeling of being hunted comes back. He sprints hard. Running over rubble and heaps of slag on the road. Veering round old cars rusted and left for years.

They give chase. Whatever they are. He cannot see them but

feels them. He hears the feet pounding and the whispered grunts and calls. The cackling laughter comes again. Meredith barks but he cannot close the distance between them. She stays at a fixed point leading him on.

He takes a corner to see Meredith outside the doorway to a church. Her mouth open, her huge tongue hanging down to the side as she takes the head rub from the big man at her side.

Blowers slows to a jog to a walk and looks on with only the barest sense of confusion inside.

'Corporal,' the man says, nodding curtly.

'Sir,' Blowers says, coming to a smart stop as he snaps out a salute.

'Sergeant not a sir,' Big Chris says, grinning with white teeth showing through his bushy black beard. Dressed in army fatigues and only then does Blowers realise he's wearing the same.

'Sergeant,' Blowers says.

'Inside,' Chris says, casting a look of distaste round at the view. He clicks his tongue for Meredith to run on through the open doors. Blowers follows. Unsure of where he is. Unsure why Big Chris is here but knowing this is normal.

Inside the church is lit with hundreds of candles that burn and flicker to fill the space with golden light. The floor is swept clean and the air smells sweet. A contrast of the sterility of the broken world outside to somewhere that has the warmth of life.

'Marine marine in a boat...living proof shit can float!' Malcolm laughs striding towards him with his hand out. 'Not bad for a bootneck.'

'Thanks,' Blowers says, shaking his hand. 'If you want a job done properly...don't ask a Para...'

'Twat,' Malcolm laughs.

'Fuck you,' Blowers grins.

The smile on Malcolm's face eases, his face earnest and sincere, 'seriously, you did well...you took loads out...'

'Thanks,' Blowers says in his simple, self-effacing way.

'When you two have finished finding a room,' Chris says, his voice as deep and rich as Blowers remembers which makes him wonder why he remembers that. Chris is dead. Malcolm is dead. Oh.

'Fuck,' Blowers says then blinks as he remembers Meredith was here. 'Oh no...no...not Meredith...'

Chris looks at him in puzzlement then round to see the dog cleaning herself by the alter. 'Oh right. No, it's not what you think it is.'

'She's not dead then?'

'She's not dead. Listen, we don't have much time.'

'Eh? What's going on?' Blowers says, wincing at the pain in his left eye then suddenly feeling a burning agony in his left hand. 'And who is that?'

'That's Meredith,' Chris says, turning to smile at the slim blonde haired woman walking towards them.

'Hello, Simon,' she says, lifting a hand in greeting.

'What the actual fuck,' Blowers mutters, 'Hello, Miss...the dog's called Meredith...' he tells Chris.

'She's not,' Chris says. 'We don't have time. Ready for orders?'

'But...'

'I said ready for orders, Corporal?' Chris booms. 'Now listen up.'

'Yes, Sergeant,' Blowers snaps, coming to attention.

'You cannot let them win,' Malcolm says, walking over to stand next to Chris.

'Me?' Blowers asks.

'They will achieve one race if you stop now,' Meredith says, walking over to stand on Chris's other side.

Blowers stares from one to the other. His eye hurts. His hand too but he is a soldier and this is orders so he ignores the pain to listen.

'Blowers,' Chris says, speaking in a tone that belies the importance of what he says, 'Ask Reginald about the merging. He's on our side, you can trust him. Listen to him, the man knows what he is doing.'

'Yes, Sergeant...er, what's merging?'

'It's what Paco is now,' Meredith says softly, coming forward a step to smile at Blowers. She looks radiant and so healthy, a huge smile of clean teeth and the light shines from her blonde hair.

'I don't understand, Miss,' Blowers says.

'He is halfway from them to us,' she says, reaching out to lay a hand on Blowers arm that tingles with warmth.

'But Paco's on our side.'

'One race is what Paco is,' Meredith says. 'That's what it will achieve. A thing that cannot feel...'

She smiles warmly at him. She is beautiful in a way he has never seen before. She shines with goodness and love and the virtues a soldier longs to fight for and suddenly he doesn't want to go anywhere.

'You are so brave, Simon,' she says, holding his eyes on hers. 'So brave...' her hand reaches out to touch his cheek. 'It is your choice if you stay here...'

'Am I dead?' he asks simply, honestly.

'In a way, right now yes, but you can go back.'

He nods and tries to speak but he can't take his eyes from her. She is everything. She is purity of grace and love. She is warmth and not death and blood, she is not the heat of the battles and the things he has to do.

She holds his gaze and smiles with that warm soft hand touching his cheek. 'They cannot become what Paco is. Our species will die. Paco still has a trace left...they won't.'

'I can't stop that,' Blowers says, his voice low and muted, almost a whisper. Nothing else exists save her. All else ceases to be. It's warm here. Not hot, not cold but just right. The light is bright yet soft. Fragrance in the air. Her voice captivates him, holds him entranced. To stay here right now is all he wishes for. No pain, no sadness, no fatigue, no death or conflict. Just this woman who he doesn't know but he wants to know. He wants to know her forever. For always.

'You can,' Meredith says. Her eyes full of pain, sorrow, love and hope all in equal measure. 'But we want you to stay with Howie. You are what holds them together. You are the glue that binds. Without you, Howie will go on his own with Dave. He will not risk the lives of the others.'

'Mr Howie won't fail,' Blowers says quickly with a surge of defensive pride.

'Simon,' she moves closer, staring into his brown eyes normally so hard but now full of anguish and hurt. She falters, hesitating as though not wishing to say the words she knows must be said. He is in pain. He has done enough. He has given all he can and it's wrong to ask more. She stiffens, lifting her head and speaks softly, warmly and with regret. 'Right now Cookey is outside the house. His will to fight is gone. Charlie and Heather are fighting *for* him but they cannot do what Cookey is capable of doing. Blinky charged the ones following her but she too feels your death and falters as Cookey is, as they all are. Some will survive but not all and those deaths will crush Howie. He will go on alone with Dave.'

He watches her speaking. Entranced by the way her mouth forms the words and the way the tip of her nose moves ever so slightly as she speaks. What she tells him goes deep into his heart and causes distress but his fight is over. He has done what he can. To go back is to go back to pain and suffering but then Cookey is down and she said others will die.

She pauses to stare deep as though scrutinising his bare soul. 'Howie is an exceptional man. What he has inspires others to follow him but...' she pauses again, biting her lip before continuing. 'Every time Howie turns round, you and Clarence are there. You and Clarence validate him. You give him the courage to make decisions and lead. You give him that power to inspire. More will come, Simon. More will join you. Your team will grow and so will your responsibility but it's you that has to be there to guide them.

Without you holding them together, Howie will become a killer as cold as Dave. He needs you…'

She smiles with the sadness he feels inside and reaches to take his hand in hers. His palms calloused and hard from fighting, his knuckles bruised, his hands those of a warrior that she rubs and holds close.

'Time here is different,' she says quietly, thoughtfully and suddenly she is but a girl holding the hand of a man, shyness creeps into her features, a coyness that bewitches him. 'And…you will come back here…' she adds lightly.

'I will?' he blurts.

She nods with a wide grin spreading across her face that melts his heart, 'you will,' she laughs.

'When? Tomorrow?'

'Not tomorrow,' she laughs.

'Ah that's too late then…'

'You must do what has to be done first.'

'I will…I'll go do it now…will I see you when I've done it?'

She bursts out laughing with a sound that brings delight to the church, 'you will…and I will see you too.'

'Okay…so I'll get it done really quickly and come back.'

'Do you know what coming back means?' she asks, trying to be earnest but laughing with delight again.

'I don't bloody care,' he says, grinning at her laughing. 'If you're here.'

'You,' she says, holding his eyes on hers, 'are worth more than you will ever know, Simon Blowers.'

'Thanks,' he says in the Blowers easy way of taking praise. 'You're so pretty.'

'And you are most handsome,' she says, dropping her tone to show she means it. 'Everything you have done is right. Do not for one second think you have done wrong, Simon. Will you go back to Howie?'

'I will. I promise…but I'll come back here yeah?'

She laughs again, unable to stay serious. 'Yes! Yes you will come back.'

'Okay. So like...that's a date?'

'A date? Yes. Yes, it is a date. I'd like that very much.'

'Yeah?'

'Yes.'

'Okay, so...er...if you're Meredith what's the dog's name?'

'Bear, she is called Bear.'

'Okay. I can't wait to come back though.'

'I cannot wait for you to come back...but...there will be work when you do come back.'

He shrugs, unbothered, 'always work to do.'

'So you will go back to fight?'

He stares at her with a raw honesty pouring from his features, 'I'll fight for you, Miss.'

'Okay,' she says, with equal raw honesty. 'And I will wait for you.'

'I'd like that,' he says with a vulnerability that makes her move a step closer.

'I will. I promise.'

'Okay,' he says, wanting to kiss her but figuring they only just met so that's probably not a cool thing to do right now, even if he is dead somewhere.

She kisses him. A peck on the lips but slow enough for him to feel the lasting impression of her lips on his. 'I'll wait...'

'AHEM,' Chris says aloud. The room comes back. Blowers blushes furious and deep at Malcolm shaking his head in disbelief and Chris rolling his eyes.

'Sergeant,' Blowers says, stiffening to attention.

'Sergeant indeed,' Chris says, tutting with a grin at Meredith. 'Ready for orders, Corporal?'

'Yes, Sergeant.'

'Let Maddox go with the child. He poses no threat to Lilly and isn't worth your time. So far?'

'So far, Sergeant.'

'Go north. They're massing. You need intelligence on numbers. Reginald knows this but he needs a boot up the arse. So far?'

'Boot Reggie in the arse, so far, Sergeant.'

'Very good, Corporal. Stick with Howie. He needs you. Lead your team and train them when you can. Tell Reginald he is right, the species will merge and Paco is what they will become, oh and tell Howie not to be so complacent next time. That's it.'

'Roger. Understood.'

'By the way, you're blind in one eye and your little finger on your left hand has been bitten off.'

'What?'

'Flesh wound now get up and get back in the fight...'

'Tell Clarence I called him a fat Herbert,' Malcolm adds.

'But...'

Blowers spins round at hearing the dog barking wildly behind him, bouncing on the spot in the church with her tail swinging.

'What's going...'

'I SAID GET UP AND GET BACK IN THE FIGHT...'

CHAPTER THIRTY-TWO

'*Get up and get back in the fight,*' Dave says, dancing back from the infected with his hand pressing the radio switch under his shirt. Howie fights with tears streaming. Clarence feels crushed, broken. His heart in pieces. Nick falters, lashing out with his axe but his blows are weak. Roy slashes but his face shows the emotions he feels. Paula's heart breaks as Clarence's does. Her face contorting with the instant grief of such a loss and the void within them of where Blowers was. Blinky fights but she too feels the draining of energy. Charlie and Heather cover Cookey but the press coming is too great. Paco rages. Untouched by anything other than his care for Heather. In the hallway, Meredith barks non-stop with her feet planted either side of Blowers dead body.

Dave pauses in the space he gained from the kills he just scored. His impassive face shows a mild irritation at his orders not being complied with. '*Get up and get back in the fight...*'

The rest hear his voice but if anything, it makes the pain worse. A perception that Dave's autism prevents him from understanding Blowers is dead, but in the press of the battle, they can neither do nor say anything to him to make him understand because only Dave is good enough to find space to transmit.

Dave blinks. His right hand flashes out to cut a throat. He pauses, listening. His left hand stabs forward to drive the blade through the eye of one coming. His head tilts, his mouth purses. He kills two more and steps into the space created while drawing breath.

'*I SAID GET UP AND GET BACK IN THE FIGHT...*'

The voice roars. The voice bellows with a pulse of energy that sweeps through the horde and sends a jolt through everyone else. Cookey's eyes snap open. Faces grow hard from a feeling coming. A feeling growing. Something inside surging up.

Later, people will say Dave made it happen. They will say Meredith made it happen and people will talk about this day. Some will lie for the glory of the association and say they were there and they saw it. Others will think it an urban legend. A myth. A story made up.

In truth, only one man can say he saw it. Only one man in the kitchen of a house where he protected a newborn child in his arms from the infected coming from the hallway.

Maybe it was Dave that made it happen. Dave's belief that his orders that are always complied with. Maybe it was the dog who refused to let him die in peace and dragged his soul back to keep fighting. Maybe it was both of those things or, maybe, it was the kiss from a woman who gave love when love was needed most of all. A woman who gave the gift of a laugh and the touch of a hand on the hard arms of the warrior who was weary to the bone. A woman who simply *asked* him to keep fighting. A woman with warmth, grace, goodness, and the virtues that a soldier longs to fight for.

His heart booms. It doesn't beat but it booms to fire with a power that sends energy surging through his veins. It flows into him like fire that heats the core and drives him up on his feet. He stands bleeding. He stands battered, cut, raked, bruised, swollen, one eye gone, a finger bitten away and his face caked in blood and for one glorious second they cannot touch him. The love of the woman holds them off and buys him the time to find his feet and bunch the energy needed. Her touch comes through to form a glow that cannot be breached by the filth of what they have. He is Howie. He has that power to keep them back with will alone. Fear ripples. Hope grows. Aggression manifests. Tears cease to flow and snarls come from both sides.

In that frozen second, Maddox sees Blowers turn his head to face the backs of the infected charging at the child and in that second Maddox knows his judgement of Blowers was very, very wrong.

The dog at his side. The dog given the name Meredith by mistake. The dog who lowers her head and pulls her lips back with hackles that rise.

Pack fight.

Meredith goes for the doorway and those outside. Blowers goes to the kitchen with a rage that burns bright and glorious. He grabs one from behind and snaps the neck to cast it aside. He scoops, grabs a knife and rises to stab up into the groin to open the artery. He sidesteps and drives the point of the blade into a neck. He steps forward, grabs a handful of hair to yank the head back and cuts a throat from behind. As that body drops, he steps through, dips down and explodes up with an uppercut that smashes a jaw and kills the beast outright. At the apex of that swing he pivots round to stab into a stomach. A twist of his hand and he opens the flesh enough to reach in and pull the innards out. He twists, drawing the blade across another throat. He pivots and slams his broken hand into the face of another then stabs down into the body as it falls. He annihilates those in the kitchen. He moves through them like a hot knife through butter. He is water flowing over rocks and his arm still tingles from where she laid her hand upon him. This life is not the only life. This world is not the only world. Be it a dream. Be it a delusion. Be it a fantasy born from the chemicals pumped from his dying brain to ease his passing. Be it those things and more. Be it the transition of the same dream Howie had that passed through the hive mind to replicate in Blowers mind. It matters not. It was real. She was real. She was there and he's got a date so fuck you, fuck all of you, bring death and bring it fast because he does not fear it now. To go back is a blessing not a curse. To go there is a victory not a loss so bring it. Bring all of them. Bring them here.

The last one in the kitchen falls dead. Blowers draws air, inflating his chest in the vision of a monster. The whole of him drips with blood. The knife gripped in his good hand. Maddox holds the child in his arms. A baby boy still covered in the fluids of birth. Blowers looks upon them and smiles at the child and a beautiful thing in a place of filth.

'Go,' Blowers growls the word, turns and stalks down the hallway that builds to a run as he explodes out into the battle outside.

Maddox releases the air from his lungs in the sudden quietness of the house. He blinks several times for that's how long it takes for his mind to process what he saw happen. He turns to leave, stops and looks back to Julie lying dead on the floor. She looks at peace now. Her features relaxed in death to bring serenity. He crosses to her, lowering the child so her lips can touch his head.

'A boy,' he whispers to her. 'It's a boy.'

Time to go. He wraps the baby in a towel, takes his rifle and bag and slips quietly into the garden and away into the darkness of the night.

CHAPTER THIRTY-THREE

Carried forth on a wave of pure energy that sees him sprint from the house into the fight outside. Blowers brings with him the urge to keep going, the hope to win, the need to strive and refuse them the victory. That he is weakened and in agony does not show. That he is carried only by the memory of what could be a delusion does not matter. It does the job. He joins Cookey to fight side by side. He orders Charlie to re-mount and fight on horseback. He rallies and pushes the infected back and once their numbers are dwindled, he orders everyone to Blinky then to the precinct.

Cookey, Charlie and Heather see his awful injuries but there is no time to give voice or raise concern. There is separation when there should be unity and her words still whirling through his head force that endeavour to be completed. *You are the glue that binds. You are what holds them together.*

In the precinct, they felt his loss and the battle turned against them. They felt the surge as he regained his feet and that strength that flowed as he rallied them back to the town to turn the battle into what it should have been, a sordid scrap. A nasty fight of no real consequence.

Blowers led his few down the building line to Mo, Marcy and

Paula. He told Charlie to clear space and batter the infected out and away from the billowing smoke and crackling flames in the shopping centre. He then took them through the ranks to the middle to form the circle that turns to fight out with each protecting those on their sides and Howie the pivot on which they move.

Blowers takes the point opposite Howie. He is the counter weight that gives balance. A completion of a circle the centre of which becomes sacred ground that cannot be touched or reached by the infected.

They win as they do. They win by taking life and holding form as one. They win by attrition. By a few that are greater than the sum of their parts. Heather fights with them. Too frantic, too caught up and too swept along to question her place, and besides, Paco is busy playing his new game of skittles-with-zombies with Clarence.

The last few fall. Reginald watches from his lofty perch with his battle-swatter still gripped. He too fought bravely but in the end, it was the infection that killed the spiders off. Their tiny systems simply unable to cope with what the virus gave them and made them do. Now he looks down with one foot perched in a manly fashion upon the windowsill as he grips his weapon and views the battlefield.

Dave cuts his last one down. Howie swings the axe through the neck of the crawler. Mo stabs into a throat. Clarence breaks one over his knee. Paco snaps a spine. Chests heave. Hands, weapons and bodies drip blood as they all turn to see the last infected male standing alone down the street.

He stares back at them through red bloodshot eyes that flick from face to face until they come to rest on Simon Blowers who stands firm and glares back through one eye.

The infection takes them in. It watches to learn that its closest grasp of victory was by forcing separation. It almost took one today and although Blowers lives, it knows it hurt them. Its awful red eyes glance up to Reginald who stares back closely with a mutual analysis underway.

Dave's wrist flicks. The knife spins through the air.

'COME WE GO...'

The voice booms from the infected man but an eye for an eye and Dave's blade sinks into the infected man's left eye, killing him outright. It slumps instant and dead leaving the words hanging in the air as far away a small boy purses his lips and frowns.

Then it's done. Over. Another town laid to waste. Another town on fire. Every window in the street is smashed. Bodies everywhere. Pools of blood. Dismembered limbs. Corpses stuck with arrows. Heads chopped off that scatter the ground like footballs. They breathe hard with wild eyes still crazed and ready to fight. Jess takes a step. A skull pops. Meredith scours looking for hearts that beat and throats to bite.

'What did he say?' Nick asks, breaking the silence.

'Come we go,' Roy says.

'Oh,' Nick says.

The silence stretches.

'What's that mean then?' Nick asks.

'Don't know,' Roy replies.

All of them save Paco turn to stare up at Reginald who shrugs and waves his battle-swatter in the air. 'I have no idea what it means.'

The silence stretches.

Howie leans forward to look at Blowers. Paula turns. Clarence shifts. Nick steps out. Roy frowns. They all move to stare down the line at the sunken gory hole where his eye was, at his broken nose now at an angle, at his face swollen, bruised, cut and bit. His arms the same. His top torn and hanging in shreds that show the marks on his body, the long welts, the deep cuts, the bruised flesh. Every part of him caked in blood and wounds. They look down at his left hand and the bloodied stump where his finger was. His team look in awe of a legend born on this day in this place, to a man that cannot be killed.

'How are you still standing?' Paula asks quietly.

'I'm fine.'

'Yeah,' Paula says, biting her lip, 'that's not fine, Blowers.'

'There's tough,' Clarence says, 'then there's Simon Blowers...'

'Get off,' Blowers says, uncomfortable at the attention. 'It's fine...it'll grow back.'

'What will?' Cookey asks. 'Your eye or your finger?'

Blowers shrugs.

'Now I'm not a doctor but I don't think eyes and fingers grow back,' Cookey says. 'Roy? Do eyes and fingers grow back?'

'Nope.'

'Fucked then,' Cookey tells him. 'Unless you got the finger...we could stitch it back on or something...can you do that with eyes, Roy?'

'Nope.'

'Fucked then. Did you get the finger?'

'I think she ate it.'

Cookey thinks for a minute. 'She still in that house? We could go and get it...'

'Dunno, I didn't see who did it...'

'Should have looked properly.'

'Fair one.'

'With both eyes on the job.'

'Twat.'

'So you fingered a zombie then?'

'Oh fuck off,' he groans.

'Plenty of fingers here...you want one?'

'Do one, Cookey.'

'Willy for later?'

'What?'

'Don't give it large now cos you're all butch with your one eyed nine fingered japery...do you want a willy to play with later?'

'Er...nah, I'll be okay.'

'I'll sneak one in your pocket without anyone looking.'

'Cheers.'

'Keep an eye out for me though.'

'Dick.'

'Can you only count to nine now?'

'Mate...' Blowers snaps then chuckles.

'You can borrow mine if you need to get to ten,' Cookey says giving him the middle finger.

'I fucking hate you.'

'You smell of hairspray,' Blinky says leaning in to sniff Mo, 'why do you smell of hairspray?'

'I think we need to get out of here,' Howie says. 'We need somewhere for the night and holy fuck what's happened to your face?' he blinks at Marcy, stunned at the sight that only now he is seeing. She glares back as he looks at Paula and blanches again. 'Shit...ooh...ooh fuck...'

'What?' Clarence asks as Paula and Marcy turn round to show him. 'Oh...' he winces and pulls his head back before looking away in distaste.

'That's so bad,' Cookey says, looking from Marcy to Paula.

'Is it?' Marcy asks icily.

'Fuck yes,' Cookey says, nodding at her. 'Awful...seriously... like...like really awful...'

'I ate a spider,' Paula says through gritted teeth.

'Argh,' Howie says, turning away to yack.

'S'fucking gross,' Nick says.

'It went in my mouth,' Paula says.

'Oh stop, don't...' Howie says, still looking away.

Hair everywhere. Clumps standing up made stiff by hairspray and spider goo. Legs of spiders poke out from the strands. Squashed spiders mangled in their scalps. Red raw lumps all over them, swellings in their cheeks, on their foreheads and jaws. Spots with white heads and puncture wounds oozing puss. The same up their arms, on their necks and hands. Even Blowers stares through his one eye, stunned at the sight that somehow looks far worse than he does.

'What?' Paula asks, looking round at the gawping faces. 'We not pretty now?'

'Eh?' Howie says, 'er nooo, not at all...like so pretty...'

'Very pretty,' Clarence rumbles.

'Pretty,' Nick says.

'I would,' Blinky says, 'I meant Marcy, Miss Paula, Sir...'

'I...' Paula goes to say something in reply but can't find words to respond.

'That wasn't awkward at all, Blinky' Cookey says.

'Fist me, pencil dick.'

'Right so,' Howie says, trying to be serious again but glancing at Paula and Marcy, 'so...er...you ate a spider?'

'Yep,' she states pointedly, 'chewed it up...'

'Oh no, no no,' Howie says. 'Where's Mo? Is he the same as you? Mo?'

'Behind Clarence, Boss,' Mo says as the mountain slowly rotates and slides three people away with his bulk.

Mo looks fine. Not a mark on him. He even looks tidy, his shirt tucked in. His clothes not covered in blood. One tiny smear on his cheek is the only tell of the battle he fought.

'Mo Mo Dave Two,' Blowers mutters, squinting through his one eye.

'Is it that bad?' Marcy asks, fingering the lumps on her face.

'Yes,' Howie says.

'No but really, is it really that bad?'

'Yes.'

'Seriously, are they awful?'

'Yes.'

'Howie!'

'What?'

'Are they really that bad?'

'Er...no?'

'Better. Right, can we go please. I hate Boots now.'

'Good job seeing as you burnt it down,' Nick says.

'I ate a spider.'

'What you smiling at?' Cookey asks, seeing the weird grin on Blowers face.

'Nothing. Fuck off.'

'You're a pirate now.'

'Cookey, fuck off.'

'Like a bandit.'

'Oh for fuck's sake...'

'An arse bandit.'

'Piss off.'

'With a stumpy hand.'

'Okay, get it out your system...'

'A one eyed pirate arse bandit with a stumpy hand that can't wank properly.'

'I'm right handed.'

'I ate a spider.'

'I meant other men when you do reach arounds with your one eyed pirate arse bandit stumpy hand thing.'

'Fair one. Finished?'

'Um...'

'Enough, we're going,' Howie cuts in, looking round at his bunch of one eyed spider bitten or weirdly neat and tidy misfits.

CHAPTER THIRTY-FOUR

'How's the pain?' Roy asks, binding the dressing over his hand. 'Blowers?'

'Huh?'

'I said how's the pain?'

'S'fine,' Blowers says.

'Sure?'

'Er yeah, yeah sure.'

'Hmmm,' Roy says, securing the end of the bandage. 'Look at me.'

'I'm fine,' Blowers says.

'Yep, so it won't hurt to look at me will it,' Roy says, shining the light from his head torch into Blowers eyes. He checks his ears again and once more starts feeling for bumps on Blowers skull. 'You sure you didn't bang your head?'

'Of course I banged my head. It was a bloody scrap, Roy.'

'Stop being facetious. Do you feel dizzy? Nauseous?'

'I'm not concussed.'

'You keep drifting off,' Roy says quietly.

'Thinking,' Blowers says.

'About what?' Roy asks, lifting Blowers head to check the dressing over his eye.

'Stuff,' Blowers says, thinking about one woman and only about one woman. It felt so real and when he woke up, he was convinced it was real, but now, with the passage of time, he thinks more and more that it was just a dream.

The barn was Heather's idea. The place she found earlier that she knew was large enough to hold them all and had running water. The three vehicles and the horsebox parked on the grass outside. Jess grazing contentedly having been scrubbed down and given oats and water. Meredith washed and fed and now dozing in the doorway so she can see inside and out.

The small fire on the concrete floor crackles with a soothing sound as it bathes the room in an orange glow. Roy works with a head torch strapped to his head. Everyone else sorts kit and cleans up in a muted, almost pensive atmosphere. A day from hell that has sapped energy. Straw and hay bales split to make beds for the night and soft places to sit. Paula and Marcy work cream into their bites, wincing at the sore spots.

'It'll probably take your good eye a while to get stronger,' Roy says, nodding seriously at him.

'I'll be fine,' Blowers says, not realising this is the longest conversation he has ever had with Roy.

Outside, Heather and Paco walk across the field under a fine rain to join Howie and Dave staring down into the town now ablaze from the fires that spread fast to engulf whole streets.

'Good spot,' Howie says, glancing at her.

She looks at him as he turns back to stare down into the town. The brooding aura pours off him so thick she can almost see it. 'What went wrong?' she asks bluntly.

'I did,' he answers instantly. 'Complacent. Won't happen again.'

She has more questions. Hundreds of them. Who is he? Where does he come from? How old is he? Does he have family? How does he know how to do these things? Who taught him to lead? Why isn't he going after Maddox? What about her list?

'Okay,' she says instead because none of it actually matters and besides, she hates it when people ask her questions.

'I'm going up, Dave, you stay on watch for a bit with Heather.'

'Yes, Mr Howie.'

'With me?'

'Yes, Heather, with you,' Howie says, walking back through the wet grass. A day of days. He thinks back to the equestrian centre and the people he and Dave executed. The very thought of it makes him detest himself with a surge of utter self-loathing. A voice inside demands to know who he thinks he is to be judge, jury and executioner.

However, he would do the same thing again but the next time he wouldn't let it bog his mind down like it did this time. This, today, this *mistake* was his fault and his alone. Yeah maybe one could argue it was a culmination of events but the reality is that he is the leader and he failed. He should have gripped Maddox sooner. He should have kept them together. He should have done many things differently.

Who is he kidding? He is a supermarket manager. Not a General. Not a leader of men and women. Is this too much? Is he taking on more than he can deal with?

It's too late for that now. Learn from it. Learn the lessons and push on. That's all they can do. He stops walking as the idea of handing over to Clarence pops in his mind. Maybe Clarence should take over? Clarence is the professional soldier.

But then this isn't about being soldiers in an army. This isn't about rules of warfare or engagements. It's about sending a message. That's all it was ever about. Send a message that we won't be cowed. That we'll fight back no matter what comes. Soldiers are for war. This isn't a war. It's a survival mechanism reacting to the risk of a species being wiped out. They call it a game to give it a label and make it tidy in a box. They call it a war, a fight, a battle and all those things so they can process and understand the things they do.

If Blowers had died today, Howie would have gone on with Dave. That decision was made as he felt the connection to Blowers ending so abruptly and that in itself raises more questions. They felt Blowers die. They knew he was dead. His heart stopped. His energy within the hive mind ceased to be there. What came back was Blowers but somehow concentrated and stronger, harder, determined and his energy was different. The same man but suddenly it was like Blowers had purpose and faith in something. That's what it felt like.

It was a point in time where everything was balanced on a knife-edge and now, in reflection of the moment he realises how much he takes them all for granted. The assumption they will go with him is gross and offensive. To assume such a thing makes him an arrogant cunt.

'Listen in,' he stops in the doorway to the barn knowing Heather and Dave can hear him in the field. Reginald's chair creaks in the back of Roy's van that tells Howie Reggie just turned round to listen too. Everyone looks up and over at him. The lads and Charlie now clustering round Blowers, mugs of coffee in hands made from water heated on the fire. Paula and Marcy being checked by Roy while Clarence stands with them watching on. Howie sees them for what they are. For people. For individuals who have chosen to do this.

'What happened today was my fault...'

'Wasn't just your fault,' Paula cuts in. 'I told the lads to make you coffee and it was my idea to take our time...'

'I could have said something,' Clarence says. 'You can't take the blame, Boss.'

'It was my fault. I had my head up my arse after what Dave and me did...which is what I wanted to ask about. Is anyone here uncomfortable about that? You can say if you are...now's the time to...'

'Mr Howie?'

'Go on, Charlie.'

'I should not have broken his finger...no,' she says as several start protesting. 'It was unnecessary. He posed no threat and as Maddox pointed out, we were armed and he was not. I could have simply stepped away, moved back, turned aside or even requested Mr Howie, Paula, Clarence or Blowers speak with him. Instead I used force because I *could* and that is wrong.'

'He was a rapist cunt,' Nick says.

'We established that after the fact,' Charlie says. 'At the time he was an angry scared man who thought the army were there to save him...'

'Still a rapist cunt.'

'Within my reflection of the incident,' Charlie says thoughtfully, 'I considered the reaction from Dave...or rather, the lack of reaction from Dave. Neither Dave nor Meredith reacted in detection of a threat. So why did I?'

'He was staring at your boobs,' Cookey says.

'He was also staring at Marcy's boobs while drooling but neither Dave nor Meredith showed any threat detection. It was a loss of control. I used force because I knew I could use force. There was no temperance or restraint. He stared, his tone was offensive so I broke his finger. How can that ever be the right thing to do?'

A blast of air from Clarence who folds his arms and nods thoughtfully, 'Charlie, if you were my daughter I'd be the proudest man on Earth...but I do agree with you.'

'Thank you,' she says with real meaning.

'I don't agree,' Marcy says. 'I've been round men like that all my life. Dirty perverted bastards that can't control where they put their eyes and if they can't control their eyes then sure as shit they can't control their hands or their dicks. Fuck him. He stared. Howie told him to stop. He carried on being a pervert so Charlie reacted. His actions made it happen so yeah...fuck him.'

'Agreed,' Nick says.

'And,' Marcy adds, wincing as she touches one of the spider bites on her face, 'and he came out being a dick too...if that was me after twenty days of hiding and seeing what I thought was the army I'd be like...like...well I wouldn't be like he was. I'd be thankful and a decent human being instead of a complete dick. Sorry, I don't have the nice words like Charlie does...'

'Marcy,' Paula says at what came out as a harsh tone that made Charlie flinch and everyone else looks sharply at Marcy.

'Fuck,' Marcy groans, 'I didn't mean it like that, Charlie. I'm sore, my head hurts, I'm hot and tired...'

'Of course,' Charlie says.

'Indeed you have a delightful way with words,' Reginald says, walking into the barn with his hands clasped behind his back.

'And you can fuck off,' Marcy mutters darkly.

'Reggie?' Howie asks, 'what do you think?'

'Well,' Reginald says, coming to a stop near the fire which he knows is the central position and the light from the flames will bathe him in the right way. He appears to think for a moment. Studious in his reflections as he gives weight to the issue. 'I must say that I rather agree with both Charlie and Marcy. Charlie is correct in her observations that she used force *because* she could but that in itself tells us what a bully that chap was. Of all those present, he turned to Charlie to vent his actions. He did not point and shout at Clarence and you had already told him to stop staring at Marcy. He chose what he perceived to be a very attractive young lady instead of any one of the others who, and forgive me being so blunt, but who all look extremely tough and capable. So yes, Charlie was correct that the use of force was perhaps unnecessary but then Marcy was also correct in that he did indeed, and to use a common phrase, *have it coming*.'

'Right,' Howie says, scratching his head.

'Sometimes there is no right or wrong answer,' Reginald muses. 'Sometimes a course of action is chosen and one must retain the strength of character to hold that course.'

'Okay,' Howie says thoughtfully, 'what about after that?'

'The six people you killed?' Reginald asks lightly.

'Yeah.'

'I gave you my opinion.'

'Oh right, I thought that was to shut Maddox up.'

'It was, but it was also my opinion.'

'Fair enough then.'

'And on that subject, may I ask what our plans are regarding Mr Doku? Are we going after him?'

'Blowers? You had the most time with him. What do you think?'

Blowers goes back to the church to the orders given and the light and warmth and the kiss he can still feel. 'Er,' he clears his throat, blushing lightly at the memory that is thankfully hidden in the shadows of the barn. 'I don't think he's worth our time...he's a complete dickhead but I don't think he's a threat to Lilly. Besides,' Blowers shifts, thinking back. 'He found that woman and stood by her...he could have legged it, ditched her...done anything but he didn't...even when I was in the hallway trying to hold them back he carried on. He's a tosser but he's fucking brave as anything.'

'He is that,' Clarence says.

'And he took the baby with him,' Blowers adds.

'What was it?' Paula asks.

'Little boy,' Blowers says with a faint smile. 'Maddox did everything to get him out. So er...so I think he'll be alright. Maddox just isn't a team player.'

'That'll do for me,' Howie says. 'We'll leave him to it then.'

'Um maybe we could go north?' the words come out before Blowers can apply the brake on his mouth.

'Do what?' Howie asks.

'North?' Cookey asks.

'Fucking north?' Nick asks.

'Why north?' Paula asks.

'What's in the north?' Roy asks.

'Northern people,' Cookey says.

'Coal mines,' Nick adds.

'Racing pigeons,' Mo says.

'Everyone has ferrets in the north,' Cookey says.

'How far north?' Roy asks. 'Scotland north or the midlands north?'

'The midlands aren't the north,' Paula says.

'They are from here,' Roy says.

'Everywhere is the north from here,' Clarence says. 'Unless you go south obviously.'

'My auntie lived in Scotland,' Cookey says. 'Auntie Angela. Ran a taxi firm in Glasgow.'

'We went to the north for a match once,' Blinky says. 'It rained.'

'Might get zombie ferrets,' Cookey says, clearly thinking on the subject.

'We've had zombie rats,' Nick says, 'at that motorway service place with the bloke on the roof...we nicked his trousers.'

'Yes!' Blowers says, bursting out laughing. 'You remember that?'

'Er yeah, I just said it,' Nick laughs.

'And zombie spiders today,' Cookey says.

'We are not mentioning that ever again,' Paula says quickly.

'So we might get zombie ferrets,' Cookey adds.

'They'd be mean little bastards they would,' Marcy says. 'I got bit by a ferret once...'

'On the arse?'

'Cookey!'

'Alex.'

'Sorry, Marcy. Was only a joke.'

'It's fine,' she says waving a hand at him. 'If anyone else said it I'd go nuts.'

'Ferrets go for nuts,' Blinky says.

'Oh good one,' Nick laughs.

'Get fucked.'

'Anyway,' Cookey says, 'we've got t'speak t'language in t'north up ladder lad in a flatcap eating t'pie...'

'This is bordering on racism,' Paula says.

'It's not racist to take the piss out of northern people,' Nick says.

'You are so politically correct, Miss Paula.'

'Someone has to be, Mr Howie.'

'Reggie? Will it do zombie birds?' Cookey asks.

'How on could I...'

'Don't be baited, Reggie,' Paula says.

'What about zombie worms, Reggie?' Nick asks.

'Zombie cats,' Blinky says.

'Enough,' Howie calls out, 'why north, Blowers?'

'Ignore me, I think I banged my head...'

'You okay?' Charlie asks.

'Mate, you alright?' Nick asks.

'Roy, is he okay?' Paula says as the ripples of concern go round the room which make Blowers squirm and wish he'd kept his bloody mouth shut.

'I'll er...I'll get some fresh air if that's okay,' Blowers says, standing up from his straw bale with too many people trying to help. 'I'm fine...honestly...just get a bit of air. Nick, you got a smoke?'

'That won't help,' Roy says.

'Ah be fine,' Blowers mutters.

'I'll come with you,' Nick says. 'Cookey?'

'Yep, coming...'

Blowers rolls his eyes as Howie smiles at the whole of Blowers team escorting him outside.

'Might have one actually,' Paula says. 'Howie? You coming for one?'

'Aye.'

'That's what northern people say,' Cookey calls out, 'they say *aye* a lot.'

'Well,' Roy says to Clarence, Marcy and Reginald, 'just us then. Did you see the longbow earlier? I've got it right here if you wanted to see it.'

'Quick,' Paula mouths rushing outside with Howie to escape the longbow lecture that's just starting behind them.

'Forgive me, Roy. I have work to do,' Reginald says gravely, adding a sincere nod before turning to rush off.

'Did you feed Meredith?' Marcy asks Clarence.

'No! No I don't think I did…I'll go do it now.'

'She had food,' Roy says, holding his longbow.

'Did she?' Marcy asks weakly, sitting back down.

'Big dog though,' Clarence says, 'she probably wants seconds.'

'Pudding,' Marcy says, rising again with Clarence.

'Pudding,' Clarence says, lifting a hand at Roy.

'Dogs do not eat pudding,' Roy mumbles, staring forlornly at his longbow then realising everyone is now outside smoking. 'I'll come out with it,' he adds brightly, rushing after them to the door.

LATER. Much later. Very much later, after Roy has discussed the merits of the compound, recurve and modern bows and given examples of firing speed, aiming and the draw weight, which was of course shared by *suggesting* everyone have a go at pulling it. After he then switched to the longbow and discussed the history, design and usage in battles and again *suggested* they each have *a pull* to feel the draw weight. After that, and of course the show of firing at a static target.

After all of that, they quietly disperse to drift inside with much yawning and stretching of limbs from being lulled into boredom by the very long and detailed lecture. Blinky even said *this is boring as shit* but it had no effect.

Blowers stays outside leaning against the side of the barn as his mind once more drifts back to the church and the thing he now considers was definitely a dream. He listens to the quiet conversations inside and the rustling as they move about and prepare for the night. Marcy comes out to check the Saxon is ready for the first watch before smiling and heading back inside to brew up.

The air is cooler than it was. The pressure eased by the brief storm. He casts his gaze towards the town and the glow of the immense fires reflecting off the low clouds. Meredith comes out for her nightly check on who is where. She moves out to Jess, sniffs and wags her tail then looks down to Paco, Heather and Dave further down the field. She goes to the back of the van and looks inside at Reginald then turns to walk back towards the barn.

Blowers watches her. The calmness of her manner and now she seems just a normal dog and not the thing inside their heads when it starts going bent. He looks round quickly, furtively and thinks for a second.

'Bear?'

The reaction is instant. Her head snaps to him. Ears cocked. Eyes fixed. Her whole manner poised and alert. He smiles at himself being such a dick but again checks round.

'Bear?' he mutters again, pretending not to be looking at her.

She comes to him instantly, responding to the name she was given by her old pack. Not that Blowers knows that.

'Bear?'

She whines and pushes her nose into his hand. Her tail wagging furiously.

'Is that your name?' he drops to a crouch, his right hand rubbing her head and down her long neck. 'Bear yeah? Bear? Are you Bear?'

Each utterance gains a response. She licks him, whines, wags her tails and cocks her head to the side. Her eyes fixed on him.

'Good girl,' he rubs and pats, fussing her head and ears. 'I wish that was your name eh? Bear? Is it Bear?' he chuckles at the response, grinning widely and knowing it proves fuck all.

'Ah bless, she's enjoying that,' Marcy says, walking towards the Saxon with a blanket.

'She looks like a bear,' Blowers says, laughing at her whine and head tilt when she hears the name.

'She does doesn't she,' Marcy says, ditching the blanket inside then walking back. 'You okay? Need anything?'

'Nah I'm fine, thanks, Marcy.'

'Okay, I'm brewing up for me and Howie if you want one.'

'Er...nah, I'd better get some sleep...Marcy?'

'Yeah, what's up?'

'Ask a question?'

'Of course,' she says, walking over to stand closer. She drops down to join him fussing the dog. 'Blowers?' she asks when he doesn't say anything. She sees the trouble on his face. The hesitation at speaking his mind.

'Ah nothing...'

'No it's not,' she says softly, 'come on...'

'I er,' he scratches the end of his nose, his face so bruised, swollen and sore. His nose still broken at a slight angle. His right eye glances to her and for once the hard glare is gone. 'I er...had this dream.'

'Dream? Last night?'

'No like today...when I...'

'Oh honey,' she reaches out as the single tear spills from his eye. He stiffens, embarrassed at his own emotions. An instant transition and the composure is gained. The hardness of the man returns.

'Simon, it's okay,' she urges, seeing him recoiling into himself.

'I'm fine.'

'Simon, what is it?'

'Nothing. It's nothing.'

She smiles sadly, seeing the chance is now gone. 'There's tough,' she mutters, 'then there's Simon Blowers.'

'Yeah,' he says in that Blowers easy way of taking compliments.

'I'm here if you need me.'

'Thanks.'

'Seriously. Wake me up...come find me...anytime.'

'Yeah, yeah cheers, Marcy.'

She moves forward to kiss his forehead, giving him a hug regardless of whether he wants one or not. The emotions surge up and threaten to come out. He swallows them down with composure gained by that same will power that held the line for so long.

'Howie would have been devastated if he lost you,' she says, rising to her feet. 'Come get me if you need me.'

'Yeah, yeah I will. Thanks.'

Bear licks his face. Sensing the turmoil inside. Feeling his pain. He died today. His heart stopped. Everything else that happened was magical and wonderful but he still died today. His heart still stopped. He felt it. He felt that second when it happened. The sense of mortality. The awareness of being finite, of there being an end. She pushes into him. Unjudging, unquestioning, loyal and forever pack.

Was she real? He has to know. He will fight to the end if he knows. How can he know? Take a chance. Take the risk of looking like a dick. He rises and crosses to the van, slowing at the last few steps.

Reginald senses his approach and turns in his chair as Blowers appears at the back door. Reginald respects Blowers immensely. More than the man could ever know and like the dog he senses the turmoil bubbling under the surface.

'Is it raining?' Reginald asks lightly.

'Raining? Er no, no it's stopped,' Blowers says, looking up.

'That is good,' Reginald says, standing from his chair. 'I wish to have a walk. Will you come with me?'

'Er yeah, yeah sure,' Blowers says.

'I think I am to have a guard,' Reginald says in the way of a joke, 'and there is none finer than Corporal Blowers eh?'

'Okay,' Blowers says, smiling his easy smile.

'Good,' Reginald says dropping from the van to look up at the sky then down to Blowers. 'Come on, walk with me...tell me about this dream...'

Printed in Great Britain
by Amazon

50803559R00267